The Creators

Book Three of the SHANJI trilogy

James C. Glass

AN [e-reads] BOOK
New York, NY

Copyright © 2002 by James C. Glass
First e-reads publication 2002
www.e-reads.com
ISBN 0-7592-5312-9

For Becky, Steven, Marybeth and Sarah

Author Note

This work is the third book in the SHANJI trilogy, and makes reference to both SHANJI and its sequel EMPRESS OF LIGHT. Each story stands alone, but is part of a single tale, and the books are best read in series.

One

Yesui and Nokai

There had been light rain during the night, and in the morning glow from Tengri-Khan water droplets sparkled in rainbow colors as if diamonds studded the transparent dome high above Shanji's capital city. Across the valley, a black buttress of rock rose to scattered forests among mountainous craigs giving the planet its name. Three peaks glowed in a mottling of red and yellow, and there was a flash of gold from the roof of a pagoda nestled within their summits.

Yesui yawned, and raised her arms in ritual greeting to the morning, the palms of her hands turned outwards to receive the light, drawing energy from it in a smooth flow through arms, chest and legs. The ritual was a daily reminder she was an intimate part of this world and the universe containing it. A special part, yes, for she was Mei-lai-gong, the Empress of Light. Within the hour she would return to the gong-shi-jie, the place of creation, to do her daily work. There had been a time when the gong-shi-jie was her prefered place to be, her manifestation floating within swirls of the light of creation, the vortices of stars peeking through from real space, all peaceful, without ambition or agenda, so unlike her interactions with people. But then she had met Nokai and now he was with her on Shanji, and it seemed her heart constantly ached with the love she felt for him.

As Ambassador of Lan-Sui, Nokai kept a suite of rooms in the Hall of Ministers, and from where she stood on the balcony of her palace apartment Yesui could see that the windows of those rooms were still shuttered. Nokai was not an early riser, often retiring after midnight and ending each day with an hour of deep meditation and prayer to First Mother. *How unlike we are*, thought Yesui, *yet I love him so much and he loves me, too. I feel it even now; it's as if we're constantly connected.*

1

Yesui sighed, and watched as the city of Wang Mengnu Shan-shi-jie awoke below her. Here was the city of Shanji's Empress, Yesui's mother, called Mengnu by the people and Kati by those who knew her well. Even in early morning the cable cars were running up and down the steep upper slopes of the city, and little dots of people were waiting on pagoda-roofed platforms to receive them. Others scurried to and from buildings of steel and polymer colored red, yellow, green and blue rising as high as ten stories to the left of the cable cars, while to the right a cascade of hanging gardens swept down the slope in a single mass of color. The gardens were empty of people, except for one place where a small group was performing morning exercises by a pond. Likely they were elderly people, for this was a workday on Shanji, and even at first light many would be engrossed in their tasks.

Her grandfather was no exception to this.

Good morning, sweet one. It seems too nice a day to work, but your father and brother are expecting you and you are again distracted by love.

Gong-gong! I didn't even sense your peeking. You're being naughty again.

Then you shouldn't broadcast your feelings so loudly without shielding yourself. Every Moshuguang in the city is probably feeling heartache at this very moment. And your father's ship needs that jump in space-time within half an hour if he's to reach Tengri-Nayon on schedule.

I can put them within an hour from orbit, Gong-gong. You've seen me do that before today.

Not when distracted, dear.

Even the Chancellor of the Moshuguang could not shield the good humor in his mind, but then Ma was suddenly there to defend her daughter.

Mengmoshu is such a tease in early morning before his desk is heaped with work, dear. It will pass. Good morning, Father.

Ah, you also work early.

What else am I to do when my husband is away? Yesui, I've written a note for your father, and Tanchun is bringing it to you. We have family on that ship, so do try hard to focus on your work when you get there.

Oh, Mother. Yesui left her balcony and closed the plasdoor behind her. I'll go right now, then.

Good, said Mengmoshu, then, Kati, we must talk in person. Would you join me for noon tea at Stork Tower? It's about . . . well . . . please excuse us, Yesui.

And they were suddenly shielded from her.

"Now what?" said Yesui. She took one step towards her bed, but then there was a soft rapping at her door. When she opened it, Tanchun was standing there holding out a sheet of vellum to her. The servant of Shanji's Empress and also Weimeng, first wife of its former Emperor, was rapidly greying but still slender and graceful. "For you, from your Mother," she said softly, "and you have another visitor here."

Yesui took the note, read it quickly and peered past Tanchun to see Nokai standing there dressed in the robe of a Lan-Sui priest, his eyes twinkling with amusement. She was suddenly aware of her disheveled hair and the rumpled old robe she wore. Her heart pounded, Tanchun smiled shyly, bowed, and glided away from them.

"Nokai! You were right here, and I didn't feel your presence," she gasped.

"I wanted to surprise you, and succeeded," he said, stepping up close and taking her hands in his. "I know you have work to do, and I have an unusually early meeting to attend. Yesterday you asked me what I would like to see next on Shanji, and I've finally decided what it is: the pagoda, the memorial shrine in your honor at the summit of Three Peaks. I wish to go there with you late this afternoon and perhaps hear the story about a shrine I understand you have not yet seen, even though it honors you."

He squeezed her hands gently and she was lost to his will. "Near sunset," she said. "I will arrange a flyer."

"Not by horse?" he said.

"I don't ride horses," said Yesui. "Mother is disappointed by this, of course, but I wasn't raised in the mountains like she was. Besides, the trip is hours by horseback and a flyer can have us there in minutes."

"Very well," said Nokai, but Yesui sensed his disappointment at not experiencing a ride on an animal, something the people of Lan-Sui only read about in stories.

They set a time, Nokai kissed her hands and let them slide from his as he turned away. Moments after he left she could still feel his now unshielded emotions, and her own heart continued to flutter as she flopped down on her bed. When she stared up at the white cannopy of silk, Nokai's face was there, long, delicately boned, brown eyes with green flecks, beautiful, then fading as she breathed deeply, slowly. Her heartbeat slowed, and she closed her eyes.

If only you could go with me like Mengjai. My brother understands. He has seen the beauty of the place of creation, and understands my attraction to it. But you cannot go there, my love. In this we are so different, and I hope it will not be a barrier between us.

In relaxing she gained initial focus, first physical, then mental, for her body was but a shell when she was gone. Sensation ceased in her feet and hands, then legs and arms, then chest. She let out a deep breath in a sigh as the matrix of purple stars appeared in her mind, and she remained with it for a long moment. For that part of her special mind that had come from a mixing of Tumatsin and Moshuguang bloodlines, her body ceased to exist. She was now pure spirit, soul, a thing not yet understood but conscious, hovering in real space and aware of the matrix of entrance points to the higher dimensionality called the gong-shi-jie, the place of creation. Long ago, before humans, or planets, or stars, there had been only one point in the matrix, and from that point had come a single burst of light colored purple beyond purple, giving birth to an ever expanding universe. The matrix had expanded with it, now filling all space. The distance between each point of purple light in her view was small beyond imagination.

Now she moved towards the matrix of purple lights, still points as she drew closer, their spacings increasing, one looming straight ahead of her and she fell into it, briefly aware of the lace of green threads as she went through the interface, the purple vortex forming to mark her return path as she came once more to the gong-shi-jie.

Swirling clouds of purple laced with blue enveloped her and in every direction were the vortex manifestations of stars in real space, colored deep blue to red in a pattern immediately familiar to her, a pattern compressed, for in this place there was no continuum of space or time. Still, the pattern remained constant, connected to real space by the quantum electrodynamical interface in which her day's work was to be done. Close by the small, purple vortex marking the return path to herself was a large swirl in red-orange that was Tengri-Khan, and even from here she could see a similar stellar manifestation showing the presence of Tengri-Nayon. Yesui drifted towards it, a ghostly presence in a place of chaos beneath order. When alone there was no need to show the green flattering manifestation of herself to someone, and maintaining it was a distraction when her work was delicate.

Her father's ship was now nearly two light years out from the Tengri-Nayon system and well beyond the great cloud of icy debris surrounding Tengri-Khan. Her control over the space-time wave was still imperfect; it encompassed not only the point of origin as defined by contact with Mengjai aboard the ship, but everything along a line thousands of kilometers parallel and antiparallel to the ship's trajectory. Safety demanded that space around the ship be as empty as possible during a jump.

First she must find Mengjai, and that was the easy task. Her sneaky brother probably sensed her even now. This was verified when she neared the vortex of Tengri-Nayon and called out to him.

Mengjai, I'm here.

His response was immediate. Yes, you are, but taking your time about it. Are you enjoying the view, or just thinking about Nokai?

Both, dear brother. He's taking me to see my shrine on Three Peaks after I'm finished here. We're going to make mad love there. Yesui adjusted her course, homing in on Mengjai's presence. The vortex of Tengri-Nayon was huge as she dipped down near it to enter the interface.

You're dreaming, Yesui. If you insist on marrying a Lan-Sui priest you'll have to wait until your wedding night. Are you in the interface yet?

Yes, but you needn't talk now. I have found you.

All around her were the green threads, sparkling like spider-web in morning dew, the manifestation of space-time in this strange place separating two vastly different dimensionalities. Near her the threads were roughly parallel, slightly curved, but in the distance they joined others in the whirlpools that were the sister stars Tengri-Khan and Nayon. Locked on Mengjai's presence, she came in closer, closer to a single thread, at first sparkling, but uniform, then not so uniform, then a series of bright, oblong spots, closely spaced, pulsating in brightness. Without conscious thought she rushed towards one point, swallowed by it in a flash and suddenly the colors were gone. The blackness of real space was punctuated with thousands of stars, two of them quite bright to her left and right.

5

Her father's ship was right in front of her, less than a kilometer away. *So, here I am. Are you ready to jump?*

I am, but father is asleep and I'm going to leave him that way. The last two jumps gave him a headache because he insists on keeping his eyes open.

But Ma gave me a message for him.

I'll pass it on to him. Trust me, I have a brain.

Really? Well, the message is short. I suppose you can handle it.

Yesui gave him the message, most of it actually for Empress Yesugen on the capital planet of Meng-shi-jie in the Tengri-Nayon system. There was a meeting planned for two Empresses, to take place in the gong-shi-jie, and a time-line on production of carbon-nanofiber-reinforced polymer. Ma sends her love to both of you, she said.

I'll pass it on. And say hi to Nokai for us. He's a nice guy, Yesui, the only person I've ever met who can calm you down. Better marry him, and give us all some peace.

I will when he asks me, and Nokai isn't here now. Let's see how close I can get you to orbit this time.

You were close enough last time, so don't get cocky. That's why we have engines on this thing.

The ship was a Meng-shi-jie freighter, wedge-shaped and uunarmed, its cargo bays crammed tight with polymer beams and panels destined for housing construction on that planet. Lan-Sui emigrants remained a problem there, most of them choosing to remain even after peace had been restored and Yesui had renewed the warmth of their gaseous world by transfering mass to it from the gong-shi-jie. The issue was living space, and with new materials provided by trade with Shanji, Empress Yesugen was making every effort to solve the problem.

Okay, here we go, said Yesui. A flash of green and she was just back inside the interface, a single oblong spot of green now fringed in purple, how she did not know. The high level creator she still named 'Mind' had done it for her on her first jump, but now it just happened. It was now her twelfth jump, at a familiar distance, freighters streaming to and from Shanji with her guidance, Mengjai logging some forty light years of travel in less than one year real-time. She paused, the oblong spot flickering back richly at her, and used the mantra her Mother had taught her for focus.

I am Mei-lai-gong, the Empress of Light. I call the light, and it comes to me — so.

There was a brilliant flash of violet, fading rapidly, a wave of flickering points radiating from the oblong with symmetry identical to it, then slowing. Yesui returned to the gong-shi-jie to receive her brother's critique on the work.

Well? How close?

Hmmm. I'm checking. Meng-shi-jie is on screen. Strobe on. Time is — one-point-six seconds, and convert — that's two hundred fifty six thousand kilometers from orbit. Not a record, but close to last time. That's fine with me, Yesui. A comfortable margin. Let's keep it that way.

Okay. I'll be back in a week, then. Behave yourself in port, brother.

I have no choice; I'm a guest of The State, and the women here are anything but delicate flowers. Not my taste. Hurry back to Nokai, now, and thanks for a good trip.

Bye, she chirped, and did what he said, drifting quickly to the purple vortex of herself and falling into it. A flash, and physical sensation returned. She was on her back, arms at her sides. She opened her eyes and saw white silk draped above her. Here in her room only a few minutes of real time had passed, yet she'd traveled nearly six light years in performing her task. She sat up on the bed and yawned, and then Ma was there again.

Ah, you've returned. All went well?

Yes, Mother. And your message is delivered.

I'm having breakfast on the balcony. Will you join me?

Yesui felt the lonliness in her mother. Even after twenty six years of marriage, Mother still missed Da terribly when he was away. *In a few minutes,* she said. She got up and spent the few minutes fighting with the tangled mass of her hair, then changed into a yellow robe and matching slippers and left the suite of rooms once occupied by an orphaned Tumatsin child destined to become the Empress of Shanji.

The royal suite was only meters away. She knocked softly on the door, and Tanchun answered it, smiling and bowing politely. Past the huge bed canopied in gold, double doors were open to the balcony and Mother was sitting at a table there, sipping tea. Her eyes went from brown to a beautiful emerald green in an instant as Yesui approached.

"Good morning, dear. I'm having my usual barleycakes, but Tanchun will bring whatever you want."

Yesui hated the Tumatsin staple. It tasted like heavy paper when chewed. She asked for honeycakes and a hardboiled egg and poured tea for herself as Tanchun hurried away.

"Mengjai was his usual grumpy self this morning," she complained. Mother munched, and smiled. "He doesn't have a love to soften him." Yesui took a sip of tea. "You're probing me, Mother. And Mengjai says the women on Meng-shi-jie are not to his taste."

Ma chuckled. "His time will come. Your time *has* come. It's been a year, now. Have you and Nokai talked about marriage?"

"Mother, not now."

"I'm not prying, dear, but the two of you practically glow when you're together. And I was only twenty one when I sat on this very balcony, feeling your special presence inside me. I remember that first time we were together in the gong-shi-jie and my realization of what you might be. First Mother has blessed me with my children. I want the same for you and your brother."

Tanchun thankfully interrupted by arriving with honeycakes and an egg for her. Yesui cracked open the egg and let it cool while she nibbled at a cake. "Nokai and I will visit the shrine on Three Peaks this afternoon," she said absently. "It was his suggestion."

"How wonderful!" said Mother. "You've seemed so reluctant to see it, and it *does* honor you, dear."

"As the Mei-lai-gong."

"Yes. That is who you are."

"I am Yesui, Mother, a person, not a god, not a thing to be awed by or worshipped."

"The shrine isn't a temple. It commemorates an event that turned the Three Peaks into colorful glass, fused by hot dust from our own star. *You* did that, Yesui, before you were even born. It is a symbol of the power First Mother has blessed Shanji and our family with, nothing more."

Yesui had quickly gouged out the egg, and plucked a piece of shell from her mouth. "I don't remember doing it. I don't remember anything from that first time."

Mother reached over and put a hand on hers. "Oh, my sweet, the feelings inside you are so familiar to me: the time when I first saw myself as a changeling, then the way people revered me when I was healing them. You feel as I did when I went to Jensi City and saw the garden of miniatures dipicting my entire life, then the Church of The Mother, who they thought to be *me*, everyone carrying the little red books filled with sayings stolen from conversations I'd forgotten.

They revered me, *worshipped* me. I found it frightening and appalling. I told them I was a servant of First Mother, an emissary, and only gradually over the years have most of them come to believe it. Our powers are supernatural to the people, Yesui, but it's up to us to show them our humanity, our oneness with them. We are special *and* human. I've accepted that, and found serenity in what I am. It's time for you to do the same."

Mother drew back, embaressed by her outburst, her eyes red for a moment, then quickly green again. She nervously fingered the collar of the black Moshuguang robe she wore. "Sorry, but I had to say that. It's been coming for a long time."

Yesui was stunned, but managed a wan smile. "Sooner might have been better. But you *do* understand. I don't want to be worshipped by anyone, Mother — including Nokai."

"Ahhh," said Mother, leaning back in her chair. "Now we come to it."

Yesui wiped honey from her lips. "Sometimes I think he feels himself unworthy to marry me, yet the love inside him makes me ache."

"A very spiritual man, no doubt, and a devout believer in First Mother. It is She he worships, not you."

Mother's voice was nearly a whisper. "He is not ordinary, that man. His shield is inpenetrable when he wills it. A gentle soul, yes, but I sense great strength there, a power deep within him, without ego. Many Moshuguang have sensed it, including your grandfather. Nokai is respected by them, though they see his role as Ambassador as a friendly political gesture by Lan-Sui and Yesugen. Nokai, I think, is more than that. The two of you fell in love so quickly, so naturally. Sometimes I think forces other than love are involved."

Yesui frowned with the sudden return of a memory. "Do you remember that presence in the gong-shi-jie, the one I call 'Mind'?"

"The one who warned us away from the area of new star formation in Abagai's galaxy, yes."

"More than that to me, Mother. Also my teacher, my observer. She even said 'they' had been watching me, and you, for sometime. And when I was moving Lan-Sui City, she helped me while I was terrified over Nokai's safety. At one point she said, 'Find your man. That is very important to us'. I just remembered that."

"Oh, Yesui," said Mother, her eyes glistening. "There is a plan behind all of this — and it comes from beyond our perception."

They spent several minutes in silence, each thinking about what that plan could be.

Yesui had arranged a flyer and a Moshuguang pilot for the short hop to Three Peaks. Tanchun had spent two hours combing out her long hair and fastening it near the scalp with a comb of red and green mollusk shell. She wore no jewelry and was dressed in the black robe of the Moshuguang, with matching soft-soled slippers for the climb to the shrine.

Two hours before sunset she went to the palace rail platform and met Nokai, who was the only passenger on the cable car. Nokai still wore his white robe, but had added a black sash of rough wool at the waist, giving him a less formal look. His eyes appraised her as he took her hand, and she felt warm all over. They sat down in silence, shoulder to shoulder for the half-minute ride to the flyer field above the palace. Two guards at the gate bowed and passed them through. A young Moshuguang in military blues bowed stiffly and smiled. "A lovely night for the flight," he said.

Forty flyers were lined up in four rows. Another sat in a circle of strobing yellow lights, and they went to that one, a circular aircraft four meters across, open cockpit with plas windshields rising a meter above the edges of metal. They sat in the seat directly behind the pilot and buckled up tightly.

"A new experience," said Nokai, but Yesui had felt his excitement before he said it. She held his arm as they lifted off, felt him tense then relax. They rose straight up to the dome, a panel sliding back to let them through, and suddenly cool evening air swirled around them.

The pilot banked the craft slightly as they headed south, and there was a brief glimpse of golden palace turrets and colorful buildings below them, then the blackened western valley mottled green with insistent new life poking through soil made glass. Yesui was reminded of the terrible purple light her mother had used to win the war bringing her to power. *Could I do such a thing?* she wondered.

Nokai turned, and smiled at her.

The flight seemed only slightly longer than their ride on the cable car. A rocky cliff passed below them, then the tops of trees, the smell of *Tysk* heavy in the wind. For just an instant they saw light reflected from the great lake far to the south, the place where the Tumatsen still lived their simple lives. Her mother's people — and *her* people as well, yet Yesui hardly knew them. *I've seen so little,* she thought, and Nokai squeezed her hand.

"Perhaps we can see it together," he said, and she looked up at him, surprised, for she'd not felt any probe of her mind.

They descended toward a high plateau ringed with jagged peaks: Emperor's Thumb prominent to the east, the Three Peaks west. The colors on Three Peaks seemed like the work of a giant artist's brush. The east sides now turned grey in shadow, three steep fingers of rock interlaced at a single summit.

The flyer came down at the base of the peaks a few meters from an archway of glistening black polymer, and beyond it a paved path wound out of sight around a vertical rock face. "I will remain here as long as you wish," said the pilot, "but there's no lighting up there and a descent in total darkness can be quite dangerous."

"We'll be down before then," said Yesui. Once on the path, she looked back and saw that the pilot had settled into a back seat of the flyer for a nap.

The path quickly ended at the base of a narrow staircase carved right into the glassy rock, a steel handrailing on the outside edge, each step covered with rough material that grabbed at her slippers when they climbed. A warning sign indicated a climb of two hundred meters to the shrine and they took it slowly, neither of them experienced in vigorous physical activity.

The staircase spiraled upwards around one pinnacle, then crossed to another via a short, steel-mesh bridge and upwards again. There were three places along the way where niches were cut into the rock, each with a little bench on which to rest, all of which they used. The last bridge was near the summit, crossing a terrifying span of four meters with nothing but two hundred meters of air below them.

They came around a corner, the steps ending at a second gate in black polymer and a box where they were instructed to deposit slippers and shoes.

The pagoda was nestled within a triple summit of rock spires rising a few meters above its roof, resting on pillars driven into ground where grass and flowers had once grown. The steep roof rested on tall mahogany columns, an open structure with a circle of benches looking out on the plateau east and south and the distant dome of the city to the north. The mahogany floor was polished to a mirror finnish and at its center, rising from a circular golden plate covered with a hemisphere of glass, a blue flame burned brightly.

Nokai took her hand and they ascended three steps to the pagoda floor, where they watched the flame silently for a long moment.

It was not what she'd expected. "There's nothing here to tell the meaning of this place. How is it a shrine?"

"The blue flame is enough," said Nokai, "burning steadily, a sign of eternal energy. A simple, peaceful place of quiet serenity, a place of silence to turn inwards and examine oneself. It's lovely."

He turned, and cupped her chin in his hand, his brown-green eyes now so close. "Lovely — like Yesui," he murmured, then kissed her softly, then firmly as her arms went around him. For seconds, the only sensation was physical, his lips on hers, the pounding in her chest, but suddenly they were together in another way, his feelings filling her.

Oh, Yesui, I love you so much. I need you so much.

And I love you. I want us to be together forever.

Their lips parted, Yesui pressing a cheek against his chest, Nokai's chin resting on top of her head.

"I — I would be a very devoted husband, if you would have me, Yesui," he said. "It has been a year, now, time enough for you to decide if I'm suitable. I'll respect your decision, whatever it is."

"Suitable? Nokai, I *love* you. I want very much to be your wife."

His elation brought her to tears. Nokai wiped one tear away with a finger and kissed her softly again. Now her skin tingled powerfully and there was a buzzing in her ears, in her head, a new presence suddenly there with a powerful voice.

The blessings of First Mother are given to you and your offspring. May you nurture each other with love and share supportive strength in times of difficulty, both in this world and others. Know that we bless your union and watch over you at all times, for you are one with us and The Mother. Our love to you, Yesui and Nokai. We are most pleased.

Yesui clung to Nokai and opened her eyes. They were enveloped by a soft purple glow extending a meter from their bodies, which faded rapidly to nothingness as they watched. She looked up at Nokai, and he smiled at her.

"We are not alone," he said.

"We are never alone."

Two

Mengjai and Tirgee

Mengjai and Huomeng were the last to leave the ship, the cargo unloaded and servicing begun. Only three days in port and one gone, the last of the crew now in city streets doing what crewmembers did on short leave. But Mengjai would not be with them this time, for he and his father had been invited to dinner at Yesugen's home and would spend a night and a day there.

They were dressed in crisp military blues, a sight not uncommon on Meng-shi-jie, but there was still the occasional stare as they walked through the reception area, and the stares were directed at his father. There was the prominent bulge of the forehead, the delicate veins there identifying him as a Moshuguang, a mind-searcher, and even on Meng-shi-jie the special powers of the breed were known. There were no such features on Mengjai's face nor his sister's, even though their powers far exceeded those of their father's. Mother's features were more subtle, but still there, and then there were the constantly changing colors of her eyes. Her children had inherited none of this, yet they were Moshuguang and more.

It was late in the afternoon when they caught the public underground to the city twelve miles distant. The ride was short, but long enough for them to be examined by their fellow passengers sitting on benches facing each other along the train. The rough canvas clothing of the passengers, mainly natives and emmigrants from outlying villages, made Mengjai conscious of his uniform.

Two fierce looking little men had actually glared at them when they first got on the train. Small, but hard-muscled, their eyes had blazed red, mouths opening slightly to display short blunt tusks, but then Huomeng had raised a closed fist to them and given them a short salute. In return the men had nodded stiffly, and the glaring ceased after that.

"Warrior class," Father had explained. "Perhaps their fathers fought in the war against Shanji. Perhaps they even died there. They are part of your bloodline, son. The Tumatsin came from them a long time ago."

The port facility and the underground train had been blessedly air-conditioned, but when they reached the city and stepped out onto a platform near ground-level the air seemed to come from a blast furnace. A short flight of stairs up to the street and they were sweating. The sky was the usual orange haze of dust blown in from dry plains, and although Tengri-Nayon was nearing the horizon the heat was oppressive.

Construction was everywhere and the sidewalks were jammed with people jostling for routes around and beneath scaffolding. One lane of the street was blocked off by a team of workers laying bricks, and an endless line of little bubble-canopied two-seat cars was waiting for a chance to dart around them. Buildings of steel and reinforced polymer soared high on both sides of the street, most of them unfinished skeletons of metal several stories up.

As usual it was difficult to breathe, each breath more dust than air, but it was only four blocks to Yesugen's residence at city center, a four square block area where traffic was not allowed and construction was for the most part complete. The streets ended at a circular area of dark earth mottled green with the first shoots of grass from hybridized seed imported from Shanji. Baby *Tysk* only a foot high dotted the area, and in the center was a white quartzite basin with an obelisk rising several meters above it. The basin was empty, only filled with water during special occasions. Water was still a precious commodity on Meng-shijie and not to be wasted on a display of grandeur.

Yesugen's new residence was in the new building on the other side of the basin, a long, three story structure in yellow polymer surrounded by a high steel fence with a single entrance guarded by four men of the warrior class. Mengjai and his father presented their papers and Yesugen's formal letter of invitation at the gate. Each piece was examined carefully and a telephone call was made. The guards were polite, but watched them closely, laser rifles slung casually. One guard several inches shorter than Yesui returned their papers and bowed stiffly. "You are expected," he said, and opened the gate for them.

The grounds in front of the building were being tilled for planting, and they followed a red brick walkway to the entrance where two guards ushered them inside. Suddenly cold air chilled them. The building seemed empty, a large circular hall of black stone and a high dome ceiling in yellow, without decoration. A ring of indirect lighting reflected off the dome, but the room seemed gloomy to Mengjai. Austere, perhaps. Hallways radiated away like spokes of a wheel, all dark. A guard came out of one to their right. He was dressed in a black leather tunic with a silver chest plate, a pistol holstered at his side. "This way, please," he said, and bowed stiffly.

They followed him down a curving hallway dimly lit by tiny panels next to the floor, their footsteps echoing from the walls. "Not many people here today," said Huomeng.

"The meetings are on second floor," said the guard. "The residence is on the third." He stopped before a blank wall and held out something in his hand. There was a chirp, and a portion of the wall slid upwards, flooding them with light. An elevator. They stepped inside, the guard coming in after them. Steel walls, ceiling and floor. There was a control panel with several unmarked buttons and a slot for a key; the guard pressed a button, inserted a key into the slot and turned it.

The elevator moved slowly and groaned as they were lifted upwards. The door opened and two guards were facing them, rifles slung. Beyond them another guard sat at a console, face illuminated by the light from several screens and beyond him was a huge double door in black wood. The door suddenly opened and Kabul was standing there, the first friendly face they'd seen. "Come in, come in," he said, and the guards stepped aside for them.

They shook hands with Kabul, whose grip was crushing. A tall man in black leather and high boots, his face was crinkled and brown, with a mass of hair turning white, but he had a warm smile.

"Tight security," said Huomeng.

"Absolutely," said Kabul, then to Mengjai. "Tirgee is about to wake up. She doesn't know you're coming — at least I *think* she doesn't. One never knows with her."

Mengjai had last seen Tirgee when she was six months old, a beautiful child with huge eyes. She had traveled the gong-shi-jie with

Yesugen since birth, but at that moment when he was bouncing her on his knees and she was happily burbling, she was a baby girl who turned his heart into putty.

The residence was large, but simply furnished with lounges, chairs and tables rough-hewn from wood. Kabul touched an end table. "I made this," he said proudly. "It's that new variety of *Tysk* you've sent us, and even an amateur like me can work it. I used it for all the furniture in these rooms. It's a sort of hobby, and practical. Yesugen is quite pleased with the results."

A gentle man, thought Mengjai, yet quietly strong, for he had first stolen Yesugen's heart and then softened it. And now the children were there to soften it further. "Is Niki awake?" he asked.

"Soon. He should remember you quite well. And so far he's a good big brother to Tirgee. No squabbles yet."

Mengjai laughed. "Well, good luck."

Huomeng shook his head. "Indeed. We certainly had problems with *our* two when they were little."

Kabul showed them all the rooms, including the large dining room with a huge table and metal flatware set for five. Delicious odors of food cooking came from the kitchen, where two women were preparing the evening meal.

They ended their tour at the childrens' rooms, Niki's door ajar. Mengjai peeked inside, saw the three-year-old on his back, eyes open. The boy saw him and smiled. "Mengjai!" he said sleepily and yawned. "Are you really staying with us?"

"Yes, but don't hurry to get up. I'll see you at dinner."

"Okay," said Niki, rubbing his eyes as Mengjai closed the door.

Kabul opened Tirgee's door and the three of them went in quietly to see the new traveler in the gong-shi-jie. What they saw was a beautiful little girl asleep on her back, tiny hands by her head on the pillow. Tiny full lips, and a pug nose, her hair black but still short, she suddenly frowned as they looked down at her.

Mengjai felt a new presence in his mind just before Tirgee's eyes opened wide and locked on his. In a flash she was awake and animated, arms waving, legs kicking.

"Ghai!" she cried, and held out her arms to him. Her smile made him giddy. He picked her up and she gurgled happily, patted his face with both hands, then hugged him tightly, her little arms around his neck. "Ghai," she repeated, and continued her hug for seconds.

The men grinned at him. "Obviously she remembers you," said Kabul. "Quite a conquest."

Tirgee gave Huomeng a long appraising look, then pointed at Kabul and smiled beautifully. "Da!" she said, and squirmed in Mengjai's arms. Mengjai handed her to Kabul, where she nestled against him and burbled again.

As they left the room, Mengjai whispered to his father, "I felt her in my mind the instant she came awake. It was *strong*, like Yesui."

"I felt it too," said Huomeng.

They went back to a sitting room to talk. Niki came out of his room a few minutes later with a hand reader loaded with a disk of all the various ships, commercial and military, of the Shanji-Meng-shi-jie alliance. Mengjai sat him on his lap and went over each ship with him. Tirgee squirmed to get down, Kabul released her and she crawled quickly to Mengjai, stood up unsteadily, a hand on his knee. Her attention was rapt, eyes following the scroll of the reader, looking at him when he talked. Mengjai had the feeling she understood everything.

Yesugen arrived moments later, looking tired, but the children rushed to her, Tirgee crawling nearly as fast as her brother could walk. Yesugen swept Tirgee up into her arms and hugged Niki to her side. The three men rose to greet her. Even with an audience she kissed Kabul firmly, while the children clung to her. With her guests she shook hands with a firm grip. "Another day and little progress," she said. "All those men want to do is talk, talk, talk."

They went straight to table, for the servants had begun serving the instant Yesugen had arrived. She disappeared for only a moment to change from her military leathers into a rich burgundy robe, and sat down at the head of the table. Niki had his own place at table, sitting on an ingenious riser chair built by his father, but Tirgee sat in Yesugen's lap and was fed by her from a little bowl brought by the servants.

The meal was simple: squash, onions, a leafy green somewhat bitter to the taste, and goat's meat. There was tea laced with honey, and chunks of crumbly cheese to finnish the meal. Huomeng gave Yesugen the message from his wife, and Yesugen snorted. "At least when *we* talk, something gets done."

Still tough on the outside, thought Mengjai, and once a formidable adversary of Shanji. But times change, and so do people. Now they were connected by trade and something else — those special people who traveled in the gong-shi-jie. As he thought it Mengjai looked at Tirgee and saw she was watching him.

Do you hear my thoughts, little one?

Tirgee gave him a beautiful smile, then clenched her hands open and closed as Yesugen slid another spoonful of food into her mouth.

Talk quickly turned to politics and Mengjai had nothing to contribute. He was immediately bored. The children became restless and Niki asked to be excused. As her brother left the table, Tirgee squirmed and complained, so Yesugen put her down and the baby crawled quickly after Niki. A moment later Niki was back tugging at Mengjai's sleeve.

"Will you play with me?" he asked.

Mengjai looked at Yesugen, who nodded and smiled, and so he excused himself and followed Niki to his room. The room had been neat before, but now it was cluttered. Tirgee sat in the middle of the floor, a fuzzy red bunny in her sleeper. She had emptied an entire box of colorful polymer blocks all over herself. The blocks were paired with matching male and female links of various shapes and she was busily assembling them into a chain.

Niki showed him a collection of stuffed animal toys neatly arranged on a shelf, and in a drawer lovely crystals from the mines of Meng-shi-jie were lined up in rows. In another drawer a large box was filled with metal miniatures of fierce looking warriors and two attack cruisers of Meng-shi-jie, each in its place in soft polymer. Niki took them out one by one and for nearly an hour Mengjai helped him arrange them in various attack formations on the floor. All formations were historical; Niki's play was education, for he was successor to the throne of Meng-shi-jie and did not yet know it.

Tirgee mostly ignored them, glancing over occasionally, intent on her work. But then four blocks were left over and nothing would fit. She got up on all fours, pushed off the floor and stood, then *walked* to a closet in a stumbling gait and rummaged in a box there. Came back with five more blocks clutched in her little arms, sat down again. Still two blocks remaining unattached. She repeated the process again, walking to and from the closet, two more blocks found and her chain was completed. She draped it over her head, stood up and paraded around the room, dragging the chain behind her like the train of an Empress' formal robe. And looked over her shoulder at Mengjai.

A beautiful gown, my lady. You are very clever, he thought.

Tirgee, Ghai, and she smiled.

But then someone was coming; the girl dropped to all fours and crawled towards the door. Kabul was suddenly there and picked her up. "Ah, doing your chain again," he said, then to Mengjai, "Come have a drink with us, something relaxing before sleep."

"Thank you. I didn't know Tirgee was walking yet."

"She has taken her first steps," said Kabul.

"Well, she's been walking all around this room for the last ten minutes." Tirgee frowned at him.

"Really? Well, she *can* be a secretive little girl. Put your troops away, Niki, and you can have a sweet drink with us before bedtime."

Niki rushed to obey.

The rest of the evening was spent in the sitting room. There was gossip about Yesui and Nokai, and Yesugen wanted to know about their sensations during a space-time jump. The adults sipped a clear liquid from small, chilled glasses, Mengjai commenting he'd just discovered a new auxilliary fuel for their ship. Yesugen laughed. "It is slowly distilled from the juices of various desert succulents, and one small glass is sufficient for a good night's sleep."

Something was wrong with Tirgee. She was pouty and wouldn't smile at him. When Mengjai tried to pick her up she crawled away from him and spent most of the evening in Yesugen's lap scowling at everyone, and Mengjai in particular. He'd angered her, no doubt, but how? Yesugen sensed his concern. "She gets like this when she's tired," she explained.

Tirgee didn't complain when Yesugen took her to bed, but when Mengjai waved goodnight to her she turned her head away from him. Niki formally excused himself minutes later and went to bed on his own. The adults soon followed, deliciously warmed by their drinks. Mengjai and his father slept in separate beds, matresses hard and cushioned saddles of wood for pillows.

Mengjai's eyelids were heavy as his head hit the pillow. But as he drifted off there was suddenly an angry presence in his mind.

Ghai! Na se Tirgee ba-ba, Ghai! Na!

Now what was *that* about? wondered Mengjai, and then he fell into a blissful sleep.

In the morning, all seemed normal. Tirgee burbled and hugged him when he picked her up. "Whatever happened, it seems I'm forgiven," he said, and held her little hand. Yesugen had left before daylight, but Kabul remained until noon, talking with Huomeng while Mengjai played soldiers with Niki and Tirgee nestled in his lap. When it was time to leave, Niki was upset and near tears, but Mengjai assured him they would see each other again and then the boy brightened. In her father's arms Tirgee only smiled when Mengjai gave her a goodbye hug. "Someday, if I'm lucky, I'll have a little girl just like you," he whispered.

A final handshake with Kabul and they were gone, walking the dust-choked streets towards the underground taking them back to port to live on the ship five days while loading and servicing were completed.

Father was saying something to him, but Mengjai heard little of it.

There was a strange empty feeling inside of him.

Nearly three light-years from Meng-shi-jie four men sat down at a table for afternoon cakes and tea. All were dressed in tailored bodysuits of white leather currently in fashion among middle-class citizens of Jensi City, though one of the men had come to this meeting from a place far to the west. The men were all in their forties, with the first strands of grey showing in long shining hair they wore as tails held in place by small bands of pure silver. Their fingernails were manicured and polished to a gleam, eyebrows trimmed and shaped into arches accentuating their eyes, and with a close look the pores on their skin could be counted.

The table was shielded by an umbrella and sat on a veranda at the second level of a substantial house in white marble that enclosed a lovely garden and central fountain. There was a spectacular view of the surrounding forested hills, and to the east the spire of The Mother's Church rose with tall buildings into a clear sky.

The owner of the house, a man named Sheng-chih, poured tea for the others, then broke a sweetcake into four pieces and performed the distribution. "In the name of First Mother, who has honored us with Her blessings," he said solemnly.

"We give Her our thanks," they said together, and ate.

Sheng raised his cup, and the others did likewise. "To Wang Mengnu, good health and wisdom. May her reign be long and prosperous."

"With the blessings of First Mother," said the others, and they drank.

Sheng passed the rest of the cakes around, each man filling his little plate and waiting politely until their host began eating. "Such a lovely day we have, so close after the rainy season," he said.

"There is still light rain in Wanchou and some flooding north, but the Dahe should be within its banks in a day or two," said the man who had traveled far.

"Zao and Tuen have relocated their offices to Jensi City, and you could do the same. All our dealings with production matters can be done electronically, and it's so much nicer to live here," said Sheng.

"Yes, Chuen, we have only the occasional high winds here, and the rainy season is short," said Zao.

"In the future, it would be best if we could meet regularly like this," said Tuen. "I don't trust the security of our net."

"Nor do I," said Chuen. "I will give consideration to such a move. There is logic in having an office at the banking center of Shanji. My board will understand that."

"Good," said Sheng. "We will then keep our discussions to a minimum this evening, and have time to enjoy the splendid meal my staff has worked all day preparing for us. I've also arranged for our entertainment, four lovely and talented young women from the city. All are healthy and from educated families. I must insist, however, that you stay here overnight in order to fully enjoy their company."

"We are honored, Sheng-chih," said Zao, and the others nodded in agreement.

The men ate silently for a moment, each with pleasant thoughts about the evening to come. It was Tuen who broke the silence.

"I suppose you've heard by now that Shiang liaw is gravely ill."

"Yes," said Sheng. "I understand he's not expected to last the month. What a shame he has no children to carry on the family business. I hear his wife is also quite frail."

"There is talk she intends to sell a good portion of the family holdings," said Tuen. "A four thousand hectar tract of timber to the north of us has been mentioned specifically, and two other noble families have expressed interest in the acquisition. It is necessary to acquire the entire tract, and Madam Shiang will be putting it up for bids.

"But nobles sell to nobles," grumbled Tuen.

"Not under present law. She must accept the highest bid, and there can be no bias regarding the class of the bidder. Our enlightened People's Empress has seen to that," said Sheng.

"Four thousand hectars," said Tuen, "the price will be far beyond our reach."

Sheng steepled his fingers in front of his face, and smiled. "Ah, but *that* is the topic of discussion this evening. So many have profited well under the new reign of Our Empress, but they remain independent. They have not organized themselves into something greater and stronger like we have. They must see the value of cooperation, the increased profit in being a single cell in a much larger, healthy organism. We must bring them into our fold, Tuen, and show them the way to fortunes they haven't dreamed of."

"The sale will take place within months," said Tuen. "Can we organize so quickly?"

"Perhaps, but not likely. There will be other opportunities," said Sheng. "We must think in the long term. But you might make inquiries among your contacts and find out what bids are being offered for this property."

"The bids will be sealed," said Tuen.

Sheng chuckled. "Of what use are contacts unless they provide us with advantages in business? With usefulness comes their profit. Without it, their reason for existence ceases. Our methods for obtaining advantages are irrelevant, as long as they are discrete."

"I understand," said Tuen.

"Good," said Sheng, and he poured tea for each of them, then picked up his cup.

"Gentlemen, the days of the nobles are nearing their end. The families are soft from luxurious living, their political position softened to weakness by the new order on Shanji. Power is now in the hands of the people, and wealth will come to those smart enough and ambitious enough to take it. People with vision — like us."

He raised his cup. "Let us drink to the *new* nobility on Shanji."

They raised their cups, and drank deeply.

Three

The wedding was delayed three months by squabbling.

The problem was mostly between Yesui and her mother. Yesui wanted a small private ceremony with only immediate family as guests. Mother wanted something grand. "You are Mei-lai-gong," she declared. "The people know what you did for Lan-Sui and how you hurry our ships to and from Meng-shi-jie, but many don't even realize you're my daughter. They have never seen you in public, never seen us together. You've become a creature of mythology to them, you, the person who will someday rule in my place!"

That issue alone was enough to sidetrack them into an entire week of heated argument, for Yesui still stubbornly refused to consider being Empress of Shanji or any other world except the gong-shi-jie. Even in the place of creation she had no responsibilities for rule. There were beings of higher order than her, beings who had taught her, guided her to wonderful new places. She wanted only a life of learning and exploration, and chances to use her powers for good as she'd done for Lan-Sui. Let First Mother rule the universe if She wished. Yesui wanted no part of it. She only wanted to experience wonderful new things — and to be married to Nokai.

There were external pressures on the Empress of Shanji, but Yesui had no patience with them. The Wazera family had requested a service on Lan-Sui, but Yesui rejected the idea and Nokai firmly supported her. "Even with jumps it would take us *months* to be married and resume our lives," she complained.

Then there were the priests in Jensi City who wanted a grand ceremony in Church of The Mother, the wedding to be held two days after a public reception in honor of the Mei-lai-gong and her work. Yesui could envision the media circus certain to accompany such a plan, and she threw such a tantrum even Nokai was shocked by her behavior. But he was there to comfort her when she threw herself sobbing into his arms right in view of the blazing red eyes of her mother.

Gong-gong and Father gave her support, but Mengjai was no help at all.

"Kati, the girl's wedding is perhaps the most memorable day in her life. Forget politics for one minute and let her have what she wants," said Mengmoshu to a furious daughter. "There will be plenty of time later for public receptions."

"I agree," said Huomeng. "When we were married you only wanted a private ceremony here, and you were newly crowned as Empress. Even the ceremony your Tumatsin gave us was a simple thing, and they hurried us off to our gert so we could be alone."

Huomeng put an arm around his wife and Empress. "I still remember some wonderful nights we spent with your people, Kati," he said, eyes narrowing. "Hmmm."

Mother smiled for just an instant, touching Huomeng's shoulder with her head, eyes flickering green, but then red again. "So do I, dear, but that was for us. I was commited to being Empress and meeting the people. Yesui is not."

"Again, there is time for that," said Gong-gong. "This is a wedding, not a political act. Kati, you fight against a will that is inherited from *you*. How well I remember it from the time you were a little girl."

"And so do I," said Huomeng.

Mother was not amused, but seemed to soften. "All right. If anyone has an idea for compromise I would like to hear it."

Mengjai had been silently watching all of this, smirking, and shaking his head. "Compromise! What an incredible suggestion! Grand or simple, what difference does a ceremony make, Yesui? When you're married you're married, the ceremony is over and you have the rest of your lives together."

Yesui remembered a time she'd been deliberately cruel to her little brother by transfering a favorite toy of his to the gong-shi-jie. Now, she wanted to strangle him.

"Could you please leave us along for a while so we can discuss this?" Nokai asked suddenly and firmly.

Everyone seemed surprised, even Mother. "Well — I suppose."

"Sure," said Mengjai, moving to leave the room. "This has gone on long enough and at least you can talk to her. Good luck."

Mengjai left, but the others hesitated.

Nokai held Yesui tightly against him, and there was a tone of command in his voice she's never heard before.

"We'll call you when we're ready," he said.

The men nodded, took Mother by the arms, and firmly yet gently marched her out of the room.

We'll be right outside that door.

YES, Mother, I hear you.

The door closed, and they were alone. Yesui burst into tears and pressed her face against Nokai's chest, body shuddering. Nokai held her tightly, hands carressing her back.

"I wish we could just run away somewhere," she sobbed.

"Shhhh, my darling. Whatever happens, we'll be together. Remember, we are not alone. Wherever we are, First Mother is with us and She has blessed our marriage. Even now we are as one with Her. All else is ceremony to satisfy others."

He took her face in his hands and kissed her so softly her lips tingled. "You are my wife, and I love you. I will go where you go, and your wish is mine."

Yesui smiled. "I wish you could go with me to the gong-shi-jie so we could hide there for a little while and escape all this arguing."

Nokai carressed her cheek and ran a finger over her parted lips. "All that happens is by First Mother if you only listen to your heart, my darling. If you are calm and listen carefully, the choices you make will be pleasing to Her. But She has made us one, and that will not be changed by ceremony. Our love will not be changed by it. Whatever the ceremony we are joined together as husband and wife. And a compromise is not so hard to make if you yield yourself to it. Now turn inwards, and listen to your heart."

He held her tightly for a long moment, then asked, "Are you ready?"

"I think so," she said, and kissed him.

They went outside to meet the expectant family members.

And within half an hour had agreed on a plan for a wedding that greatly pleased the Empress of Shanji.

Three months of preparations, though not the usual things for an expectant bride. Everything was done for her, everything decided for her. Yesui's single task was to jump the ship bearing Yesugen and the Wazeras from Meng-shi-jie to Shanji. She did it in one jump, bringing the ship within a week of orbit around Shanji and hoping that collisions within the cometary cloud would damp out the disturbance she'd caused there in moving the ship through it.

Before the jump Yesugen had joined her briefly in the gong-shi-jie and shown her a regal manifestation with high crown and flowing robe. *You do your work in a place I cannot penetrate*, she said sadly, *but both your mother and I suspect Tirgee is capable of it. Would you test her abilities and teach her what you can?*

I would be honored to, said Yesui, and was delighted by the idea of having a student to work with. Tirgee, grand daughter of Abagai, she who had instructed both Yesui and her mother in the place of creation, would be the first of a new generation to travel here. What would the higher order creators think of this? The Chuang shi. Creators of stars. Yesui hadn't heard a thing from the being she called 'Mind' for nearly two years, yet she knew the Chuang shi still watched her. Perhaps they watched Nokai, too. How else would the two of them have received that wonderful benediction on the evening they'd pledged their marriage?

So Yesui made the jump, and returned to herself. She endured a day of instruction on how she should act and the signs she should show to the people. Yesui only saw herself being dragged into a future role she did not want, her role as Empress of Shanji.

"You must accept it, if your heart says so," said Nokai when she was fuming again. "You're still not listening. In a few days this will be over and for a while we can live our lives the way we wish to, but your future responsibilities as Empress will not go away. Your mother won't live forever, and you are her oldest child."

Yesui listened to her heart, but it said nothing either way, and so she endured. The agony was softened by the arrival of Nokai's parents, who loved her immediately and gave her crushing embraces. They were gentle loving people, and in their minds Yesui found no political ambitions regarding the marriage of their son to The Mei-lai-gong. To them, she was only a sweet young woman their son had fallen in love with. They tried hard to stay in the background, but were guests of the Empress and occupied rooms next to Yesugen's near the royal suite.

It was the first time Yesui had met Empress Yesugen in person. Not once in her life had Yesui seen the changeling face of her mother, and now here was Yesugen, tall, with a chisled gaunt face, oval eyes, and short blunt tusks showing in her upper mouth when she talked. Yesui's first sight of Yesugen was disturbing, but the woman sensed it and understood.

"You appear so delicate," said Yesugen. "Yet you have the power to destroy a star. You've not inherited the Changeling traits of your mother, I see. In battle, she was terrifying to behold."

"I am not my mother, Yesugen. I'm pleased to meet you face-to-face at last," said Yesui, but then Mother came up and rushed the Empress of Meng-shi-jie away to some meeting.

They ate several meals together in the royal suite, the families of bride and groom well mixed in their places at table. Conversation was light, even between Empresses. The Wazeras were fascinated by the gong-shi-jie and wanted to hear everything about it, including what Yesui saw and did there. Yesui described it as best she could, but at one point she sensed a terrible thought in the mind of Nokai's mother that drove her to tears.

Oh Nokai, my baby! What can this supernatural person possibly see in you? And what kind of life will you have while living in her shadow?

Yesui burst into tears in mid-sentence, covered her face with her hands and bolted away from the table. She left the room, leaned against a wall in the hallway, her body shaking from the sobbing. Nokai came after her. She felt him before his touch, leaned back into his embrace.

"What is it?" he asked softly, and kissed her ear.

Yesui masked herself furiously. "It's nothing — just all the talk — the waiting — I'm so tired of it all."

Warm in his arms she composed herself and he took her back inside. Everyone was staring at her as she sat down. "Sorry," she said, "but isn't a bride entitled to a single fit of nerves? It's over, now. I'm fine."

Everyone smiled, except Gong-gong. Five Moshuguang at table, and only Yesui had sensed the concern of her future mother-in-law. Or not? Gong-gong continued frowning at his soup, then finally came to comfort her.

I heard it too. It is nothing, the concern of a mother hanging on to her only child. She thinks him ordinary and he is not. Now put it out of your mind!

Yesui smiled at him; he wiggled his bushy eyebrows at her and went back to his soup. Conversation resumed and the incident seemed quickly forgotten.

But Yesui did not forget it.

Getting married was a four day affair.

The first day was more the way Yesui had imagined it might be, a ceremony taking place by a pond in the hanging garden just below the palace. The garden was in full bloom, the air perfumed. Only the immediate families were present. Mother was disappointed by the absence of Weimeng, her foster mother, who was now in hospital with a viral infection. Even Gong-gong seemed concerned about the woman's health.

Both Yesui and Nokai wore the white silken robes of purity. Garlands of tiny wildflowers were laced in the hair Tanchun had patiently combed out into a cascade down Yesui's back. In the presence of their families they stood to face a magistrate under a canopy of yellow silk laced with gold threads, and held hands.

The ceremony lasted one minute; they exchanged simple vows of love, loyalty, respect and honor, and the magistrate pronounced them man and wife. They kissed, and signed the wedding contract, then received the congratulations of their families.

There was no time for a relaxed reception, no time yet to be alone as husband and wife. They went straight to the cable car station and filled a car going to the flyer field. There they boarded several aircraft for a hop over the mountains north and to the city of Wanchou where a parade and reception awaited them. Mengjai did not accompany them on this diplomatic journey, but stayed behind to ready the first flight of one of the descent vehicles that had brought people to Shanji ages ago. It was a task originally dreamed of by his father.

The wind had blown Yesui's hair into a frazzle by the time they landed, but Tanchun was there to comb it all out again. The day was hot and Yesui felt sticky beneath her robe.

The media snakes were thankfully out of sight, but were snapping their pictures through telescopic lenses while Yesui, Nokai and their entourage piled into several cars with transparent bubble tops. They were soon joined by several other cars painted in military blue and filled with armed troops of the Moshuguang elite. A caravan was formed and they drove with terrifying speed to the city, the military vehicles clearing the way for them with flashing lights and sirens.

They slowed before turning onto a large street of brick, tall buildings lining it on either side as far as she could see. Ahead the street was empty, Moshuguang standing guard at blocked off intersections. The sidewalks were a mass of people pushing against each other for position, many arms raised to wave greenstone pendants at her. The people cried out to her, but no sound penetrated the bubble of the car. Still she heard them, in their minds, the cries of joy, of supplication, the confusion when they saw her.

The Mei-lai-gong is coming! There! No, it's only a young woman in white — but there is our Empress! Mei-lai-gong must be near. Look for the glow of her presence. Mei-lai-gong! See the amulet of my belief, and hear my prayers!

Nokai squeezed her hand. "Yesui, you must give them something of yourself. They are your people."

As instructed by Mother, yes, but the storm of thoughts in her mind was crushing her and she was compelled to do what she'd agreed to do. She took a deep breath, let it out slowly as she drew in the energy of her surroundings. The car's interior suddenly chilled and was filled with an aura colored emerald green, and with it came the strongest greeting she could muster.

WE ARE JOINED BY FIRST MOTHER, AND COME WITH HER BLESSINGS TO WISH YOU LIVES OF PEACE AND HAPPINESS.

Yesui waved regally to the crowd as she did this, and Nokai joined her, looking pleased.

The crowd was stunned at the sight of her, the sudden presence in their minds. Men bowed solemnly, women burst into tears, held out amulets towards her and little children stared at her with huge eyes.

The prayers came at her with a rush and seemed to go on forever. Prayers for a sick child, the loss of a job, the wish for a departed loved one to be taken into the arms of First Mother, they filled her, drowned her in feeling until she began to shiver. Nokai put an arm around her and she felt safe again, feeling his warmth, his love. Her aura flickered, then held steady, and she continued her mental greeting as a kind of mantra to keep her focus.

An eternity later it was over. An entire block of the street was barricaded against foot traffic. The caravan pulled up in front of a long, seven storied building sided in yellow polymer and with many windows.

Heat blasted her as she got out of the highly chilled car. Mother organized them into a line and they filed inside, Empress and her husband leading, then Yesugen, with Yesui and Nokai behind her, the rest following. A line of dignitaries awaited them. Mother made the introductions; a mayor, ministers of planning, sewers, culture, et cetera, et cetera. Yesui could recall none of their names when it was over.

They went up a long flight of stairs to a large room filled with linen covered tables and huge crystal chandeliers. They sat down at a long table on a raised dias, only the mayor sitting with the honored guests, but all the other tables were soon filled. Yesui worked hard at maintaining a serene expression as she looked out at all the unfamiliar faces staring back at her. And her stomach was grumbling from hunger.

The mayor gave a short speech. Yesui didn't hear it, but was conscious enough to join the applause when it was finished. Glasses at each place were filled with a golden liquid. Mother gave a short speech of thanks for their reception and proposed a toast to bride and groom. They drank. The liquid burned a fiery path into Yesui's empty stomach, and she wouldn't touch another drop of it the rest of the evening.

The meal arrived in eight courses, a hundred servers attending the gathering. Yesui nibbled at bits of meat she could not identify, and filled herself with noodles. The meats were hot and spicy, and did not set well in her stomach. The sour pudding they had for desert was even worse. But Nokai seemed to enjoy all of it, sampling everything and smiling his approval.

Everytime she looked up it seemed like all eyes were on her, and she had to maintain her composure. All energy seemed drained from her, and her stomach was being uncooperative in the digestion of her food. She was nearing tears.

Just when Yesui thought she might make a fool of herself Mother called an end to the event, explaining they must rest before traveling to Jensi City the next morning and thanking all for kindness and hospitality. The entourage paraded grandly from the room, mayor and Empress leading the procession. More handshaking at the waiting cars. Mother seemed to have more energy than hours before, while daughter was ready to faint.

I can't do this, thought Yesui behind a hard mask. If this is what's required of me as an Empress, I cannot, I WILL not do it!

Rooms were reserved for them on a secured floor in a hotel near the flyer field. Another drive at terrifying speed, and they were there. At dusk Yesui found herself at last alone with Nokai in a simple windowless room with two chairs, writing desk and a single bed. It was their wedding night. Yesui flopped down on the bed to test it. Her eyelids seemed heavy. She sighed, looked lovingly up at Nokai, who smiled back and began fumbling with the sash on his robe.

"My darling," she murmured —

And awoke.

Nokai sat on the edge of the bed rubbing his eyes, his naked back to her.

"Wha — what time is it?" she asked sleepily.

"Six, and now there's pounding on the door. No wonder we're awake. We have to be at the field in twenty minutes!" He stood up, back to her, and slipped his robe down over his head. For just one instant the view was wonderful.

Yesui was fully clothed, her robe barely rumpled. Nokai sat down on the bed, leaned over and kissed her firmly on the mouth. "Hurry," he said.

She looked at him sadly, tears welling in her eyes. He kissed her again, and smiled. "You were so tired last night, and fell asleep before my eyes. I couldn't bring myself to wake you."

"It was our *wedding* night," she sobbed.

"I know. Tonight, then. Now hurry, or they'll start pounding on the door again!"

By the time a Moshuguang trooper came for their bags, Yesui was in a state of quiet fury. She scowled at everyone in sight, including Mother.

What's wrong with you?

It's nothing. My marriage is starting out as a ruin, but it's no matter to you.

Mother's eyes were red until the squadron of flyers touched down near Jensi City. After a three hour flight Yesui was ravenous and even Nokai, in his usual good mood, was rubbing his stomach when it grumbled. The only food on the flight had been a single honeycake washed down with cold bitter tea.

Another caravan sped them towards the city: tall, colorful buildings and a single spire from the Church of The Mother thrust up into a clear sky, a monument to the new Shanji. A city of banking, commerce, new technology, its citizens were chosen carefully for their skills. Everything seemed new and clean. The surrounding hills were dotted with sparkling homes of those most successful under the new democracy, homes of quartzite and white marble, nestled in thick forests of tall trees. Yesui was impressed, yet the newness, the freshness of the place strangely bothered her.

There was no parade this time, no crowds of people clothed in canvas. They sped down streets without slowing and the few people they saw only gave them a glance. All were dressed in tailored form-fitting suits in white or black, and seemed in a hurry to get somewhere.

They neared Church of The Mother and there was a crowd cordoned off around the front entrance. The building was a block of white stone without ornamentation, its black marble spire rising like a spear fifty meters above it.

I know you're angry, but please remember our agreement. Just this one day, Yesui, and it will be better. Please! said Mother.

Yes, yes, and yes!

Yesui breathed deeply to prepare herself, and Nokai held her hand. As they got out of the car Yesui let the aura come to her, and the two of them were enveloped in green.

People cried out, amulets waving among a crowd of well-dressed people held back by barricades, and Yesui's head was instantly throbbing from Mother's greeting to them.

I come as a servant to First Mother, and bring her greetings to you. Know that She watches over you and blesses your lives.

The crowd was hushed. A few knelt in reverence. Mother had summoned her own aura, and was enveloped in a lovely blue glow. All had been previously orchestrated. Mother held out a hand to her and Yesui approached, tightly gripping Nokai's hand.

This is Yesui, my daughter, and her new husband Nokai Wazera, son of the Governor of Lan-Sui.

Yesui's head buzzed from the force of her mother's presence, but knew she was more than equal to the rehersed task. She took Mother's hand and turned to face the crowd, auras of blue and green melding together.

A few more people knelt in the crowd as Yesui paused an instant for focus. And Nokai squeezed her hand gently as she showed her true self to the people.

I AM YESUI, DAUGHTER OF WANG MENGNU-SHAN-SHI-JIE. I AM MEI-LAI-GONG, GIFTED BY FIRST MOTHER TO BRING LIGHT AND MATTER WHERE I WILL IT. TODAY I CELEBRATE MY MAR-RIAGE TO NOKAI, AND THE UNITING OF OUR WORLDS. I BRING YOU GREETINGS FROM FIRST MOTHER, AND HER WISH FOR YOUR LIVES TO BE PEACEFUL AND HAPPY.

As she said it, her aura changed from green to a rich, deep purple, a great fan reaching meters above her head.

The crowd knelt in unison, as if struck down flat by a great hand.

Yesui hated the sight of it. For one horrible moment she felt like a charlatan, but then it passed. Nokai squeezed her hand again and smiled, and the bad feeling passed.

The procession into the church was led by two Empresses, side-by-side, Yesui and Nokai behind them, then the rest of the entourage. They went down a center aisle between filled pews, the parishoners all standing and gawking at the aural displays. No altar, no decorations, only a lecturn and four chairs on a raised platform at the front, one occupied by a lay priest in a tailored white suit. He rose as they approached.

Nokai released her hand and she followed Mother and Yesugen up three steps to the platform. They stood by their chairs as the man with them went to the lecturn and opened a little red book there. "Page ninety five," he said, and the rustling of pages being turned was heard throughout the church.

"We welcome Yesugen, Empress of Meng-shi-jie, our friend and ally. May our friendship continue for many generations. We welcome Yesui, The Creator of Worlds, Empress of Light and energy in all forms. She is Mei-lai-gong, and comes to us from First Mother to do Her work."

The crowd stared at her and Yesui stared back, feeling a strange uneasiness in the presence of these people. Her aura responded, brightening, and the feelings of awe she felt from the congregation were somehow satisfying.

"Finally, we welcome our beloved Empress, Wang Mengnu Shan-shi-jie, she who guides us in the ways of The Mother and watches over our lives. Now hear her words."

Heads were bowed as people looked at the little red books they held. Yesui felt disgust rising within herself and caught Nokai looking at her as if he knew it. *If you're in my mind, why don't I feel it?* she said to him.

"And when they were quieted, she said to them, 'Now hear the Will of First Mother. Those who heed the plight of the sick and the poor, of those who cannot help themselves, these are blessed in My Sight. Those who ignore it are cursed'."

A strange choice of quotation, thought Yesui, and there was passion in the priest's voice when he said it. Again she felt unease, and wondered if she was sensing something from the hushed crowd and not herself.

"Our honored guest from Meng-shi-jie would now like to say a few words. Please be seated," said the priest, and went back to his chair.

Yesugen went to the lecturn and began to speak, but Yesui barely heard it. Her turn was next, and she'd never spoken to such a close formal crowd before now. Nerves, yes, but something else was disturbing her: growing uneasiness, even a sense of hostility was there. Her words were rehersed, the same greeting she'd given to the masses outside the church, and thanks for hospitality, yet now she felt suddenly compelled to say something more and that something was certain to make Mother unhappy. The compulsion was growing with each beat of her heart. She looked at Nokai, but he only closed his eyes slowly and opened them again. His expression seemed stern and then she heard someone say 'Mei-lai-gong' and her heart skipped a beat.

Yesugen had turned away from the lecturn, and was holding out a hand to her. "Yesui?" she said.

Mother didn't look at her, staring straight ahead with eyes blazing red.

Yesui went to the lecturn, breathing deeply to calm her nerves, but the compulsion remained, growing each second. Still, her voice was steady as she repeated the rehersed greeting she'd given to those outside the church. But as she neared its end she felt a terrible force strike within her, a thing compelling her to continue when all she wanted was to be finished with it. Her aura seemed to have a mind of its own and was now illuminating the first ten pews of the church in deep purple. People were stirring uneasily in their seats and staring up at her with wide eyes. Nokai and Father had never looked more serious, and Gong-gong was actually scowling.

Yesui paused a long moment and let her gaze wander over the congregation. Gong-gong later told her that at this instant red streamers suddenly radiated upwards within the purple of her aura, an effect he found most impressive.

Yesui paused, and felt a new feeling from the people before her. Terror.

Now she spoke softly, but all could hear her, for more than sound carried her words. "I am a woman gifted by First Mother," she said. "I am Mei-lai-gong. I am Moshuguang, and I sense a disturbance among you. Perhaps it only comes from a few, but it is there, and I have only felt it in this place. You must examine yourselves to be certain you follow the Will of Our Mother in all things. If you do not follow Her Will, then all you have built here is without meaning. And without Her presence, your lives will be empty."

There, it was out, but from where? Yesui felt her face flush as she turned from the lectern, fearing a look at her mother's face, but doing it. Mother's eyes were blazing red, her face gaunt, horrible, two glints of ivory protruding from her upper lip. Mother didn't look at her, yet brushed by her in taking a daughter's place at the lectern.

Oh, what have I done? thought Yesui. She saw the priest still seated, holding his face in his hands.

Yesui sat down, face burning, and tried to still the hammering of her heart. What evil force had suddenly entered her to cause such humiliation for herself and her family? What must Nokai think? Now he wasn't looking at her, but at Mother, standing tall at the lectern.

Yesui felt salty tears welling in her eyes and fought back a sob. It had taken only an instant to realize that for the first time in her life she was seeing her mother's changeling face and now hundreds of people were shuddering at the sight of it, most of them Hansui being reminded their Empress was indeed a Tumatsin. This was certainly *not* what Mother wanted, for she'd said it many times. It was a countenance brought about by fear, or anger, a thing inherited from bioengineered warriors of Yesugen's world, marking her as a foreigner.

It was a countenance last seen in a short, but terrible war.

But Mother just stood there for a long moment, letting all see her as she was. The church was horribly silent, except for a few nervous coughs. Yesui risked a blurred glance at Yesugen, but the woman only sat there calmly, her mouth slightly open to display her own short tusks.

Mother gripped the lectern with her left hand, turned to point at Yesui with her right. Yesui blinked, and felt a gush of wetness on her cheeks. *Oh, Mother, I'm so sorry*, she thought hard.

Mother pointed, her blue aura now laced in red and yellow, voice deep and gutteral.

"Hear the words of The Mei-lai-gong," she growled, "and obey them, for it is she who follows me on the throne of Shanji!"

No! No! I can't! Not after this! I can't do it! I won't! thought Yesui.

"She has dared to tell you a thing I have personally felt since entering this church, a thing that was not here during my last visit. I will be more specific in my observations. What I feel is coming from more than a few of you. It is arrogance, selfishness and greed, and these are not the ways of First Mother, It is not *my* way. I did not perceive such things in the mass of people outside this church, but I feel them *here*. It occurs to me I'm speaking to a select group of people with influence to obtain seating in this coolness rather than standing outside in the heat. Yet many of you still follow The Way. You work for the betterment of *all* people, not just yourselves. Let it remain that way. What you have done here is a marvel, and is an example of what can be done anywhere on Shanji. But do *not* become elitists, for that is the very thing I fought against when I first took the throne. And if necessary I will fight against it again."

Yesui was happily surprised by her mother's words, but still felt new tears on her face. When she looked at Nokai, his smile made her face flush again.

"I have been negligent in not visiting here more often," said Mother. "This will not be so in the future. In the meantime, I bring you best wishes from First Mother for happy and productive lives in Her service."

The people were stunned. More than a few were weeping, and some heads were bowed, perhaps to hide shame. Mother went to the seated priest and put her hand on his head. Face covered by his hands, he wept in short sobs, as if trying to catch his breath.

"The guilt is not yours, Lao," she said softly, "and without your warning I would not have been prepared for what is happening here. Now stand up, and take your station as spiritual leader of this church. And let us leave these people to think about what has been said."

Lao stood, eyes red and moist. His self-control returned with amazing swiftness. He bowed to his guests, then led them from the platform and down the long aisle of the church. The entourage followed, Yesui gripping Nokai's hand tightly, for her Moshuguang mind now swirled with feelings of sorrow, anger and hostility in a great wave from the people. Energy draining, she lost her aura by the time they reached the high double doors at the entrance. The doors opened as Yesui felt something darkly threatening, but it passed quickly when she head the cheers of the people outside.

Smiling faces, amulets waving, the people strained at the barricades. Mother embraced Lao, whispered something and he was weeping again. She turned to Yesui and held out her hand. The fierce countenance was gone and her eyes were emerald green.

Come, she said.

The two of them broke away from the entourage standing by waiting cars and they went to the barricades, guards hurrying to follow them. Yesui was suddenly euphoric from the new feelings, her smile automatic. The surging crowd saw them coming and gave a collective gasp. Some knelt, others held out their hands. Babies were thrust forward for a blessing.

Yesui followed Mother down the line of barricades, touching hands and faces, smiling, feeling the touches of other hands on her robe. In seconds she was near tears from the wonderful feelings inside her.

May The Mother bless you with peaceful and happy lives.

The minutes were seconds and then they returned to the cars waiting to speed them away to a nearby hotel.

These are the people, Yesui. These are YOUR people, said Mother, and then the crowd, the church, all the feelings were gone and Yesui was pressed up against the man she loved as her car careened down an empty street.

That night was spent in an exclusive hotel of palatial opulence at city center, a place frequented by nobles and more successful members of the new emerging middle class on Shanji. Mother thought it excessive: plush red carpets, wall tapestries of country scenes, dome ceilings guilded in gold. Even the palace of Mengnu was not furnished so grandly.

They occupied the entire top floor of the hotel, a structure of forty levels. Food was brought to them on trays of pure silver and served by hotel staff in a large dining room in the Empress's suite. Large chandeliers in brass with hanging crystals of citrine and amethyst lighted an ebonite table. Dishes and cups were laced with flower patterns in gold, and they ate with golden sticks.

Mother had provided the menu and so the meal was simple, though served in eight courses: carrousels of spices, into which they dipped slices of mutton, goat, and fish from the southern sea, then a thick barley soup which they ate with spoons, two courses of vegetables, one raw, one cooked, followed by honeycakes and sour berries in thick sweet cream.

It took them three hours to consume the meal. The Wazeras were exhausted and excused themselves early. Tanchun was preparing beds for all of them when Huomeng took Nokai away for a 'conversation between men', leaving Yesui with her mother and grandfather at table.

Yesui felt abandoned, but Mother smiled and said, "They won't be gone long, dear, and then you and Nokai can be alone. You did well today. Your instincts are good."

"I thought I'd done a horrible thing," said Yesui.

"Because you didn't know what was happening," said Gong-gong. "Your mother and I were ready to flee the church when we first entered it."

"Such animosity," said Mother.

"Particularly towards the rear of the congregation, but I couldn't pinpoint it. We're going to have problems here, Kati. Watch this place closely."

"I certainly will," then to Yesui, "We've neglected your Moshuguang training, dear. You must learn to quickly search the minds of all people you deal with, particularly in political matters."

Oh, no! "I don't want to talk about that, Mother. I'm tired."

"It is only a matter of drill, Yesui, and I will direct you," said Gong-gong. "Will you please this old man?" There was now a smile on his grizled face, and he playfully wiggled a bushy eyebrow at her.

Yesui nearly laughed at him. "Yes, Gong-gong, I will work with you on the Mind Search."

Nokai was suddenly back and Father was giving Yesui a sly smile while strongly masking himself. "A long day, and an early start tomorrow. Time for bed." He held out his hand to Mother, and her eyes glowed green.

In all these years their passion has not cooled, thought Yesui. She stood up and took Nokai's hand in hers as the royal couple left the room. Her grandfather smiled and waved a half-eaten cake at her.

"And I will pleasure myself with the rest of these honeycakes," he said.

Yesui kissed him on the cheek and Nokai led her to their suite several rooms away, passing through two sitting rooms, a ballroom and a second dining room before getting there.

Thick warm carpet, wall tapestries of storks flying from jagged peaks, a plush bed canopied in gold silk, and there was an adjoining bath with a huge marble tub.

Nokai closed the door and they were alone. "Would you like to take a bath?" he asked.

"I don't think so," she said. She stepped up to him and fumbled at the sash of his robe. "Not now."

Yesui removed his sash as he took the shell comb from her hair, allowing it to fall around her shoulders. She felt no nervousness, no fear, only love as they undressed each other and came together with a soft yet deep kiss. The bed was prepared for them, coverlet pulled back. Nokai picked her up and lay her gently on the bed, then reached to turn off the lamp glowing beside it.

"Leave it on. I want to see you," she said softly.

They cuddled together, Nokai's soft hands moving over her. His body was not hard, but smooth and firm, and he smelled like musk. She kissed his ear and whispered, "I'm not experienced, my darling."

"Nor am I. We'll learn together, Yesui, my Yesui. I love you so much," he murmured.

Their lovemaking was fumbling, awkward and wonderful. When he finally dared to enter her she felt a small stab of pain, but washed it from her mind with the heat of their embrace. And exhaustion overtook them before they could complete what they had started.

Bedside light still on, they fell soundly asleep in each other's arms. And in the morning, Yesui found a small spot of blood on the silken sheet beneath her. She quickly covered it up so Nokai wouldn't see it.

After that, there was the mad rush back to the flyer field for the trip to visit Mother's people by the southern sea.

Beginning at the front pews, people filed out of the church in order after the Empress and her entourage had driven away. In the last few rows white-suited men waited patiently, but exchanged nervous glances with each other. One man stared straight ahead with narrowed eyes while his companion, pudgy and round-faced, figited beside him.

"There," said Tuen. "Now Lan-Hoi looked at me and shook his head. He's terrified like the rest of them."

Sheng sighed. "Most unfortunate, indeed, but understandable. I've never before felt the Moshuguang presence, and it *is* a fearful thing. The old man in particular, I think. When he passed us, my mind seemed to cloud. One needs to maintain a pleasant memory in the presence of these people, and the best thing is to stay away from them."

"People will abandon us, Sheng-chih. I can see it in their eyes. We can avoid The Searchers, but the Empress is suddenly the enemy of all we wish to do. How can we proceed against her opposition?"

Sheng folded his hands together in a pose of meditation. "It is an interesting problem, but solvable. Each cell remains small and visable. The organism grows cell by cell, remaining invisible. The fact it exists must be protected by any means necessary. I will talk to the others, convince them this can be done."

"But the land deal, Sheng," said Tuen, wringing his hands together.

"Forget it. We're taking a backward step before moving forward again."

"Wang Mengnu will know it," grumbled Tuen.

Sheng clenched his teeth. "Then we will deal with her as we must. She is suddenly a great disappointment to me. Now relax, Tuen, cease your talk and wipe the sweat from your forehead. It is not a good thing for out associates to see at this moment."

The man obeyed.

Sheng placed his hands palms upwards on his knees and closed his eyes as the last rows of the church emptied out. It was a pose of prayerful meditation in the presence of First Mother, an apparent turning inwards to examine a flawed soul.

There was no reverence in his thoughts, only the building of dark scenarios regarding how far he was prepared to go in dealing with opposition from the Empress of Shan-shi-jie.

Four

Revelation

It was a five hour flight to the southern sea, and Tengri-Khan was half-way up to its zenith when they touched down in seven flyers on a sandy plane. Water stretched south to the horizon. Yesui had dozed for most of the trip and so had Nokai, but they came awake during the descent to see the deep blue of water ahead and a mass of low round dwellings and long buildings as far as the eye could see to the east. To the west were green foothills rising to meet jagged peaks of mountains, and a brown delta, where a river flowed into the sea. Far out to sea, a line of boats with white sails formed into a crescent.

The air was filled with the odor of salt, fish and animals when they touched down. Twenty people were there to greet them, mostly women on horseback, and there were several riderless horses in a cluster beside them. The women wore robes striped red, yellow and green, while the men were in brown leather pants and tunics.

Mother's excitement pushed in Yesui's mind. Oh, there's Goldani, and — and BABAR! Look at him! His hair is turning GREY! And I smell meat cooking, and ayrog, and horses. It's so wonderful!

Also horse dung, added Yesui.

So many for you to meet, Yesui. You were so little when they last saw you. Try to be pleasant, dear.

Yes, Mother.

They stepped out of the flyers and assembled in a group: Mother, Father, Yesui and Nokai, Yesugen, Gong-gong, the Wazeras, Tanchun and several guards from the Moshuguang elite. But once assembled, Mother left them quickly and walked towards the women and men on horseback, her arms outstretched. A woman and a man got off their

41

horses, running towards her until they came together in a happy, back thumping embrace.

Mother motioned to her entourage to join her, and they went forward. Father, Yesui and Nokai went first, closely followed by Yesugen, who seemed nervous.

Yesui recognized Goldani from her time at Festival as a little girl, but now the woman's hair was steel grey and fell down her back in a tail fastened by a leather thong. Now in her sixties her body was still erect and hard, but her leathery wrinkled face made her look even older than she was. She smiled at Yesui, eyes brown, then yellow, and held out her hand.

"May your marriage be long and fruitful," she said formally.

Yesui shook her hand, introduced her to Nokai.

"I'm honored," said Nokai, and nothing more. So quiet, yet his expression made it clear he was delighted to meet these people.

Mother turned and motioned to Yesugen. Goldani's eyes turned red in an instant.

"Yesugen, Empress of Meng-shi-jie and the worlds of Tengri-Nayon, this is Goldani, the leader of our Tumatsin people," said Mother.

Goldani bowed stiffly, eyes still red. "You'll find our accomodations inadequate, Madam, but it's the best we can offer and we're honored by your presence," she growled. Her face was suddenly gaunt, voice deep.

Yesugen also bowed, even smiled. "The honor is mine to meet a people who fought so well in a war we all regret. You were very strong that day."

"We are not political, Madam. We keep to our simple ways and our lives are happy here," said Goldani, and now her eyes were yellow again. "But we do hope for continued good relations between your worlds and ours."

Mother beamed a smile. "The Tumatsin *are* represented in our People's Congress, of course, and now I'd like to introduce you to their newest representative who begins his three year term in just a month from now." She turned to the tall man standing by Goldani and hugged him proudly.

"This is Babar, and he is also my baby brother," she said.

"Two years in age is not such a difference," said Babar, and his smile was quite friendly. His skin was burned brown by Tengri-Khan, for he was a fisherman, his hands large and gnarled from hard work at sea. Like his sister his face was long with a prominent nose resembling the beak of a bird, giving him a somewhat hard look. But the twinkle in his eyes betrayed the happy man within.

To Yesugen, he bowed and said, "I'm not a political person, but it's my turn to serve in Congress and I'll do the best I can."

Babar shook hands with Nokai, gave a nodding bow to Yesui. "I hope you will enjoy the same happiness I've had with my wife and children. My oldest daughter, Ala, looks much like you, Yesui."

Yesui smiled politely. *How long will we stand here?* she thought.

"We have horses for you," said Goldani. "It's a three kilometer ride and we'll go leisurely for those of you who haven't ridden."

Nokai's eyes lit up like lasers, but his parents looked terrified.

"They are gentle animals," added Goldani.

All were mountain horses, small, and by hitching up her robe Yesui had little difficulty mounting up. Goldani put the reins in her hands, and said, "Just hold them, and enjoy the ride."

Yesui's buttocks instantly hurt, her inner thighs stretched taut, and she hadn't even moved yet. The animal swiveled its head to look at her; for one instant, she thought that he, she, it might try to bite her.

Can we move, please, and get this over with? But still she had to smile at the excitement written all over Nokai's face. The dream of a Lan-Sui child had become reality.

Goldani went back to her horse, returned with a folded robe and held it out to her Empress and friend. "To us you are Tumatsin, and will remain so. Will you wear this?"

Mother said nothing, but smiled; in front of everyone she pulled her own golden silk robe up over her head and replaced it with the coarse woolen one striped in red, green and yellow. The momentary sight of Shanji's Empress in her underclothes was astonishing to everyone, men averting their gaze but still managing a quick peek.

They moved out at a walk, Goldani leading with Mother and Yesugen beside her. Next came Yesui with Nokai, Father, Babar and Gong-gong, then the rest, both Tumatsin and Moshuguang men bringing up the rear. The ground was sandy and they followed a path along the edge of a cliff dropping several meters down to the sea. A salty breeze cooled them. There was now a strong odor of fish, but not unpleasant. To the north, goats and sheep cropped grass on slopes rising gently towards the high plateau. Soon there was a scattering of gerts on the slopes, dome-shaped dwellings covered with animal hides, fresh wash drying on their sides, a few dogs barking, even fewer faces peering out from dark doorways.

After two kilometers the few gerts were now many, each on a block of land a hectar in size. People had come down to the trail and were lining it, all smiling, all dressed in coarse woolen shirts and pants, men and women. Children of all ages were everywhere. Another crowd, but different. They looked at Yesui and smiled. No turmoil of thoughts, no prayers or reverent stares, no amulets, only curious and interested observation. So Yesui was startled when one of the women trilled, and others joined her, the sound coming like a wave from far ahead. Yesui found it somewhat thrilling, and when she looked at Nokai he laughed. Two young children raced by them on horseback, paralleling their course. Neither could have been older than seven, and moved as one with their animals.

The trilling grew louder, the crowd larger. They were entering a village; ahead there was a mass of gerts around four long buildings with flat sod roofs. Now there was the odor of meat cooking, and ayrog, Father's favorite drink. The crowd pressed forward, waving. "Kati!" they cried. "Kati!" And Yesui was hardly noticed. *They don't know me*, she thought. *I'm a stranger to them.*

Mother was waving and smiling, having a wonderful time. Yesugen waved regally so Yesui followed her example. A smile came to her face, and at once people noticed her, waving back. Suddenly she felt relaxed and welcome in this place.

The odors of meat cooking were now dizzying. A mob of people congregated around great open pits by two long buildings, smoke swirling upwards. Horses and goats mingled with the crowd. Sacks of ayrog were suspended on steel poles, men and women raising ceramic cups to fill them. Women were carrying baked goods and steaming pots to rough-hewn wooden tables lining the barbeque pits. The noise was deafening, and few people seemed to notice the arrival of the royal party.

They got off their horses, Yesui grunting with effort and pausing to massage her sore buttocks from the brief ride. *I'm too fragile*, she thought as she looked at the people.

Mother led them through the crowd, and again there were shouts of "Kati!" Cups were raised. People reached out to shake Mother's hand or touch her shoulder. Yesui was astounded by such intimacy with an Empress, but nobody touched her in such a way. The people only looked at her curiously and gave her a friendly smile.

"Kati! Cook our meat faster and there's more time for drinking!" shouted a man, and Mother laughed at him. A full throated laugh, lusty, like nothing Yesui had ever heard. *She is not the same person here,* she thought.

Because she has come home again. These are the people she came from as a child. You met them once, and have forgotten all of it.

It was Mengmoshu who spoke to her without words.

Not true. I still remember Mengjai and I watching the children getting their first horses at Festival. I remember everything, Gong-gong!

Mother led them to one of the large buildings adjacent to the barbeque pits and pointed to a doorway. "If you wish, we can eat inside to get away from the dust and the noise," she said.

"Please!" said Nokai. "Could we eat out here? I want to see what's going on. Yesui, let's stay outside. I've never seen anything like this!"

"Of course you can," said Mother. "After all, this is your wedding celebration."

"It *is*?" said Yesui.

Goldani sent several men into the building and they returned quickly with decorated saddles, two larger than the others, all festooned with ribbons in red, yellow and green. Low tables were brought out and placed in front of the saddles. Yesui and Nokai were seated in the large saddles, crossing their legs in meditative position beneath the tables, Mother, Yesugen and Father to their right, the Wazeras with Gong-gong to their left, and so on.

"Tea for the bride, and ayrog for the groom!" shouted a man.

A woman brought cups of ayrog for both of them. Both were familiar with the brew, but when they tasted it they gasped in unison, "This is *strong*!"

The crowd cheered. "Now you must kiss!" shouted someone.

They kissed, and the crowd cheered again.

A woman brought them eating sticks, and knives sharpened to a razor's edge. Another brought them plates heaped with meat and cheese, and chunks of white vegetables like turnips, only sweet. *There's four meals of food here,* thought Yesui, and began sampling everything.

"You must try the fish!" shouted Babar from four places away from her. More saddles had been brought out and he'd been joined by a woman, tall and lithe, and two girls in their late teens. The face of one girl was familiar. *Ala*, thought Yesui.

She'd barely begun eating when the crowd became hushed. A young girl, perhaps sixteen, approached and knelt before her. She was lovely, her almond shaped eyes sparkling yellow, then red, then yellow again as she smiled.

She is the most recent bride in the village, Yesui. This is an unbelievable honor for her, said Mother.

In one hand the girl carried a small bowl filled with smouldering sweetgrass, in the other, two wreaths woven of grass and laced with purple wildflowers shaped like little bells. She placed the bowl on Yesui's table, waved her hand to move the smoke first towards Yesui, then Nokai. She leaned forward, holding out a wreath with both hands. Yesui instinctively bowed her head as the wreath was lightly placed there.

The ritual was repeated with Nokai, who bowed and pressed his palms together in a prayerful attitude. The girl resumed her position in front of Yesui and took two leather thongs from the pocket of her tunic. Now Yesui felt joy coming from the girl, and anticipation.

"Will you love your man, and stand by him as long as you both live?" The girl's voice was soft and reverant.

Yesui was a bit startled. "Yes," she said.

The girl took Yesui's right wrist, tied a leather thong around it, then turned to Nokai.

"Will you love your woman, and stand by her as long as you both live?"

"Yes," said Nokai, and a thong was tied around his wrist.

The girl stood up, turned to the crowd and held her hands over her head.

"These two are now one!" she shouted.

The crowd cheered, and cups were raised. "Drink — drink — kiss — kiss!" they chanted.

Yesui and Nokai obliged them, and the crowd roared its approval.

Mother had tears in her eyes and Father's arm was around her. When she caught Yesui watching her, she said, *Memories. It seems yesterday I sat in your place to be married in the presence of my people.*

This was a wedding? thought Yesui, but then Nokai was kissing her again, quite deeply this time and totally into the spirit of the moment.

In between sips of strong brew and more kisses they managed to finish their meal. Little girls brought them simple gifts from the village: polished agates of good luck from the sea, pairs of ceramic plates and cups with motifs of fish and flying birds, necklaces of colorful shells and two small bowls for the burning of incense and sweetgrass.

For Nokai there was a beautiful knife, and something else. The knife had a handle of bone and a twenty centimeter blade, razor sharp. The other gift was wrapped in soft chamois, a short tube of rough wool open at one end. Nokai looked at it curiously. Father took it from him, and demonstrated.

"It goes over index and middle fingers — like this." Tube over his fingers, he wiggled it at Nokai, and the crowd roared with pleasure.

"But what *is* it?" asked Nokai.

"Later," said Father.

Mother's emerald eyes flashed, she blushed, and the image in her mind made Yesui's heart thump hard.

Well, THAT should be interesting, thought Yesui.

Eating and drinking were continuous throughout the day and evening. Towards dusk the air was filled with the sound of music from wooden flutes and three-stringed instruments held in musicians' laps. People came and went, but most stayed until after dark, the barbeque pits now filled with deep red embers.

There was dancing, couples swirling to fast thumping beats, then circles of people stepping sideways and singing. Yesui and Nokai tried a few steps, feeling awkward at first. By the end of the evening they were stepping lively in a circle with their families, and even Gong-gong was enjoying himself.

But well after dark, people began leaving. For most of them the new day would begin before dawn when their boats put out to sea. When only a few men remained drinking the last of the ayrog by the barbeque pits, Goldani escorted the wedding party members to their sleeping places and Yesui and Nokai were finally alone in the building in front of which they'd sat for hours.

It was a single large room with wooden benches lining the four walls and a large fire pit in the center, above which a hole in the ceiling was slightly open to air by an elevated pane covered with animal membrane. Oil lamps flickered around the room. The bed was a thick mattress of straw covered with hides, and two small saddles covered with thick wool served as pillows. The bed had been placed on the floor next to the fire pit, in which a small pile of embers glowed dully. No windows, and the doorway was covered only by a hide blanket.

They undressed, and Nokai placed their clothing on a bench. Yesui lay down on the bed to test it. "It's squishy," she said, feeling soft hide against her back. Nokai looked down at her with a faint smile, and Yesui felt his anticipation.

"Are you going to try your new toy?" she asked.

"If you like."

"I like," she murmured.

Minutes later she was writhing on the bed, gasping for breath. Nokai seemed to sense when she was ready, entering her, thrusting, the wonderful sensation in her body peaking and making her cry out as he suddenly shuddered and she felt something new inside her.

There was raucous laughter from the men outside by the barbeque pit.

Yesui giggled, clung to Nokai and he kissed her long and deeply. She stroked his back, felt his breathing slow with hers. "My love," she murmured, and drifted quickly into sleep.

Much later, it seemed, she awoke and felt wetness beneath her. Nokai still held her, but was sound asleep. The night was still, the revelers gone home to their beds. Flickering oil lamps cast mesmerizing shadows on the ceiling. Stillness, and flickering light, yet she remained strangely awake, caressing Nokai's back and shoulder with a hand.

She closed her eyes to concentrate on the smoothness of his skin and suddenly the matrix of purple stars was there to beckon her. A call. She felt a presence, a tingling on her skin, and one purple spot of light flickered at her.

Yesui.

Yes? Who is it?

It has been a long time, Yesui, but there are things that must now be said and shown to you. It is the wish of First Mother.

A familiar presence, quickly remembered. 'Mind'? she asked.

As good a name as any. It's necessary for us to meet in the place of creation, and I've marked your way. Will you come now?

Must I? I don't want to leave Nokai.

You won't, I promise you. Come, now, and follow my marker. Nokai is a part of this.

The single point of purple light flickered again, drawing her to it, the feeling of Nokai's cool skin fading, then gone. She went through the interface rapidly; a flash, and the swirling clouds of creative light, the vortices of countless stars surrounded her again. Her place. The working home of The Mei-lai-gong.

'Mind' was there to greet her, but again did not show a manifestation. She, as Yesui thought of her, was simply there and understood.

Hello again. This has been an important day, said 'Mind'.

Nokai and I are now married, said Yesui.

We know. First Mother is much pleased by your union, and wants you to know that. That is Her first message. The rest must be said to both of you.

I will repeat it for Nokai, said Yesui.

No, he must be here to receive it himself.

But how? He is an ordinary man.

First Mother is in him, and has chosen him to be with you. All power comes from Her. Call him, Yesui; call him to this place.

Yesui thought about Nokai and how they'd met, that first sensation she'd had of someone gentle and pure in spirit sending out a prayer to a mystical being called Mei-lai-gong.

Nokai! she called. Likely he was sound asleep. Dream with me, darling. Come with me to the gong-shi-jie. I want you with me.

No answer, but she felt something, a kind of awareness. Nokai, please come. I'm waiting here with someone to see you.

I hear you; I feel you beside me, and your breathing is very slow. This dream seems real, he said. I see — something — colors.

Just think him here, said 'Mind'. Pick a point close to your manifestation, and think him to that point. He's on his way, Yesui. Hurry!

Yesui thought it.

Oh, said Nokai, then, Ohhh. Like my first vision of you when I was on Lan-Sui. I fell in love with you that night, Yesui. What a nice dream to end a wonderful day. All the beautiful colors, just like before.

What? said Yesui. This is not a dream, Nokai. You are here with me in the place of creation. I can feel you here.

She felt amused doubt in Nokai, as if he felt she was playing with him, but then a bright spot of purple light suddenly flashed near her, and grew into a vertical ellipsoid the size of her manifestation.

There, that's better, said 'Mind'. A marker for your man.

Who's that? asked Nokai.

Someone once organic, but now different. Yesui calls me 'Mind', so that is my name. I come from First Mother, and you have been brought here by Her power.

You are of the Chuang shi, he said. You are a Creator.

Of fifth order, yes. There are several orders, Nokai, but it is First Mother who has chosen you to be with Yesui, and Yesui to be with you. That's why you're here, for there is something I have to say to both of you.

Yesui listened impatiently. You've seen this place before? she asked Nokai.

In dreams. This place and others, beautiful things like pillers of clouds with new stars forming. Once I saw Lan-Sui City as if I was outside of it. I thought it was you who showed me these things.

It was First Mother, said 'Mind', acting through myself and others like me. It is necessary to understand this part of Mei-lai-gong's world so you can aid her in the future, but you will not see all that she sees or be able to go everywhere with her. There will also be special tasks for you alone, if you're willing.

I follow the word of The Mother in all things, Nokai said solemnly.

Good, said 'Mind'. Now, this is for both of you. As of this day, your work has begun. There will be good times and bad, dreams, ambitions, not all fulfilled, and disappointments. It is important your love for each other remain strong. Your hearts must be your guide to First Mother's Will, for I will only guide and test you at critical times. There are many unanswered questions to be considered, and your futures are not pre-determined. Much will depend on what you choose to do, or not to do.

We will listen to our hearts, said Nokai.

Yes, said Yesui.

Then there's nothing more for me to say. Go with the blessings of Our Mother, and all the Chuang shi. In your own ways, you're a part of us. I'll see you again soon, Yesui. There's some testing to do. Goodbye until then.

Goodby, said Yesui, then hesitated, the purple vortex of herself swirling nearby.

Nokai will follow you there, said 'Mind', and his manifestation with him. In the future, you will know when he's here.

A flash, and Yesui's hands felt Nokai's cool skin. His face was near, eyelids fluttering. His eyes opened to slits, and looked at her.

"It was not a dream, darling," she murmured.

"I know," he mouthed, and then his eyes closed and he was asleep again.

Yesui snuggled close, forcing her mind to think random thoughts until she fell asleep in his arms.

They slept late the next morning, and said their goodbyes, and there was another ride back to the flyers. In minutes Yesui was missing the good earthy people who'd given her such a wonderful welcome. Still she felt happy as they came down through the opening in the great dome over her city. Her new married life was about to begin.

Mengjai met them at the flyer field, and he had horrible news.

Lady Weimeng had died peacefully in her sleep two nights before, and her body was being prepared for burial.

Mother became hysterical with grief.

And it was the first time Yesui had ever seen her grandfather cry.

Five

The Chuang Shi

The Empress of Shanji seemed to change after the death of her foster mother, and Yesui was the first to notice it.

Weimeng was entombed next to her husband in the cavern of the emperors deep within the mountain slopes north of the city, just beyond the flyer field. It was a cool place, walls and ceiling of polished granite, markers on walls at each place of eternal sleep, a single flame forever burning on a raised altar in the center of the great room. Even in dim light Yesui could see the places reserved there for Mother and Father, herself and Mengjai. Standing there, looking at her name carved on a slab of black granite, she wondered about death. Would it be the same for her, or Mother, as it had been for Weimeng?

Abagai had surely died, her body buried on Meng-shi-jie, yet there had been that final meeting with her in the gong-shi-jie, the incredible transfiguration of her manifestation at the instant of death. The body had died, but a part of Abagai had become something new, only to be taken away quickly by the Chuang shi. Yesui often wondered if she would ever see or hear from Abagai again. She wondered if such a transfiguration awaited herself, or Mother, or if there would only be cessation of existence and the slow decay of a body encased in cold stone.

After the death of Weimeng, Mother was suddenly conscious of her health. "She was only in her late seventies, and should have lived longer. It was a sedentary lifestyle that shortened her life, and I've been living the same way for years. Well, I'm going to do something about that," she said.

Master Yung was long dead, but his oldest son Tzisong now ran the School of Ancient Arts, and Mother resumed her lessons with the sword after an absence of twenty years. Yesui went to two of them, watched her mother sweat and growl while swinging a heavy, curved sword, and decided it was not for her. After each lesson Mother's arms were corded and muscled like those of a man, but when Yesui pointed it out with dismay to Father he only smiled strangely. "Hmmm," he said, and nothing more.

Mother also began riding again, twice weekly in late afternoon, and was soon riding wildly, several Moshuguang troopers chasing after her over rolling hillocks in the valley outside the city. Yesui again refused to participate. She hated horses, hated their sweat, smell and wary stares whenever she was around them. Mother was angered by her refusal. "You are soft, and so is Nokai. You cannot think properly if your body is not healthy and strong," she growled.

This went on for weeks until finally they found something Yesui was willing to do, and only because it caught the interest of her husband. The exercises were simple, rhythmic, and did not cause her to sweat, though after the first few times she performed them her muscles were quite sore. Gong-gong had provided the idea and pronounced them 'good exercises for the soft and elderly' with a glint in his eye. Nokai was interested because they exercised in early morning when it was cool, and so it was not necessary for him to take another bath before rushing off to the Hall of Ministers.

Each morning they arose at dawn and assembled by the pond in the hanging garden below the palace. Gong-gong directed their movements, for he'd practiced the form for fifty of his seventy years. Mother, Father, Yesui and Nokai were now his pupils, and he enjoyed his role as teacher.

The Hwu-dye-meng was performed with a short, light sword in the right hand, a long streamer of red silk in the left. Thirty minutes of continuous movement with knees slightly bent, short, slow steps to turn the body, arms moving synchronously to produce spirals in red around each participant.

For Yesui it was more dance than exercise, and enjoyable. After a few weeks of it she indeed felt stronger and more energized. A few more weeks and her appetite was increasing; she found herself consuming vast quantities of meat and fruit, and no longer found honeycakes appealing. Her weight began to increase, her breasts swelling and becoming more sensitive to touch, though not painfully so. Nokai seemed energized as well, especially in their lovemaking. At times, she even felt his lust for her in his gentle soul, and was excited by it.

Other changes were distracting, and then a concern. Sudden flushes of heat would come to her face, without reason. If she waited longer than two hours to eat, her stomach would not only grumble, but give her a vague nausea. Tears would come to her eyes without provocation, and stop just as quickly as they'd come.

She described these symptoms to her mother, who masked herself fiercely, yet smiled and then sent her to the Moshuguang physician who'd attended Yesui's birth.

The physician examined her, made tests with her blood and called her the following day. "You're in perfect health," he said, "and your symptoms are not unusual."

"Then what is the cause?" she asked nervously.

"You're pregnant, Yesui, over three months along."

Yesui was euphoric. "We're going to have a child," she murmured, and tears rolled down her cheeks.

"Children," said the physician. "You are carrying twins, and both are developing well. Would you like to know their sexes?"

"Oh, no. I want to be surprised!" she cried.

She told Nokai that evening; he was wonderfully shaken by the news and held her tightly. That night, when he began caressing her, she assured him she was not suddenly fragile, but the tenderness of their lovemaking was as much in mind as in body and she felt him with her when she sent out a prayer to a being unseen or understood.

Thank you for this man and his love, and the gift of our children.

For one brief instant, the vision of a matrix of purple stars was in both of their minds, then gone.

During the next few months her only purpose in life seemed to be the physical nurturing of the babies growing inside her. Everyone else was quite busy. Nokai continued his ambassadorship for Lan-Sui and remained a citizen of that world. He never talked about his work, but seemed content with it. Mother was now traveling more, making regular visits to Wanchou and Dahe, and gone for two or three days at a time. Father and Mengjai spent all their time inside the mountain as the date neared for Shanji's ancient landing craft's flight.

Mother was quietly terrified about the flight test of a millenia old vessel, for her husband and son would both be part of the four man crew and eight passengers. She had shared this fear with Yesui, who was optimistic.

"It's well preserved in structure, the fuel I brought in from Lan-Sui is adequate in supply, and all the electrical and computer systems have been up-dated. What can go wrong?"

"Everything," said Mother.

For Yesui there was constant eating, the growth of her babies, morning exercises and her meetings with Gong-gong to develop her way with the Moshuguang. The ability was there, only a few lessons necessary, and there was time to talk of other things. Mainly he taught her to keep a part of her focus on the continual background of thoughts coming to her at all times, thoughts for which she'd developed an unconscious filter over the years.

They met in his office with its computer displays, shelves of books and disks, and simple plastic furniture. He brought in subjects for her testing, calling them 'rabbits', and had her scan their minds. The 'rabbits' had private thoughts, some interesting, none political except for those deliberately suggested to them secretly by her grandfather. She sensed all of them and Gong-gong was pleased. The first subjects were average citizens, all lacking the ability to mask themselves. Difficulty increased when the subjects were Moshuguang: several scientists and technicians who worked inside the mountain, and also a trooper from the flyer field.

Yesui suddenly realized how strong her abilities were, for she easily penetrated their masks and even found that the trooper had a schoolboy's crush on her, a nice thing to learn in her present physical state.

Gong-gong's mask was absolute when he willed it, but he allowed her some peeks to test her limit. "Even the best of us does not constantly retain a mask, and you must be alert for opportunities," he explained.

Nokai was an open book to her, but she wondered if there were more things to see. And dispite the fact he was not Moshuguang she was certain he was sometimes in her mind without her knowing it.

So one night when he was deep in sleep she scanned him slowly and carefully so as not to disturb him. On the surface were random thoughts and snatches of dreams: stern faces of men seated at a long table, her own face, smiling, a glimpse of swirling colorful clouds of energy in the gong-shi-jie. She dug deeper and there was resistance, a stubborn blackness as if she were trying to enter another part of his mind. She closed her eyes for focus, pressed harder, and suddenly there was light, as if two black curtains had been drawn aside.

A great orb of golden light was there, radiating streamers in all the colors of the gong-shi-jie, and Yesui heard herself gasp. It was not a sun, for the swirling clouds of purple, violet and blue around it betrayed a presence in the gong-shi-jie. Yesui was mesmerized by it, feeling a strange euphoria, and then it was gone, the black curtains drawn again.

She opened her eyes. Nokai's eyes were open, looking at her. He smiled, and she suddenly felt as if she'd somehow just violated him. He gave her face a single caress, closed his eyes and was asleep again without a word.

Yesui lost two hours of sleep that night, wondering about what she'd seen, and the following day could not bring herself to ask Nokai about it.

'Mind' came to Yesui again in the sixth month of her pregnancy. The call came in the morning, after Nokai had gone to work and Yesui was resting on her bed.

Are you feeling well?, asked 'Mind'.

I'm fine. Everything's going perfectly well so far. What will we be doing today? As she asked it, Yesui was instantly in the gong-shi-jie, feeling 'Mind' there, but without manifestation, as usual. *You never show yourself to me*, she complained.

I'm a kind of energy, Yesui, without form to manifest. I could show you something from a time long past, but it would only be distracting for you. I have some simple tests for now. Our work will become more serious after your children are born.

I'm ready, said Yesui.

Then follow me. We go to what you call 'Abagai's Favorite Place'.

Yesui was thrilled with expectation. *Will I see her?*

No, Yesui. She works elsewhere, but I can tell you she's happy and content. You'll have to wait until another time, but it will come.

They went quickly past the vortices of stars to the dull glow of violet light surrounding the great wheel of Yesui's galaxy, yet Yesui knew that back in her room her unconscious body had drawn perhaps a single breath. In the gong-shi-jie she was an entity of pure thought, conscious of time even though there was none, and traveling with an indefinable speed. "Even pure energy has its limitations," Mengjai had explained to her. "Light-speed, and no more."

I am something other than energy, thought Yesui, in a kind of mantra, and energy goes where I will it to.

So far you have used it well, said 'Mind'. They were now bathed in violet light, that peculiar manifestation of matter invisible in real space, and the great wheel of star vortices was behind them. Far out was another wheel glowing faintly, and it was over two years since she'd been there.

"Ah, yes, the Stork galaxy," Mengjai had said after her first visit. "Member of our local group, type Sb spiral, four hundred thousand light years out and approaching us at a hundred and twenty million kilometers per hour. Don't hold your breath for the collision."

The violet light disappeared, then reappeared as they approached Abagai's galaxy and homed in on a spiral of vortices near its center. Yesui looked for remembered signatures near Abagai's favorite place, but saw nothing familiar.

Everything changes rapidly here, said 'Mind'. You'll have to learn them again.

No time for study, a tangle of vortices rushing past her, then a flash and she was back in real space.

Abagai's favorite place had indeed changed in a short time.

A wall of roiling clouds laced with black lanes of dust now seemed to glow, for within the cloud a cluster of new blue stars had appeared, their intense radiation blowing a clear bubble around them outwards by several light years. Other proto-stars were caught in the expanding bubble, the disks of dust and gas around them now distorted and being blown away, the births of new planetary systems aborted.

Well away from the bubble, pillars of cloud were topped with bright globs of compact nebulae with streamers in red and green, the first cries of life from smaller and cooler baby stars. Everywhere Yesui looked new stars were forming, some still compact irregular bits of nebula glowing faintly, others spewing forth terrible emissions of gas and dust as the first heat from internal thermonuclear reactions reached their photospheres. A horrific violent place, yet wonderfully beautiful.

I see the work of the Chuang shi, Yesui said reverently.

We only initiate it, said 'Mind'. The rest occurs naturally, according to natural laws we do not govern, Yesui. There are forces here we have not defined, but they are available for us in this universe.

This universe? There are others?

Many. Countless numbers of them, and all are connected. Energy can be made to flow from one to the other, Yesui. Energy from one can create another. You call us the Chuang shi, but we are not truly creators. Most of us work with the energy at hand to make new things. But the most advanced of our kind are called upon to make new universes from the old. It is First Mother who made your universe, bringing energy from another to form it. She is not of this universe, but now dwells here. Even She is not a true creator, you see. Much is left to chance, and natural physical laws beyond Her powers to control.

Yesui's mind whirled with questions. There must have been a beginning, then, a time when there was nothing, then a first universe. And Mengjai says the laws of physics are universal, with forces understood in terms of particles created in the first seconds after the birth of our universe. He calls the laws elegant and orderly. So how and when, and by WHO were they defined?

If there was a first universe it is lost in memory, Yesui. This process was going on long before your universe was created and long before First Mother was a living being in the sense you understand life.

WHAT?

Yes, She once lived, as you do. The Chuang shi, all of us, have lived as organic beings at one time. You still don't see, Yesui. You've forgotten what you were told here during your last visit. Your mother is Chuang shi, of the first and lowest order. YOU are second order, perhaps more. You are Chuang shi as well. You ask WHO dictates the forces of nature. A better question might be WHO creates the seeds of the Chuang shi in each and every universe. And we don't know the answer to that, Yesui.

Yesui started to ask about Abagai, but 'Mind' stopped her.

Oh, so many questions you have! Time for answers later, and you're here for some sensory tests. Nothing crucial, but we're really not certain about your order. I want you to relax and put your questions away for a while.

For awhile, said Yesui grumpily. So what do I do?

You don't DO anything. Just follow my directions and tell me what you see. Last time here you were trying to peek inside that cloud and I wouldn't let you.

There are new hot stars there, now, said Yesui.

But outside their radiation bubble the cloud is unchanged. What do you see there?

The cloud was opaque in real space. Yesui flashed to the gong-shi-jie and saw a shimmering of violet light there. In the interface the threads were fairly uniform, roughly parallel, but kinked ever so slightly at one point. I see a slight discontinuity in the interface here, she said.

What happens if you put energy into it? asked 'Mind'.

Yesui used the violet light, thinking it to the discontinuity in an unfocused flash. The discontinuity was suddenly more severe.

It made it worse, she said.

Not worse, said 'Mind'. The cloud's uniformity, its symmetry is disturbed. It will now contract to form a new star or a cluster. At this point natural forces take over, but you initiated it, Yesui. Prematurely. Eventually the radiation bubble from the hot stars nearby would have reached this place and caused the same thing, but not as neatly as you did it. Is the violet light gone?

Back to the gong-shi-jie. Nearly, much fainter — no! It's getting brighter again!

Being renewed?

Yes.

From where?

I — I don't see. Yesui looked hard, saw sparkles within the violet mist. Little flashes at random places. Purple flashes. What are they?

Later. Let's do something else, said 'Mind'.

You're teasing me, said Yesui.

Yes I am. Follow me now. We're going to the core of this galaxy.

'Mind's presence was enough, but Yesui wanted more.

It would be easier if you showed me a manifestation, she said.

Only to satisfy your curiosity about me. In my organic life I was nothing like you. It's better if you think of me as one of your own kind. Come on now.

More teasing, and so many questions unanswered. Yesui felt herself growing irritated.

Just one more thing, said 'Mind'.

In the gong-shi-jie the density of vortices seemed to increase as they approached the core. The distribution changed dramatically, vortices no longer arranged in great arcs, but more uniform, and there was an absence of violet light. Even the vortices were different here, most of them small in a band of color from yellow to green, but some were huge and colored the deep, deep red of the one Yesui had been temporarily trapped in when she was a little child.

All the stars here are old, said 'Mind', and many have died, but some of the dead ones can be important to us.

The gong-shi-jie was suddenly empty of vortices, a large expanse of swirling clouds of creative light, yet not far ahead the vortices reappeared, following the surface of some invisible, slightly squashed bubble. But when she looked closely, Yesui saw something monstrous in the center of the bubble, the largest vortex she's ever seen, and its color was red beyond red, nearly invisible to her.

It is as old as this galaxy, said 'Mind', and has a mass two hundred million times that of your Tengri-Khan. Long ago it swallowed up all the gas and stars in this great space here and no longer grows. Though it seems huge, it is small by comparison to other objects like it.

'Mind' was suddenly amused. *If it had a billion times more mass, you would see First Mother Herself here, scurrying around to examine its potential.*

For what? asked Yesui.

Why the creation of a new universe, of course, said 'Mind'. That is Her work, and the work of high orders. It continues as we speak. Now look at this wonder from the interface.

A flash, and Yesui was looking at a swirl of twisted, green threads in the shape of a giant inverted cusp. At first glance it could be the space-time signature of a giant star, but with differences. This was a true cusp, its bottom a singularity, at least from this distance. For such a large mass, its size is very small, she said.

Move in closer, said 'Mind'.

She did, but the singularity remained. At that point, however, she now saw a flickering, a tiny region at the singularity seeming to flash in and out of existence at a rapid rate. Even the threads of space-time were fuzzy and distorted, close to the singularity. Yesui told 'Mind' what she saw.

Ah, hah! This is good, said 'Mind', seeming pleased.

I'll see more, closer up.

No, not this time. Moving close to where space-time becomes chaotic requires special skills, Yesui, and careful teaching on my part. We'll come back another time. What you've seen tells me you're at least third order of the Chuang shi, and I must say I'm excited about working with you. We will proceed slowly and in the meantime you have a life to live, with other responsibilities.

I would spend most of my life here, if I could, said Yesui with enthusiasm.

Yes, you're a child of the gong-shi-jie, but your life is more complex than that. You have many responsibilities, Yesui. Only some of them are here.

Yesui read a terrible thing in those words. Must I be Empress, then?

It seems so, said 'Mind'. Your husband and babies are also important.

Another revelation? You think our children will have powers greater than mine?

It would be natural, yes, but we have to wait and see. Now one last look, this time from real space.

Another flash, but the view was not so spectacular as she'd thought it might be. There was only a diffuse spiral of glowing gas clouds with a few embedded stars, then a brighter ring of glowing gas and at its center an extremely bright spot of light. Beyond was dark void, a few clouds of dust and gas, and beyond that the space was filled with a myriad of small red stars in every direction. Still it was beautiful, and Yesui wished to dwell there a while.

Time to go home, said 'Mind'.

Yesui reluctantly followed the presence. A flash to the gong-shi-jie and the journey was too rapid to absorb details of vortical signatures. In a blink they were out of the core and moving out of the plane of Abagai's galaxy, the distant wheel of her home system winking at her. To her consciousness, which still related events according to time, they crossed the distance between two galaxies in no more than five heartbeats, homing in on a spiral arm, vortices flashing by in a blur and then suddenly frozen in position.

The purple vortex leading to herself was right there, and suddenly she wanted to laugh.

I've had much more practice than you, said 'Mind'. Be patient, now. Give birth to your children and then we'll work together again. Don't forget that Nokai can be with you here whenever you will it and that First Mother blesses both of you. Goodbye, Yesui.

'Mind' was gone.

A flash, and Yesui was back in herself, on her back and staring up at a silken canopy. The instant of her arrival she felt something and put her hands gently on her stomach.

There had been a distinct movement from deep inside her.

Six

Birth of Dreams

"It was your father's dream when we were young, and now that the day is here I'm terrified", said Mother, and she gripped Yesui's hand.

They were in a lounge which had been cut out of the western flank of the mountain. Thick plas windows looked out on the high butte where Abagai had landed her troops to face a mountain girl who would be Empress of Shanji. The valley was three hundred meters below them and a large crowd from the city had gathered there for the event. The sky was clear and there was no wind at ground level, ideal conditions for liftoff.

The room was walled and beamed in steel painted white, the carpeting grey. There was a scattering of polymer chairs in clusters, where people sat and talked with animated gestures in anticipation of the moment. A few were stationed by the western window with bulky cameras on shoulder mounts, media representatives from Wanchou and Jensi. A Moshuguang trooper kept guard on places for his Empress and her daughter.

Most of the people there were Moshuguang, scientists and engineers who had worked long and hard to ready an ancient vehicle for flight. Gong-gong was also there, not as royal guest but as the aging Chancellor of the Moshuguang. He gestured for Yesui and Mother to follow him.

"They're about to enter the spacecraft," he said.

He led them to a series of short windows along the northwest wall of the room where they could look out onto the monstrous steel tunnel like a pipe going far back into the mountain. The shuttle was a hundred meters away, looking like a wedge-shaped bug on three legs, venting white mist. Small cockpit windows were barely visible above a blunt nose of heat-resistant composite in white, the rest of the fusilage dull black.

Twelve men in blue pressure suits, and helmets under their arms, came out of a door in the tunnel and walked to the shuttle without ceremony. Leading the procession were Huomeng and Mengjai, the others carefully chosen from their freighter crew and equally experienced in space flight. But this time, Yesui would not be there to push them once they were in space,

They weren't going far. The space station had been moved by remote to a seven hundred kilometer orbit. There, they would rendezvous with it and spend two months setting up both biological and metallurgical laboratories for specialized experiments by the Moshuguang.

Drama of the flight was not in its mission, but in the fact that the superstructure of the shuttle was over a millenium old.

Drama of the liftoff was in the anticipated noise from hydrogen-powered fusion engines.

Freighters from Meng-shi-jie were much more modern, with magnetic lifters quickly carrying them to the edge of the atmosphere before the engines were turned on. For the shuttle, so tiny by comparison to cargo vessels, the lifters were small, and first blast from its two engines would occur only meters above ground level.

The crew climbed a ladder up into the belly of the craft, and was gone. Hours before, Yesui and Mother had met with Father and Mengjai in the suit-up bay to wish them good luck. Both men were giddy with excitement, like little boys off on a grand adventure.

"Five minutes to liftoff," announced a loudspeaker in the room.

The wait seemed longer. In her mind, Yesui heard Mother tallying up all the things that could go wrong, even though the spacecraft had received continuous meticulous care by the Moshuguang over its long history.

"It's a simple flight, Mother", she said out loud. "Quit worrying so much."

Mother smiled wanly. "I have to worry, because your father will not. This flight has been his dream for over thirty years. I still remember when he first showed me this ship, deep inside the mountain. I remember the passion in his voice when he talked about flying it. And now he's doing it, with his son. Our son." She laughed. "Who could have guessed it would be that way? We weren't even getting along well together at the time."

"One minute to liftoff!"

There was movement behind the cockpit windows, Father as pilot, Mengjai his second. Now there was a humming sound in the tunnel, lifters coming up to full power. The craft shuddered, lurched a bit and lifted centimeters from the floor before moving slowly forward. There was a rumble as a huge door rolled upwards, and light spilled into the tunnel. Cameras were clicking, people rushing from the tunnel viewing to get a place at the western window as the spacecraft neared the exit.

Yesui and Mother joined the rush, the Moshuguang trooper stepping aside for them as they took their place. The craft was a meter off the floor when it exited the tunnel, and rose smoothly to a hundred meters to hover there. Movement in the exhaust nozzles of the engines, steering vanes being checked, then a glow, dim, then bright, then an explosion that smacked the plas window against Yesui's nose.

Sound came in waves that rippled the window, and the light of Tengri-Khan paled before the glare of the engines. The ship went from horizontal to near vertical attitude before reaching the butte at the end of the valley, air glowing eerily in its wake. In seconds it was a speck, the exhaust train expanding behind it.

"Five kilometers, all nominal. Ten. Fifteen."

And so on. They waited expectantly. Yesui's ears still buzzed from the horrible avalanche of sound, and she wondered what it had been like for those observing from the valley floor. Ten minutes later, the news they'd hoped for came.

"Insertion complete. Rendezvous expected in two hours and twelve minutes. A preliminary packet is now available for registered media representatives, and may be obtained in Room G."

Mother let out a sigh of relief, her eyes turning from red to yellow, then brown. "There is still the descent to think about," she said.

"No more difficult than bringing a freighter in," said Yesui, "and they'd better be back on time. I want everyone here when the twins are born."

"Of course, dear," said Mother. They joined the exiting crowd, but took a private elevator down to the maglev rail car awaiting them deep in the mountain. The Moshuguang guard with them never looked at them directly, and remained stoically silent.

"Your father is getting too old for spaceflight. I wish he would leave it to Mengjai," said Mother. "He complains of headaches and aching joints, and then he goes up again. It makes no sense to me."

Yesui bristled slightly at that remark. "He loves space travel, Mother. You don't have to understand it. I love the gong-shi-jie and what I do there. There was a time when you also loved it."

Mother caressed Yesui's face. "Yes, I did, but that was when Abagai was there. I still miss her." *Like a mother to me.*

"I miss her too," said Yesui, "but in a week I begin work with her grand-daughter. Yesugen will bring her to me." She gripped Mother's arm suggestively as she said it.

"I should talk to Yesugen about my problems in Jensi City," said Mother.

"Then come along with me. You can talk with her while I work with Tirgee. If nothing else it will be a good distraction for you."

Mother gave her a knowing look. "All right, I will."

And there were no discernable worries in Mother's mind when they reached the maglev car.

Tirgee showed them a magnificant green fan in the gong-shi-jie, but nothing indicating what she looked like in life.

It is her way, explained Yesugen. I don't think she holds a good image of herself yet. Kati, it's good to see you here again. It has been a while.

Yes, it has, said Mother.

Tirgee, do you remember Yesui? She's going to be your teacher here.

I remember, said Tirgee, and Yesui was surprised by the strength of the child's presence. Are we going somewhere else? I know all of this place.

I'll show you new things, said Yesui. Now, come with me, and we'll leave our mothers to talk.

A short while later Yesui was wondering what she might teach to this new traveler in the gong-shi-jie, for Tirgee seemed to sense everything. She saw all the vortical signatures of stars, even to the deepest red, which Yesui warned her about. When quizzed about colors in the clouds of creative light Tirgee even saw the wisps of violet when they neared the galactic edge.

Yesui pointed to the faint wheel of light far away and said, That's where your grandmother went. She's working there now, but we can't see her. Someday I'll take you there.

Why can't we see her? asked Tirgee.

I don't know. She's alive, but in a different way and so we can't see her. I don't understand it either, Tirgee.

Tirgee didn't seem concerned about it. I've been here before. What do we see next?

They retreated from the galactic edge, and Yesui found an orange vortex at the edge of a spiral arm. This is a fairly large star and we're going to look at it in a different way. Follow me closely.

Ever so slowly, Yesui made the transition to the interface, where there would be no manifestations of herself or Tirgee, only presence. Transition made, she instantly felt Tirgee with her.

Pretty, said Tirgee.

A little further, said Yesui, and felt Tirgee move with her.

A huge orange star filled their view, with large black spots in clusters erupting great plumes of glowing gas.

Oooo, said Tirgee, very impressed.

This is what a star looks like in life, Tirgee. Its light keeps us warm and makes things grow, like Tengri-Nayon does for your world.

Tirgee enjoyed the view, but didn't know what a star was and made no connection with the sun in her sky. Hot, she said.

Yesui had a sudden idea for the end of their first exploration. Let's see a planet, now. I'll show you where I live.

When they reached Tengri-Nayon's position, Mother and Yesugen weren't there. A short drift and they reached Tengri-Khan. Finding a planet, especially a small one like Shanji, would forever be a delicate task for Yesui. Only from the interface could she see the tiny perturbation of space-time for an object that size. But this time was different. Mengjai was working on the space station, and could serve as a target for her entrance into real space.

Mengjai, it's Yesui. Can I borrow your attention for just a second?

Ah, spying on me again. What do you want?

Mengjai! It was now Tirgee who called him.

Who's that with you? he asked.

At that instant they flashed into real space. The station was a kilometer away, a great wheel bristling with instrumentation, the shuttle docked nose to nose with a cylindrical pod jutting from the hub. Shanji seemed huge below it, an orange ball with splotches of green and whirling wisps of white clouds.

It's Tirgee, brother. I'm taking her around the gong-shi-jie.

Tirgee, how wonderful! said Mengjai. You're following in your grand-mother's footsteps.

And mine, corrected Yesui. She's a talent, Mengjai. She sees the interface.

But are you having a good time, Tirgee?

Yes. It's all pretty. I can't see you, Mengjai.

I'd wave to you, sweet, but I'm working in a cargo bay, getting the last of these instruments unpacked.

So when will I see you again? You promised, said Tirgee.

In a year or so. This project will take some months to complete, but I'll see you again soon.

I just wanted to show her Shanji, said Yesui, and she sensed a great wave of affection passing between her brother and Tirgee.

Maybe Tirgee can visit us someday, and see our mountains.

Mountains? asked Tirgee. The ones on Meng-shi-jie had been errod-ed away to smooth hills by millenia of high winds and dust.

We should go, said Yesui. Mother and Yesugen are probably wait-ing for us right now. Take care, brother.

You, too. Bye, Tirgee. See you soon!

Bye, said Tirgee, not wanting to leave, but depending on Yesui's presence to find her way back, and so she followed.

Mother and Yesugen were just returning and Yesui's guess was they'd been out to the galactic rim where they could see Abagai's new home.

Yesugen looked expectant. *Well, how did she do?*

Quite well, and all by instinct, without my coaching. Her sensing talent goes beyond what I had at her age.

I heard Mengjai, Ma. He talked to me! said Tirgee.

That's nice, dear, said Yesugen, then to Yesui, You think she'll be able to move our ships in space, then?

Oh, yes. It's a matter of time and training, once I see she can com-mand the movement of energy, and we didn't try that today. She's too young to even understand the concepts yet. I think I only did it because Mother moved energy during the war and I was with her. We shared memories of it. Tirgee also needs time to have a good grasp of physics and astronomy. Another ten to fifteen years, I'd say.

Soon enough, I suppose, said Yesugen reflectively. Kabul and I will begin her education right away.

Mengjai says he's coming to see me soon! shouted Tirgee, totally oblivious to their conversation.

Yesugen smiled. Mengjai is so good with the children. They miss him, she said. Well, it's time to go home.

When should I work with Tirgee again? asked Yesui.

Let's say in thirty days. I will bring her here.

No, Ma! I can come on my own! cried Tirgee.

Before Yesugen could object, Yesui said, She needs to learn that right away. I will call her from here, and see if she can target me.

Very well, said Yesugen, then, Kati, I hope I've said something helpful, and what you said has made me feel better. We need to talk here more often, for both of us.

We will, said Mother.

They drifted apart after saying goodbyes, and went leisurely to the purple vortices leading to themselves. Mother seemed subdued.

You had a nice talk? asked Yesui.

Oh, yes, but Yesugen is still quite militant compared to me. She would take immediate undercover police action in Jensi City, and has no Congress to answer to. I'll find another way. Mostly we talked about Abagai, and the Chuang- shi. I passed on what you told me about them. How they were all once living beings.

Mother looked at her somberly. We talked about death, Yesui, and wondered if it's death or transfiguration that awaits us.

That's morbid, Mother.

No, it's practical. Didn't you hear Yesugen? She now sees Tirgee as a possible replacement in moving our ships if something happens to you. I see you as my replacement if something happens to me. There are now only four of us who can truly work in the gong-shi-jie, and only one who can move our ships. We are a rare breed, Yesui.

My children should add to our numbers, said Yesui, but wondered if it would be so.

That is my hope. I hope for many grandchildren, Yesui. You are about to bless me with two of them, but your brother shows no interest in marriage.

His current love is space, Mother, and he's barely in his twenties. His time will come. At least he's made one conquest. Tirgee is crazy about him.

He would be a good father, said Mother, if only he would settle down for a while.

They paused at the purple vortices guiding the way back to their physical consciousness. Mother looked around at the clouds of creative light, and said, This place was my refuge for many years when Abagai was with me. I still wonder if I'll ever see her again, if I'll be transfigured as she was, or if she was specially chosen for it.

We are Chuang-shi, Mother. I think we'll both see Abagai again someday. But first I want to see my children born.

A nice thought, said Mother.

A flash, and they were both back again, living as organic beings on the planet called Shanji.

It was nine months to the day since her wedding ceremony in the Tumatsin village. Father and Mengjai had twice been delayed by complications and were still working on the space station.

Yesui arose at dawn and waddled down the stone path to the garden with Nokai firmly grasping her arm. She was a behemoth, a bloated dead fish too long out of water, and she wondered how he could still bear to touch her. Her slippers were too tight and threatened to explode with each step, and she was sweating by the time the downhill walk had ended. *I'll have my babies right here before I walk up that hill again,* she thought.

She dabbled her feet in the pool without removing her slippers. She dared not sit down for fear of not being able to get up again, and even leaning over a tiny bit made her lower back ache. She was still puffing breath from the effort when the rest of the family arrived for morning exercises.

Twenty minutes of continuous slow movement and she was dripping wet. Only Nokai seemed to notice her difficulty and kept watching her, but Mother and Gong-gong were oblivious to it. When it was over they were at least kind enough to help Nokai roll his gargantuan ball of a wife back up the hill again.

Nokai changed his robe and went off to work, but he must have said something to Tanchun because suddenly the woman was bothering her when all she wanted to do was sleep. Yesui was on her side, knees drawn up, and just drifting off to sleep when Tanchun knocked softly on the door and came into the room.

"Please sleep, My Lady," she said softly. "I will sit with you and get whatever you need."

"Thank you, Tanchun," said Yesui, too weak for opposition at that moment. She was aching all over, and the tiny breakfast she'd eaten was contemplating an exit before digestion if she dared to move.

Tanchun sat down in a chair beside the bed as Yesui slipped into a doze. There was movement inside her, localized, perhaps a heel being dragged. Yesui wished for more of it, just to know her twins were still alive. They were not active babies, not like their mother had been. Mother had told Yesui all about her birth: the constant activity leading up to it, the strong feeling of presence, then her first miracle in the gong-shi-jie. Yesui felt little of this, and there was no presence she could detect. She'd tried hard to use her Moshuguang mind to make a connection with her babies, but nothing was there. It frightened her a little, for even the mind of an unborn child would be aware of sensations. Even the mind of an ordinary child should be aware of that.

The doctor had recently assured her that nothing was wrong; there was no evidence for any defects in either twin. He was Moshuguang, the man who'd delivered her, and so she opened her mind to him in trust.

"Each birth is different, each child is different, even among twins," he said. "You must put away all expectations. Your children may be more or less than you in ability, but they are still your children. I can only tell you they're healthy and full-term, and I'll do my best to make their birth safe and keep you comfortable."

But Yesui remembered what 'Mind' had told her. It is normal that my children be more than me, for that is the way of the Chuang-shi, she thought.

So far, it didn't seem to be that way.

Yesui dozed, but was jolted wide awake when the first contraction struck in early afternoon. Tanchun was startled from light sleep in her chair, and leaned forward as Yesui arched her back.

"What is it, My Lady?"

"Something is happening. I feel a squeezing — here."

Tanchun left the room for a moment and there were voices in the hallway outside the door. She returned with a cloth soaked in warm water and gently wiped Yesui's flushed cheeks and forehead.

"Everyone has been alerted, My Lady. Your work is about to begin," said Tanchun, smiling.

Mother arrived before the next contraction had a chance to strike. She took Yesui's hand in hers and said, "Nokai has been called, and your doctor is assembling his staff in the hallway. Are you certain you want to give birth here?"

"Yes," said Yesui. "You gave birth to me at home, and I can do it, too. Besides that, I do *not* want to be moved."

"I certainly understand that, dear," said Mother, and squeezed her hand.

In minutes the room was crammed with people. Mother got Yesui up and walked her around the room while Tanchun changed the sheets on the bed. The doctor arrived with an assistant, two nurses and three carts of instruments.

"When does the *rest* of the palace staff arrive?" asked Yesui irritably, and Mother took her outside to walk up and down the plush red carpet of the long hallway. Forever, it seemed, and then the first forceful contraction came. "Ohhh," she groaned, and Mother guided her back to the room.

She lay down on the bed, and the doctor examined her. "Two centimeters," he said. "Things are just getting started, so relax. I'm staying right here."

Oh, gooood, thought Yesui. But two hours later her water broke, and they tortured her more by getting her up to change the sheets again. The contractions were suddenly more forceful and regular. One more examination, poking and prodding, and she suppressed an urge to kick at the doctor's face.

Nokai finally arrived, breathless, to kiss and hold her hand.

It is time for serious work, said Mother, time to do what I've taught you.

Birth without pain, Mother had said. The body would perform the necessary functions, but it was not necessary for the mind to be aware of pain or effort accompanying it. Nokai held her hand, wiped her forehead with a damp cloth. "I'm here, darling," he said. "I'm here."

Mother took her other hand. *Together*, she said, and Yesui closed her eyes.

The matrix of purple stars was there, and physical sensation was dulled, then gone. A sense of loss, and an overwhelming compulsion, and she cried out, *Nokai!*

I'm here. It's beautiful, he said.

You're HERE? How —, said Mother.

There was a sudden flash, a spot of light growing into a golden orb with radiating streamers overwhelming the purple matrix in brilliance. *What in the name of Our Mother is — , began Mother.*

We are not alone, said Nokai. They've come, Yesui. Oh, First Mother, I ask you to give strength to Yesui, and grant us a safe birth for our children.

The golden orb blazed forth, warming her, mesmerizing her. It was a thing she'd seen before in her husband's dreaming. She felt a thrilling presence, not just Mother and Nokai, but others, and suddenly knew that the Chuang-shi were with her as well. I am honored, she said, and bathed in their presence for what seemed a long time. The orb pulsed slowly with a hypnotic rhythm and she was slipping away to a dark place filled with sparkling violet mist, tiny points of light flickering, beckoning to her —.

The golden orb suddenly faded, the matrix of stars rushing away from her.

Someone was crying high-pitched and shrill, and then another, a softer cry more like a whimper.

She opened her eyes in near darkness, a single lamp glowing to her left. The doctor and two nurses were crowded around a cart at the foot of her bed, backs to her. There was a sucking sound and another shrill cry, something banging on the cart.

"Oh, she's a feisty one," said the doctor, and the nurses laughed. "You can wrap her now. She's clear."

"A girl?" asked Yesui.

The doctor glanced over his shoulder at her. "You have *two* girls, Yesui, over two and a half kilograms each. Good job, mother. Now for the other, the calm one. Come here, sweet."

Sucking sounds again, and a complaining mumble. "There, that wasn't so bad. Now wrap her, too. Here, a red ribbon for the feisty one, yellow for the other. Otherwise, we won't be able to tell you two dears apart."

Nokai was squeezing her hand so hard it hurt. "Are you all right?" she asked.

"I — I really didn't see anything," he stammered.

"Two girls," said Mother. "How wonderful."

Two nurses brought the babies over and placed them in Yesui's arms. Two tiny bundles of new life, eyes closed, ribbon bows

73

clamped on wisps of dark hair. Their faces were identical, round, with button noses and bowed lips. One was frowning, the other relaxed and sound asleep. Nokai leaned over to look closely at them, then kissed Yesui softly.

"What will you name them?" asked Mother.

"We were thinking Bao shi for a girl," said Nokai.

"Jewel is a nice name for a girl," said the doctor, "but now you have two jewels. For the red-ribboned one, I suggest Shaan diann."

"Lightning?" said Yesui.

The doctor chuckled. "I think it will be appropriate for her."

It was decided. Bao shi and Shaan diann would be their names.

The new parents looked them over, and so did their new grandmother. She coaxed them with a prod to open their eyes. There was no glow from those eyes, no special focus or recognition. The color of their eyes seemed black in the gloom of the room. Their little bodies were perfect, with no marks to distinguish them. And Shaan diann was the first to complain about hunger.

Mother seemed disappointed.

In every way, it seemed that two perfectly normal children had been born to the Mei-lai-gong and her husband.

Until they were twelve years old.

Seven

For some people time may be regarded as the fourth dimension in a four-dimensional space that condensed out of a parental space of ten dimensions at the very beginning of the universe. For the pragmatic, however, time is only a measure of a span of consciousness separating two identical events, say, that occur at the same position in three dimensions. As such, for most people, the measure of time is a subjective thing and is related to experience.

For a youth everything is new, each minute, each hour a new experience. Time crawls forward from one event to another, new dreams come and go and everything is possible. The future seems vast, and life is immortal.

For the mature adult time speeds up. The long hours of formal education are past, a profession achieved, with short-term goals and ambitions. There is marriage, a permanent and hopefully loving relationship dreamed of over countless agonizing hours in youth. Children arrive, whimpering to be fed one day, going out on a first date the next, getting married the day after that. Dreams and ambitions remain. There is a future, but life is now mortal.

For the middle-aged and elderly, time moves at a blur. Much of their life is now past experience. It is a time of evaluation, a summing up of dreams, ambitions realized or unfulfilled. For the fortunate the balence sheet is positive. For the fortunate, dreams remain, dreams that can be fulfilled in a short time. For many there is nothing left; life is not only mortal, but rapidly approaching its end. They cease to function and dwell only in their past.

For Kati, now well into her fifties, time seemed to move in a blur, but she was fortunate. Over the thirty five years of her reign, most of

75

her reformation plan for Shanji had been accomplished and the end was in sight. The slums of Wanchou were gone, the population stabilized, and there was good medical care for the sick and elderly. Unemployment was under two percent, lowest in the history of the city. The new sewer system had dramatically reduced the spectre of disease that had once haunted the streets of Wanchou. There was a University there, with a medical school. Cultural parks had been added, and the northwest quadrant of the city, with its unique shops and theatres, had become a home for the visual and performing artists of Shanji.

Over fifty thousand tourists had visited Wanchou in just the past year, and added their coins to the coffers of the new middle class growing there.

Kati was proud of this, but did not take credit for it. The people had done the work and initially, at least, the nobles had financed it. Kati had only provided the incentives: new, undeveloped lands for the investing nobles, privately owned business and dwellings for the common people.

In Wanchou, the system had worked as well as it had in the great industrial complex north of it along the Dahe river. For the past fifteen years the foundries, machining and rolling plants had operated three shifts per day, with only one day each week set aside for maintainance. Employment was a hundred percent yet people were still moving in, drawn by high wages for skilled labor. A school of technology had been built there, students carefully selected for their abilities, the number of graduates never allowed to exceed that of the experienced workers about to retire.

Trade with Meng-shi-jie provided a demand still exceeding supply. Finished materials moved through the warehouses like water through a pipe and then southeast on the new maglev line to the great landing field for Meng-shi-jie freighters. With a push from the Mei-lai-gong the rountrip time for each freighter was less than seven months, yet there was still a continual flow of finished materials.

Profits had skyrocketed in the past decade. Workers owned their own apartments and drove madly in bubble-topped cars. They shared in company profits according to their seniority, a thing Kati had lobbied hard for with the nobles. Production had leaped four-fold after her initiative had been vetted. Businesses had moved in to serve the needs of the workers and share in their new affluence. The place was now a small city and there was talk of incorporation.

In the countryside home life was little changed, at least outwardly. The people still lived in their huts, raised their cattle and crops, and had too many babies. But now there was a medical clinic in each village, with nurses and new doctors rotating in residences from the medical school in Wanchou. Infant mortality rates had fallen substantially and Kati could only hope that birth rates would eventually follow by shear necessity.

The farmers and herders lived simply, their lives devoted to the land and to First Mother. When Kati granted them new lands and seed as payment for their produce, they simply made more children to help tend them. The maglev line now transported two crops a year and there were no longer the great bins and graineries filled with rotting foodstuffs.

Her own people, the Tumatsin, lived lives unchanged except for ownership and freedom. Their pastures and barleyfields now extended to the high plateau and would go no further. Villages now covered some forty kilometers along the shore of the great sea where they fished and tended their animals. Like their compatriots to the north their lives were devoted to hard work in the service of The Mother. They were never seen in the great cities, never left their lands, their only connection with the outside world the few trade items they manufactured for pleasure: knives, shell jewelry, and finely made clothing of lamb's wool.

And then there was the problem of Jensi City.

Kati was not sure what had gone wrong there. She wasn't even certain she should be worrying about it.

If there was a monument to Kati's rule on Shanji, then Jensi City was the most obvious. In the beginning there had been only forests, and it seemed the city had arisen overnight: tall, clean buildings, the spire of a church dedicated to First Mother clearly visable among them, then the beautiful cultural parks, especially the one where Kati's early life was shown to the people in miniatures.

But that had been in the beginning. Now Jensi City was something more than that. And that something bothered her deeply. In the beginning, Jensi City was to have been a city of new technology, a place for engineers and scientists to adapt transfer technology from Meng-shi-jie to the needs of Shanji and develop offshoots from it. That had been the initial investment by the nobles: computers, superconducting cores for the maglev, the new carbon nanofiber reinforced polymers, and pharmaceuticals. The laboratories had been there before the city began to rise from the forested hills. Its first citizens had been the most highly educated people on Shanji.

They were elite from the beginning, thought Kati. Could that be the problem?

First citizens of Jensi could only take residence if they had high skills, and jobs awaiting them there. Investment by the nobles was substantial; they were quick to request grants of untouched forested lands in the north as return on investments, and Kati had given them without question.

Salaries were huge compared to the average working class on Shanji. Jensi was isolated, its citizenry educated, sophisticated, with good tastes for living. It was natural that businesses would be invited in to provide for their comforts and pleasures. And Kati's new privitized banking system soon followed them.

Banking now dominated the reputation of the city.

And every major company on Shanji, whether noble family owned or shared ownership by workers, had an office there.

Kati wanted to find out why that was so. She called the Hall of Ministers and spoke with Minister Shiu in Economics. The man was a friend; he'd been the earliest supporter of her reformation plan before she'd even taken the throne.

"I have some concerns about the lack of economic diversity in Jensi City," she said.

"How so?" asked Shiu. "Much of our planet's wealth is centered there."

"That's my problem. It was intended to be a city of high technology, not of banking and commerce. Why have our banks become so centralized?"

Shiu paused before answering. "A sign of our progress, perhaps. All cities have major branches, of course. All accounts and transfers are handled electronically. Centralization of corporate headquarters has no effect on everyday business, Madam."

"Why not Wanchou, then? It's closer to our manufacturing and agricultural regions."

Another pause. "Setting, perhaps. Jensi City is new and clean, surrounded by forests. There is no poverty, no crime. The air is clean, the climate moderate. The accomodations are quite elegant. If I were a corporate head I would think seriously about moving there myself."

"This was not done without cost, Shiu. Where has the money come from? The nobles? I've signed very few land grants in the past ten years."

"Ah, yes — let's see," said Shiu. "I seem to recall looking at that ..."

Clicking of a keyboard as he checked something. "Yes, you're correct. Minimal activity until four years ago, and then a dramatic increase in investments by several families. It's likely they're allowing investments to reach a high level before requesting further land grants. The market value of forested lands has tripled in the last few years, you see, and thirty percent of it is already under private ownership. You might want to consider setting some land aside for —"

"We can talk about that later, Shiu, and I think it's a good idea," said Kati. "For now, I want an overview of where the money has come from for construction and development of new business in Jensi City over the past decade."

"That is easily obtained from tax records, Madam. I will see to it immediately. Is there anything else?"

"Not now. Thank you for your help, Shiu, and I'm grateful for your support over the years."

"My pleasure, Madam," he said. "You have done well for all your people."

Perhaps some more than others, she thought. Kati hung up, and sat thinking for a long moment. Minimal investment by nobles during a time when monumental construction was being completed in Jensi. So how was it funded?

Mengjai had not seen Yesugen and her family for the past seven years, and Yesui had brought him a terse message from her after a meeting in the gong-shi-jie. "She says that if you do not visit soon, her children will make life unbearable for her."

"That seems extreme," said Mengjai, and laughed.

Yesui glared at him. "They are friends and important political allies, and you are the only one with opportunities to visit with them on Meng-shi-jie. At least you can do *that* for us."

Us? "Motherhood hasn't softened you, sister, and you're beginning to sound like Mother," he snarled.

"Mother won't do it so I'll have to speak for her," said Yesui. She had taken the time to ride the rail car into the mountain to confront him in the privacy of his laboratory office, and neither of them was happy about it.

The office had once been his father's and overlooked an empty bay where two shuttles had once been housed. Now they were docked with the space station, flown there by crews of young astronauts getting first experience in space.

"There isn't another man on this planet who has more freedom with his time than you do," continued Yesui. "When you're not off somewhere you bury yourself in this mountain. Your own family hardly ever sees you."

"I'm designing new experiments for the station. It takes time," he said defensively.

"Not *all* your time. Forget about Yesugen for a moment; your own nieces miss you. They're growing up and you're missing all of it. They ask about you and I make excuses. I'm tired of it!"

"I see them as regularly as I can," he said.

"Every six months is *regular*? Mother is Empress of this planet, and she sees them at least every *week*!"

"All right, all right, I'll try to get out of here more often," he said. *At least she isn't nagging me again about marriage.*

"I heard that," snapped Yesui, and looked around at an office cluttered with papers, books, disks, and electronic bins in various stages of repair. "So, you don't look so busy here now. I want you to have supper with us tonight, promptly at six, and no running away afterwards. I want you to spend the evening with us. *One* evening, Mengjai. Surely that will not alter the future of spaceflight for Shanji."

Mengjai sighed. "I will do it if you promise not to nag me for at least a week," he said.

Yesui smiled. "One week, no more."

"Fair enough," he said.

Mengjai arrived promptly at six and was dressed in military blues. When Yesui gawked at him he said, "Isn't this a formal affair? Haven't you invited some sweet young thing to meet me?"

He said it because it had been so his last two visits with them.

"I was serious, Mengjai. This is a family evening," said Yesui, and closed the door behind him.

The suite was an expansion of Yesui's old rooms, the entrance a few steps down a red-carpeted hallway from the royal quarters. Sitting room, dining room, two bedrooms, bath, and a small office for Nokai. White marble floors and ebonite furniture were in stark contrast. The walls were painted red, with little adornment except for several brass framed mirrors lending depth to the rooms. There was an occasional lamp in brass with shades of leaded glass, but most light came from ceiling panels in each room.

Nokai came out of his office to give him a firm handshake. "Good to see you, Mengjai. I'm supposed to send you right into the girls' room. They want to show you something." He put his arm around Yesui as he said it. Both of them wore white robes and seemed the perfect picture of a serene happy couple.

"Not too long, though. Supper will arrive shortly," added Yesui.

So Mengjai made the short walk through the dining room to a door just beyond it, where he softly knocked. "Are you ladies open to visitors?" he said loudly.

"Mengjai!" answered two identical voices. The door flew open and Shaan diann grabbed his arm to pull him inside, then kicked the door closed behind her. The room was small and in shambles. Two unmade beds filled most of it. Unwashed clothing was piled in an open closet and there was a musty odor, even though fresh evening air was coming in through an open door leading to a small, railed balcony. Walls were covered with printouts of abstract computer-generated artwork in bright colors: geometric shapes fitted together like tiles on a floor, others great sweeps and roils of colored inks that seemed vaguely familiar to him.

Bao shi was robed in black, like her sister, and sat in front of a computer console, a screen there showing one of the gaseous giants of the Shanji system. She looked up serenely at Mengjai, and smiled. "We have a new disk from grandma, one of her learning disks from when she was a little girl."

Shaan pushed a chair against his legs until he sat down. "Ma says you will tell us all about it," she said.

Even at age ten, the girls were turning into heartbreakers. Their features favored Nokai: long faces and necks, delicate cheekbones, noses more prominent than Yesui's. Still, it was their eyes that first caught one's attention: deep set, almond in shape, a color so deep blue and with flecks of violet that in proper light made them seem purple.

Identical twins, yes, but different, some of it artificial. Shaan's hair was cut short and combed back above her ears. Bao had never cut her hair and it lay as a great, black stream halfway down her back. Shaan's eyes twinkled and she was a darting gnat, never still, and full of fun. Bao was quiet, contempletive and serene, with a look in her eyes bringing peace to the observer. *One could drown in those eyes*, thought Mengjai, as he sat down beside her.

"Hurry!" said Shaan. "Ma will be here in a minute." She sat down on the other side of Bao, and leaned against her.

Always touching, thought Mengjai. Every time he'd seen the girls they were in physical contact whenever in reach of each other.

Yesui was not so quick to interrupt them. For fifteen minutes he went over the learning machine disk with his nieces, describing the planets and their differences for both the Tengri-Khan and Tengri-Nayon systems.

"Is that all?" asked Shaan, when he was finished. "Where is the gong-shi-jie?"

"It's not in real physical space, Shaan. You can't take pictures of it," he said.

"But Mother goes there all the time," said Bao. "It's like she goes into a dreaming state and her heart is barely beating. We wait and watch, and then in a minute she's back again."

How do you explain the physics of the gong-shi-jie to ten-year-olds? he wondered.

"It's a real place, but of a higher dimensionality than the universe we see around us." *Oh, boy, I just lost them.* "Sorry, but it's hard to describe it without using mathematics. Anyway, it exists, and there's a special part of your mother's brain that allows her to go there and manipulate the tremendous energies stored in the place."

"She's told us all about it," said Shaan, "and what she sees there. We've tried making pictures of it."

"Yes, I see them," he said, looking at the walls. "They look familiar, but there is more to it than that."

"You've been there," said Bao.

"Yes, but never alone. I can't go there by myself, but when your mother is there I can be there too if I wish it. We were somehow mentally connected at birth, Bao. Neither your mother nor I can explain it."

Shaan scowled. "Bao and I are connected, too, but not to Ma. That's why we can't go there with her."

Mengjai was confused by that.

"Shaan and I know each other's thoughts and feelings all the time," explained Bao. "We even share out dreams at night."

"Well, you have Moshuguang heritage, and your father is certainly the strongest empath I've ever met. You sense nothing from other people?"

"Only what we get from words, expression, or tone of voice," said Bao softly. "Is there something wrong with us, Mengjai? Grandma thinks so, and Ma gets angry when we even ask the question."

"Ma is very defensive about us," added Shaan. "I think she feels ashamed by what we can't do."

"Now, now," he said. "You're both beautiful, intelligent and talented girls. I'm sure nobody has ever said something is wrong with you."

"They don't have to say it," said Shaan.

From deep within his Moshuguang mind, Mengjai had a sudden revelation that made his heart skip a beat. "Is this why you've wanted so bad to see me, to talk about this?"

"Yes," they said in unison, and looked as if they were about to cry.

"Oh, sweeties," he said, and hugged both of them. "Do you want me to talk to your mother and grandmother about it?"

"Yes," they said.

"And Father," said Bao, "but please don't make them angry with us for telling you."

"I promise," he said, and then there was a knock on the door.

"Time to eat!" It was Nokai. And Mengjai had a few seconds to mask himself firmly before the girls followed him out of the room.

Conversation at table was pleasant enough, though Yesui seemed to sense something was wrong and kept trying hard to probe him. Nokai had arranged a direct line of trade between Shanji and Lan-Sui, and was quite pleased with the results. Yesui talked a lot about her work with Tirgee and raved about the girl's progress like a proud mother. With each compliment given to Yesugen's daughter the mood of the twins sank deeper and deeper into gloom. They remained silent and picked at their food, sitting so close to each other their shoulders touched. Finally, Mengjai could stand it no longer.

"I'd like to hear what the girls have been doing," he said, cutting Yesui off at the end of a sentence. "My, how you've grown in just a few months. And all that artwork in your room, that's something new. Tell me about it. Where do you get your ideas?"

Yesui looked surprised, and Nokai frowned. The twins seemed terrified, but Shaan fought through it in an instant.

"From pictures, and things Ma has told us," she ventured.

"What things?" asked Mengjai.

"The gong-shi-jie," said Bao timidly.

"I describe it as best I can," said Yesui. "Their art is mostly from imagination."

"But it's beautiful, it really is. The girls have a talent, Yesui. Who knows what other talents they might have?"

Yesui and Nokai caught his meaning instantly, and looked stunned. The girls smiled faintly at a compliment received.

"When your mother and I were little, she had a great talent and it seemed I had none. But I surprised her one day."

Mengjai then told the girls how Yesui had suddenly discovered he could be with her in the gong-shi-jie, and acted out the drama of her shock. Even Yesui smiled at that.

"And you're still sneaky, brother," she said.

"I can still do it, you know, but the gong-shi-jie is your world, not mine. I have my own talents and work I enjoy and that's the important thing. Don't you agree, Nokai?"

"Of course," said Nokai, his chin in his hands. "Happiness and honest work are the will of Our Mother, regardless of talent. Nothing more is required by Her."

Sensing something, empath? thought Mengjai. He was trying hard to read the mind of the man, but there was a total blank. Yesui had warned him about this.

"So, let's nurture the budding artists with details for their pictures. Yesui, tell them about the star vortices, your minifestation, and Tirgee's, and let's see what Shaan and Bao can do with it."

Yesui was now completely aware of what he was up to, for he'd opened his mind to her. She was both horrified and saddened by what she'd sensed from him; her eyes were moist, but her voice controlled as she described in detail the things he'd asked for.

The twins listened in rapt silence, often looking at each other. They seemed to brighten, and Mengjai could already see new pictures forming in their minds. As their mother finished talking they were squirming in their chairs, eager to get away.

"Can we be excused?" asked Shaan.

"We need to try doing some of these things before we forget them," added Bao.

Yesui looked at Mengjai, and he nodded. "Well — I suppose. We have some nice berries for desert, but that can be later."

Shaan and Bao rose together, holding hands, and rushed away to their room, talking excitedly. Their door closed, cutting off the sound of their conversation.

Silence.

Nokai was looking down at a plate half-filled with food. Yesui put her face in her hands and sniffled.

"Oh, Mengjai," she sobbed, "what have we done?"

Mengjai sighed. "Made your children a bit miserable, I think, but it's not just you. It's Mother, too. Maybe even the Chuang-shi. Your expectations came from them. They never promised anything, Yesui."

"They said it was normal for abilities to increase in each generation of our line," said Yesui, now glaring at him. A tear ran down her cheek.

"Well, it hasn't happened yet. And those two lovely girls of yours don't even know what expectations you have for them. They think they've failed you *and* Mother, and they don't even know how they've done it. If it's going to happen, it'll happen. Both of you always talk about having faith in First Mother, but where is *your* faith right now?"

Yesui opened her mouth to shout at him, but Nokai stopped her.

"You're right," he said, and looked at his wife. "Admit it; there was disappointment soon after they were born. They were nothing like you; your mother said it. That was the beginning. We've been impatient and have no faith. It's true, Yesui. Mother help us, it's true." His voice faltered, then cracked.

Yesui began to cry softly. "I dreamed of taking them to the gong-shi-jie and training them there with Tirgee. I've been dreaming about it for ten years, Mengjai. Ten long years."

"We love our children," said Nokai. "We do things with them and show them affection. They *must* know we care about them."

"I'm sure they do," said Mengjai, "but that just makes the hurt all the worse. They want you to be proud of them. Surely an empath like you can see it."

Nokai rubbed his face with his hands. "I — I thought it was self-generated, the expectations they had for themselves. Shaan and Bao are so tightly connected they're like one child. They don't readily share feelings with anyone but themselves."

"They shared plenty with me this evening," said Mengjai.

"Oh, dear," said Nokai, and Yesui gushed tears with a sob.

There was a long moment while two good people wept.

"I'm the outsider in this matter," said Mengjai, "so *I* will talk to Mother. No sense in getting her angry at you over a confrontation."

Yesui sniffled and wiped her eyes. "And *then* what?"

"Have faith and love your children. Accept whatever happens. It's that simple."

Yesui smiled faintly, and then the most marvelous thing happened; she gave him the nicest compliment he could remember getting from her.

"You should have had children before me, Mengjai, and then I could have learned from you."

"Someday — when I find the right woman," he said.

Yesui laughed, and Nokai shook his head in humor.

"Speaking of children," said Mengjai, "tell Tirgee that I'm leaving for Meng-shi-jie in a week, and I promise to see her this time. I'm sorry it's been so long, but my last two layovers I didn't even get out of the ship. This time, I'll have four days."

"I'll tell her," said Yesui, then, "She's not a child anymore, Mengjai. She's thirteen, nearly a woman. I think you'll find she's a lot like her mother now."

It sounded like a warning. "I will bow to her gracefully," he said dramatically, with a flair of his hands.

Yesui wasn't amused.

"And now, before desert, I'd like to see what Shaan and Bao are up to," he said, and excused himself from table.

The girls were happy to see him and demonstrated their paint program. A background of swirling colors and several star vortices in red, green and yellow had already been added. Bao was carefully putting in the first fractal features of her mother's manifestation, and near it was a great swath of emerald green, shaped like an open fan.

Shaan pointed to it. "That's Tirgee," she said.

Only a swath of color, without features of any kind.

I wonder what she looks like now? he thought.

Eight

Tirgee

Sheng-chih arrived promptly at dawn and knocked softly on the ornately carved bronze door. It was opened by a servant, a white-haired skeleton of a man whose black robe hung on him like a sack. He bowed and stepped aside for Sheng to enter.

The opulence of old nobility was sweet and quaint. The rooms were plush, warm, and cluttered with the treasures of generations. Thick red carpet was springy to the step, the walls and beamed ceilings gilded in gold leaf. Large mirrors framed in brass were on every wall. The upholstered furniture was deep and plush, end tables and lighted curio cabinets displaying vases, cups and figurines of gold-inlaid porcelain. Two sitting *Shizi* in brass, and with rubies for eyes, guarded a cold fireplace. The odor of incense filled the air, mingling with something heavier, and sweeter.

The servant took him through living room and dining room to a large double door of leaded glass leading to a balcony. When he opened the doors, Sheng saw three men seated at a brass, glass topped table with their dowager host. The men arose as he stepped out onto the balcony, the servant stepping backwards to close the door behind him.

Sheng bowed to the ancient tiny woman who sat so proudly erect on a thick-cushioned chair at the table; she smiled sweetly, and held out a jeweled hand. Her robe was heavy and ruby red, with flower designs in gold thread. Her arm was like a stick, her sleeve draped over it.

Sheng took her hand ever so gently and kissed a jewel. "Madam," he said softly, allowing his lips to brush her hand.

"You are prompt, Sheng-chih," she said. Her voice was raspy, her breathing rapid, for the condition of her lungs was rapidly deteriorating. This meeting would likely be his last chance to use her.

There were no introductions. Sheng shook hands with the three men and gave each of them his card. All three were in their forties, dressed in black tailored suits. Not old enough to be heads of noble families. Perhaps sons or trusted representatives, but messengers in any case. They studied his card and did not smile.

"I owe my thanks to Madam Shiang for inviting you here," said Sheng. "Your time is valuable and I will be brief. Please sit."

The three men sat down on one side of the table, Sheng joining his hostess on the other side. The balcony was large, with a two meter railing serving as a trellis for flowering vines, tiny blooms in red and violet. Young *Tysk* grew in wooden tubs at the four corners of the balcony. They were on the twenty-third floor of the building, surrounded by buildings of equal height yet hidden from view by the flowering vines.

A silver service lay in the center of the table; they served themselves, but Sheng did the honors for his hostess after inquiring after her wishes, and leaned warmly against her while serving.

There was tea and honeycakes, and a sweet pulpy fruit from the west, cut into quarters. There was no breaking of cakes, or distribution, no homilies to First Mother or Her Empress. Sheng-chih ate slowly as he talked.

"This city owes so much to our noble families. Without their investment and support it would not exist," he ventured. "Those of us who have profited from our commercial growth are deep in your debt and are aware of the sacrifices you've made."

No reaction from the men, only a glance at Madam Shiang, who smiled sweetly. "Something our Empress fails to recognize," she said.

"In time, perhaps," said Sheng. "Her intentions are good, but the new system needs tuning. The nobles have been burdened with all the costs of reform and have reached the limits of their liquid assets. Growth can not continue in such a way. Don't you agree?"

One man nodded. Another blinked his eyes slowly.

"Excuse my bluntness, gentlemen, but under the present system the noble families who've done so much for us are rapidly becoming land-poor. The process of investing, and receiving new lands in return, has led to a depletion of your liquid reserves. How can anyone expect you to develop new lands without capital, I ask you?"

The glint in the mens' eyes told him he had their attention, and Madam Shiang was nodding her head sagely in agreement with what he'd just said.

"So what do you propose to do about it?" asked one man.

"I ask you to share your burdens with those of us who have benefited from your sacrifices. You have created considerable wealth for many people in this city."

"We're quite aware of that," said the same man, undoubtedly a noble's son, much bolder than the other two. "We're also aware that few taxes are paid by these people. That burden is also ours."

"Ah, but there's a bill before our Peoples' Congress at this very moment that will allow tax credit for investments. It comes from people like myself who wish to see continued growth at a time when investment from your families has dwindled to a shadow of its former self. But even tax incentives are not enough. There must be more."

Sheng paused to sip tea. The men leaned forward in anticipation, and Madam Shiang raised an eyebrow at them. Beneath the table he gently squeezed her hand as he began to talk again.

"Gentlemen, I represent a consortium of business leaders willing to share your burden and promote growth. Individually our wealth is not extreme, but together we represent a considerable financial force which we owe to your families. Our combined liquid assets are currently at seven billion Yuan, and growing. We are conservative people, have saved wisely over many years and are now in a position to invest on a larger scale. And we are offering you our support."

The men were shocked by the figure he'd named, and the figure was accurate. It was no time for deception — not now.

"I propose the following," said Sheng, maintaining momentum. "Each noble family establishes its own investment corporation. Our consortium deposits funds in the names of family members as gifts or private debts, and the money is used for new investments. With the new tax incentive certain to pass, for each Yuan we contribute you receive two, plus the grant of new lands. Flow of capital is thus assured without the use of your reserves."

"You propose to give us free money?" The same man, again, and he laughed.

Sheng laughed with him when Madam Shiang frowned. "Of course not. We are business people, and profit is our motive. In this plan we're investing in two things: future expansion, for which we propose a generous allowance — and a small ownership of your current developed properties."

"How small?" A second man suddenly spoke, eyes narrowed.

"That is negotiated at the pleasure of the families. A small percentage of an individual business, or the whole thing. That is up to you. We'll pay according to current fair market value, and that certainly guarantees a high return on your initial investment."

"All done through a family corporation?" The second man, again, perhaps higher up the noble food chain than Sheng had first suspected.

"Not necessarily. Individuals may exchange holdings for investment shares in our consortium. This may be done discretely, and property excess may be compensated for in cash or bullion. A trade, you see, without tax consequences. And our return on investment has averaged forty percent for the past few years."

"Even more," said Madam Shiang. "Mine has been closer to fifty, and I've rid myself of lands I don't care to develop in my remaining years."

Remaining months, perhaps, thought Sheng-chih. You wouldn't be so pleased if you knew the actual return was seventy percent to the consortium, either. But still, you've done well by us. "Madam is a wise investor," he said.

Sheng asked for further questions, but there were none. Madam Shiang asked the others to remain with her when Sheng was prepared to leave. They shook hands. The wary expressions of the men were gone, and all had his card. He kissed Madam's hand again and thanked her for the audience with representatives of honored noble families.

When he left the suite of rooms, there was a bounce in his step.

He knew he had them.

The only thing unchanged was the heat. It seemed searing on Mengjai's face as he came up from the underground train station.

The scaffolding was gone, streets and sidewalks unblocked by obstructions, but filled with people and little bubble-cars. Buildings soared high, windows blackened by thin film interference, polymer sidings in yellow, green and brown and resistent to the weather. Two meter *Tysk* growing in wooden tubs were spaced at regular intervals along the sidewalks, their leaves curled up into tubes against the day's heat. The shops were all open, windows displaying clothing, household goods, also arts and crafts from the Tengri-Nayon and Khan systems. There was even a small display of Tumatsin bone-handled knives — but at a price Mengjai could not afford.

The people seemed a mix of natives and immigrants, long gaunt features of the one, round faces of the other. Their dress ranged from loose-fitting clothes of canvas to expensive form-fitting suits in black or white. Many stared curiously at his military blues, and two members of the warrior class acknowledged him with a nodding bow as he walked the streets to the Empress' residence.

The fountain was not running, its basin empty, but around it were gardens in full bloom, great sweeps of pink, red, yellow and white, and partially shaded by a matrix of leafy *Tysk* now over four meters high. There was still a guarded entrance at the gate, the guards passing him through after making a call to the residence and instructing him to wait in the reception hall.

He was met there by a tusked warrior in battle leathers, wearing a holstered sidearm. The little man waddled ahead of Mengjai to the elevator leading up to the residence.

The elevator descended.

"We're going *down*?" asked Mengjai.

"The family is not in their quarters, sir. You're to be met at another place."

The elevator doors opened. They were in a basement, a single, long hall with white walls and floor painted grey curving out of sight to his left, ending at a steel door to his right. Water pipes along the ceiling gurgled as he was led to the door. It was hot and humid, and their footsteps echoed from the walls.

The guard opened the door and Mengjai was startled by the collective scream of many voices, the sharp crash of metal on metal that greeted his entrance.

The room was monstrous, with a ten meter ceiling and an expanse of wooden floor four hundred meters square. Along one wall was a series of bench seats rising in tiers, a few warriors and guards with slung laser rifles sitting there to watch the action. Two other walls were draped with large, plain red flags with scattered chairs and piles of clothing, bags, assorted weapons along their bases. The fourth wall backed a raised platform with a simple altar spewing forth smoke from a bowl of incense, and a standing microphone into which a black-robed man was screaming his commands.

"At sword length. Fourth *dong*! Zhumbei!"

"STRIKE!"

Twenty rows of black-robed, wire-masked combatants screamed simultaneously and slashed furiously at each other with long, curved swords. Mengjai flinched at the sound of it.

"You may sit here, sir," said his escort, and Mengjai sat down on the end of a bench to watch.

"At sword length. Fifth *dong*! Zhumbei!"

"STRIKE!"

A horrible series of clashes, steel striking steel, and apparently flesh. One of the combatants went down hard and was helped to the far side of the room by his adversary.

There were five more *dongs* and three more casualties before it was over. One of the fallen ones was rushed past Mengjai and out of the room. His face was covered with blood and the mask he gripped tightly in his hand was smashed beyond recognition.

Mengjai watched in horror and fascination, for he'd never before seen such violence or participated in it. The art of the sword was still taught on Shanji; Mother continued her lessons, but only as exercise, and the classes were small. They did not hack away at each other like this. They did not draw each other's blood.

What he was witnessing was the fierceness of a people his mother had once fought against, a people who revered war and honored death in battle. She had fought them and taken lives with her steel, but she never talked about it. All he knew about the great war had come from his father and Gong-gong. Now he was seeing it first-hand.

The class ended, Participants bowed in unison to their instructor, who returned the bow with hands clasped at his chest. Masks were removed, swords held in the curve of an arm as they walked wearily to the other side of the room to rest, and change their clothing.

One student did not go with them, but fumbled with the binding of his mask as he walked directly towards Mengjai.

Two warriors with slung laser rifles walked in front of Mengjai and stood by his side. Mengjai felt apprehension for one instant and then the student was in front of him, pulling at a strap and lifting off the mask.

Black hair spilled in a mass over her robed shoulders.

"Hello, Mengjai," she said, and only then did he feel her presence in his mind.

"Ti — Tirgee?" he stammered.

Long face sweating, still breathing hard from the exercise, her open mouth displayed the tusks of her bloodline. Prominent cheekbones made her black eyes seem deep-set. She was now inches taller than Yesui, slender, but her shoulders were broad. She held her sword in the curve of an arm and stepped forward when he seemed unable to move.

Tirgee put an arm around his waist, and pressed her cheek against his chest. "It has been a long time," she said.

Mengjai overcame his temporary paralysis enough to slide one arm around her, and he felt a muscled back there. The guards shuffled their feet nervously beside him.

"I would never have recognized you by sight," he said.

Tirgee drew back, squeezed his arm with a firm grip, and smiled. "That's what happens when you stay away so long."

Mengjai shook his head. "All your little messages from the gong-shi-jie over the years have not prepared me for this. You've suddenly turned into a beautiful young woman."

Now she *really* smiled, and Mengjai's heart fluttered for a beat.

"Well, you're here now. Did you enjoy watching our sport?"

"Yes, if you call it sport. It seemed more like watching a war. I think one of your fellow students was badly hurt today."

"He'll recover, as all of us do. If his cut is clean a little salt will give him a fine scar. I have a small one, but it's not in a good place." Tirgee pointed at her own face and he could see a two centimeter long rill of scar tissue on the underside of her chin.

"I must change, now, and the day is planned. Mother and Father are in meetings and Niki is attending a tactical school in the field. He'll be back in two days and will be very unhappy if you're not here to see him."

Mengjai bowed and swept his arm in a grand gesture. "I'm at your disposal, Madam," he said.

"Then wait here. I'll just be a minute," she said.

Tirgee crossed the great room to change her clothes. One guard followed her, the other remained with Mengjai. Across the room, the black robe came off over her head, then a tight, black shirt beneath it. There was a glimpse of a broad muscled back before it was covered with a white blouse, her guard facing Mengjai. When she came to him again she wore a silken blouse with puffy sleeves, a leather chest plate over it, leather breeches, and black polished boots nearly reaching her knees.

Thirteen, or fourteen, to the casual passerby she could be in her twenties, he thought, then realized his mask was down when she smiled.

"There is a car waiting for us," she said, and took his arm when he offered it to her.

They returned to the elevator, up to ground floor and walked outside, two guards right with them. Again the heat assaulted him. Two bubble cars awaited them, each driven by a member of the warrior class. The guards got into one car, Tirgee and Mengjai into the back seat of the other. The cab was cool, even with hot sunlight beating on him from above.

The car started with a jerk; they careened around a curved drive and sped through the gate opened for them, turning left, then down another street at high speed. Behind them, the other car was nearly touching their rear bumper. "Are we late for something?" he asked.

"No," said Tirgee. "Moving quickly from place to place is a part of our security protocol and guards must be with me whenever I leave the residence. Do you mind?"

They're not chaperones, Mengjai.

I wasn't thinking that.

Oh yes, you were.

Mengjai smiled, then gasped as they swerved to pass a car and nearly hit another one coming out into an intersection.

"Traffic will soon clear. It's a workday, and we're going to the countryside," said Tirgee. "I want to show you what has happened to the underground cities my ancestors lived in."

"The mining cities?"

"Yes. The mines are still operational, but everything else has changed. It was the first thing Mother wanted to do after surface construction was well underway, and she'd thought you'd appreciate it. She thinks it could be an attraction for tourists."

The street quickly changed from brick to graded earth embedded with gravel that rattled beneath the car, but there was no lessening of speed. Low rolling hills stretched before them, covered with dry dormant grass, and a few scraggly bushes with long thorns. Mengjai found the scenery bleak, quite unlike the greenery he was used to on Shanji. Tirgee saw this immediately.

"There's little rain here, but what we get diffuses quickly in our porous soils. The aquifers are deep here. Essentially all our water is underground," she explained.

The car finally slowed, the road winding through a broad canyon, the hills now higher on either side, with outcroppings of rock that sparkled in sunlight. Soon the hills were topped with such rock and there were places where the tops had crumbled into avalanches of boulders and slabs that nearly reached the road. The rock was stained red, with veins of white quartzite and schist, the first sign of an underlying pegmatite structure. These rolling hills were old mountains worn down by countless ages of high winds and blowing debris. Mengjai could not imagine the force of such winds, deriving their energy from the violent outbursts from Tengri-Nayon until only recently.

The first people here had lived underground like moles until the coming of Empress Abagai, Tirgee's grandmother. Many still lived there. But now there was life on the surface, a single city and a few scattered towns, tiny patches of green on Meng-shi-jie's blasted surface. It was no wonder her people were so hard.

Tirgee read every thought. "The Lan-Sui immigrants have been a great help. They had no other place to go, and are dedicated to hard work. Sunlight, an open sky, a far horizon are probably their greatest rewards. Mother does not fear them as she used to, but further immigration is still closed. Our main problem is water."

"There must be full aquifers all over the planet," he said.

"We've only just begun exploring that possibility," said Tirgee, then looked at him. "It's another thing we need help with."

The talk of a young adult, yet he still remembered bouncing her on his knee.

Ahead, the dirt road suddenly ended at a graveled lot where several cars were parked. Beyond it a concrete pill-box of a building sat next to the huge maw of a tunnel going into a hillside cut back to expose a wall of sparkling rock. Tirgee pointed a few degrees to the right of it and said, "The first city is ten kilometers further, and we'll go there by flyer when Niki gets back. But this is the new project Mother wants you to see. The initial public viewing is coming up in only two weeks, so you're one of our first visitors, Mengjai."

She squeezed his arm and was excited, acting her age for one instant. They got out of the car and two guards followed their crunching steps to the concrete building. Steel tracks came out of the tunnel, with two cables overhead, moving, the grumble of an engine coming from inside the building. A man clothed in grey canvas stood on a platform at the end of the tracks and bowed to them as they approached. They had just stepped up onto the platform when a box of a railcar came out of the tunnel and screeched to a halt in front of them.

The car could hold eighty people, but was empty. Out of forty thick leather seats they chose one in the middle of the car, the guards sitting in the back by the entrance. The car lurched forward, moved into the tunnel, into darkness — then dropped.

A steep descent, perhaps thirty degrees below horizontal and the air was suddenly chilled. Rock was all around them, illuminated dimly by regularly spaced yellow lights. Mengjai was by the window, and he was quite conscious of Tirgee pressing against his side to look past his shoulder. They rode in silence and it was fifteen minutes before the tunnel suddenly widened, then disappeared.

And Mengjai beheld Yesugen's new marvel.

The cavern was so large it seemed they'd stepped out onto the surface of some mystic planet under an open night sky. Blue lights were like stars in the ceiling, their light reflected by a still, black lake stretching far. Clusters of yellow lights glowed from window-shaped openings in the walls around the lake, and at the base of each cluster, right at water's edge, quarter-bubbles of transparent material glowed in red. Handrailed foot trails ran off in both directions around the lake. They went down steps from the railcar platform and Tirgee led him along the trail to their right, each step on solid rock until they reached the first glowing canopy at water's edge. Eyes adjusting to low light , Mengjai found the setting surealistic and enchanting. A place of retreat, or meditation.

Heat lamps dotted the canopy, and lounge chairs had been placed beneath it on a thick layer of black sand over gravel over the bare rock.

Beside the canopy a short, steel- mesh dock went out a few meters over the water. When he looked at it Mengjai saw a boat coming towards him, a dark silhouette with a man standing in the stern, swaying back and forth. The lake was not as large as he'd first thought.

Tirgee went to water's edge, scooped up a handful of water to splash her face and neck with, her guards only steps behind her. "Do you swim?" she asked.

"Never learned," said Mengjai.

"Neither have I," she said, "but the boat is quite safe. You'll enjoy it."

Mengjai looked at the black water, and thought otherwise. Now he imagined he smelled food cooking, and thought he must be getting hungry.

"The hotel — behind you. A meal will be ready for us when we return," she said.

The boat arrived, docked smoothly by a boatman pulling expertly on a single, stern oar. The boat was wide, with an upswept bow and cushioned seats with backrests along the hull. They stepped out onto the dock and the guards crowded in behind them. Tirgee turned to them and said, "You will remain here."

The guards looked pained. "Our orders, ma'am. We must do what —"

"Your orders come from me, and I take full responsibility for them. Stay here, and wait."

No argument. It was a command as ever he'd heard one, a command of a thirteen-year-old-going-on-thirty. *You sound like your mother.*

"I'm told I favor her," she said sweetly, then grabbed his hand and pulled him into the boat after her.

They settled themselves into soft cushions as the boat pulled away from the dock. They did not go far out into the lake, but stayed near shoreline and made a complete trip around that took over an hour. The water was mirror smooth, the single oar a whisper in the stillness. Tirgee leaned against him as she pointed out certain features.

"Seven hotels are cut into the rock, and all rooms face the lake. The canopies cover artificial beaches, but swimming areas are small. The shoreline falls off steeply most places and the lake is over a hundred meters deep at its center. This is meant to be a place of rest, not activity. And there is no cooler place on our planet," she said.

Tirgee trailed one hand in the water, and looked up at him. "I love coming here. It's so peaceful, even romantic, don't you think?"

Oh, oh. "Absolutely. You can bring all your young suitors here when they're clamoring for your attentions," he said.

Tirgee smiled beautifully, then firmly took his wrist and pulled his arm up and around her shoulders. "I don't have any suitors yet, Mengjai, so you'll just have to do for now."

"Now, now," he chided, but his arm refused to move and his hand involuntarily closed on her shoulder. *Oh, my, this isn't right,* he thought.

Tirgee nestled against him and closed her eyes. "What's the harm, Mengjai? We're only pretending. Mmm," she murmured. In minutes, it seemed she was nearly asleep. Mengjai held her, and rested his cheek against the crown of her head. They remained that way until the boat was nearing the dock and they were within sight of her guards.

Mengjai worked hard to keep his mind blank the entire time.

After they'd docked, a wonderful meal awaited them in a state-owned hotel carved out from the rock of the cavern walls. The interior walls were rough-hewn rock with *Tysk* columns and beams and sturdy wooden furniture, all rooms lit by electric lamps with yellow panes of glass. The setting was rustic, warm and intimate. The two of them ate alone at one of twenty tables, the guards hovering at the entrance nearby. They talked about Mengjai's work in space, and Tirgee's in the gong-shi-jie, and Yesui's twins.

"I will have two children," said Tirgee, "a boy and a girl."

"Children would be nice," said Mengjai. "If I ever settle down, I'd like to have a family."

Tirgee put her chin in her hands and gazed at him. "And when will that be?"

Mengjai laughed. "Who knows? As soon as I've had my fill of spaceflight, I suppose. I don't think it's right to be flying off when the children are small. You're a good example, Tirgee. I missed some important years while you were growing up. I missed all the years you were a little girl."

She smiled. "You're not my father, Mengjai."

He smiled back. "Like a much older brother, maybe." Mengjai struggled to keep his mask up, and could read nothing in Tirgee's mind.

"Maybe," she said, and her eyes twinkled with amusement. In the dim lamplight, she looked oh so far beyond her thirteen years. In that light, she was a vision that he knew would return to haunt him.

And it did.

That first day was the most wonderful. They returned to the residence for dinner with Yesugen and Kabul. Talk was political, as usual. The after-dinner drinks were strong, as usual. He went to bed early, but was awakened soon after falling asleep.

Hello, brother. Here we are again. Want to join us?

In the twilight of sleep he slipped away to join his sister for a heartbeat or two, seeing through her. Swirling mists, and a glorious fan of green.

See? I told you, said Yesui.

I feel him, said Tirgee, but is he really here?

Yes, really, said Mengjai, and he described her manifestation to prove what he'd said. She altered the colors and intensity of her manifestation to test him, but still seemed doubtful.

If you don't mind, ladies, I'd really like to sleep. So, goodnight, he said, and was instantly back in himself.

But only moments later, before he was in sleep, the door to his room squeaked open. He looked up and saw Tirgee silouetted in the doorway.

"You were there?" she asked.

"Yes, sweet, I was there. Now let's both of us get some sleep."

"Happy dreams, Mengjai," she murmured, and closed the door again.

The next day was spent with Kabul on a tour of the city and the housing complexes for immigrants ringing it. Niki returned that evening, and Mengjai talked with him until bedtime about the education of a young prince destined to be Emperor of Meng-shi-jie. At fifteen, the lad was as tall as Mengjai and hard muscled. He favored his father in both appearance and personality: handsome sculptured features and deep set eyes giving him an intense look, highly disciplined by military training, yet soft-spoken, gentle and compassionate. *He will be a fine leader,* thought Mengjai.

The day after was Niki's, and Tirgee was conspicuous by her absence. Mengjai spent much of the day in a flyer with Niki and two guards to fly over outlying villages at locations where local aquifers had been found at depths less than thirty meters. Around the villages they saw hectar after hectar of baby *Tysk* growing under umbrellas of fine cloth, and single hectar-sized bubbles of plas-sheet stretched over hydroponic vegetable crops grown from Shanji seeds.

The greening of Meng-shi-jie had indeed begun, but over ninety percent of the planet's surface was still barren for most of the year and there were many generations of work yet to be done. All of it depended on aquifer availability and water content, and Mengjai found himself thinking about the various Moshuguang techniques that could be used in making a survey.

For Mengjai there was another marvel when they flew to one of the old cities some kilometers east of the spa he'd seen with Tirgee. Two hundred meters below ground level he saw a city of apartments and small shops built on the floor of an enormous cavern hollowed out for the veins of copper, iron, zinc and cobalt it had once contained. There were buildings up to four stories, and brick paved streets with monstrous light panels in the cavern that dimmed or intensified according to the time of day or night. Railcar service ran through tunnels connecting to other such cities further east. The one Mengjai saw had a permanent population limited to ten thousand. It was one of the smallest, he was told.

An active mine was their last stop. He saw diamond drills the size of a bubble car cutting new bores to expose mineral veins, then laser drills working those veins, flashing them to ions, electromagnetic scoops sucking metal ions to separators to be deposited on metal sheets of their own kind. Drilling and ore processing were as one on Meng-shi-jie. *Another idea for technology transfer*, thought Mengjai, and he took literature about it for the Moshuguang scientists on Shanji.

In the evening he talked about the tech-transfer possibilities with Yesugen and Kabul, and they seemed receptive. He talked about various tracer and electric field techniques he was aware of for mapping out the distribution of aquifers, and they were impressed. They asked him if he might be interested in pursuing the work himself.

"I'm not a geologist, but it *is* an interesting problem," he admitted.

Tirgee said only a few things the entire evening, but watched him constantly, hanging onto every word he said. Even in normal light it was hard to believe she was so young. *Why can't you be older?* came a sudden compulsive thought, so sudden he failed to mask it.

Tirgee only smiled.

Niki talked about his schooling: history, politics, science and mathematics. He attended the state school for military officers and would receive his commission in three years, with flight school to follow. He talked about flying in space with Mengjai. Tirgee only watched and listened, and smiled at appropriate places in their conversation, but her eyes never left Mengjai.

And in the morning, when it was time for him to leave, Tirgee only shook his hand warmly, without an embrace. "I will call you from the place of creation," she said, "and you must promise to visit us every-time you're here."

"I do so promise, my lady," he said jauntily, and grandly kissed her hand.

Yesugen and Kabul smiled and took him to the door. Niki had said his goodbye the night before and had left the residence before dawn. Tirgee remained where she was, but gave him a little wave goodbye.

At the door, he shook their hands and said, "I've been negligent in not seeing you more often. One day the children were babies, and now they're grown. You must be proud. Niki will be a fine emperor someday, and Tirgee will move our ships. You have a fine looking son and a lovely daughter. Very soon there will be suitors banging on this door."

Kabul chuckled, but Yesugen smiled faintly and said, "For Niki, this will likely be true. But for Tirgee, there are only three men in her life, and I think this will be true in the future.

"There is her father, and her brother — and you, Mengjai. Hurry back."

Mengjai blushed.

And what Yesugen had said was still gnawing deeply at him when he reached the spaceport.

Nine

Frustration and Disappointment

Mengjai's strong rebuke hurt deeply, but in her heart she knew he was right. Nokai seemed devastated by it, for he'd been accused of a lack of faith and thus found wanting in the eyes of First Mother. For an empath priest of Lan-Sui, this was a serious matter.

They vowed together to accept their daughters the way they were, to put away any ambitions for the girls as future members of the Chuang-shi and to simply love and nurture them as people. Yesui ceased talking in front of the children about the work she did with Tirgee, because it only made them feel badly. It was easy to do, because she could discuss such things privately with Nokai.

Mother was a more difficult problem. Mengjai had not been diplomatic with her, and made her angry. He then left Yesui with his mess. Mother refused to admit she'd hurt the girls in any way and insisted they were Chuang-shi, that it was only a matter of time before their powers would be revealed. In preparation for that moment she had provided the finest Moshuguang tutors for her grand-daughters' education. Science and mathematics came first, followed by history and political science. The girls dutifully studied their lessons and did well enough, but neither showed real interest in the subject matter. The passion they shared was for art in any form. It consumed every waking moment for them. And where there is overwhelming desire to do a thing, there is also a talent for it.

Yesui wondered when the hurt had begun. It had started subtly, perhaps, when the girls were quite young. Even then, expectations had not been so great. Her own powers as Mei-lai-gong had been revealed before her birth, but that seemed exceptional. She'd been conceived during a great war, when her mother was most active in moving the terrible light from the gong-shi-jie to kill and destroy. Even Mother used that to rationalize Yesui's precocious abilities, for she herself had had no inkling of her Moshuguang powers until she'd reached the age of four.

So for the first few years there had been no immediate expectations for Shaan and Bao. The problem had begun after that.

One scene came back to haunt her. The girls were six, and full of energy. Tanchun had taken them out into the hallway to play hoops and hopefully exhaust them before it was time for their afternoon nap. Yesui lay down on her bed to do the Mei-lai-gong's work; her memory was vague, but Mengjai had been involved, so it must have been something to do with a space-time jump. Whatever it was, she did it and came back to herself with the usual lazy awakening.

She was not alone on the bed. Tiny hands held hers at her sides, and she heard a gasp.

"Ma?"

She opened her eyes.

Bao and Shaan were pressed against her sides, like reflections in a mirror. The deep, deep blue of their eyes was already wondrous.

"Were you dreaming, Ma?" asked Shaan-diann. "We listened to your heart, but it was beating so slow."

"Yes, I was dreaming," she said, and yawned. Drowsy, she then said a stupid thing. "I dreamed of the gong-shi-jie, a place where there are beautiful swirling clouds of light in all colors. I dream about it often."

"Is it a real place?" asked Shaan, eyes wide.

"When I dream it, it's real to me."

"Can we go there with you?" asked Bao-shi. "Shaan and I can share dreams sometimes."

The imagination of children, but they *were* twins, so perhaps it was true. But Yesui wasn't thinking about that; she wasn't thinking right at all. At that moment it was ambition and expectation that had overcome her. She'd seen that moment as an opportunity to test her children, as one might test the intelligence of a trained pet.

"Do you want to try and share my dream with me?" she asked.

"Oh, yes!" the girls said together.

I didn't realize what I was doing, thought Yesui. She'd instructed the girls to relax, close their eyes, and allow themselves to drift towards sleep. They did it well, since it was near their nap time.

Can you hear me, dears?

Yes. Two voices, as if one.

Then come with Mother, and tell me what you see. Her excitement had been so real, so joyful at that moment.

The matrix of purple stars was instantly there, a sight that had thrilled Nokai the first time he'd seen it. She paused, moved closer, waiting again for a reaction. Moved closer still, feeling leaving her hands as the mists of purple, blue and violet appeared in her view. There was no presence, nobody there — except herself. She withdrew instantly to the matrix of stars, and feeling returned. Her right hand was being squeezed very hard.

Do you see it?

No, Ma! We're trying! Again, one voice.

Her heart sank. You don't have to try. Just relax and see what's here.

Nothing happened. She waited an eternity, and nothing happened. Well, maybe we can try at another time, she said, and opened her eyes. The girls still lay there with their eyes tightly closed.

"All I see is darkness," said Shaan.

Bao was gripping her mother's hand hard. "If I squeeze my eyes tight shut, I can see little flashes of light," she said excitedly.

"That's not it, dears. We'll try again, maybe at night when you're very sleepy," said Yesui.

The girls opened their eyes and sat up. Shaan-diann scowled, and said, "Oh, it was just a silly game." Bao-shi said nothing, but the look on her face registered a terrible disappointment. Something had been there to be seen, and she hadn't seen it. She had not been able to do what Mother expected of her.

Yesui felt the sting of tears when she thought about that day and others like it when the girls had tried to see her world of creative light. They'd given up on it quickly, and perhaps it was even then that their distancing had begun. Over those few years since, with Yesui's increasing talk about her work with Tirgee in the *real* place called the gong-shi-jie, the girls had gone into themselves, always together, spending more and more time isolated in their room.

Exactly when they'd discovered art, she didn't know, but one thing was certain. Art was no longer solace for her daughters, but life to them.

Yesui was helpless to repair the past, but could nurture the present. She talked it over with Nokai and they hired a young artist to tutor the girls in their passion. His name was Jie-huang. He was Moshuguang and had received his general education within the brotherhood. His grasp of science was average, of pure mathematics less than that, his knowledge of history and politics only superficial. Gong-gong had recommended him because of his skills in computer imaging, and also because he was highly regarded for his potential with inks and brush by the contemporary artists who frequented Stork Tower.

Jie-huang was only eighteen, but his work had already appeared in three one-artist shows in Wanchou galleries. He was quiet, respectful, and patient as a teacher. He began meeting with the girls two days a week. The lessons were split; one day inside on the computer, the other outside with inks and brushes. He took them to the hanging gardens, the summit of the mountain overlooking Wanchou, the *Tysk* forests beyond the valley, and they visited with other artists over tea at Stork Tower.

The girls worked relentlessly, without pause. They barely made time for eating. Most of all they seemed happy and fulfilled. Yesui saw this and felt satisfied she had done well for her children. There was nothing more she could do for them unless First Mother saw fit to give them powers requiring training in the gong-shi-jie.

Yesui left her girls in the care of Jie-huang, and returned to her own work.

It was not the gong-shi-jie that occupied much of her time these days. There was the routine task of space-time jumps for the ships, but these occured at intervals of weeks and each only took a few minutes of real time. She worked with Tirgee once every month as she had for several years, and left the girl to practice on her own. Her progress had been slow, and Yesui was not a patient teacher.

Tirgee's sensory abilities had been acute from the beginning, but it seemed she could do little else without coaxing. *I call the light, and it comes to me — so,* thought Yesui. Not so for Tirgee. When Yesui moved light energy it was by instinct. She thought it, and it was so. There was no conscious thought of the mechanism involved, and had to do with the wiring in her special brain. So how do you teach the transfer of light energy to someone who doesn't have the mental wiring for it? Yesui had wrestled with the problem for a year before coming to a conclusion.

The wiring must come first.

Yesui's Moshuguang mind had provided the solution. In dance, music or sport, a complex series of movements can be hard-wired into the brain by visioning, but the vision must first be there. Tirgee lacked the vision, but Yesui did not. In the gong-shi-jie, presence was of the mind, and Yesui could enter it. Tirgee was quite receptive to this, once she heard what Yesui was trying to accomplish.

Yesui worked from within the girl's mind to transfer violet light from the gong-shi-jie to the interface. For that brief instant they were as one, with Tirgee an equal participant. Yesui expected the process to be slow, and it was. Working once a month it was over a year before Tirgee began showing the first signs of being able to move the energies of the gong-shi-jie on her own. But once she'd reached that point she could visualize the process herself and enhance the new neural network now growing in her brain.

Yesugen was never told about her daughter's difficulties. Tirgee was most appreciative of that, but there was a deadline of sorts. Yesui had told Yesugen that Tirgee would be ready to move ships by age fifteen, and that time was rapidly approaching.

In some ways, it was as if she had a third daughter. Yesui had never seen the girl face-to-face, and Mengjai had never thought to bring pictures back from Meng-shi-jie. She had felt, rather than watched, the girl's growth. Tirgee was intelligent and disciplined, becoming more like Yesugen each month, and yet there was a gentle, even spiritual quality about her that probably came from her father. Her emotions had erupted at puberty, and on several occasions she'd fled shrieking to the vortex of herself, frustrated when the light wouldn't move for her.

But now, Tirgee moved light in the gong-shi-jie.

Yesui kept her focused. The single task was to create a space-time wave. Once Tirgee was regularly moving violet light in and out of the interface she wanted to do other things: creating mass in real space, and transfering light there.

Entirely different processes, and we have no time for it now. You must first learn to do this one thing.

They began to squabble regularly over this, but Yesugen's expectations rather than Yesui's stalling tactics always prevailed in their arguments.

And squabbling over that particular issue ceased on the day Tirgee created her first space-time wave.

It was a tiny thing, damping out to nothing in less than a light week, but it was there and Tirgee was thrilled. Yesui knew that progress would now be rapid, for now the vision was there, and the wiring behind it.

Yesui made her announcement of the event to a proud Yesugen when Tirgee was barely fourteen years old.

I must tell Mengjai, said Tirgee, still excited.

Good luck, He's holed up in his mountain on Shanji.

Tirgee darted away towards the vortex of Tengri-Khan, but Yesui followed her easily.

Mengjai!

Tirgee! Hello again. What is it, sweet?

Straight out of the gong-shi-jie, and at full speed. Yesui was astonished at Tirgee's quickness in reaching him. How regularly did they do this?

I made a space-time wave, Mengjai! It was a little one, but I can do it now!

I told you it was only a matter of time, but congratulations! Does your mother know yet?

She's pleased, Mengjai, but the wave only went a light-week or so. We still have months of work to do, said Yesui.

Ah, well, teacher is never satisfied. But I'm proud for you, Tirgee. Hear from you soon?

Oh, yes, said Tirgee.

Bye, bye, then, and he was gone.

Yesui was stunned and shocked by the wave of silent affection that had just passed between her brother and Tirgee. No longer was it affection shared by adult and a little child, but something between a man and a woman.

You like him, she said.

Yes.

No, you like him a LOT, and he's twenty years older than you.

Age has nothing to do with it, said Tirgee, and it's no concern of yours.

Tirgee's great green fan of manifestation actually flickered with her annoyment.

Very well, I won't mention it again, but there are some things you need to know about my brother.

I already know everything I need to know, said Tirgee. Now, let's get back to work!

If a manifestation can be said to turn in a huff, it did so and moved quickly away. And that was the end of that conversation.

In other ways life passed slowly for Yesui in that first decade of marriage. Even her work in the gong-shi-jie became a repetitive, though infrequent routine, and she yearned for something new.

That something seemed illusive and by the end of the decade Yesui began to feel a certain forboding about her future in the place of creation. The forboding was brought to a terrible climax when 'Mind' came to her only weeks after the girls had begun their tutoring by Jie-huang, and Mengjai had again left for Meng-shi-jie.

'Mind' had called her only three times during the decade, each time taking her to the great mass lurking at the core of Abagai's galaxy. They went to the interface and closed in on the sharp singularity there, the point of its cusp fuzzy, then flickering, a chaos in space-time. But it was never more than that to Yesui, though 'Mind' took her in quite close. As usual, 'Mind' never told her exactly what she was supposed to be seeing, but Yesui knew something was there, something beneath the chaos, another structure, a higher dimensionality, perhaps.

The third time she tried it, Yesui felt her first pangs of failure. I'm sorry, she said. All I see is the chaos of space-time very close to that mass, but no other signature of the mass itself. I'm just not seeing it.

'Mind' was kind, but truthful with her. We could try looking at a much larger mass, but I think the results will be the same. There is something else there, Yesui, at the point of the cusp, a tiny region where only space exists, a space of ten dimensions. Do you see any distortion at the point of the cusp, anything new to you at all?

Yesui tried again, and saw nothing new. It's the same, she said, and her heart sank. I'm afraid we've found the limit of my abilities, 'Mind'. You are seeing what I cannot see.

There is no shame in that, Yesui. You are only second generation of a Chuang-shi line, and still an organic being. Your powers are truly extraordinary, and that's why First Mother sent me to work with you.

But my limits have been reached, Yesui said glumly.

It seems so, said 'Mind', but your talent is close to fourth level. That makes you unique in this universe, Yesui. Try to think of it that way, and remember that your line continues.

My children show no powers at all. They are as normal as can be.

You're impatient, Yesui, and we are not. It could be generations before higher talent surfaces in your line, or it could be here right now. We simply don't know yet, but we're watching.

My children?

Yes. And their children after them.

There was somehow a feeling of finality, of closure, in what 'Mind' was saying. Yesui had reached her limit, and there would be no new wonders for her to explore in the future. At that moment, the talents she possessed seemed unimportant, at least to the Chuang-shi. They had expected greater things for her and she had failed them. But *how* had she failed? What was it they'd wanted from her that she could not *do*?

'Mind' sensed all of this, and quickly responded.

Oh Yesui, dear Yesui, listen to me carefully. You are the mother of a Chuang-shi line, whatever happens in this generation. You move light and mass at will, you've given life to a cold dying planet and enabled instantaneous travel between two stars. Ask yourself what more you can do with the abilities you're blessed with? There are no limits, Yesui, except within your own imagination. Put your ego aside and think about the possibilities! You're not so limited as you think you are.

But you expected more of me, and I've failed to do it!

Ah, expectations, said 'Mind'. These are dangerous, Yesui, as you're learning in your organic life. No, we only think of the possibilities, and test for them. You have not 'failed' us in any way.

But there WAS a new possibility for me, and now it's gone, said Yesui.

Yes, there was , but to exercise it you would have had to leave your husband, your children, your very existence in this universe — forever. In a way, I'm relieved. You have a wonderful life and deserve to live it fully before transfiguration. It is best that way.

What WAS it? Please, 'Mind', I have to know. I have to know what might have been for me.

And will be, but after your transfiguration, said 'Mind'. Very well, I'll tell you. It is a fate that awaits me, and will happen soon. I will go to a place much like I showed you, but with a much larger mass. I will bring mass to it through the violet light as you did with Lan-Sui, but on a much larger scale and in a galaxy far, far from here. And when I'm satisfied with the mass obtained, I will enter that place you could not see, and manipulate a force you can not sense. And a new universe will be born, Yesui, a new universe created from this one. My existence here will cease, for I will be First Mother to a new universe.

Yesui was stunned into silence and thought for a long moment, trying to even imagine such an event.

Could you have left your loved ones to do this? asked 'Mind' ever so softly.

Gone forever from the world she knew, alone in a new universe, waiting for stars, planets, galaxies to form, then somewhere, life. And after that? The seeds of the Chuang-shi are in each universe, 'Mind' had told her. How long before they would appear? A billion years? Ten billion? Alone, a solitary traveler in the gong-shi-jie, searching for that first cry of an entity who sensed she was there, an entity who could connect with her and share a life.

No, said Yesui. *I — I could not have done it.*

And so it will be, said 'Mind'.

It seemed there was nothing more to be said, and Yesui was feeling a great sadness.

Will I ever hear from you again? she asked.

Oh, yes, but our work together is finished. I will call you again, but it will be a while. I have my own work to finish, but we'll come together at least once before I'm gone.

You've been my best friend here, 'Mind'. I'll miss you.

Save your goodbyes for later, Yesui. We are always together, you and I. We are one with the Chuang-shi.

We are never alone, thought Yesui, and 'Mind' was suddenly gone.

Lin-po had managed the Tranquilities shop for seven years, and enjoyed a reasonable success. His wife Mei-ling had helped with the decorations and waited on customers as much as he; they lived in two rooms above the shop, connected to it by a short flight of stairs. In recent weeks the stairs had been increasingly difficult for Mei-ling, for she was eight months pregnant with their first child.

For seven years their lives had been devoted to the business, the entire time of their married life together. They'd met, and fallen in love, while working as clerks in a similar shop in Wanchou. The pay there had been quite low, but they'd lived with their families and other families, six people to a room, and the small incomes of many had been sufficient for the whole.

Lin-po was diligent in his work and had a wonderful way with customers, for he truly liked people and wished to satisfy their needs. His effectiveness was noted, and his promotion to assistant manager had only been in force for three months when the invitation from Jensi City came. For Lin-po, it was a blessing from First Mother, received at the very time he and Mei-ling had decided to marry.

They were married in a civil ceremony, and moved to Jensi City with all their belongings contained in two suitcases, their transportation expenses paid by whatever noble family had hired Lin-po. Their identity was never revealed to him. The new store was an empty shell when they arrived, but their two room apartment was furnished and they had never known such a wealth of space.

The first two years they worked day and night, seven days a week. The line of credit at a local bank seemed unlimited, the business under his complete control. He placed the orders and they were received. Mei-ling supervised the placement of plants around the shop, then the tranquility areas, benches beneath overhangs of trellised flowering vines with self-circulating waterfalls of stone and ceramic in their centers. The shop filled with urns, amulets, small altars for use in the home, and bells of all sizes and tones. The air soon smelled of incense and sweetgrass, and there was tranquil sweet music of stringed instruments to please the ear and soothe the soul.

It was the scientists who first discovered their shop, people who appreciated a place of peace and tranquility. They bought a few little things, then spent some time in the tranquil zones reading, or just listening to music, tinkling bells, the whisper of falling water. They returned with their families. Altars began selling, then more expensive items such as the self-contained waterfalls.

Other shops opened in the little mall containing Tranquility Corner, but all sold clothing and were quite expensive. An elegant restaurent moved in to occupy the mall's center, trellised with flowing vines, and menus from which a single selection cost more than Lin-po and his wife spent on food for an entire week.

Their clientele changed, though the scientists continued to come in. Now their customers were dressed in richly tailored suits of black and white, their ladies elegantly coiffed and wearing embroidered robes. Their tastes matched their appearances, and nothing in the shop was too expensive for their consideration. The men returned often, without their extravagant wives, to enjoy a few moments in a tranquil zone and escape the stresses of their days.

Over the years, business grew steadily. There was a bonus for Lin-po from the appreciative owners. His apartment was now rent free, and for every Yuan that Lin-po invested in the shop, out of his modest salary, the owners would invest two in his name.

By the end of their seventh year, Lin-po and Mei-ling had five percent ownership in the shop they had built, and business still flourished. They had a modest savings account, and their first child would arrive in only two months. For this they gave thanks to First Mother, for they both had devoted their lives to Her service.

So it was that they were horrified to learn one terrible day that the shop was to be closed, and they would lose their apartment.

A man entered the shop in mid-afternoon when there was a lull in business. He was dressed in a tailored black suit and did not identify himself, only handed a notice to Lin-po that said the first three floors of the building, including all businesses and apartments, had been sold and would be taken possession of by their new owner within two months.

"I don't understand," said Lin-po. "I'm part owner of this business and nobody has asked me about selling it."

"I'm just a messenger," said the man, and left the store.

Mei-ling was already in tears when Lin-po called the bank and discovered his business account had been frozen; he was unable to make new purchases of stock. "Five percent of that money is mine!" he shouted. "Where has it gone to?"

"All funds have been transfered to Fangzi-yin. They are the new owners," came the reply.

He was familiar with the name, a new company that had erected its own twenty-storied building in less than one year.

Lin-po was given a number and called it, transfered several times before reaching a knowledgable person who handled commercial transactions. There was the constant background clacking of a computer keyboard as they talked.

"It's not just your business, but all the others as well. The first three floors of the building will be converted into a nightclub and casino, with several resturents on each floor. It will be a showpiece for the city, sir. This is the way of progress."

"But I don't want to *sell!*" screamed Lin-po.

"Our representatives will be there in the morning," said the man. "I'm sure you'll feel differently after you've talked to them."

And in the morning, two men *did* come to see him, two men in tailored black and carrying briefcases. They were polite and smiled and presented him with a most generous offer for his portion of the business. No names were offered, and he asked for none. He was furious, and Mei-ling was near hysteria.

"It's not just the business, but a dwelling we're losing, and under the law we'll have to leave Jensi City, don't you see?"

"You can go to Wanchou and live well there, start a new business with what we're offering you. What's the problem?" said one man. He patted his briefcase. "The money is right here, in cash. All you need to do is sign for it, and you can be on your way."

Lin-po bit his tongue to contain his fury. "The business was illegally sold without my consultation or approval. I will *not* sell my portion of it in such a way." He stamped a foot to emphasize his words.

Both men looked at him sadly. "We have no time for argument, sir. You have until this evening to reconsider your decision and see its foolishness. Perhaps you'll be less emotional when we return."

"I don't want to see you in this shop again. Please leave," said Lin-po.

And they did.

They did not return that night, either, but others did, when the mall outside was empty, and Lin-po was preparing to close the shop.

Mei-ling was just beginning her labored climb up the stairs when three men entered the shop. One was a sharp-faced man in a business suit, carrying a briefcase. The other two looked like thugs from a holovision action film, as broad as they were tall.

"We're closing," said Lin-po.

What happened next was brief, and would forever remain a nightmare for Lin-po and his wife.

"Yes, you are," said the well-dressed man. "Have you reconsidered your earlier decision about selling this business?"

"I have not. It remains the same."

The man nodded to one of his companions, who took an expensive vase from a shelf and threw it to the floor, pieces scattering in all directions.

Mei-ling screamed and came down the stairs shouting curses Lin-po never dreamed she knew.

"The money is here, in this briefcase. Just sign the paper, and its yours."

"Get OUT!" screamed Lin-po.

The man nodded again, and his thugs began breaking everything, sweeping entire shelves clean with thick arms. Mei-ling shrieked like a *Shizi* and charged one of them, her hands clawing at his face. He picked her up as if she were a stuffed toy, and held her high over his head, as if preparing to slam her to the floor.

The tailored man took a thick wad of Yuan notes from his pocket and lay some on a counter, then pointed at Lin-po's struggling wife.

"This will compensate you for what we've broken so far. Now, how much must we pay to break *that* piece?"

Lin-po's voice failed him, then, "Don't —", he croaked.

The man put the briefcase on the counter, opened it to show the neat packets of notes inside, then presented a small piece of paper to him.

"Sign it," he said, and motioned for Mei-ling to be put down gently.

Lin-po signed.

"Good," said the man, then put the rest of his wad of Yuan notes on the counter. "There is your bonus, a travel allowance to wherever you wish to go. But you'll be gone from here by the day after tomorrow, and if you talk to anyone about this we'll know it. The dead can not begin again anywhere, sir. Remember that for both of you, and, oh yes, my congratulations on the coming birth of your child."

He pocketed the signed note, smiled, and the three men left the store like customers, closing the door gently behind them as Mei-ling threw herself sobbing into Lin-po's arms.

They touched nothing in the shop, and left the door unlocked without care. That night they packed the few new possessions they'd accumulated over the years, and in the morning closed their savings account, adding a cashier's check to the contents of a black briefcase that never left Lin-po's hand.

By evening they were on the maglev to Wanchou, and Lin-po was thinking about who he could confide in about what had happened to them.

He decided that nobody could be trusted on a planet ruled by money.

Perhaps he could begin again, and be a part of that rule.

Ten

The Twins

Yesui was depressed for several days after that last meeting with 'Mind' in the gong-shi-jie. The people in her life, however, would not allow her to remain that way. The first night, she cried in Nokai's arms, and he was the first to comfort her.

"You've lost none of the powers First Mother has blessed you with," he said. "You've discovered your limits, Yesui. We all have them. Build on what you have. The gong-shi-jie has never been your entire life, or your only destiny. Like it or not you will be Empress someday. Maybe this is a sign from First Mother that you should pay more attention to that."

This didn't help much, and she cried again when she went to see Mother, repeating what 'Mind' and then Nokai had said. By the end of it she was nearly hysterical and Mother called Gong-Gong to join them in her suite. They were on the bed, Yesui's head in Mother's lap when he arrived.

Gong-Gong held her tightly. "Shhh, Yesui, shhh," he said, rocking her like a little child. "Think how lucky you've been to do so much in such a short time and still have a long life ahead of you. For your Gong-Gong, there is Kati, you and Mengjai, and now the twins. You are my legacy, the only important things I leave behind when I'm put into the ground. Everything else I've done is not important, even though I wanted it to be."

Mother stroked her hair as Gong-Gong held her. "All of our lives change, dear, and not always to our liking. Disappointments are a part of it. I don't know how much First Mother directs our lives, but I do think She's involved with us if we are truly Chuang-shi."

Mother seemed suddenly wistful. "My active life in the gong-shi-jie ended when I became Empress, but you were there to do what I could not have done. I like to think that what I have done as Empress is good in the sight of Our Mother. Perhaps another change has come, or is about to come.

"My days as Empress are numbered, Yesui, and there is only you to replace me. You have a loving husband and two daughters to nurture, and your work in the place of creation can go on with little loss of real time. Your future is full of possibilities, dear, don't you see?"

Yesui sniffled. "You think Nokai is right, that I should prepare to be Empress?"

She could see Mother hesitate, for they'd argued for years about this very thing.

"It is a definite possibility," said Gong-Gong. "Yes, indeed, and not just because your mother wishes it. I wish it too. The rule of Shanji must continue with the powers of the Chuang-shi on the throne! This, I believe, was meant to be, the day your mother was born."

"Even so, Father, the choice is still Yesui's," said Mother softly.

Yesui sat up rigidly and wiped her eyes with a hand. "Being Empress is certainly not my first choice, but now things have changed for me. I — I need to think awhile," she said.

She *did* think, for most of a day, but then she was lying on her bed in the middle of the afternoon and she started to cry again.

The twins heard her and came into the room. When she saw them, Yesui held out her arms to them because they looked so concerned. They snuggled up against her on the bed. "What's wrong, Ma?" asked Shaan-diann.

Yesui told them everything, including how she'd failed in the gong-shi-jie. She even tried to explain the singularity to them, the little blur of space that seemed to come and go. "I've never failed at anything before," she said, "and I'm sad about it. It will pass. I have many other things in my life, including you two."

Yesui hugged them tightly. "I love both of you so much, just the way you are. If I've made you feel otherwise, I'm sorry. A mother can say and do foolish things, sometimes."

Two pairs of deep, deep blue eyes looked at her closely. "It's all right, Ma, we love you, too," said Bao-shi.

In her uncertainty, Yesui tried to scan their minds, but nothing was there. No sign of masking — just nothing.

"That's very important to me," she said. "Well, I've had my time of tears. Now I will move ahead. Are your lessons with Jie-huang going well?"

"Oh, yes. He's wonderful," said Bao.

"We're practicing with fractals, now," said Shaan. "Would you like to see it?"

"Yes, in a few minutes, but first I have something to say to your grandmother."

The girls left excitedly, for it was the first time their mother would actually come just to see their work. Yesui went to the royal suite, was admitted by Tanchun and walked into the bedroom where her mother sat working at her desk.

"Yesui," said Mother. "What is it, dear?"

"I've made my decision, Mother."

"And?"

"If I'm to be Empress, I have much to learn. Just show me where and how to begin."

Mother sighed, and smiled. "I'm so happy, dear. This is a great weight taken off my shoulders."

Yesui only nodded, turned, and walked out of the room.

Listen to your heart, Nokai had told her. Well, she'd listened, but her heart was hurting too much to say anything, so for once she'd listened to her head, instead.

A pattern was developing, a great whorl spreading out from a black singularity as if it had a mind of its own. Shaan pecked furiously at the keyboard, Bao resting a chin on her shoulder to watch the screen.

"It could be a fern, or an abstract tree," said Bao.

"Too artificial. You can still see individual fractals. We have to make it larger. Here, I'll make another one, close to the first."

Another singularity appeared on the screen as a black spot, and a new pattern began to grow. "Let me try it," said Bao.

"All right. My fingers are tired, anyway."

They exchanged places, Shaan's chin now on Bao's shoulder. The pattern grew rapidly, similar to the first, but different, all of it a combination of randomly generated clusters of pixels in both size and shape.

"Still looks artificial, and there's no symmetry, no geometry to it," said Shaan.

"More symmetry," mumbled Bao. "I'll make it an initial condition, with the placement of the singularity. Let's use four of them, on the corners of a little square."

They'd barely begun the third pattern when Mother called them for supper. They were back in minutes after gobbling their food, but their parents didn't seem to mind. Both were having their own deep discussion of the banking economy at table.

"Looking better," said Shaan, after they'd worked for another hour. "Not bad, in fact, if you realize the pattern is built from random bits of space."

"But I can still *see* those random bits," said Bao. "All I have to do is look long enough. What if we switch from one pattern to another at a high enough speed the eye can't follow? The detail will be gone, but the pattern should still be there."

Another hour was spent programming in several switching sequences between the four files composing the pattern, and a recycling of the sequence every second or so. Their initial test used all four files.

"Ready?" asked Bao, her finger poised above a key.

Shaan grasped her shoulder. "Go," she said, and Bao hit the key.

"Ooooo," they said together, as a beautiful, pulsating pattern appeared on the screen.

They laughed. They hugged each other and rushed from the room to get their parents. "Come see!" they shouted. "Come see what we've done!"

Their parents watched from the doorway. "It's beautiful," said Father, "like a flower opening up over and over again."

"It's all just random bits of space," explained Shaan, then, "we can make anything this way."

"If it pulsed more slowly it could be hypnotic," said Mother. "Can you change the speed?"

"Oh, yes," said Bao, but she hit a wrong key and the pattern pulsed much faster for just a second before she found the right one.

"Ah, that's restful," said Father. "I could go to sleep watching that."

Mother frowned. "Could you speed it up again where you had it for a second?"

Bao did it.

"Not so good," said Father. "That fast flickering would keep me wide awake. It's even disturbing."

Bao went back to slow pulse, but Mother continued to frown.

"What is it, Ma?" asked Shaan.

The question seemed to break Mother's reverie, and she flinched. "Oh — nothing. For a time there it reminded me of something I've seen before. This is beautiful work, both of you. Jie-huang has taught you a lot in a short time, and I'm pleased. Be sure to show us more of this when you have it. We want to keep up with your progress. But don't stay up all night with this. It's past time for sleep right now."

"Yes, Mother," said Bao. "We'll continue tomorrow, *after* our other lessons."

Mother kissed their cheeks. "You've read my mind, dears," she said, then bid them goodnight.

The door closed. The twins looked at each other, and giggled.

"Does she know?" asked Bao.

"Of course not. After ten years, she has ceased to even imagine it," said Shaan. "Let's go to bed right now, while all of this is fresh in our heads, and we'll continue it in our dreams."

Their beds were covered with clothing and printout, and they shoveled everything onto the floor with their hands, then pulled one coverlet up tight. When they dreamed together they slept in one bed, bodies touching. They pulled off their robes over their heads and threw them carelessly on the floor. Bao turned off the lights and they climbed into bed in their underclothes. They snuggled together with the coverlet thrown back.

"The same pattern?" asked Bao.

"It would be easiest. Why don't we try it in three dimensions? We can make a cube, with singularities at each corner, then put in the patterns and see what we get," said Shaan.

"Okay, here we go. Goodnight, sister," said Bao.

They rolled over and lay pressed together, back to back. Sighed together and drifted off, the momentary feeling of falling coming, then going.

Darkness, and absence of being, of time. In sleep, Bao was suddenly aware of something dimly lit within the darkness. It grew brighter, a pattern of eight glowing balls, as if placed on the corners of a cube. Four of them flickered at her, Shaan's signal to begin.

They spoke little to each other in their dreaming, but used pictures for communication. Words involved a different part of the brain, and were usually distracting. The four flickering balls were Bao's to work with and she began quickly, the fractal pattern growing from fresh memory of what they'd done on the machine. Converting to a three dimensional image with such high symmetry required only a ninety degree rotation. She tried it, felt a mental tug. Shaan was not ready, had started behind her. Bao kept a light pressure on the image, ready to turn it, and suddenly it did.

The image was lovely, great plumes of color roiling in all directions. It immediately reminded Bao of a picture she'd seen of a distant massive star near the end of its life. The star was blowing off its outer atmosphere in great billowing jets with a cylindrical symmetry. What she and Shaan had made looked like three such pictures put together with a ninety degree rotation between each.

The pattern rotated ever so slowly, and individual fractals could be seen, somehow mottling the beauty of the effect. *Faster*, she thought, and the rotation speeded up.

More, thought the part of her that was Shaan-diann, and the pattern was spinning rapidly, a pulsating blur of color that seemed alive. So beautiful. She wanted to watch it forever.

It did not last long.

Without warning, the pattern began to dissolve while it was still spinning. Dark voids appeared within it, and individual fractals were suddenly flying away from its boundaries.

What's wrong? asked Shaan. Are you waking up?

No. I'm not doing anything but watching.

The pattern fell apart, crumbling as if smashed by a heavy blow, and the pieces flew away in a blink, leaving only darkness and a single spot of strobing golden light where the pattern had been.

So what's that? said Shaan.

I don't know. Bao was suddenly afraid. She'd not consciously wished the pattern to be erased, yet it was gone, and now there was this strobing light in its place. *You're scaring me, Shaan,* she said. *Stop it!*

I'm not doing anything! said Shaan.

The strobing light brightened and began to grow. It was not one light, but many. It seemed as if it was not truly growing, but that they were getting closer to it. There was indeed a sense of motion, of falling, and what had been one light was now thousands, filling her view. *Shaan!* she cried.

Bao! I'm here! What's happening to us?

The huge cluster sucked them into it, smears of color whipping past, and they were falling, falling, falling ...

MA!, they cried out together, in terror.

No answer, only a dream become nightmare, and they were helpless in leaving it, yet Bao knew she was not far from consciousness. She was dimly aware of Shaan's warm back pressed against hers. Yet she was falling, golden lights rushing past, penetrating an endless cluster of the things, a core ahead still solid in appearance.

Then not so solid, a scattering of golden points, then darkness, and something quite dim, straight ahead of them.

Oh, Shaan, I'm so scared! she said.

So am I, but it's just a dream, Bao. I can feel you at my back.

But what IS this? I didn't make it up.

Neither did I. Ma! Are you there? Are you doing this?

The object ahead grew brighter, and was colored deep purple. It was shaped like a fat teardrop, with a dimple on its bottom. Something was in the teardrop, swirling like liquid as they drew closer, and closer. The dimple was much smaller, and was shaped like a bean, with little ripples running around on its surface.

Closer still, it was not liquid in the teardrop, and not swirling, the motion more random and flickering like fractals popping in and out of view. But it wasn't fractals they saw. Something simpler, like pieces of thread, moving fast but coming and going at the same time. Little purple pieces of thread. Over much of the teardrop, the threads were bent into loops, their ends vibrating so fast they were nearly a blur. Near the bottom the threads were open and seemed to be moving into the bean-shaped dimple through a tiny neck attaching it to the teardrop.

Bao was mesmerized. For a moment she forgot her fear, did not wonder how this marvel had come into her dream, for it was something she could never have imagined. Shaan was mute, but Bao felt her sharing the wonder of the dream, her fear also slipping away with the certainty that she and her sister were lying on a bed in a dark room in a real world, and what they were seeing was not real at all. It was something they'd conjured up between them without knowing how.

Whatever it was it ended quickly. Bao was trying to follow the motion of a ripple on the bean-shaped dimple when it seemed she was suddenly jerked away. The teardrop was gone in a blink and golden lights were rushing past her again at terrifying speed. *Shaan!* she called.

I think we're waking up, said Shaan calmly.

Rushing lights became a receeding cluster of golden stars, then a small orb, then a single pulsating point of light which disappeared when their pattern suddenly popped into view, rotating slowly, fully constructed as before.

Back where we started, said Shaan.

I think I'd like to wake up, now, said Bao.

Me, too.

The pattern fell apart into pieces and disappeared as if blown away by a gust of wind.

Shaan was warm at her back. They did not move. "How could we have made up such a thing?" murmured Bao.

"Bits and pieces from here and there," said Shaan. "Our minds put them together in a new way, is all."

"Those stringy things weren't fractals, Shaan. We've never seen anything like that."

"No, but they made a pattern, so they must be bits of space, just like the fractals."

"Space doesn't vibrate either, Shaan. Those little loops had ends vibrating like mad, and stuff was flowing into that little bean-shaped thing. I swear it was growing, getting bigger while we watched."

"Me, too," said Shaan, and then she suddenly sat up on the bed. "Let's draw a picture of what we saw."

Bao's feet hit the floor. "Yours, and mine. We can compare."

They got up, turned on a light at the computer console, and spent half an hour drawing with pen and ink.

The drawings were virtually identical.

"We can study these before sleep, and maybe the dream will come back," said Shaan.

Bao yawned. "Maybe, but right now I'm sleepy, and I don't want to dream anymore. Good night, sister."

They turned out the light again, and this time each went to her own bed. Bao's head was swimming when it hit the pillow. The drawing was still pictured in her mind, but she made it fuzzy by thinking random thoughts until it finally went away and she was sinking — sinking —

A bright, golden star appeared in her view, pulsed one — twice — three times.

She fell soundly asleep, and there were no more dreams that night, at least none she could remember.

But in the weeks to come, Bao-shi and Shaan-diann dreamed again and again about a dimpled teardrop filled with stringy fractals, and each time they were taken there through a magnificent cluster of golden stars.

Nokai awoke, and heard distant murmurings coming from the girls' room. Yesui was sound asleep, lying on her back, and did not stir. He was tempted to get up and order the twins to bed, but then the murmurings stopped.

He lay strangely awake and aware of every little creaking in their room as the palace contracted in the coolness of night. It was only two hours since they'd gone to bed. He rolled over onto his side to look at Yesui, his wife, his love, his Mei-lai-gong. Her lips were slightly part-ed, breathing slow, but not so slow as when she went to the gong-shi-jie. At those times it was like she was dead, but he'd learned not to be frightened by it.

It was three nights since they'd made love. He was tempted to kiss those parted lips and awaken her, but something held him back. Still, he moved closer until he could feel Yesui's warmth and smell the flowery odor of the soap she'd used that evening.

His awareness was more than scents and sound. There was a pres-ence, though he and Yesui were alone in the room, and suddenly it was stronger, a precursor familiar to him.

Nokai rolled onto his back and closed his eyes to await Her coming. *Your servant awaits you*, he thought.

The golden orb was there, then the same familiar dense cluster of stars with radiating streamers.

Nokai, She said, and he was shocked. Never before had he sensed speech coming from Her apparition.

I am here, First Mother. What is your command for me?

I do not not come to command, Nokai. Have you not yet forgiven yourself?

Yes, I've forgiven myself. I'm only a normal being, with imperfec-tions. My faith is not perfect, but my will, and Yesui's, are now in your care. Our ambitions for the children are put aside, and Yesui has resigned herself to her limitations. She now works hard in preparing to be Empress, though she has no ambition for it. And the children seem happy and fulfilled.

It is the children I've come to talk about, and both of you must hear this, She said, then called, Yesui!

Yesui stirred in sleep, and Nokai instantly felt her in his mind. Nokai? What is it?

He heard a little gasp, and knew the vision of golden stars had appeared to her.

Yesui — dear Yesui — I am First Mother, the first of the Chuang-shi, and we are become as one. Blessed is your line. I have watched over your mother, and you, and now I will watch over your offspring. All you are doing for them you must continue to do, and all else must be left to Me. Can you accept this?

I — I have committed my will to you, First Mother, but there are days I wish to take it back. Some dreams are hard to give up, said Yesui.

An honest answer, She said, but beyond their everyday lives, there's little you can do for them. They go where you do not, and see what you can't see. It is I who must test and instruct them.

Nokai's heart ached from the feelings of euphoria and hope washing over his wife. Your will is ours, First Mother, he said.

Yes, said Yesui, so excited now she was nearly awake. YES!

You are happy, now, and that is good, for I know you've been disappointed, said The First of the Chuang-shi, but you must not try to instruct them in the gong-shi-jie. It will only confuse them and slow their progress. Their vision of the place of creation is far different from yours. Do you understand?

I do. I will not interfere, First Mother. I promise.

Then it will be so. My blessings on both of you. Live your lives well, and know that I'm with you. I am most pleased, Yesui and Nokai. Most pleased.

The stars rushed away, a cluster, an orb, a point of golden light, then gone.

Yesui was wide awake. "Oh, Nokai!" she squealed, and rolled into his arms. He'd never seen her so elated. He held her tightly, kissed her forehead, her lips, and she pressed back hard. "Mmmm," she murmured, then pulled back to look at him.

"You were there before I was. She came to you first, and She's come to you before. I remember those golden stars from a dream of yours, only it wasn't a dream, was it?"

"She comes to me in my prayers, but until now it has only been a soothing presence. There were times I felt I was being told or shown something, but this time there's no doubt about it. Oh, Yesui, you're so happy, and that makes me happy, too." He kissed her softly.

"Something happened with Shaan and Bao tonight," said Yesui. "I just know it."

"I woke up a few minutes ago and heard them talking, but then it stopped," he said, and rubbed his nose along hers.

"Shouldn't we check on them?" she asked, muffled as his lips brushed hers.

"Not now. They must be asleep, and we're the ones who are wide awake." His mouth found hers again and his hand moved up beneath her sleeping robe.

"Oh," she said.

And the next half hour made them ready for sleep again.

But in the morning, before dawn, when they were up for daily exercises in the garden, they crept into the twins' room. Bao and Shaan were both on their backs, sleeping peacefully. Nothing seemed changed from the night before, except for two identical drawings in pen and ink, lying by the computer.

Yesui studied them for a long moment.

They showed something she had not seen before, or even imagined.

Eleven

Differences

Problems have a way of solving themselves, thought Kati.

Once she'd made her decision, Yesui was working hard in preparing herself for her civic responsibilities, and now there was the announcement regarding the twins. It was no surprise to Kati. Hadn't she always told Yesui it was only a matter of time before their powers would be revealed? What those powers were, of course, nobody seemed to know. There was only the assurance from First Mother that She must test and train them. They saw what Yesui did not, and yet Yesui was far beyond Kati in that regard. So what more *was* there to be seen in the gong-shi-jie?.

Whatever it was, Yesui was adamant in not interfering with First Mother's work with the twins. There was to be no talk about the gong-shi-jie in their presence and no questioning about what they were doing there. They were to be treated as perfectly normal children, when they were not. Kati went along with it only because she had a plentiful supply of things to worry about, and also because she had total faith in First Mother.

Another comfort was the presence of her husband. After decades of space travel, Huomeng had announced on his sixtieth birthday that he was retiring from it. He'd had his fill at last, and no regrets, but now he looked for new things to do.

Their days together were now regular, exercises and breakfast in the morning, supper together in the evening, then Huomeng reading in bed while Kati finished her day's work at the desk. The evenings were the most wonderful. When they exchanged ideas on the problems facing her it was the way it had been before they even realized they were falling in love, nearly forty years ago.

That love had not diminished, and although passion had cooled over the years they were both physically fit and enjoyed regular intimate moments after the lights had been turned out.

For the moment, at least, Huomeng had something to do in training young astronauts for both shuttle and freighter flights, and consulted with his son on new experiments for the space station. He and Mengjai remained close, after years of space-travel together, but Kati rarely saw her son and their last meeting regarding the twins had not been pleasant.

Kati worried a lot about Mengjai. He was becoming a loner, secluding himself in the mountain when not in flight to and from Meng-shi-jie. He'd even grown apart from his sister since her marriage to Nokai. She was aware of no friends of his outside the family, and he certainly showed no inclination towards marriage. It seemed he was becoming a hermit, going deeper and deeper into himself. So she was surprised by what Huomeng said one night when they were cuddling each other before sleep and she was thinking about her son.

"I haven't seen Mengjai in ages. Did you see him today?"

"Yes. He was reading geology in my old office over the bay," said Huomeng.

"Geology? What does that have to do with the space-station?"

"Nothing at all. Meng-shi-jie is trying to survey their aquifer system, and Mengjai is researching the problem. He's been asking for a lot of advice from other Moshuguang regarding survey techniques. I believe Yesugen asked for the information."

"Oh," said Kati. "Well, that's nice of him. He's leaving again soon for Meng-shi-jie, isn't he?"

"Three weeks."

"He's on every flight, now. Can't your young trainees handle that?"

"Some can, but I'm not flying anymore and someone has to handle in-flight training. Mengjai is best qualified for it."

"Oh," she said, and there was a long, silent moment.

Huomeng squeezed her gently, and said, "If you're wondering, I think there's another reason Mengjai goes to Meng-shi-jie so much, especially in the last two years."

Kati looked at him expectantly, and he grinned.

"Tirgee is there," he whispered, and raised an eyebrow.

She caught the meaning instantly. "Tirgee? She's a child, not much older than the twins."

"She's a beauty. You haven't seen her," said Huomeng. "She's well beyond her years in many ways."

"Still a child, dear. You're speculating."

"No, I'm not. Mengjai talks about her all the time, now, and Tirgee contacts him regularly from the gong-shi-jie. *That* has been going on for years. I think it's serious."

Kati counted in her head. "Huomeng, there is an eighteen year difference between them!"

"Seven years between you and I, even more for Yesugen and Kabul. Women who prefer older men are certainly not rare," he said, and smiled lecherously at her.

Kati patted his cheek. "Seven is not eighteen, dear."

"And we've had a wonderful life together, Kati," he said, and kissed her.

Her attention was turned to other things, but now she had a new worry about Mengjai.

Kati met with Yesui and Father at breakfast to discuss the Jensi problem. They'd begun their day with exercises, and returned to their apartments to change clothes. The table had been set on the balcony, although it was a heavily overcast day, and an earlier rain shower had sent rivulets of water down the sides of the great plas-bubble covering the city. Tanchun had put out tea and covered dishes of barley soup, hard-cooked eggs, and honeycakes for their meal.

Yesui was the first to arrive, and looked hurried. "The girls were sleeping so soundly I had to shake them awake," she said. "They will *not* go to bed on time." She sat down, poured tea for herself, and looked hungrily at the covered dishes. "Is Gong-Gong coming?"

"Soon, dear. You won't move so quickly either when you reach *his* age."

He arrived a few minutes later, and Yesui was uncovering the dishes as he shuffled out onto the balcony. "A lovely morning," he said.

"It's been raining, Gong-Gong," said Yesui, shoveling an egg onto her plate.

"Ah, but I awoke this morning, and so it is a lovely morning," he said.

Kati pulled a chair out for her father and carefully positioned it beneath him as he sat down. Yesui laddled some soup for him and poured his tea, but he refused the offer of an egg or honeycake.

128

Yesui ate hurridly and waited with impatience, drumming her fingernails on the table. "Is this about Jensi City, again?"

"I'm afraid it is," said Kati. "We have the figures on production costs, now, and they don't correlate well with investments claimed by the nobles. There's a difference of nearly half a billion Yuan."

"In favor of the nobles, of course," said Yesui.

Kati munched a honeycake. "According to tax records, yes."

"So have them audited," said Yesui dismissively.

Kati sighed, and Father looked at her darkly as he sipped his soup. "That has never been done, dear. I've had an honorable agreement with the nobles for thirty-five years, and it's backed by mutual trust. The Ministry is checking the figures again. Perhaps there's an error."

"Half a billion Yuan buys a lot of land, Mother. I assume you'll hold up the land grants until the error is found."

"That would be a bad precedent, Yesui. It's a sign of mistrust."

"Land grants *can* be revoked," added Father. "Your mother has the power to do that."

Yesui drummed her fingernails on the table again. "Mother has the power to do anything she wishes, Gong-Gong. The Ministry, the Peoples' Congress, everyone answers to her."

"I'm not a dictator, Yesui. The success of my reign has been built on mutual trust and my belief that the people must have control over their own lives."

"You didn't live under our last Emperor, Yesui," said Father. "The needs of the people were not a concern to him, and he would not permit change. Life here was not good before your mother took the throne from him."

"I've read the history," said Yesui, "and I'm not questioning motives here. You asked me to look at problems as if I were Empress, Mother, and I'm doing it. If the nobles have made an honest error, why should they mind an audit? It's not a matter of trust, but of financial accountability, especially when you're giving them land grants."

Father took a sip of tea, looked at Yesui, then Kati. "Even if the figures are found to be correct, there's no need to upset the nobles. A quiet audit can be done electronically by the Ministry. They have access to all accounts in every bank."

"Without the families knowing it? Father, I'm surprised at you!" said Kati.

"Oh, Mother," said Yesui, "this is *not* about trust. *You* are Empress, and the final authority on Shanji. You govern the planet and have veto power over any bill passed in the Peoples' Congress. Why is a little thing like an audit so disturbing to you?"

"A secret audit," said Kati. "It's like the Searchers' probing of our private thoughts under the Emperor's rule. We hated it."

"I haven't heard you use that term in a long time," said Father. "Searchers." He held the word on his tongue, as if tasting it.

"At least the Emperor knew when people were trying to fool him," said Yesui. "I think Jensi City could use a good searching, right now!"

"Yesui!" All the arguments before Yesui had agreed to prepare herself to be Empress, and all that had happened was that the arguments had changed. "You have a very poor attitude about this," said Kati.

"Impatience is more like it," said Father. "Now calm yourselves, ladies. Kati, I agree with Yesui on one thing. If the figures turn out to be correct, an audit must be made before further land grants are made. Overt, or covert, the choice is yours, but it must be done. We've never had this problem before, and it's only happening in Jensi City. I haven't forgotten what we sensed when we last visited there. Have you?"

Kati thought for two bites from a honeycake, while Yesui scowled at her. "No — I haven't. Are you certain that an electronic audit can be done with complete discretion?"

"Absolutely," said Father.

Yesui's face softened. "You don't have to do all the families, just a couple, but choose the highest investors and include every family member. Nokai tells me that on Lan-Sui people even invest in the names of their children, and have special accounts for them."

Now Father frowned. "Children pay no taxes here, Kati. The problem could be worse than we thought."

"All right. All right!" said Kati. "I'll call the Ministry and order a discrete audit, but *only* if the figures we have are proven correct."

She looked at Yesui. "Satisfied?"

Yesui nodded. "It's a start. I haven't forgotten what we felt in Jensi City either, Mother. I don't like that place, not at all. I think we should watch it closely."

"I think we can all agree on that," said Father. He pushed back his chair, and stood up slowly. "One issue at a time is enough for me, and other work awaits my attention. Kati, thank you for my breakfast.

"You ate very little of it," she said.

"It was enough." He smiled, then put his hands on the table, and leaned over to look closely at Yesui.

"Tell me, grand-daughter, if you were Empress, would you send the Moshuguang to Jensi City to search the minds of the people?"

"I would," said Yesui, without hesitation.

"I see," he said, then, "I think we need to have a private talk about what it's like for common people to have their minds invaded and paralyzed. I know it well, because I did it for years, and only to keep a man in power. If power is the motive, I will not do it again, for your mother — or for you."

He turned, shuffled to the doors, and was gone from them.

Yesui sat with her mouth hanging open, and started to get up. "What was *that* all about?" she asked.

"He'll tell you. Please sit, Yesui. There's one more thing I want to ask you about."

Yesui sat down with a sigh of resignation. *Now what?*

"It's not politics, or finance; it's about your brother," said Kati.

"Mengjai? What has he done now?"

"Nothing I'm aware of, dear, but your Father seems to think something is going on between Mengjai and Tirgee."

Yesui smiled. "Oh, *that*."

"That?"

"I meet with Tirgee regularly, Mother. I know how she feels about him. I personally think it's infatuation, but for Tirgee it's love."

"And for Mengjai?" asked Kati, pressing.

"He has affection for her. I've felt it when Tirgee talks to him from the gong-shi-jie."

"No more than that?"

"Maybe there's more. Ask Mengjai," said Yesui, then, "Has Yesugen said something?"

"No, only your Father, but he made it sound serious."

"When I asked Tirgee about it, she was defensive, and said their age difference was no matter. At the time it sounded like she could be thinking marriage. I wouldn't be surprised if Yesugen encourages her. A marriage between Mengjai and Tirgee would be a tie between two ruling families and a new mixing of Moshuguang and Chuang-shi bloods."

"I wasn't thinking about that," said Kati. "I want to know why Mengjai is so restless and spends most of his time in space to and from Meng-shi-jie."

"Well, I think about it. Mengjai could be a good political catch for Tirgee, and begin a new Chuang-shi bloodline on Meng-shi-jie. Tirgee also wants to learn the transfer of energy from the gong-shi-jie to real space, and I won't teach it to her. I know they're allies, Mother, but it would be like putting a new weapon into their hands."

Kati was disturbed by the new turn in the conversation. "You and I think differently, Yesui. I don't know why it is, but you don't seem to trust anyone. You're always looking for alterior motives and something sinister."

Yesui didn't even blink. "They exist, Mother. Sometimes I think you're too good-hearted to see them. You trust people too much."

"Perhaps I do," said Kati, "but an Empress must have trust as well as love and compassion for those she rules."

Again, not a blink. "She must also have distrust and a strong hand over those who would subvert that rule," said Yesui.

Kati sighed. "You're right. We're not alike."

Yesui smiled coyly. "Do you still want me to be Empress after you?"

"Right now, you're doing a good job of talking me out of it," said Kati. *Is that what you're up to?*

"No, it's not," said Yesui, "and I'm still learning, Mother. As for Mengjai, that's all I know, except that if he ever *does* get married I think he'll be a very good father. I've even told him that."

"That was nice of you, dear," said Kati, and stood up. "Well, then, I'll try not to worry, and let things happen as they will. Any new signs from the twins?"

Yesui walked with her arm-in-arm to the door. "No, except that they're sleeping so soundly, now, and often for short times during the day. Testing, perhaps, but I don't ask."

"If you don't mind, I'd like to see them this afternoon and look at their work."

"That's fine, Mother, but no quizzing about dreams unless they offer something."

"Agreed." Kati kissed Yesui on the forehead, and grasped her arm. "Dispite your sharp edges, I love you, dear."

Yesui smiled. "I love you, too, even when we're different."

The door closed, and Kati was alone, thinking, Yes, we're different. I'll have to somehow smooth those edges or you will be a harsh Empress. Or maybe my edges aren't sharp enough. I think you're right about one thing, though. The problem in Jensi is more serious than we see right now. There is something foul there.

Yesui busied herself with study and research during the day, going through disked bios of Ministry personnel and representatives of the Peoples' Congress. She noticed a disturbing trend of wealth among these people, but with exceptions. The Ministry was composed of nobles and Moshuguang, half and half, as it had been for centuries, and even with recent retirements. It was the Peoples' Congress that had a high proportion of wealthy individuals, and most of them were from Jensi. A broad spectrum of wealth existed for the representatives of Wanchou and the Dahe district, while those from the Tumatsin and other rural districts would be considered poor by city standards. Representation of the nobles was fixed by law at twenty percent of the vote, but over thirty-five years it was now sons or grandsons who represented them, *not* the heads of families. And it was the family heads, fathers and now grandfathers, who had originally supported the economic and social reforms on Shanji.

The twins returned from their lessons in early afternoon and talked excitedly about a fieldtrip they'd taken to study the flowers and vines in the hanging gardens below the palace. A little while later Mother arrived to admire their artwork, and left with a piece of it to display in her rooms.

Nokai came home on time and the girls repeated details of their fieldtrip for him over supper, dominating the conversation. When they went to their room to study, Yesui talked about her day, then asked Nokai if he had access to payment records for goods received on Lan-Sui.

"Of course, for both Lan-Sui and Meng-shi-jie," he said. "They are on the same system. But Yesugen must approve it and you'll have to wait months for hard copy."

"That's soon enough. I'll talk to Yesugen," said Yesui.

After supper, Nokai read while Yesui continued her scan of bios, and then it was time for bed. Nokai went straight to their room. The twins had been very quiet all evening, and so Yesui went first to check on them. She knocked softly on their door and there was no answer, so she pushed it open.

The lights were on. A beautiful flower pattern that looked three-dimensional rotated slowly on the computer screen. The room was amazingly neat: clothes hung in closets, papers and drawings in little stacks on the computer console.

The girls were stretched out on one bed, eyes closed. They lay on their backs, arms at their sides, and were holding hands. Their breathing was extremely slow.

Yesui went to the bed, and sat down slowly next to Bao. No movement, no fluttering of eyelids, the girl seemed in deep, deep sleep. Yesui watched her for a long moment, then dared to touch her on the cheek. The flesh was warm.

She ran her finger lovingly along the cheek, then flinched back in surprise.

Bao had suddenly opened her eyes, but only half-way.

The lovely deep blue, violet-flecked eyes were now as black as a starless night, and Bao slowly closed them again.

"What is it?" whispered Nokai from the doorway.

Yesui smiled. "They're gone away," she mouthed to him.

She left the lights on, left everything just as it was, and closed the door softly behind her.

Twelve

Lady of Dreams

A memorial service was conducted in the chapel of Church of The Mother the morning after Madam Shiang's ashes were interred. Only a small circle of close friends attended, all of them nobles, except for two. One of these was Quantou, a prominent businessman now favored by the polls in his bid for mayorship of Jensi City, and a strong advocate of law and order. The other was Sheng-chih, Madam Shiang's close friend, and now the executor of her estate.

The light was dim: a few candles on an altar with a bowl of smouldering sweetgrass, and tiny purple lights like stars in the domed ceiling. The priest Lao said a few words, and there was a long moment of silent prayer for the departed. People shook hands and exchanged kind words about the last member of the Shiang family once so prominent in Jensi society.

Sheng-chih and Quantou were the last to leave, and Lao met them at the exit, nodding curtly to them.

"It was a service of loving respect," said Sheng-chih, and held out a thousand Yuan note to the priest.

"You may put it in the offering box by the door," said Lao, averting eye-contact with him. "We'll use it in Our Mother's service, but it will buy you no favors, Sheng. Your prayers are worth more to Her, and to Her Church. If you pray for forgiveness, She will hear you."

"Forgiveness? For what?" asked Sheng.

"You are an arrogant man, for a priest," said Quantou.

"I'm the spiritual leader for this city, and the goings-on in your nightclub and casino are well known to me. You and your kind have created an abomination in Jensi, and it will not be tolerated."

135

"Dear Lao, I assure you nothing illegal is taking place there. What offends you so?" said Sheng.

"Pleasures of the flesh and the lure of easy money are corruptions of the spirit, and you are responsible for them. I can pray for you, but it's *you* who must repent."

Sheng-chih laughed at him. "Pray for your own soul, Lao. I'm comfortable with mine."

Lao's eyes narrowed, his voice a hiss. "We will oppose you, Sheng-chih, if you do not change your ways."

"We? This congregation? You are a single percent of the population, Lao. Many of our citizens regard this church as a momument to superstition and mythology. It is *they* who tolerate *you*, not the other way around," said Sheng.

"Tend to your flock," said Quantou, "and leave the city's business to the rest of us. It's none of your concern."

Lao nodded. "Very well. Take your money, then, and leave this church. I don't want to see you here again." He turned from them, and walked away.

Sheng-chih felt some discomfort. "I think I've just been excommunicated," he said.

"Does it matter? You were never a part of these zealots, anyway. Your friends will leave with you. Their money is better spent elsewhere," said Quantou.

"Open opposition by the church is of concern to me, friend."

"If I'm elected mayor, it will not be allowed," said Quantou. "The police force you'll fund for me will see to that."

Sheng put a hand on Quantou's shoulder, and smiled.

"Then I will put my trust in your leadership," he said.

They left the church and drove away in separate cars, Sheng in the back seat of his while a driver assigned to him from Fangzi-yin negotiated heavy traffic to the center of the city. They stopped at a building only two blocks from his office, and the car sped away at his order as he entered a rich foyer of white marble with hanging embroidered tapistries the size of rooms.

He took an elevator to the twenty-third floor and went to Madam Shiang's suite, where he was admitted by a small slender man with delicate features, and hair tied in a tail down his back. The tight silk shirt he wore gave him a feminine look.

"The inventory is complete, sir. I've been waiting," he said sweetly.

"We have laid her to rest, Tian," said Sheng-chih. "A great family line has come to an end."

"No heirs. It's a tragedy, sir."

"They wished to have children, but were unable to, at least not with each other," Sheng-chih said sadly. "Shiang liaw had quite a reputation with the ladies through his middle-age, of course, but if he fathered a child out of wedlock he did not care to acknowledge it in his Will."

Sheng ran a hand softly over the head of a ruby-eyed *Shizi* by the fireplace. "When will you auction all these lovely things, these memories of times past?"

"The sale will be in two months, sir. My estimate is two hundred thousand Yuan for everything."

"A small, but useful addition to Madam's Charitable Trust, Tian. I will make it grow. The Shiang family will forever fund the arts on Shanji, even though they're gone."

Sheng-chih fingered a photograph framed in gold that stood on the mantal of the fireplace. "Must this also be sold?"

"The frame is brass, with gold plate. A hundred Yuan, perhaps."

Sheng took a wad of notes from his pocket. "I will give you five hundred, for her Trust. This photograph will be displayed in my office, in memory of the Shiang family."

The photograph was of a formal pose, Madam Shiang and her husband in robes, shoulder to shoulder, her hand on his knee. Taken in their forties, Madam was delicately lovely, her husband sharp-featured with a mouth pressed into a thin cruel line. Sheng rubbed a thumb over the image of the man's face.

You kept us well, Father, but Mother sacrificed much of it to give me my start. I do wish you would have acknowledged your son, but I will not hold it against you. Your name will be paramount in the funding of Shanji's arts as long as I live.

For this service, of course, you will understand that I require a considerable fee.

Bao-shi and Shaan-diann dreamed of stringy bits of space.

Since that first time the dream had always begun the same way, with a terrifying fall into a cluster of golden stars. Now, in their fourth dream, it no longer frightened them, but was exciting.

137

They always prepared in the same way, by studying the drawings they'd made of the teardrop and its little bean-shaped dimple, adding additional details after each new experience.

Preparation was no guarantee the dream would return, for they did it every night before it was time for sleep and the dream had come back only three times in as many months. Once it had come in the middle of the day, when they'd become strangely sleepy and lay down together just to rest. Shiann thought it had to do with the continual processing of old data in their heads. When new details were ready to be added to an old model, the dream would occur.

There were new details to be seen this time.

Threads looped in bizarre patterns swirled as before inside the teardrop, their free ends vibrating madly, but now other threads were joining them, as if attracted to the object from outside. These were different, more open, like segments of thread twisted into helical spirals. Before the twins' dream-eyes, the helical segments came together with others of their kind, or closed loops, to form patterns even more complex. These existed a short time before cracking apart into simpler patterns. The overall effect was the creation of new closed loop patterns inside the teardrop, and it was happening very fast.

The teardrop was growing in size.

Something was happening to the bean-shaped dimple as well. *Closer*, thought Bao, and its image swelled in her view. The throat of the protuberance connecting it to the teardrop had increased in size since the last time, and patterns of looped thread were squeezing through it. As they squeezed through they were breaking up and forming helices of such a short length they were barely visible as anything but a point.

The light becomes mass, then light again as it moves from one to the other.

What? thought Bao. How do you see that, Shaan?

The light in the dimple is hot beyond imagination. That's why the little helical things are so short.

Very profound, Shaan.

I'm not saying anything, said Shaan, but I hear it, too.

Right, said Bao, growing irritated.

Little rills were racing around the surface of the dimple, looking like waves on water, with crests and troughs.

The bean is unstable, you see. When it's much larger, it will separate from the teardrop and then burst, releasing all the hot light stored within it.

I didn't think that! said Shaan.

Well neither did I! said Bao angrily.

Then listen, and learn. Listen to the lady of your dream. I am both of you, and more. We are dreaming this together. We're making pictures, together, and they're dynamic things. We make them happen in the dream.

Bao was again frightened, and she felt Shaan's fright as well. The vision began flickering, pulling away from them. She was dimly aware of physical sensation, something squeezing the fingers of her left hand hard enough to hurt her.

Stop it, now! You are linked together. It is your collective mind operating here, beyond your conscious awareness. I am that mind. I am both of you, thinking together. There's nothing to be afraid of.

We're talking to ourselves? asked Shaan.

Your collective self. Call me Lady. It will make me seem like a real person when we're here.

The vision of the dimple had steadied, and was coming closer again. Bao's fright was replaced with amusement. We're a strange pair, sister. Together, we're another person. Better not tell Mother about this, or she'll send us to hospital for observation.

Agreed, said Shaan.

That's better. Now, watch this. Talking as one again, it seemed.

I bring light to the teardrop from somewhere else — so.

A swirl of helical threads suddenly surrounded the teardrop, appearing out of nowhere, and quickly diffused inside it.

Light becomes mass, all by itself. There's nothing we need to do.

Bizarre patterns of looped threads formed, and broke into simpler things, as Bao had seen before. A gush of pattern through the throat of the protuberance, and more tiny helices had been added inside the dimple.

Mass becomes light again. Someday we'll see the force that causes this. Something more for our imagination to work on.

That, and where the light comes from in the first place, thought Bao.

The helices, said Shaan.

From somewhere else. Where's that?

We'll save that for next time, said Lady, or themselves. *Whatever*, thought Bao.

That's enough for now. Before we continue this, we need to study astronomy, especially cosmology, and see how the Moshuguang think stars and galaxies, even the whole universe is made. That's what we're doing here; we're making a picture of a new universe about to be born. We must study hard if we want the picture to grow in our next dream.

The teardrop was now becoming dim, and the first golden stars swirled around them.

Ma's old learning disks won't be enough, but the Moshuguang will find more for us, said Shaan.

Or Mengjai, said Bao, lights rushing past her, then the cluster, orb, strobing point of gold, and she was awake.

Her left hand hurt, where Shaan had nearly crushed it in her fright. She flexed her fingers. "Ouch," she said.

"Sorry," said Shaan, "but I was at least as scared as you were. Was that really us — together?"

"I don't know," said Bao, and suddenly she was thinking about things her mother had told her about the times she'd spent in the gong-shi-jie. "It seemed like another person, Shaan."

"It seemed like a dream, too, sister," said Shaan.

"I've just been thinking that."

"I know, but why? We're not like Ma, or the Moshuguang."

"We dream together," said Bao.

"Ma once told us she dreamed the gong-shi-jie, but it's real. She had a real friend there who taught her things."

"A Chuang-shi friend," said Bao, and felt Shaan's excitement building with her own.

Shaan grinned at her. "Maybe we're not so ordinary, after all."

Bao nodded rapidly in agreement.

"And maybe the Lady in our dreams will tell us about it, if we ask her," she said.

"Your suspicions have been confirmed," said Kati. "In the annals of tax collecting on Shanji, the Ministry says it has never before seen such a convoluted mess like this."

"Our noble supporters," said Yesui, looking pleased with herself. She tapped the palm of her hand with the flat of a blade she'd just used in exercises, and sat down on a bench by the garden pool, where her grandfather was changing his slippers.

"Not just the nobles," said Mengmoshu. "The real mess is in trying to trace the flow of investment money. It seems there are people in Jensi City who provide the nobles with funds for investments, for which the families receive both tax credits and land grants.

"In exchange for what?" asked Yesui.

"We don't know yet, but we're looking into it," said Kati. "Strictly speaking, nothing illegal has been found except the differences between actual costs and investments declared."

"Then the numbers were correct," said Yesui.

"Yes, and now I have seven new requests for land grants on my desk. Right now, it seems I'm too busy to get to them, but this investigation could take a long time. I can't hold the grants off forever."

"I would get to the bottom of this mess in a hurry," said Yesui.

"Is that a challenge?" asked Gong-Gong.

"It is, but only if I'm free to use my own methods. I might have to stir things up a bit, Mother, and I know how you feel about confrontation. I also know you're busy with many other things, and this Jensi matter is mostly a job for an accountant, right now. I happen to be married to a good one. Nokai can help me unravel this if I'm free to talk to people."

"With the Mind Search," said Mengmoshu, giving Yesui a scowl.

Yesui tapped her forehead with a finger. "I can get what I want without them even realizing it, Gong-Gong. You know that. And I don't have the features of a Moshuguang. In fact, most people don't even know what I *look* like, outside of the capital city. Some creative work with my clothing and hair and I'm an accountant sent by Empress Mengnu to solve a puzzle for her."

"That is absurd!" said Kati.

"Maybe not," said her father. "We've been so cloistered here. The last public photograph of Yesui was taken when the twins were born. But everything would have to be done with complete discretion, Yesui, and I'm not sure your impatience with people will allow you to do that."

"There's only one way to prove that," said Yesui, slapping her hand with her blade again.

"And it's not going to happen," said her mother.

The argument went on for another hour, but in the end they agreed on one thing.

Yesui would work with Nokai to identify the source of imbalence between reported costs and investments declared.

The idea of the Mei-lai-gong acting covertly as an accountant for the Empress was dismissed as an impossibility.

The Lady of their dreams showed them a cloud of light that seemed extended forever beyond the teardrop, only it wasn't light as they knew it in waking life, but a myriad of helical thread segments moving in random directions. Lady moved a bit of the cloud towards the teardrop in demonstration, a stream of helices from cloud into a spiral path around the tiny space where looped threads spun wildly. The spiral of helices decayed rapidly and was absorbed, as they'd seen before.

Now you do it, said Lady. Just think it, and it will be so. You can do anything in your dream.

Where should we begin? asked Shaan.

Where I did. Both of you — together.

Shann thought it, and felt Bao with her, just as they'd done when making their flower pattern of fractals. The process was not new, only the picture they were making, a spiral of helical segments around a fuzzy teardrop with a dimple.

Light moved. A spiral was formed, then gone, exactly as Lady had done.

How wonderful! First try! We're having fun in this dream, said Lady.

Only it isn't a dream, said Shaan. This is a real place, isn't it? What we're doing here is real, not imagination, like when Ma goes to the gong-shi-jie to do her work.

And you're not us, but someone else, added Bao. We're not afraid anymore. You don't have to fool us. You're like Mother's friend in the gong-shi-jie. You are a Chuang-shi.

Yes, I'm your friend, said Lady. I'm here to teach you, while I do my own work.

A Chuang-shi, insisted Bao.

Yes, I am, and so are you. A fascinating pair, the two of you. Together, you're a single being to me. Our Mother's choice of your empath father was brilliant indeed. You're totally connected in intellect and emotion.

Our Mother, not yours, said Shaan and Bao together. Neither understood what had just been said.

Of course, said Lady, then, Well, you have found me out. I hope we can be friends like the one your mother had. My work here can be lonely, and it's nice to share it with someone else. Does all this interest you?

Oh, yes! they said together.

Good. I think we're going to have a wonderful time.

But what are we doing here, besides making pictures? asked Shaan.

You must study your astronomy as I asked you to before I can give you a good answer, said Lady. We are Chuang-shi. We are creators.

And together, we're going to create something wonderfully new.

Thirteen

Rani

Rani-Tan slept soundly for over an hour on the mag-lev trip south out of Jensi City, but remained somewhat groggy when the train pulled into the terminal at Congress Center. Her legs were stiff from sleeping in a cramped position across three adjoining seats in the train, and her stomach now growled insistently from hunger.

The flight north from the sea had been bad enough; it was her first experience on a flyer and the flight had been full, sixty people crammed in shoulder to shoulder with hot sunlight beating down on them, and no food service. Babar had warned her about this so she'd eaten a full meal before liftoff, but was hungry again at touchdown in Jensi City. No problem, she thought. The mag-lev terminal was three levels directly below the flyer port and she had over two hours before the departure of her train. Plenty of time for a bowl of gruel passing for barley in this part of Shanji, and perhaps some fresh fruit. Her mouth had watered at the thought as she came out into a terminal crammed with white-suited people who stared at her tri-colored robe as if she were an alien being. Their staring was not friendly, and she thought it rude. She ignored it, and followed the signs to the baggage claim area.

Moving walkways sped her down a long corridor of white marble lit softly from ceiling panels. Three walkways ran close together in parallel, at slow, intermediate and high speeds. They ran far into the distance, so following the example of her fellow travelers she hopped from one to the other to obtain maximum speed. Not only hunger drove her; after a four hour flight, her bladder was now urging some haste in locating a restroom.

At the end of the ride someone jostled her as she attempted a hop to the slow walkway and she exited at intermediate speed, nearly falling on her face. People laughed at her as if she were a peasant from the countryside — which she was. The fact she was also a Tumatsin representative to the Peoples' Congress would likely make no difference to them. It was another thing Babar had warned her about. The arrogance of Jensi citizens was well known everywhere on Shanji, but now Rani was experiencing it. And there were new surprises awaiting her.

She found a restroom, but a heavy woman in a beige uniform sat at a little table just inside the entrance, her hand outstretched. "Fifty ban," the woman said sullenly.

Rani bit her lip to avoid a rude answer. She fumbled the traveling purse from her robe pocket, found a fifty ban piece and slapped it down on the table. The woman glanced at it and frowned.

The stalls were closed, with coin-operated locks. Another fifty ban. She found another coin, but it wouldn't fit the lock. She rattled the door. "What's wrong here? My coin doesn't fit!"

"You must use Jensi-ban," said the guardian of the restroom. "If you have no money, go to the end of the stalls to do your business. I'm not allowed to exchange funds here."

The last stall had no door, no stool, no paper, only a large pipe sticking several centimeters out from a white tiled floor. Rani lifted her robe, pulled down her panties and squatted low, pressing her hands against two walls for balence and feeling like half of a crouching spider. But blessed relief followed within a minute.

She reassembled herself, now furious, but the woman handed back her coin as Rani reached the door. "Sorry. I'm not allowed to keep this. Only Jensi-yuan are legal tender in the city now. It is a new thing. There is an exchange office near baggage claim. Be sure to get some change for next time."

Rani bit her lip again, snatched the coin from the woman's hand and stormed out of the restroom. Ten minutes and she reached baggage claim, found the chute for her flight and seat number. The chute was empty. She stomped a foot in anger.

Others waited with her, most of them from Wanchou. A man in a neat black suit shook his head and smiled at her. "Another delay, and they accomplish nothing by searching every bag that comes in from outside the city. There have also been thefts, but one can prove nothing. The new mayor treats us all like foreigners, and something should be done about him," he said.

"Our Empress will hear about this soon," said Rani smugly, but the man chuckled and shook his head again.

"She is far away, and receives all taxes due her. No matter that Jensi City has suddenly become a place for elite isolationists, as long as she's paid well. Nothing will happen."

Rani was stunned into silence, and it was another fifteen minutes before a loud thunk announced the arrival of her single suitcase. She now had an hour and a half to board her train.

Beyond the baggage claim area, restaurents and shops were visible through a clear polymer wall with four exits, each guarded by three uniformed men with holstered sidearms and severe faces, busily searching each piece of luggage as it came through and questioning its bearer. There was a long line at each exit, and another half hour before Rani plopped her single bag on a table for inspection. One guard, looking bored, zipped it open and peered inside as if actually interested in its contents. A second guard held out his hand, glowering at her from beneath the bill of his military-style cap.

"Identity papers, please," he snapped.

Rani hesitated an instant, never before having heard such a request, and her mind blanked. "I — I'm Rani-Tan, Tumatsin Representative to the Peoples' Congress," she stammered, and felt her face flush.

The guard raised an eyebrow, and smiled. "Then show me your travel card. Your eyes alone tell me you're a Tumatsin."

"Oh," she said, and found the photo-ID card that gave her free transportation anywhere on Shanji. The guard took it, made a show of comparing her face with the photograph, and handed it back.

"You have business in Jensi City?" he asked.

"No. I'm catching the mag-lev to Congress Center," she said. The other guard had zipped her bag closed, and was looking bored again.

"Ah, in transit only," said her inquisitor. He rubber-stamped a white slip of paper and handed it to her. Rani looked at it, saw 'MAG-LEV ONLY' in black letters.

"Give that to the conductor, and enjoy your trip. Next, please!"

Rani took her bag and brushed past a third guard just outside the exit, feeling him flinch in surprise at the near collision as she stared at the paper in her hand.

The man who'd spoken to her in baggage claim was there again, and smiling. "Freedom at last," he said.

Rani showed him the paper. "What does this mean?"

"You must get on the mag-rail train. No exit from the terminal. There are more guards at the entrance."

Rani flushed again. "Are you telling me I can't leave this building to see the city if I want to?"

"Not without this," said the man, and showed her a yellow slip of paper stamped 'EXIT' in bold, red letters. "Access is controlled, has always been controlled to some degree in Jensi, but the new mayor has added to it. Tourists are allowed only by presentation of an invitation from a citizen of the city. Visits without an overnight stay are forbidden. The hotels work with the new police in registering all visitors. For me, it's easy. I do regular business here and have an open visitor's permit from my company in Wanchou. Jensi is separate from Shanji, now. It has suddenly become a foreign place, with its own money. I heard you say you're a representative in the Peoples' Congress. Haven't you heard about these changes?"

"No, I haven't," she said, and they walked together. Her stomach growled again at the odor of food cooking. Ahead of her, on both sides of a milling crowd were brightly lit shops, a resturent with little tables. "This is my first real day as representative, and the person I replaced told me nothing about this."

"It's all recent," said the man, then lowered his voice as they passed a pair of armed policemen who studied Rani's colorful robe for more than an instant. "Jensi is behaving like a separatist state on Shanji. I will be very disappointed in our Congress if they allow it. Our Empress doesn't seem to care."

Rani bristled. "I promise she will care when I tell her what I've seen here. This is not what she intended for Jensi City, or any other city on Shanji."

"You can talk to her?"

"Yes. Her brother is my friend for years. We come from the same ordu— village. Oh, there's a money exchange, and I'm starving! I only have half an hour to catch my train!"

The man stayed with her, seemed protective yet somehow furtive, eyes darting around to see if someone might be listening to them. Rani pulled Yuan notes from her purse as they reached a window through which a young woman looked at them expectantly.

"Exchange only what you need," said the man. "A modest lunch here will cost you forty Jensi-yuan. That's a hundred and sixty in our currency."

147

Rani looked at him in horror, but slid two hundred Yuan into a slot beneath the window, and also asked the woman for some small change in fifty ban pieces. The woman calculated carefully, taking her time. Rani held out a hand to the man. "I'm Rani-Tan, and thank you for your help" she said, and smiled.

The man shook her hand gently, and lowered his eyes. "If you don't mind I won't give you my name. It's better that way. My hope is you can have some influence on what is happening here."

He bowed slightly and walked quickly away from her as the clerk shoved Jensi-yuan notes and change underneath the window to her. She carefully stored the change, kept the notes in her hand and spent it all in the restaurent for a bowl of rice sprinkled with bits of vegetables and meat, one large plum and a single cup of tea.

Service was quick, her eating quicker, and then there was the dash down stairs and one escalator to catch the mag-lev to Congress Center via another two hours of traveling.

She arrived with ten minutes to spare, but on boarding was reprimanded by the conductor for nearly forgetting to present her little white slip of paper to him. *Goodbye, Jensi*, she thought angrily, but soon was safely away from it, speeding south.

Little sleep, inadequate expensive food. Her mood was dark when she got off the train at Congress Center. The atmosphere brightened her somewhat: no police, no identity checks, no crowds in a small station with bright lights, two shops and a man selling fish cakes for two Yuan each. She ate three of them, then hailed a bubble-top cab that drove her three kilometers to Congress Center.

It was indeed a center, not even a village, in the sense there were no individual dwellings there. Congress Hall was a massive pill-box of concrete, without windows, sprawled at the center of a circle of five-story dormitories, shops and eateries, and separated from them by a lovely park with green grass, trees, and scattered benches made from stone.

The cab took her to dormitory D, and she checked in. Her room, her home for the four months each year when Congress was in session, was on the third floor and looked out over the roof of Congress Hall. There was a small bed, bathroom with shower, easy chair with lamp, a desk, console and bookcase for her use. The walls were white, the floor bare wood, and black curtains were pulled back from the single window. A telephone was on the desk, but there was no television or holovision set to be seen. Rani liked the room immediately; it was simple, yet functional, a good place for quiet work.

She spent an hour touring the dormitory, saw the cafeteria where she would eat her meals, the meeting rooms, a single lounge with holovision, and computer console for electronic mail. It was late afternoon when she made the five minute walk to Congress Hall to check in there, even though Congress would not be in session for another week.

The interior of the building was in granite, a circular space with wide stairs leading to a second level which was the congressional meeting hall. Ground level was offices along four hallways radiating outwards from the reception area. A flat white ceiling with light panels was far above it, and the granite walls were undecorated. There were no guards, only two unarmed men behind a console in the center of the area. Rani checked in, presented her travel card, and her time of taking residence was recorded for public record.

Her office suite was room seven, and two familiar faces were there to greet her. Cela and Tanzin had been Tumatsin representative staff members since the beginning of Peoples' Congress. Both were now white-haired, and remembered her as a little girl. They had honeycakes and tea ready for her, and quickly caught up on ordu news.

Her formal office seemed ornate, with plush brown carpet, paneled walls, a huge desk on which a copy of Wang Mengnu's sayings lay open to face a visitor. A tapestry showing a Tumatsin village scene graced one wall, another lined with portraits of all previous Tumatsin representatives to Congress. Rani gasped when she saw her own portrait there, and Cela laughed.

"There is a local artist who makes a decent living doing those. He did it from a photograph, and we put it up this morning. You're a part of our history now, Rani."

"Thank you so much, Cela, but I haven't even begun working," said Rani.

"Soon enough. There's a small stack of proposed legislation there on your desk. The Jensi City representatives have been quite busy, you'll see. And two of them came by this morning to see if you'd come in yet. Of all congressional representatives, they are by far the most active."

Rani frowned. "I just came through Jensi, and I didn't like what I saw there." She stepped over to the desk, opened a file containing a centimeters thick packet of papers in small, closely-spaced type, and thumbed a few pages.

"I've heard stories," said Cela. "You might want to skim those bills right now. The Jensi people might be back shortly."

Rani slapped the file closed, and picked it up. "I haven't arrived yet, Cela. I won't be here until the day after tomorrow. In the meantime, I'll be in my dormitory to carefully study these things before their instigators start trying to persuade me."

She clutched the file to her breast. "One other thing. I represent the Tumatsin. In the future, I will see any Tumatsin who comes here. But any other person, any lobbyist, must have his or her representative contact me. You might also pass the word that my loyalty to Our Empress is absolute. I will support nothing she opposes."

Cela smiled. "I hope you'll still feel that way after you've been here a while, Rani. I've been here a long time. My advice is that you say little and listen carefully at first, and also make friends with the people from Wanchou. Their political strength will be important to you, because all the others have developed ties to Jensi. Things are changing fast in that city, mostly while Congress was out of session. If there are grumblings about it, they will come from Wanchou — and from you. I fear you'll have few other friends in this congress."

"Then I'd better get going on it," said Rani. "I appreciate your advice, Cela. Don't ever hesitate to give it while I'm here. I have to learn as fast as possible."

"The day after tomorrow," said Cela.

"Yes. Early in the morning. I'll be ready for them."

"I'm sure you will. And we'll be here to help you."

Rani hurried from the office, down an empty hall to the reception desk and checked out. "I have a favor to ask," she said to the man there. "I just came in to pick up something, and won't be officially in my office until eight o'clock the day after tomorrow. If people ask to see me, could you tell them that?"

"Of course," said the man, and made a note of it in his computer.

Outside, she passed two black-suited men on the front steps leading to Congress Hall. They looked at her expectantly, and she was suddenly conscious of her tri-colored robe.

"Madam Tan?" one man called after her, but she didn't respond and kept walking, then risked a peek over her shoulder and saw the men were entering Congress Hall.

She went straight to her room and settled down at her little desk to read the file. There were four bills, all from Jensi City. The first requested a planet-wide census every four years to up-date the number of representatives from each province according to population, but made no change in the formula for representation. Reasonable enough, though costly. She turned to the second bill.

The telephone rang harshly, more like a buzz.

"Yes?"

"Two men are here to see you, Madam, representatives Peng and Tuzi. Will you receive them?"

"I do not receive visitors to my room at any time. My office hours are eight to eight, and begin the day after tomorrow. Please tell them to call my office for an appointment."

"Yes, Madam," said the receptioness, and hung up.

So it begins, thought Rani, and returned to her reading.

The second bill called for a reduction of tariffs on gold wire received from Meng-shi-jie, thus reducing costs of electronic industries not only in Jensi City, but Wanchou and the Dahe complex as well. Again reasonable, in view of the huge imports of materials to Meng-shi-jie that fueled the Shanji economy.

The third bill caught her eye instantly, a request for an extension of the mag-rail line into Tumatsin lands and all along the shore of the southern sea. The economic benefit to her people was obvious: increased tourism, rapid transport of fish, meat, cheese and cultural products, a real connection to the rest of Shanji. The idea excited her, but would her people feel the same way?

Her elevated mood sank when she read the fourth and last bill in the file, and she had sudden suspicions about why the Jensi representatives had proposed the third one.

Jensi City wanted to be declared an economic development zone, with lower taxes for established businesses and a two year exemption of taxes for new businesses to be established there.

Economic development zone, indeed, when internal efforts were already underway to make them a separate state!

Enough. Rani looked at her watch. It was after six. Not the best time, perhaps, but no time was the best time. She picked up the telephone and punched in a series of numbers. Waited until a man answered.

"This is Rani-Tan, Tumatsin representative to the Peoples' Congress. I have an urgent political matter to discuss with Empress Mengnu if she's available, please."

"One moment," said the man. There was a click, then another man on the line and she had to repeat her introduction. Another click. She waited, her fingernails drumming on the desk. There was an impulse to hang up. Perhaps she was going too far, too quickly. Her position would not officially begin for another week.

"Rani? Is it Rani-Tan from the Dorvodt ordu?"

A familiar voice, yet she'd not heard it for years. "Yes, Madam. I'm calling from Congress Center, and have some concerns to share with you if I may be permitted to."

"Why of course, dear. How wonderful it is to be speaking to a female representative of our people at last. Goldani has spoken to me about you. She says you will be leader of the Dorvodt in the near future."

"If it is the will of the people," said Rani, relaxing. "For my present position, it was Babar who nominated me and persuaded the voters. Right now I'm not sure whether I should praise or curse him for that. It's only my first day on the job, and I already have some deep concerns."

"Well, then, tell me about them," said the Empress of Shanji.

Rani did so, for nearly half an hour, describing everything she'd seen and heard in Jensi City, then the bills lying on her desk.

"Special status for Jensi is out of the question. I won't allow it if it's passed in Congress," said the Empress.

"I'm new here, Madam, but I'll do my best to rally opposition to the bill. I'm sure the delegation from Wanchou will not support such favoritism."

"I will also make my wishes known to them. Now, these other things you mention, you say they are recent changes?"

"Weeks old, Madam. They seem to be coming from a new mayor in Jensi City."

"We are aware of his election," said the Empress, "and some of the reforms he campaigned for seem to fit with things you've told me. We've been watching Jensi City for several months, Rani. Troubles have been brewing there for some time. Whatever happens, I want to

152

proceed as diplomatically and democratically as possible. I did not become Empress to be a dictator, but I do have veto power over the Peoples' Congress, and if necessary I *will* exercise it."

Rani shuddered, for many people would see a veto as dictatorial. "Your will is mine, Madam. I'll do everything I can to avoid the necessity of your veto."

"Careful, Rani," said her Empress. "Your loyalty is first to the Tumatsin, then Shanji, and only thirdly to myself. You must think in those terms. Do not support me if you think my cause is unjust. Remember our history, our heritege, and the injustices of the past."

"I will, Madam, but I welcome your opinions on issues that bother me. I must know where you stand on issues before planning my strategies in Congress."

The Empress chuckled. "Oh, I think you will be a fine representative, Rani. You may call me anytime for my opinions, and feel free to voice your own on any matters."

Rani hesitated, then, "There is one thing, Madam. I think you should go to Jensi City and see what is happening there." *Our Empress doesn't seem to care*, the man had said, but Rani could not bring herself to say it.

"That has been arranged, though I'll not personally go there at this time. We must proceed cautiously, Rani. This is a potentially dangerous situation we're facing here. If we're about to do anything that impacts on congressional matters, you will be warned.

What does she know that I don't? thought Rani. "Thank you, Madam, and I appreciate being allowed to talk to you directly like this. The blessings of First Mother are upon you."

"And you, Rani. Goodbye for now, and be strong. This congressional session might be the most difficult one in our history, and I'm sure you'll be an important part of it."

The line went dead.

Rani felt a quivering in her stomach, a strange uneasy feeling as she hung up the telephone. Towards the end of the conversation, her Empress' voice had seemed cold, even hard, and it was the voice of a woman who had once wielded terrible powers in the distant past before Rani's birth. Had the people forgotten that? Had they forgotten their freedom in democracy was at the pleasure of a woman who could destroy armies, even cities, with a wave of her hand?

She turned to her computer, ran the list of congressional delegates and wrote a letter introducing herself to each one of them. In the letters to Wanchou delegates she added a paragraph describing her opposition to favoritism being shown in establishing Jensi City as an economic development zone. Finally there was a letter to Goldani, describing the bill to extend the mag-rail into Tumatsin territory, and a request for her reactions.

It was well after midnight when she got to bed, and there were dreams. Bad dreams. In one of them, the small figure of a robed woman stood at the outskirts of Jensi City, her arms outstretched.

The city was engulfed in flames.

Fourteen

Disturbances

The House of Kuai-le suffered a disturbance.

Darkness had fallen, and the building was brightly lit indirectly in green and red from recessed light panels in the block-long facade. Above first floor there were no windows in the white granite structure, but wide plas-panels at street level allowed view of the casino inside and all the beautiful people who were there. Music blared from speakers above the revolving doors of two entrances now in constant rotation as the elite of Jensi City arrived for an evening of pleasure: drinks and a fine meal, the games, entertainment, perhaps a hot bath and arousing massage followed by other diversions, either individually or in groups, to be found on the third floor.

Several doormen in golden gowns hurried to assist both men and their jeweled ladies from bubble-topped cars provided by hotels for the occasion, cars with lush interiors and portable bars to encourage a gay mood. The cars would return regularly and often until dawn, picking up exhausted, satiated, often drunken patrons who had reached their limits for pleasure. Entrance was by permit, permits issued only to hotel patrons who had a room to return to after their night's fun, and these were checked by two burly, armed men who guarded each entrance. Such precautions, it was argued, were in the interest of safety. To drive while intoxicated was a serious offense under the new laws governing Jensi City. The few people who had tested those laws had not been seen again.

The sidewalk in front of the House of Kuai-le was crowded, and so at first there was no notice of a group of people who approached on foot, huddled together as if for warmth and carrying with them placards nailed to stakes of wood. They were led by a man dressed in a

155

white robe who carried a thick sheaf of papers in his hands and walked with a determined step as if urging his flock ahead, for fear was written on all their faces, both men and women.

The group stopped just short of one entrance, and placards were raised overhead.

'HOUSE OF ABOMINATION', said one.

'SIN CENTER', said another.

'FORNICATION FOR THE RICH' still another, and so on.

The man in the white robe began offering leaflets to passerbyes. Most refused his offer, a few didn't, and then he began shouting above the music blaring from the speakers.

"Do not yield to the temptations offered by this den of iniquities! It is a place of sin, of fornication! It will take all you have, and leave you empty. The House of Kuai-le is an abomination to our city, and to The Church of Our Mother. Do not enter here!"

The group with him took up his chant and waved their placards high. People began to notice, and frowned. "Freaks", growled one man, but his well-dressed lady looked back fearfully as he propelled her into the casino. Another woman started to get out of her car, then ordered the driver to take her away when she saw what was happening.

One doorman ran inside to report the incident, another approached the man in the white robe.

"Save your money and your souls! Do not patronize this place of sin!"

"Shut up and get out of here while you can," growled the doorman. "We've called the police."

"Those who do wrong in the eyes of First Mother are lost to Her!" screamed the robed man.

The doorman pushed him, and the man went down hard, leaflets scattering. The small crowd of supporters shrieked in protest. A placard smacked the doorman in the back of his head. He grabbed it, twisted it away from a frail looking woman with fire in her eyes.

"Go home, grandmother. You're too old for prison," he snarled.

The crowd surged against him, but help came, a burly door guard and the manager of the casino floor, Wan-sen.

"Stop this! Stop it, now! The police will arrive any second!"

The robed man struggled to his feet and pointed at the entrance. "There! Sit down there!"

His followers moved as a mass to the entrance, placards waving, and sat down in front of it, chanting, "SIN, SIN, SIN!"

The burly guard reached for the gun at his waist, but Wan-sen stopped him. "Don't. Wait for the police."

"They're blocking the entrance," said the guard.

"I said *wait!*" Wan-sen turned to the robed man, and shouted over the din of the chanting demonstrators.

"Who are you people? Why are you doing this?"

The man had been helped to his feet by two young women who now clung fearfully to his arms as if holding him up.

"I am Lao-sun, a priest of First Mother, and these are Her servants. This place of business is an abomination to Our Mother and the tenants of Her Church. It must be closed at once!"

"You'll all be arrested for this. Go away!" shouted Wan-sen.

"Not until these doors are closed forever," said Lao-san.

There was no time for debate. Red lights flashed, cars and black vans coming in from two directions and turning to block the street in front of The House of Kuai-le. Several police officers got out of the cars, carrying long stun-sticks.

"They're blocking our entrance, and this man is their leader!" shouted Wan-sen.

"We have the right of protest, and have commited no violence!" said Lao-sun.

An officer pounded on the side of a van. Back doors flew open and more officers got out, wearing face shields and carrying sticks. There was no questioning, no discussion. The police moved as a single organism, rushing the seated demonstrators and beating them on heads and shoulders. People screamed, placards were dropped, bodies curling into fetal positions to avoid blows to their heads, but the beatings continued.

"No! You don't have the right!" screamed Lao-sun.

"Now," said Wan-sen.

The burly guard beside him struck Lao-sun hard in the face with a beefy right hand. The priest's nose was a flattened mess of bloody goo before he hit the ground. The women holding the priest screamed, and backed away.

The guard kicked Lao hard in the ribs once — then again.

"Run!" gasped Lao-sun. "Tell Kati!"

The two women ran away.

Beaten and stunned demonstrators were being dragged by their ankles to waiting vans and thrown inside like sacks of grain. Their faces left smears of blood on the sidewalk. The placards were picked up and thrown in the vans after them. Leaflets were fluttering in the evening breeze. Offices scurried to retrieve them, but a few were picked up by onlookers who then hurried away from the scene. Others pocketed them and remained staring, customers who had come out of the casino to see what was going on.

The priest groaned and writhed on the street. Likely his ribs had been broken. Wan-sen pointed at him. "This man is the leader," he said.

Two officers brushed Wan-sen and his guard aside. "We need no help in this work," said one. They picked up the priest roughly by shoulders and ankles, and the man shrieked in pain. A bloody foam drooled from his mouth.

"This man and his people have cost us business tonight!" complained Wan-sen. "They're from that *church* again."

"So file a complaint," said an officer.

Lao-sun, drooling blood, was thrown into the van with his battered flock and shrieked again as his body hit the floor. He was still shrieking as the doors were slammed closed and the van pulled away.

No questions, no information gathered for incident reports, for there would be none. A disturbance had been quelled, and criminals arrested. They would be taken somewhere without trial, a prison perhaps, or be deported from the city. Whatever happened to them, they would never be seen again in Jensi City.

The officers got back into their cars and a van and drove away, leaving behind only the sound of music blaring from two speakers. Well-dressed patrons remained in shock on the street as if afraid to return to the casino. A man in beige uniform came out with bucket and mop to scrub off the smears of blood left on the sidewalk.

A leaflet fluttered at Wan-sen's feet. He picked it up, held it out towards his patrons. "I will pay a hundred Jensi-yuan in chips or tokens for each one of these you bring to the cashiers' windows if you do it within half an hour," he shouted, then stepped up to a young woman in black evening wear. "This one, Madam, is for you."

She brightened. Her escort smiled. Around them, leaflets came out of pockets. Other well-dressed patrons were suddenly chasing down stray leaflets in the street, and laughing at the game of it.

"Please, the evening has just begun. The fanatics are gone, but our Lady of Fortune awaits you inside if you care to meet her. Come in, come in."

Wan-sen herded them all back inside. The blood was gone from the sidewalk. Hotel vans pulled up after the anxious minutes of waiting for the police to go away, and new customers emerged for an evening of pleasure and hopeful profit.

Peace returned once again to The House of Kuai-le.

Sheng-chih spoke patiently past clenched teeth. "You force me to repeat myself, sir, and I only do so because you're such a valuable client of ours, but surely you can understand our position. We cannot consider land for collateral if it is not yet obtained. Such matters are not within our province, and you must contact the Economic Ministry for an explanation."

The office door opened slightly, and Tuen peered in at him, a handkerchief in his hand. Sheng gestured him to enter, then rolled his eyes and held the receiver away from his ear as a new stream of invectives gushed from it. "Please, sir, there's no reason for hysteria. It is only a bureaucratic delay, I'm sure, and your investments with Fangzi-yen are more than sufficient collateral if that becomes necessary. I have the figures right in front of me."

Tuen sat down on the edge of a red velvet chair in front of the enormous desk of Fangzi-yen's chief executive, hands on his knees and twisting at the handkerchief. Beads of sweat on his forehead glistened in sunlight coming in from a picture window facing out to a view of forested hills. The room was mahogany paneled, shelved walls filled with figurines, urns and miniature paintings dating back a thousand years to the middle dynasties of Shanji and the period of finest art. Many were gifts from solvent noble families, a few others temporarily housed as collateral for personal loans to those in a sudden period of financial decline.

"Yes, yes, your loan is assured. Now calm yourself and call Minister Shui right away. You have his number? Good. And call me when you hear something. I have the final papers on my desk."

Sheng-chih hung up the telephone, swiveled merrily in his chair, and laughed. "Oh, the hysteria. I should feel badly about enjoying it so, but I cannot. All the years of opulent living, the corruption of political influence and now the lack of it, all is coming home like a diseased bird to infect the nest. The families are going under one by one, Tuen, and much of their capital rests in our hands. I should send flowers to our beloved Empress for her aid in our success."

"I don't understand," said Tuen, wiping sweat from his forehead.

"The land grants, of course. She has issued none of them for the past two years, the careless fool, and gives no explanation for her inaction. She drives the nobles deeper into our camp, Tuen, both financially and politically. That is the fourth such call I've received in the past week. The families are growing desperate for collateral. They need loans, and depend on our good will. Things could not be better. Now, why were you in such a rush to see me?"

Tuen gulped, and wiped his face again, fearful of upsetting his superior's good mood.

"My — my office accounts have been examined by someone outside of Fangzi-yin. The entry occured five days ago. I discovered it this morning when I was looking up a previous entry date of my own accounting." Tuen clutched at his stomach, as if in pain.

Sheng-chih's smile turned into a scowl. "The mainframe file?"

"Yes, but the transfer account files are in my personal machine. They have not yet been accessed, and I just took them off-line."

"That was quick thinking, Tuen. Tell the others to do the same." Sheng turned to his own computer, fingers stroking the keyboard. "Five days ago, you say?"

"Yes."

In the green light of the monitor, Sheng's face looked suddenly lined and drawn. "There it is. My files also. Nine thirty in the morning. Someone is working quite early."

"What?"

"The time difference. Only the Economic Ministry has our access codes. Someone has entered our files from there."

"An audit?" New sweat appeared on Tuen's forehead.

"There's precedence, but notices are sent, and I've received nothing."

"Nor I," said Tuen.

"A formal audit, or someone else with access to the ministry and the power to command their cooperation," said Sheng-chih. "Well, they don't have my transfer files, either."

"Hard copy is so risky, sir. I wish you'd put them on disk or cube. If there were a fire in your home, the —"

"There is a second copy here in my safe, Tuen. The red book. The blank pages are written in phosphor and can be read in black light, just like the original. My precautions are sufficient. We are secure for the moment, but I do not like this at all. If someone looks at the grand picture they will see our mainframe files are incomplete, but that will require an audit of all the nobles. And who knows what those fools have claimed for their tax writeoffs?"

"So what do we do?" asked Tuen, wringing his handkerchief.

"Make sure our colleagues have their transfer files out of the mainframe, and then wait. There's a chance this was a simple audit done by someone who neglected to send notices. And you really *must* do something about your sweating, Tuen. Your appearance does not command confidence or trust from those who don't know you."

"It is a condition since childhood, Sheng-chih, and I'm taking medications for it," said Tuen.

Sheng-chih grunted, and waved a hand in dismissal. "Inform our colleagues at once, and tell me if their files have been entered. And try to remain calm, or appear to be so. I do *not* want to see you sweating if we're questioned by the Economic Ministry. Go."

Tuen arose, and fled from the office.

Sheng-chih sat back glumly in his chair, and fingered the telephone. What could he say to the nobles? *Land grants obtained through the use of Fangzi-yin funds have been discovered, my dears. I'm afraid you'll lose those lands and have many back-taxes to pay unless we do something soon. It is a time for creative bookkeeping, you see.*

A sudden thought struck him. *An audit without notice. Not the ministry, but someone outside it, someone higher, making what they thought was a covert probe. Royalty? Perhaps our Empress is not so naive about finance as her lack of interest indicates. Perhaps she's not our benefactor after all.*

Perhaps now is the time for a major political change on Shanji.

Lin-po worked at the dining table while Mei-ling put the baby to bed. The dishes had been cleared and washed, and prayer sticks lit

161

to overcome the lingering odors of cooked food. It was well after dark, and street noise was subsiding, only the tinkling of tin chimes fluttering in a cool breeze coming in through the open window of the apartment.

A quiet time before another storm, thought Lin-po, but things had so far gone much better than he'd expected. The apartment was even more substantial than what they'd had in Jensi City; they had a lease, with option to buy: living and dining area, kitchen, bath with tub, and two bedrooms. All furnishings were their property, and new; the remainder of their Jensi hush money had been sufficient to obtain a business loan through Wanchou's Cultural Arts Center once they'd established a six months residence. Now he worked on the final lay-out of the shop, thinking, visioning, scribbling down a detail and thinking again.

Mei-ling came to the table, bringing with her two cups of tea. She wore a yellow robe cinched tight at her waist, and had let down her long black hair. Lin-po looked up at her, smiling, and made no effort to hide the travel of his gaze over her body.

She smiled. "I did not feed you enough. You look hungry."

"For you, not food," he growled.

Her laugh was a tinkling bell. "We have another room for that, and you have work to finnish." She sat down opposite him, pushed forward a cup of tea, and sighed.

"Are we really prepared to do this all over again?" she asked.

"I am. We're experienced now, Mei-ling. It will be easier this time, and we have more space to work with."

"And our own building," she added.

"I trust these people," he said. "It is not like Jensi City at all, and the tourist trade is much greater here. I think our profit will come from little things, not the costly items, and the manufacturers are right here in Wanchou."

Mei-ling smiled again. "You're excited, husband, and it infects me."

"I can hardly wait to begin," he said, then jerked in surprise when there was a knock on their door.

Mei-ling's eyes widened in fear. The memories of her experience in Jensi City still followed her.

Lin-po went to the door, and opened it. A man and a woman stood there, both dressed in neatly tailored white body-suits. The man was taller than Lin-po, had the long face of the northern rural people, his hair tied in a pig-tail. He held a huge basket of fruit wrapped in clear polymer, and bowed.

"I am Xun-su, and this is my assistant Huan-le. We've come from the Wanchou Business Association to welcome you to our community. May we come in for a moment?"

Mei-ling stood up as her visitors entered. Xun-su put his basket of fruit on the table, and Huan-le presented Mei-ling with a bouquet of white and purple iris. "Welcome to Wanchou," she said.

Huan-le was tiny but lovely, her features small, and her hair was in double buns. She peered at them through thick glasses giving her the appearance of a little owl.

Lin-po shook hands with Xun-su. "You honor us. Please sit. We have tea, if you are thirsty."

Their visitors declined refreshment, but sat down with them at the table. Xun-su gave Lin-po some literature. "Our meetings are monthly, and you do not have to be a member to attend. Our purpose is to control the distribution of businesses so we all have equal opportunities for profit. Your shop will be unique here, and we have high hopes for your success," he said. "When do you plan your opening?"

"In one month. Our furnishings are just arriving, and merchandise has been ordered locally. We already see great savings in transportation costs here."

"There is not the competition for space here that you undoubtedly experienced in Jensi City," said Huan-le. "I understand the business climate has become quite restrictive for small shop owners there."

Lin-po scowled, and Mei-ling reached over to put a hand on his.

"Jensi City is a place I will try hard to forget," said Lin-po.

"Their loss is our gain," said Xun-su. "Several small businesses have come here from Jensi; the owners all seem bitter about their experience there, and seem eager to put it behind them."

"Indeed," said Lin-po, and the nightmare of thugs smashing his Jensi shop raced through his mind at lightning speed. The vision of Mei-ling held aloft by a burly hoodlum remained for more than an instant.

As he thought it, something else passed through Lin-po's mind. His head buzzed, his eyes losing focus, and then it was gone, and with it the starkness of the memories. They now seemed unreal, like in a dream. It was as if his memories had suddenly been cleansed, his bitterness drained from him.

"Whatever your reasons for leaving Jensi City, we're glad you're here," Huan-le said sweetly. "You have our literature. If there's anything we can do to help you get settled, please let us know."

Mei-ling sniffed the flowers given to her. "You are most kind," she said.

Their guests stood up with them. Xun-su smiled, but Huan-le did not. "Wanchou is larger than Jensi City, but you will find much kindness here. The precepts of Our Mother still rule our lives, and occasional visits by Empress Mengnu are a reminder of that," she said.

"Enjoy the fruit," said Xun-su, "and the basket is yours to keep. We wish you prosperity in Wanchou."

They exchanged handshakes, and the door closed. Mei-ling unwrapped the basket, and put the fruit away for another time. "I think we'll enjoy our life here, Lin-po. Such nice people," she said.

"It was a short visit, but pleasant. My memories of that terrible night in Jensi seem suddenly faint, as if it didn't happen," said Lin-po.

"I feel that also," said Mei-ling, and she smiled radiantly at him.

They retired soon after that smile.

Fifteen

Visitatation

Kati personally escorted Huomeng and her father to the flyer field, and acted like a mother to them.

"I know it must be done, but I don't like it without an escort," she said, her arms folded in a pose of judgement. "This was a poor time to have the Moshuguang elite out on maneuvers."

"It would only inflame Quantou's arrogance, dear. It was enough just getting an audience with him without explaining our agenda. It is an official sight-seeing visit, and he's responsible for our safety," said Huomeng. "He seems to have plenty of police officers to help with that."

"That's my concern," said Kati.

"Not with my presence," said Mengmoshu. "I may be an old man, but I'm still Moshuguang Chancellor, and Quantou understands the implications of that. A single detachment of my Elite Force could overwhelm his police in hours. He did not become mayor by being a stupid man, Kati."

"Be sure to use the blanket in the flyer, father. You just got over your cold."

"Yes, yes. I don't need reminding. Has Yesui returned?"

"This morning. What she learned just supports what we've heard. We're dealing with brutal people here. I don't want either of you to inflame them. Bring up the issues, but don't argue. Let them think our concern is real, but not threatening."

"We've heard all this, Kati," said Huomeng. "Now kiss me goodbye."

She kissed him very hard. "Be careful, husband. If anything happens to you, I'll —"

Huomeng kissed her back even harder, and held her tightly.

"Ahem," said Mengmoshu.

165

Kati hugged him tightly. "I wish you would retire," she murmured. "And do what? Write my memoires? That's enough, now. Let me go."

Huomeng watched with amusement; his gruff father-in-law was obviously enjoying himself. "We'll call tonight, dear," he said, climbed into the flyer, then helped Mengmoshu in beside him. Turbines were whining before they were buckled in. Kati stepped back several paces and waved as they lifted off.

"She won't sleep tonight," grumbled Mengmoshu.

"She will if we call her," said Huomeng.

They lifted through the open panel in the bubble over Mengnu's city, banked sharply and accelerated northeast to high speed. Mountains passed below them, then the checkerboard pattern of farms on the high plain. Mengmoshu tucked the blanket over and beneath his legs, as instructed by his daughter, his thick, leather tunic sufficient to retain body heat.

"I didn't like deceiving her," Huomeng finally said.

"It was my decision, as Moshuguang Chancellor. It is a sign of Moshuguang response, not a show of power by an Empress," said Mengmoshu.

And one hour out from the Empress' city, they were joined by forty flyers of the Moshuguang Elite, blue craft with the eternal flame emblem, each carrying nine fully armed troopers. They came in from the south and set up in five echelons above and below them.

Another hour and there were trees below them, rolling hills, and ahead the rounded summits of ancient erroded mountains. The pilot veered southeast. The escort changed formation to a single vee with Huomeng and Mengmoshu's craft at the apex.

Isolated estates now dotted the forests below them, and there were swaths of clear land where limited clearcutting operations were underway. The buildings of Jensi City suddenly loomed ahead like an eruption of colorful stalagmites from the ground. They flew over the city at full speed at an altitude of a thousand meters, a display of considerable force to observers on the ground. Their pilot veered south, escort following, then west and north again on a glide path towards the flyer field south of the city.

They began their descent. The pilot listened to his earphones, looked over his shoulder and smiled. "They say only our craft is authorized to land. The rest must stay in the air."

"Give me those things," growled Mengmoshu, and took both earphones and throat mike from the pilot.

"This is Mengmoshu, Chancellor of the Moshuguang. Our visit is not only by invitation from Mayor Quantou, but by the order of Empress Mengnu. Do not pretend to question her sovereignty in this matter. All we require are landing points for our craft and those of our escort. It is our intent that our troops will remain on the flyer field during our visit. They are here only to prevent any breach in our security. I request landing coordinates immediately, sir, without further questions."

Mengmoshu handed the earphones back to the pilot, and they waited. They were now at four hundred meters, and the flyer field was straight ahead. The pilot suddenly turned, and grinned over his shoulder. "Acknowledge area three, blue, area seven, green and red, control. Coming in at zero-five-three," he said, then clicked off his mike. "They've run out the red carpet for you, sirs."

And indeed they had.

There was a long limousine with a darkened bubble-top sitting at the end of a red carpet guarded by two ranks of uniformed men as the craft approached the ground. Their escort had dropped behind them at final descent, reforming into four phalanxes meters above the ground as Huomeng felt the bump of touchdown.

The pilot turned off his engine, but the scream of escort turbines still filled the air. The escort touched down a few seconds later; troopers scrambled from their flyers and formed ranks in front of them with laser rifles slung.

Not a single face moved in the ranks of military-style police. All wore sidearms, and were impressive in their crisp uniforms and high boots. They stood at a brace as a door of the limousine opened. A man got out, a small man in a tailored black suit. His hair was cut short and neatly styled, and he had the round face of a pure Hansui.

Huomeng was himself dressed in military blues, Mengmoshu in his usual field leathers. Huomeng got out first, and Mengmoshu refused the aid of his arm in getting out of the craft.

Their greeter walked down the center of the red carpet to reach them, looking neither left or right, his smile broadening as he came close. He extended his hand.

"I am Quantou. Welcome to Jensi City, gentlemen, and please excuse the delay. Our personnel were not warned you might have an escort with you."

"It was not inconvenient," said Huomeng. "I am Huomeng, and I bring you greetings from Empress Mengnu. And this is Chancellor Mengmoshu."

They shook hands warmly, Quantou adding the touch of his left hand to their wrists. "It's unfortunate that our Empress could not also be with us at this time," he said.

"She sends her sincere regrets, sir. At the moment, there are several matters requiring her immediate attention." As he said it, Huomeng narrowed his eyes for only an instant, and searched the man's mind as delicately as he could.

There was only time enough to see hostility and fear there.

Quantou blinked. "Our invitation is open to her anytime she wishes it," he said, then blinked again.

Careful, said Mengmoshu without words. Not so soon. He must be distracted first.

Quantou led them along the red carpet and gestured at the ranks of his police. "These men are being honored in greeting you today. They represent our finest officers, and have brought new order and tranquility to our city through their service to the people."

Huomeng's inspection of the officers was cursory, but close enough to see the hardness in the eyes, the determined set of the jaws. Mengmoshu looked closer, using the same intimidating scowl his own troops were used to seeing.

Among the ranks not a single eye moved, not even to blink.

"They are a fine looking unit," said Mengmoshu as they reached the limousine, and Quantou bowed with a smile.

"Your opinion will be known to them, sir," he said.

The interior of the limousine was in grey velvet, with two wide seats facing each other and separated by a bar holding crystal bottles of wines and liquors and two bottles of ayrog chilled in an ebony container filled with ice. Light came in only slightly dimmed by the reflective interference filter on the outer surface of the windows. A driver closed the door after they were together in one seat, then got in and drove them away without instructions from Quantou. The driver was also a uniformed police officer with sidearm, and he drove in a compartment separated from his passengers by a thick sheet of clear plas-steel.

"Something to drink, gentlemen?" asked Quantou. "Our car tour will take well over an hour."

Huomeng and Mengmoshu chose ayrog, and Quantou filled a glass with wine for himself. The car left the parking area at the flyer field and sped down a nearly empty street towards the city. Walled estates soon sprawled on both sides of it, huge trees nearly hiding two-storied mansions in marble and white stone.

"The city has grown since we were last here," said Huomeng.

"Our climate is moderate all year and our services are complete. There's nothing you can't buy here, and our cultural arts are second to none on Shanji. Many of the noble families have taken residence here in the past decade," said Quantou.

"Most of the noble families. Yes, we've noticed that," said Huomeng, and then he peered at something through the window. "The church is still as I remember it, but what is that covering the entrance? That wooden structure, I mean."

"The church is closed down for renovation. There was a serious fire that destroyed much of the interior several weeks ago. I fear it will remained closed for some time," said Quantou.

Quantou was not ignorant of Moshuguang powers. In a way, Huomeng had to admire the audacity of the man in daring to sit next to them when questions were asked. Quantou's mind was swirling madly, as if in a cycle of dreams without focus, searching for a vision, choosing one, discarding it, moving to another. All quite confusing, but he had anticipated a question and made his choice of vision before Huomeng even asked it.

"What happened?" asked Huomeng.

Quantou sighed. "I'm embaressed to say this so early in your visit, but I suppose I must. There are problems in Jensi City, problems that had become quite serious by the time I became mayor. There were few laws. The people lived in a system approaching anarchy, and there was a small but significant element taking advantage of it. Public drunkeness was common. There were thefts, destruction of property, all types of public disturbances, and only for the sport of it. There is no poverty here; our people enjoy affluence beyond any others on Shanji."

"But what happened to the church?" repeated Huomeng, pressing.

The vision was now clear in Quantou's mind, but did not match his knowledge of the facts.

"I took my office with a pledge to restore order to Jensi City. There has been progress, but my pledge has not been fulfilled and what has happened to the church is only one example of my remaining concerns. Several weeks ago the church was entered by masked men who assaulted a few parishioners at prayer, smashed the interior of the building and then set fire to it. A few suspects are in custody, but I don't think we've found the guilty people yet. They could be vandals, or reactionaries against the church itself. We simply don't know."

I don't like this, said Mengmoshu, quietly listening.

He's clever, and prepared, said Huomeng, without words.

"I find destruction of a church a most heinous crime, though I'm not myself a religious person. I will not cease my investigations until those responsible for it are caught and punished. But I must say that the church itself has made enemies in Jensi City."

Ah, here it comes, said Mengmoshu.

"There are radicals within the church, ultra-conservatives who try to force their beliefs on the entire population. Their high priest, a man named Lao-sun, has led demonstrations in the city. Some have turned into violent public disruptions, clear acts of intolerable civil disobedience. We finally arrested Lao-sun several weeks ago, just before the vandalism of his church. I fear the crime may have been perpetrated by ordinary peaceful citizens who are outraged by the trouble he's caused. It will not be simple to find them."

"What has happened to Lao-sun?" asked Huomeng quickly.

Quantou's mind was a blank. "He's undergoing psychological evaluation at the moment, and the prognosis is not good. This may seem harsh, gentlemen, but my guess is he'll be deported from Jensi City within the year and another priest will have to be elected by his congregation. The man is too unstable for such responsibilities."

"It seems so," said Mengmoshu suddenly. "Your position is quite delicate, yet you have a pledge to fulfill. Order must be brought about and maintained. It is the will of your citizens that drives you. To an outsider, however, or a casual visitor, it might seem your methods in keeping order are harsh, perhaps oppressive. To an outsider, the vandalism of the church might even be seen as religious persecution."

"This is untrue," said Quantou indignantly, but now Huomeng saw otherwise in the distracted man's mind.

"Of course it is," continued Mengmoshu. "It is a problem of image, of communication to the world outside your city. Little news reaches us, but we've had our reports. They are one reason for our visit here. What you've told us is most enlightening, and the mind of Empress Mengnu will be relieved by what we've heard so far. Jensi City is the jewel of her Empire. She extends her support for you, if you only ask for it. Your people are hers. We are, all of us, citizens of Shanji."

"That is most gracious, sir," said Quantou, stunned by Mengmoshu's outburst and not feeling the delicate probings of his mind.

"I believe there were others arrested with Lao-sun," said Huomeng.

"Yes, a few of his reactionary followers. They were held overnight for questioning, then released, I believe. I can check on that if you wish."

"I would appreciate that being done before we leave. It is another concern for Empress Mengnu," said Huomeng. They were now well into the city, driving slowly, and tall buildings loomed high on either side of them. The sidewalks were crowded, but for a city of size and wealth few cars were to be seen and most of them were driven by uniformed chauffeurs. There were no traffic lights. Military policemen standing in concrete gazebos directed traffic at each intersection. Police were everywhere, in cars, on foot, all with sidearms and carrying long black sticks.

"The downtown area seems unchanged," said Huomeng, peering up at the buildings like a country tourist.

"Look ahead. There is a new City Hall, and the white tower is The House of Fangzi-yin, our new commercial center. It accounts for over seventy percent of the taxes paid in the city," said Quantou.

Seventy percent of his salary, jibed Mengmoshu. The House of The New Masters, Huomeng. "A magnificent structure," he said.

"Their presence has attracted many new businesses and private investors to the city," added Quantou.

"I've heard of a grand casino here," said Huomeng. "Will we see it?"

"Ahead, on our left, the long building," said Quantou, "but it's closed to the public from nine to five each day. Gambling is strictly regulated here."

He pointed out the huge building as they passed it, and indeed there seemed to be no activity there.

They drove through city center and east, buildings familiar, the street finally ending at the edge of Peoples' Park and the heritege center there. A parking area was nearly empty of cars. When Huomeng got out, he was surprised to see that two police cars and a black van had been following them. Officers piled out of van and cars and formed up in two lines on either side of them as an escort into the park.

"Is such security really necessary?" asked Huomeng.

"It's only a precaution, sir," said Quantou, and smiled. "We want nothing to disturb your visit here." He gestured to an officer, and several men moved ahead of them into the park.

Trees, rich undergrowth of ferns and broad fronds, leafy branches overhanging narrow, stone paths. Stone benches were placed along the way. Wind chimes tinkled in the breeze, and there were several stone altars with bowls of smouldering sweet grass by ponds lined with smooth green pebbles. The pebbles were the first sign Huomeng had seen of any remaining belief in First Mother, each stone carefully placed there as an offering.

No people were to be seen until they reached a clearing where many stone benches were arranged in semi-circles in front of a pagoda of dark wood and a now empty stage. Several people sat by themselves on the benches, reading from little red books. They looked up when the police arrived. They closed their books quickly, stood up and walked away without looking back.

"Little has changed here," said Quantou. "Our people work hard, and few come here anymore, but we have a cultural heritage day each fall and there are regular weekend stage performances throughout the year."

But Huomeng remembered when the park had been packed with people to celebrate the new Shanji and the Empress who had made it possible. "Is the museum of miniatures still here?" he asked quickly.

"Yes, it is," said Quantou, "but there is nothing new."

The man seemed reluctant to show them that.

"I'd like to see it again, please," said Huomeng.

"Of course," said Quantou. He nodded to an officer. A group of six men moved well ahead of them as they walked to the left of the pagoda and stage area. There was a broad, stone path lined with unlit lanterns hanging from tree branches.

172

They walked it and came to the wooden arch at the entrance to the museum. Walkways went off left and right, forming a circle along the circumference of which the life of Empress Mengnu was shown in miniature.

Huomeng's first impression was one of obvious neglect. The walkways were overgrown, the exhibits choked with weeds. Figurines of people and horses had fallen over on their sides from winds over the years, and had not been placed upright again. The exhibits themselves were unchanged: Kati as a Tumatsin child, riding her horse Sushua, then her being brought to the Emperor's City, then the great war against Mandughai's troops, and so on.

Now there were a few people ahead of them, women and young children who stepped off the path as they approached. The women looked grim, and the children stared up at the police with wide eyes. Three officers were bent over at an exhibit, pulling things from the ground and depositing them in a waste container. There was suddenly a sweet odor in the air.

It was the last exhibit on the path, and the most recent, a simple statue in green stone showing an infant Mei-lai-gong in the arms of her Empress mother. It had been erected soon after Yesui's birth.

At the base of the statue a smouldering prayer stick lay on its side, neglected by the officers in their hasty cleansing. Huomeng leaned over and picked it up, twirled it in his hand and sniffed its odor. Quantou looked away before he could catch his eye.

A little girl stepped forward shyly with a bouquet of flowers tightly gripped in her hands. Two women were with her, and looked terrified. A tiny girl, perhaps four, her miniature face was framed with straight black hair and her eyes sparkled as she held out the flowers towards Huomeng. A policeman stepped in front of the girl and gently held her back.

Huomeng felt the terror of the women, and heard their silent plea.

"How sweet," he said, then stepped around the officer and knelt before the child. "Are these for me, or for our Empress?" he asked, then accepted the flowers from her hands.

"The Empress, please," she said, and tucked in her chin as he touched her cheek with a finger.

You have been heard, he thought, as hard as he could, and tears appeared in the eyes of the women.

Both Mengmoshu and Quantou were scowling at him, each for their own reasons, as Huomeng stood up again. "Wildflowers," he said, sniffing at the bouquet. "She'll be delighted to get them."

"We must hurry along, now," said Quantou. "Our lunch is awaiting us."

They went back to the limousine and drove back to City Hall, where lunch was to be served in Quantou's office. "You and Empress Mengnu must return for an extended visit soon," said Quantou. "There are many people who wanted to meet with you, and we could have arranged for receptions if you'd asked for them."

"In the near future, I'm sure," said Huomeng. "For now, we wished only to meet you and learn about any difficulties you're experiencing. Jensi is so remote, and we've been neglectful in not keeping close contact with you over the years. Empress Mengnu *does* want you to know she's concerned about your welfare."

"And the welfare of all her people," added Mengmoshu.

Quantou nodded politely. "Then we'll discuss this over lunch," he said.

And they did so, over an elaborate meal of four courses served in the mayor's office. The room was paneled, undecorated walls, a large desk fronted by two overstuffed chairs, a large table seating fourteen people, on which their meal was served. There were spiced vegetables over rice, thin slices of lamb cooked in honey, and a fine blush wine. They ate, and exchanged pleasantries until a secretary arrived with a note for Quantou.

"As I expected," he said. "Lao-sun remains in hospital for observation and testing. Those arrested with him have been released, but are required to attend a series of lectures regarding civil disobedience and its consequences. No deportation proceedings are planned for them, or any other action I'm aware of. I hope this will ease your concern."

"It does," said Huomeng, "and we hope to ease *your* concerns if you'll tell us more about them."

What followed was a long littany of economic issues regarding public safety that caused such high taxes in Jensi City itself. This burden, plus taxes collected by the Empress was becoming opressive to local businesses, and especially to The House of Fangzi-yin. "Declaring us an Economic Development Zone can greatly reduce this burden, if it is passed by our Congress," said Quantou.

"On the other hand, one can argue that your security force is excessively large," said Huomeng. "You could accomplish the same thing by establishing a garrison of Moshuguang elite troops here at the expense of our Empress. All the other cities have done this."

"The people here might see that as control from outside the city," said Quantou, then flushed. "We're so isolated, you see, so far from the other population centers, and our growth has been quite rapid."

"You have isolated yourselves from Shanji, sir," said Mengmoshu. "It is not the other way around. Jensi is a city like any other, a part of the Empire. The intent of our Empress is to meet the needs of all her people, without favoritism being shown, and it seems to her that's what you're seeking."

"That is not so," said Quantou, "but our needs are special."

"No more so than Wanchou," said Huomeng. "Their population and problems are both more diverse than yours, and even Dahe is having complex problems during its incorporation. I must tell you that even if Congress passes the bill declaring special status for Jensi City it will be vetoed by our Empress."

Quantou looked distressed. "There are people here who will be quite unhappy when they hear that. We thought she would understand."

"So why don't you meet with her, and solicit her help in other ways? We have just made one suggestion to you," said Huomeng.

Quantou was fighting for self control. Inside, he was terrified by how his fiscal masters in The House of Fangzi-yin might react to the news. The name Sheng-chih was prominent in his mind.

"It is an excellent idea," he said. "We must arrange for such a meeting in the near future, and in the city so she can meet with the people who bear the heaviest burdens of our taxes. I will send an invitation to her at once."

Mengmoshu nodded sagely, and Huomeng smiled. "Good, and politically wise, I think. She will see your problems first hand, and will undoubtedly respond to them. In a month, perhaps? No more than two. I think it's best if we move quickly on this," said Huomeng.

"I will suggest a time within the week," said Quantou, now smiling himself. "Suddenly I'm quite excited about the possibilities." Indeed, as he said it, it seemed that a kind of pressure had been released from his mind, and thinking was clear again.

After lunch, the limousine picked them up again and there was more driving to see outlying factories and research laboratories, especially a new one concerned with composite building materials of carbon super-fiber and polymer. It was near dusk when they returned to a hotel where they would spend a night before leaving early in the morning for home. Their goodbyes were said in the limousine, and Quantou seemed in good humor when they left him with the promise of another visit in the near future.

They went to their second floor suite of two rooms plush carpeted and furnished, and large windows looking out at green hills. A meal was sent up to them. They ate in silence, then Houmeng placed a call to his wife and Empress. The call would seen quite short to any listening ears, but it was to the point.

"We've had a productive time, dear. What we've learned should please you, and alleviate many of your concerns. Quantou is doing his best with what he has, and he'll be inviting you here for a meeting to clear up any misunderstandings. Yes, we're quite impressed by the man. We should be back at mid-day tomorrow. I miss you, darling. Promise you'll be in my dreams tonight. Goodbye."

Message passed, Huomeng showered while Mengmoshu went through his slow and methodic preparations for bed. When he was finished, Huomeng noticed the flowers he'd received that day had already begun to wilt. He filled a glass with water, removed a band holding the stems of the flowers together.

A piece of paper had been rolled around the stem of a flower, and fell to the table as he moved to place the flowers in the water.

There was handwriting on the paper in a tiny neat script. Houmeng read it to himself.

'Lao-sun is dead. The others are slaves
in a logging operation north of here. The
police have destroyed our church and are
searching for all of us. We plan a major
demonstration to support our church and the
freedom Empress Kati gave to the people.
PLEASE HELP US!'

Huomeng showed the note to Mengmoshu, who read it silently, then crumpled it up into a little ball and popped it into his mouth, swallowing it.

"I'm tired. I'm going to bed," said Mengmoshu.

"Good idea. I'm not used to rising before sunrise, and this has been a rather productive day," said Huomeng.

Each climbed into his own bed, and lights were turned out. Mengmoshu was truly tired, and fell asleep in minutes, lightly snoring. Huomeng closed his eyes, and waited.

Waited for her coming.

And minutes later, she was there.

Huomeng. The lady of your dreams is here.

I'm not dreaming yet, but your father is asleep.

Father, wake up! It's Kati!

Mengmoshu grumbled; snoring ceased as he turned over onto his side. *Make it quick. I'm very tired from today.*

So, what do you have for me? asked Kati from her place in the gong-shi-jie.

It's not good, said Huomeng, and then he told her about the note in the flowers, and everything else he'd seen, searched and heard that day. *I only had brief opportunities to probe Quantou, but Mengmoshu was quite busy with it.*

Do you feel badly about it, father? asked Kati.

At first, yes, but then I got to know the man. A powermonger if ever I saw one, but he has masters. He answers to a man named Sheng-chih.

Quantou is clever, though, and has his own agenda. He sees himself as governor of a new state on Shanji, said Huomeng.

He also sees his police force as an army, but it's small. We could easily overwhelm them with a few hundred troops, Kati, said Mengmoshu.

We have no reasons for military action, father.

We might have them soon. There will be other demonstrations. We could send troops in the interest of public safety, said Huomeng.

Not without invitation, said Kati. Then, *In the case of police brutality, of course, I would be compelled to take action. Does that satisfy you?*

How do we know if there's brutality? No information gets out of the city, said Mengmoshu.

I have my own conduits, said Kati.

I could garrison my troops at Congress Center. They could be here within an hour if the need arises, said Mengmoshu, pressing.

We'll talk about it when you get home, father. In the meantime, Yesui is ready to play her role again. She seems to be having fun with it.

As long as she stays close to home, said Huomeng.

I miss you, dears. Hurry back. I'll be at the flyer field to meet you.

And she was gone.

Mengmoshu was snoring again in minutes, but Huomeng remained awake for a while. His stomach turned over uneasily as scenarios flashed in and out of his mind. He went to sleep with a final, inevitable conclusion there.

A military confrontation was coming to Jensi City, and soon.

Tirgee and Mengjai led their horses to cool beneath a stand of *Tysk*, and tethered them there. The little grove of trees was surrounded on four sides by the sloping walls and plas-roofs of hydroponic cells and there was a pond in the center, with benches used by workers during their lunch hours. But it was nearing dusk, and the workers had gone home, leaving behind a small crew to tend the growing lights throughout the night. Tirgee and Mengjai would spend the night with them before the final leg of their journey the next day, back to the chaos of the city. They had been gone for six days this time, to inspect useage rates and well flows for all the new farms in what had once been the southern mining district.

Mengjai sat down heavily at the base of a *Tysk* and leaned against it. "I can't believe I've ridden so far again today," he said.

Tirgee smiled down at him. "You're getting good at it, Mengjai. I think you even like it."

"I guess I do," said Mengjai. He reached out his hand for Tirgee's as she sat down beside him. She leaned against him, and sighed.

"So quiet, so peaceful," she murmured.

"Yes," he said, and squeezed her hand. "No complications. Just earth, sky and water."

Tirgee's leathers creaked as she turned to nestle tighter against him. "And us," she said.

Mengjai smiled, and cupped her chin in his hand.

"And us," he whispered, then kissed her.

Sixteen

Yesui was sitting on the edge of the bed when the twins awoke.

The girls had been lying side-by-side on their backs, hands clasped, their usual position when going to wherever it was the Lady of their dreams took them. They opened their eyes simultaneously, looked up at her and smiled.

"Mother. How long have you been here?" they asked together.

"Only a few minutes. I hope I didn't disturb you," said Yesui.

"Oh, no," said Shaan-diann. "Our work is done for the day."

"It is a very slow process," said Bao-shi. She reached over and took her mother's hand softly in hers. "You were watching us."

"Yes," said Yesui, and squeezed Bao's hand.

"Does it seem like we're sleeping when we're gone?" asked Bao.

"A deep sleep. Sometimes your eyelids move, as if you're dreaming."

"We're not dreaming," said Shaan-diann.

"I know," said Yesui.

"You sound sad, Mother," said Bao.

"Do I? I don't think I am. But I think of you both when you're away. I wish I could be there with you, but you go where I cannot. When you were little I imagined taking you to the gong-shi-jie and showing you all its wonders, but now someone else is doing it."

"Lady hasn't given a name to the place she takes us, but it's not like the gong-shi-jie you've described to us before," said Bao.

"I think it's a part of that place I could only glimpse. My own tutor, a Chuang-shi I called 'Mind', gave me a test, but I failed it. The place was so small, so flickering; I could not get close enough to really see what was there."

Shaan-diann frowned. "You never ask us what we do there, Mother."

179

Yesui smiled. "I want to know, but to ask questions might be to interfere with your Lady's work, and I made a promise to First Mother not to do that."

"Lady won't mind if you ask. She says she knows you," said Bao.

"Yes, I think she does," said Yesui softly. "That's what frightens me a little. There, you see? I shouldn't have said that." Yesui squeezed Bao's hand hard, and tears welled up in her eyes.

Shaan reached over to join hands with her sister's and mother's. "There's nothing to be afraid of. Lady says we're helping her to create a new universe, and what danger can there be? The new universe will go to another place we can't see, and we'll be here."

Yesui blinked rapidly. "Of course," she said, and sniffled. "I'm being silly again, worrying over nothing. I'm sure your Lady would never do anything to hurt you." She wiped her eyes dry with a hand.

"I really came to tell you I won't be home tomorrow, but I"ll be in the city if you need me. Your father knows where I'll be, but outside of our family it's a secret."

The girls brightened. "Will you wear that funny wig again?" asked Bao.

"And those glasses?" added Shaan. "How can you see through those things?"

Yesui laughed. "Oh, *you*! You're as bad as your father. I can *never* feel you in my mind. I'll be gone a day, maybe two. Don't you *dare* tell anyone what I look like!"

Yesui tickled both of them, and they wrestled on the bed, ending it when she kissed them on their cheeks and stood up to look lovingly down at them.

"Miss me," she said. "I'm so proud of you both, and I promise not to worry so much when you're with your Lady. Tell her that for me, and tell her that I love you both more than life."

Yesui left the room, and the twins grinned at each other.

"She's very emotional," said Bao-shi.

"She certainly is," said Shaan-diann, "but I'm still going to tell Lady what Mother said."

The medication was not working, though he was groggy from its side-effects. Sweat continued boiling from his forehead, and his handkerchief had become soaked while he waited for the interview.

Tuen did not travel well.

And Sheng-chih had implied he might be killed if he said too much. This only told him his position along the food chain of Fangzi-yin.

The flight to Wanchou had been long and hot, and then there was a nauseating hop over mountains to the City of Mengnu. He'd presented his summons to a Moshuguang trooper who was there to meet him and escort him to the Ministry. They'd gone up to the third floor, the office of Minister Shui. The summons was recorded by a secretary, and the trooper left Tuen there under her watchful eyes. The more she looked at him the more he sweated.

"Are you ill?" she finally asked.

"The flight over the mountains was rather turbulent," he said. "My stomach is upset. Will I have to wait much longer?"

The secretary, a grey-haired woman with a kind face, rummaged in her desk while she spoke into a telephone.

"He's been here for over an hour. Will it be soon? Ah —I'll tell him."

She gave him two large white tablets. "Chew them slowly. They will help your stomach. The accountants have arrived and it'll be a few minutes, now. This is all routine, sir. Please try to relax."

"Thank you," he said, and ground the chalky tablets between his teeth.

His stomach did not have time to settle before an inner office door opened and a tall man with a long face came out to greet him with a handshake.

"I am Xun-su, sir. Sorry for the delay. Please come in."

Tuen followed him into a small plain office with a desk and a large conference table, at which a tiny woman sat with a mound of papers and accounting books in front of her.

"This is Huan-le, our chief accountant," said Xun-su.

"Please sit," she said, and motioned him to a chair across from her.

The woman did not look old enough to be chief of anything. She had the features of a child, with short-cut black hair framing her face, and her eyes were magnified by the thick glasses she wore.

Tuen sat down. Liquid oozed from his handkerchief as he squeezed it in his lap.

Huan-le smiled faintly. "I must first apologize for not sending a notice of your audit, sir. The fault is mine."

Tuen nodded, glanced at Xun-su, who'd seated himself at the end of the table to study an accounting ledger and seemed to be apart from the conversation.

"I was surprised, of course," said Tuen. "I was even more surprised when I received a summons. What is the problem?"

"Your clients, sir," said Huan-le, and peered over her glasses at him. "For the record, are you a financial advisor for Fangzi-yin in the City of Jensi?"

"I am."

"And do you include among your clients the noble families of Shiang, Ganzing and Nanbian?"

"I do, and several other noble families as well."

"We're concerned about these three only," said Huan-le, and reached across the table to hand him a single page covered with columns of numbers.

"Our audit concerns the noble families who have land grants pending according to their investments. We've been correlating these numbers with those claimed for tax deductions and actual withdrawels from their accounts. You will see that there are discrepancies in the totals for each of your clients. Investments for land grants exceed tax deductions by four and a half million Yuan for those three families alone, and that is only for one year. We want to know why that is."

Tuen made a show of studying the figures. "Yes, I see the discrepancies, but we don't handle taxes for any of our clients. Perhaps the criteria they've used for deductions are incorrect."

"You think they've neglected millions of Yuan in tax credits? Please, sir, the nobles are not stupid people, and they have experienced accountants." Huan-le laughed softly, took off her glasses to rub her eyes, then put them back on again and squinted at him.

"Any other ideas?" she asked.

Tuen's stomach was knotted in distress, and his arm pits were soaking wet. "Not at all. I assure you our accounting of their investments is correct."

"I'm not questioning that," said Huan-le.

"You're not? Then why am I here?"

"To verify, in person, the accuracy of your accounting, and you have just done that. Perhaps you can also offer me some advice."

Huan-le leaned over her stack of documents, and spoke softly, her gaze suddenly intense. He felt drawn to her, as if she were a trusting client taking him into her confidence.

"There are multiple scenarios here. First, your records are correct, and your clients have stupidly neglected millions in tax credits. I think we can dismiss that one."

Tuen felt coolness on his forehead. His sweating had ceased, and he was amazed. The fact that he was suddenly calm was even more amazing to him, under the circumstances.

"Second, your accounts are correct, the nobles have reported accurate tax credits and lied about investment credits for land grants. Also foolish, and easy for us to spot. Do you see my logic?"

Tuen nodded numbly, feeling a strange internal peace in his mind.

"Third, other investors have contributed funds to the nobles for land grant claims and written those off for tax purposes, while the nobles have accurately reported their own deductions. This, of course, is not legal. We've searched and searched, and can find no such write-offs by independent investors."

Tuen struggled to clear an intrusive fog in his mind as he suddenly saw what his inquisitor was leading up to. He blinked rapidly.

"Fourth, and this is my favorite, there is only one outside investor, who uses the nobles' own money to buy a portion of the land grants they receive. This is done by skimming off half of their returns on other investments and then transfering the money to other accounts in direct payment for a share of the land grants. Transfers are internal, and no taxes are paid. All quite neat, I must say. Also illegal."

Huan-le stood up, and leaned over the table to look at him closely. Her eyes seemed to glow.

"I'm refering, of course, to The House of Fangzi-yin," she said.

A part of him wanted to scream. Another part urged him to run. The body received the signals, but there was no response, other than a shudder. He was hallucinating, for now Huan-le's eyes *were* glowing a fluorescent blue as she leaned even closer to him.

"Where are the records of your transfer accounts, sir? Whatever have you done with them? Hmmm?"

Tuen's mind whirled madly with memories associated with her question, her glowing eyes locked on his with terrifying intensity.

"I — I have nothing to say. This is — is all nonsense," he stammered.

"We want the records, and you will obtain them for us. In return, we will keep you out of prison and allow you the wealth you've already accumulated. Only *your* records, not Sheng-chih's or the others. We'll get those on our own."

"I — I can't. I won't," he gasped.

"Dear sir, I can call your superior right now and say you've told us everything. Within a day, I imagine, you'll be a dead man. *Or*, I can spare your life, call all your clients and tell them how much you skim off the top of their investments. You will then be alive, but you'll never work in your profession again and you can look forward to a lifetime of civil suits. There are three options, you see. And the choice is yours to make."

Huan-le stood up straight. The glow of her eyes faded, and was gone as Tuen's mind ceased its chaotic whirling. He was suddenly sweating again.

"Sheng-chih will kill me. I don't want to die," whined Tuen.

"We want your records, not your life," said Huan-le. "It will be a risk for you, but here's what we want you to do."

And she told him what it was.

It was well after dark when Tuen returned to The House of Fangzi-yin. A few windows were lighted in the upper floors, but it was likely only cleaning crews working there. Sheng-chih kept an apartment for himself, a penthouse suite on the thirty-second floor, but rarely used it.

It was ten o'clock when Tuen entered the building, the hard soles of his shoes striking the marble floor with audible clicks that echoed from the walls. The armed guard at the reception desk looked up at him, smiled and pushed a clipboard with attached sheet of paper across the counter to him.

"I'm just picking up something," said Tuen. "My clients will be charged if I sign in, and I'll only be a few minutes. Please."

The guard nodded, and withdrew the clipboard, looking disappointed. And as he entered the elevator, Tuen looked back and saw the guard still watching him.

A few minutes, that's all he had. Sweat was pouring into his eyes as he got out on the tenth floor, walked the few steps to his office and let himself in. He locked the door behind him. A baseboard night light was on in the outer office. He turned it off, groped his way to the inner office door, his hand slippery on the door latch.

Safely inside, door closed again, he fumbled his way to his desk and turned on the lamp there. Quickly, now. His personal machine was in the lower right hand drawer of the desk. He got it out, along with a blank cube, plugged in the modem, then down-loaded the transfer files and re-labeled them. Made a copy on the cube, and removed it. How long? One minute? Two? His wet fingers flew over the keyboard. He went to E-mail, put in the address Huan-le had given him, and sent her the re-labeled files in seconds.

During the sending, a faint sound had registered in his brain, but he ignored it in his haste.

Tuen erased both the original transfer files and their copy from his hard drive. He made a label for the cube, and was pasting it on when there was another sound, much louder this time.

The door to his office opened.

"Back so soon? I didn't expect you until morning."

Sheng-chih stood in the doorway, a smirk on his face.

Tuen's mind moved with rehearsed clarity.

"This is for you, a copy of my transfer files for your safe. I've just erased the files from my hard drive, but I want my machine destroyed in the morning anyway, just to be sure."

"Tuen, you're sweating again, and most profusely. Whatever is the matter with you?" asked Sheng-chih in a condescending tone.

"They know, Shen-chih. They know someone is helping the nobles to obtain land grants. They accused us of doing what we're actually doing, but it has to be a guess. They have no proof, and I denied everything, but then they threatened to confiscate all my files. Now there is nothing for them to retrieve. This is the only copy."

He handed the cube to Sheng-chih, who took it and rolled it over in his hand. "So you've acted quickly to remove possible evidence," he said softly.

"Of course. We're safe, now, Sheng-chih. There are no fund transfers for them to find."

Sheng-chih stepped over to the desk and fingered the wire leading from computer to modem. "Then what is *this* for?"

"I was preparing to enter your calendar to schedule a meeting for tomorrow," said Tuen.

"On your personal machine?"

"It was turned on, and convenient," said Tuen, his burst of panic now subsiding.

"No need for that. We can go to my office right now, and discuss what happened to you at the Ministry." Sheng-chih put a hand on his shoulder, and patted it. "You've been through a great deal, and I want to hear all about it."

"Yes, Sheng-chih, as you wish."

Sheng-chih put an arm around his shoulders and guided him from the room without bothering to turn off the desk lamp.

Out of the outer office darkness, two men stepped forward. In desk lamp light coming over Tuen's shoulder, something flashed in the hand of one of the men.

"Goodbye, Tuen," said Sheng-chih.

Tuen screamed once, and then could only make a strangled bubbling sound.

Nothing was heard beyond the tenth floor of the building.

Seventeen

Warnings

Yesugen only added to Kati's worries when she called to her from the gong-shi-jie.

I could have contacted Yesui directly, but with all the trouble you're having I thought you should hear me first. It's not urgent, but we need Yesui to jump another ship for us.

Kati had just gone to bed, and Huomeng was bathing. It was well past midnight, and they'd sat for hours discussing their strategies in Jensi City.

She wasn't expecting another jump for months, said Kati.

That was the schedule, but Mengjai has requested we move it up. He's heard about your difficulties and wants to see his mother again. It has been a while.

It certainly has, said Kati, then paused. Yesugen — is he happy there?

Yes. His work is going well, Kati; it's a great service to us. We're quite pleased by what he's done so far. We're discovering new aquifers every week, it seems, but now their connections must be mapped and more sensitive equipment is required. Mengjai will obtain that while he visits you.

Ah, so he's not just coming to see his mother, said Kati.

He misses you very much, Kati, said Yesugen. He talks about you all the time, especially since he heard about the revolutionaries you're dealing with. He's concerned about it, and so am I.

There's no revolution on Shanji, said Kati indignantly.

Yesui calls it that. She talks to Tirgee, and then I hear it. Perhaps there was a misinterpretation. Actually it's Tirgee who asked me to call and request Yesui's time in jumping the ship. Tirgee is qualified to do it, but she's terrified of making the jump with Mengjai on board. Her confidence is not what it should be, and she simply refuses to do it.

I'll have Yesui call you when she returns, said Kati, and you can arrange the jump time with her.

They were two women, talking from places of vastly different dimensionalities, yet their minds were as one. Two mothers, Empresses, and first level Chuang-shi, their bond allowed nothing to be hidden, and Kati anticipated Yesugen's question before it was asked.

You have another concern? asked Yesugen.

Yes, said Kati, unsure whether it was the proper time to pursue the matter. It would be better, perhaps, to do it face-to-face in the gong-shi-jie.

A mother's concern, said Yesugen. You'll feel better if you express it directly. We've known each other for a long time, Kati.

I know, Yesugen, but I don't want to offend you, and my concern involves your daughter.

It was silly to hesitate, for Yesugen could already see the concern that was there.

Say it, Kati, said Yesugen.

It's Tirgee and Mengjai. I've sensed a great deal of affection between them.

We are all quite fond of Mengjai. He is a fine young man, said Yesugen.

He's not so young, much older than Tirgee, but I think it's your daughter who draws Mengjai to Meng-shi-jie for such long periods of time. I think their relation has passed simple affection and turned into love. That is what concerns me.

There was a long agonizing pause.

You see? I've offended you, said Kati.

Not at all, said Yesugen. It's a concern I also had when Tirgee first told me about her feelings, and that was three years ago. I have dismissed it, Kati. Why should we fear love between out children?

But why Mengjai? I'm sure Tirgee could have any man she wished for on Meng-shi-jie.

One of her own kind? asked Yesugen.

I didn't mean it that way!

I think you did, Kati. You're forgetting the Tumatsin, the Moshuguang, all are descended from my people. We are closer to you than the Hansui in many ways. You and I are even closer. Through our mothers we are Chuang-shi. In the old times, a match between our children would have been considered ideal to continue our lines, but I want you to know that's not what's hap-

pening here. I've neither discouraged or encouraged their relationship. It has developed on its own.

I'm not accusing you of intrigue, Yesugen, said Kati. I'm only concerned with lasting happiness for my son. I want the love in his life to be real.

I want the same for Tirgee, said Yesugen, then, Why don't you talk to Yesui about it? I had this conversation with her over a year ago, and she wasn't as diplomatic as you. But she works closely with Tirgee, and knows the girl's inner-self better than I can. Yesui has come to share my views on the relationship, and has expressed no recent concerns to me. Ask her opinion.

I will, said Kati. I appreciate your openness, Yesugen. You've allowed me to sense much you haven't said.

And also from you, said Yesugen. You have much to worry about, Kati. Do not be discouraged. In any political system, regardless of fairness, there will always be corruption and dissent to deal with. You and I are different in our methods, but I'm sure you'll find the best way for Shanji. My only concern is that you remain in power. I will not allow what we've built to be torn apart by a corrupt few. But I doubt you'll need my help in correcting the problem. Remember the war, Kati, the war I remember so well from a time when we were enemies, not friends. When you will it, no foe can stand up to you. The energy of creation is at your command.

Only as a last resort, said Kati, but thank you for the encouragement. I'll have Yesui get in touch with you as soon as she arrives.

The matrix of purple stars winked out — and Yesugen was gone.

Kati opened her eyes. Huomeng was warm at her side, his arm draped gently across her stomach. She turned her head and saw he was awake, watching her.

"I only caught the last of it," he said. "Did you ask for advice about Jensi?"

"No, it was something else. We talked about Mengjai and Tirgee," she said, and stroked his forearm.

"Oh," said Huomeng softly.

"Mengjai wants to come home for a visit, but Yesui has to jump the ship because Tirgee is afraid to do it."

"With Mengjai on board," said Huomeng.

"Yes. He needs some new instruments, but I think it's an excuse to see us again. It sounded urgent."

"Perhaps he has something important to tell us," said Huomeng, and ran his hand lightly over her stomach.

"But what?"

Huomeng kissed her shoulder. "I think you know what it is."

She rolled against him, and cuddled. "There are times, like now, when it seems everything is falling apart, and I have no control over anything," she murmured.

"Not everything," he whispered. "There's us, my sweet. We are the one constant."

"Yes," she said, and kissed him softly.

They fell asleep peacefully in each others' arms.

Rani-Tan folded her hands serenely over her chest as the two men glowered at her from the other side of the conference table in her office.

"We're trying to understand your position, Madam," said Peng, a most senior representative with twelve years in office. "Exactly what is it that you hold against Jensi City?"

Rani paused for a few seconds, as if thinking, then said, "If anything, it's your elitist attitude, sir, and the attitudes of those you represent. Jensi is our finest example of economic progress, but it's as much a part of Shanji as any other city. It is not a separate state, and I see it heading in that direction."

Peng thumped his fist lightly on the table to show his indignation. "That is blatant nonsense. Declaring Jensi an Economic Development Zone would have resulted in industrial expansion planet-wide, not just in the city. There was no favoritism involved, or intended. Your accusations in debate were totally false."

"The others didn't see it that way, sir. The vote was not even close, and the division was clear. There was your delegation and the nobles on one side, and the rest of Shanji on the other. That division will remain until Jensi sees itself as only another part of the Empire," she said calmly.

"Paaa," said Peng, spitting rudely. "Empire, indeed. Jensi is the hub, the commercial center of Shanji while Mengnu sits in her bubbled city and collects taxes from us without giving anything in return. Now she opposes our progress, young woman. It is she who pulls your strings. You are, after all, a Tumatsin."

Rani's face flushed, and the reaction of her eyes was beyond her control. Both Peng and Tuzi drew back, momentarily startled by the sudden color change of those eyes.

"I'm loyal to both my Empress and her Empire, which includes the people I represent. Our Congress represents the whole empire and they have cast their vote. Learn from it, sir," she growled, and felt some pressure in her upper mouth. She breathed deeply to control herself. To see The Change come upon her would only make these men see her as more alien than they already did.

Tuzi waved a paper at her. "We are immediately withdrawing Bill 1016. There will be no mag-rail extension to the south, and no new benefits for the Tumatsin. Jensi trade with your people will be stopped as of today. Perhaps the Tumatsin will see their error in choosing you to represent them."

Rani felt calm again. "The mag-rail extension *was* of interest to me, but my people don't want it. You only simplify my work. As to trade with Jensi, it has been minimal, and there's more than enough market for our meager goods in Wanchou. So withdraw your bill. It will allow time for me to introduce two of my own, and I intend to do so next week."

She withdrew two pieces of paper from a file in front of her, and pushed them across the table. "I show these to you first because they have a direct impact on Jensi City," she said.

Peng and Tuzi scanned the pages together, eyes widening as she continued.

"Bill 1027 establishes the Yuan as the single currency for exchange on Shanji. All other currencies are forbidden, including your Jensi-yuan. One Empire, one currency.

"Bill 1028 limits local police to one officer per thousand population. A police force is not an army, gentlemen. Shanji has the Moshuguang for such purpose. This allows roughly a hundred officers for Jensi City; I believe your present number is closer to a thousand, and growing each month. You complain about taxes, but waste money on a police force in excess of your needs. I assure you the other cities will see no problems with these bills, so I will not ask for your support of them."

Peng lost control, and exploded with rage. He wadded the two sheets of paper into balls and threw them at her, striking her in the chest. His face turned a strange color, a tinge of blue as he stood and leaned over the table. Tuzi looked frightened, and grabbed at his arm. Rani winced, and looked at him in amazement.

"You — you TUMATSIN!" screamed Peng. "You PAWN of Mengnu! Haven't you read any history? There was once an Emperor of Shanji, and he opposed all change. For this, he was thrown out, and now it's happening all over again. If your beloved Mengnu can't see what she's doing, then she should step down or be removed like her predecessor! What's happening to the economic backbone of our planet can *not* be allowed to continue!"

There was terrible pressure in her mouth, and The Change was upon her. The men jumped back as she stood. Tuzi pulled at Peng's arm, dragging him towards the door.

Rani's voice was deep, and gutteral. "Your words are dangerous, sir. They imply treason."

Tuzi shook his head and pushed Peng towards the door. "He's upset. Please don't —"

"If you hear treason in my words, then run and tell your Empress!" screamed Peng, and Tuzi pushed him out the door, slamming it behind him.

Screaming in the outer office, then silence.

Rani sat down hard in her chair, and put her face in her hands. "Oh, Mother, now I've done it. I've really done it this time," she moaned.

The door opened again, and Cela peeked inside.

"Are you all right, Madam?" she asked, and then Rani looked at her.

"Oh, I guess not. You look like you're ready for war," said Cela.

"I think I just started one," said Rani, breathing deeply again to reverse The Change.

"Well, you *did* make an impression," said Cela, then, "You have a call from your friend in Jensi City. He's been holding for the last fifteen minutes and says it's important. Should I put him through?"

"Yes, right away," said Rani. She went to her desk and reached it as the telephone rang one time.

"Mister X," she said. "Good morning."

There was a soft chuckle at the other end of the line. "I sound mysterious," he said.

"The man without a name," she said. "Do you have some news for me?"

It was the man who'd helped her at the Jensi City terminal when she'd come to Congress Center to begin her term in office. Only a week after she'd arrived, he'd called to tell her new developments in

Jensi, and had been calling regularly since that time. At first she'd been cautious, thinking he could be a Jensi agent assigned to track her activities, but over the months she'd come to trust his information which she immediately passed on to Empress Mengnu. Whoever this man was, he seemed highly placed; he went everywhere in Jensi and his knowledge of the inner-workings of both City Hall and The House of Fangzi-yin was acute.

"Several things," he said. "There have been more arrests, people plucked right from the street, and some demonstrators in front of City Hall were beaten and taken away. I think now the church people will have sense enough to stay underground. Then there is Tuen, a top-level accountant of Fangzi-yin. He went to Mengnu City to be audited, and has mysteriously disappeared. Has he been arrested by the government?"

"I'll ask," said Rani, taking notes.

"Otherwise he's likely dead," said X. "Things are heating up here. The mayor has called for a rally against the negative vote on special status for Jensi. Congressional representatives will be here for it. Do not, I repeat, do *not* come here under any circumstances. Your face is known here; it's on posters all over the city, along with Mengnu's. You are the enemy, Madam. There is talk that Quantou will call for Jensi to sever ties with Mengnu and establish a separate state unless she agrees to their terms."

"I'm not surprised," said Rani.

"Then get Mengnu to move *now* before separatism catches fire with the general populace. I can't talk anymore, and this could be my last contact with you. I've been recalled; my company is pulling its branch office out of Jensi. The same is happening to Dahe companies. None of us want to be caught up in this mess."

"You have my thanks and our Empress' for the information you've provided," said Rani.

"I support her as much as you do, but she frustrates me," said X. "She sits and waits when she should be moving to restore order here, throw out the separatists and bring The House of Fangzi-yin down with them."

She had never heard him so emotional. "I'll pass all of this on to her right away. Take care for your own safety. Maybe I'll have the chance to know your real name someday."

"Maybe," said X, and hung up.

Rani sat thinking for a moment, then picked up the telephone again, punched three numbers and stopped. She picked up a file and went to the outer office. Cela and Tanzin looked at her with concern, though The Change was no longer upon her.

"Tell anyone who asks that I was feeling ill and went home. If they hear of it, the Honorables Peng and Tuzi might feel better about their morning here."

"You're all right?" asked Tanzin.

"I'm fine," said Rani, "but I have something to do. I'll be in again tomorrow morning."

She left her office, went back to the dormitory and up to her room. She called the palace on her secured line, but Mengnu was in conference and could not be disturbed. Two hours later, as arranged, she called again. Her Empress answered the call at the first ring, and they talked for over an hour.

"Have I moved too fast?" she asked. "My new bills will only inflame the situation. I could delay introducing them if you wish."

"Do not delay," said Mengnu. "That will only show weakness, and encourage them. I will take the necessary steps, Rani, and it will be painful. Military action seems likely, so stay where you are and be careful. These people are capable of anything."

With that, she was gone.

Rani ate dinner by herself in the dormitory that night, and quickly retired to her room. She went to sleep at ten, and was startled awake well after midnight.

The scream of many turbines rattled the windows of her room.

She looked outside and saw hundreds of flickering lights descending towards the flyer field west of Congress Center. More passed overhead, and her window rattled again.

It is worse than I imagined, she thought, and went back to bed again.

We're nearly finished, said Lady.

How can you tell? asked Bao and Shaan together.

The dimple's neck is nearly closed off, and the dimple itself is a nearly perfect sphere. It's important the symmetry be exact. Notice how the little waves running around on its surface are beginning to interfere with each other?

There are little crests and troughs, said Shaan.

I must wait for the exact moment when there is only a single crest, and that is when the new universe will be born. Do you remember all I've taught you so far?

Yes, said the twins.

Do you think you could do it on your own?

Right now? asked Bao.

No, but could you do it after I'm gone?

If we had trouble with it, couldn't we ask you for help? asked Shaan.

When the new universe is born, I will go with it and there will be no way for me to return.

So we can't go with you? said Bao.

I am pure energy, and you are not, except for the part of you that is here, said Lady.

Then we COULD go with you, said Shaan.

You are young, with long lives ahead of you before transfiguration into my form. Your day for creating a new universe of your own will come, but it will not be now. There are other things First Mother would have you do, and you have so far only seen the smallest of things here in the place of creation. When I'm gone there will be another Lady to teach you the whole of this place.

But we're going to miss you, said Bao.

Your mother would miss you even more if you went with me.

Our bodies would die, said Bao.

No, but the essence of Bao and Shaan would be gone from them. To your mother, you would be like people locked deep within themselves, without reactions or personalities. That is worse than death.

We understand now, Bao and Shaan said together, though Shaan in particular seemed disappointed.

Good, said Lady. She paused. There is one more thing I must teach you before I go. It requires your special gifts in seeing these higher dimensionalities, and the Lady who comes after me will not be able to help you with that part of it. I will teach you how to make tiny versions of the huge mass we've been working with. Do you know the word 'nucleation'?

Like dust for forming rain drops, said Bao.

Something for molecules to grab onto, said Shaan.

Yes. The large is made from the small; a galaxy, a cluster of stars, a single sun, even a planet can begin at a single point if sufficient mass is there to begin with. I will show you how to make that mass, and it's a small version of what we've been doing here.

Yes, show us! said the twins excitedly.

Another time, said Lady, but it will be soon. There is little time left for me. When I'm gone I'll miss you both very much. I will miss all the Chuang-shi I've known in this universe.

A feeling of great sadness was suddenly there.

Go, now. Your mother is waiting again. She worries over what might happen to you. Tell her that she and I will meet soon in the place of creation.

Lady's presence faded, was gone as the cluster of golden stars appeared and swirled around them, drawing them back to themselves in the usual rush.

They awoke on their bed, and Mother was sitting there, looking down at them. Tears gushed from their eyes, and both girls began crying softly when they saw her.

"What's wrong?" asked Mother, and stroked their cheeks.

"The new universe is ready to be born, and Lady will be *leaving* us!" they sobbed together.

"Oh sweets," said Mother, and bit her lip. There was a strange mix of fear and relief in her mind.

"She says if we went with her we couldn't come back, that our bodies would be like —"

"Shhhh, Bao," said Mother, and now *her* eyes brimmed with tears. "It's not something I want to think about."

"But Lady will be *alone* in the new universe, with nobody to talk to," sobbed Shaan-diann.

Mother caressed their foreheads with a warm hand. "They will come in time. In any universe the Chuang-shi are eventually there to work with their First Mother. To your Lady it will not seem a long time, believe me."

"Are you sure?" asked the twins simultaneously.

"Absolutely," said Mother, smiling, and wiping their tears away with a finger.

"Our lessons aren't over yet," said Bao, and then she told her mother what they would be doing.

Mother's brows knitted in thought. "Condensation centers. How interesting. Seeds for the formation of planets, even stars."

She laughed. "If I could do that I would have had a much easier time with Lan-sui."

"You've done so much, and we haven't even started," said Shaan. "We haven't done anything on our own."

"We don't know enough, yet," said Bao, "but Lady says someone else will come to teach us when she's gone."

Mother looked startled. "Who is it?" she asked.

"Lady didn't say," said Shaan, "but it sounds like we have a lot more to learn."

"Oh," said Mother, and the twins felt a sudden, new sadness within her.

"Ask her," said Bao. "She says she will call you from the place of creation."

Mother nodded, but minutes later she was trying hard to hold back her tears as she left their room.

Eighteen

Plans

There was a knock on the door, and then it opened. Yesui peered around the edge of it.

"Is he here yet?"

"No," said Kati.

"The freighter's in. I called." Yesui came in and sat down on an ebony chair by Kati's desk. "Well, here we go," she said

Kati frowned at her.

"You know what he's going to say, Mother," said Yesui. "Tirgee was so giddy today I couldn't work with her. She's also afraid."

"Afraid?" asked Kati.

"Afraid of what you'll say, the way you'll take it."

"As if I have the power to do anything," said Kati bitterly, and neatly arranged the stack of papers in front of her.

Yesui lowered her eyes and was silent for a moment, then, "He loves you, Mother, very much. Your blessing will be important to him if you give it. If you don't it will only drive him away from us."

"Have you forgotten your own suspicions?" asked Kati.

"Oh, that was years ago. They're all gone. I had a long talk with Yesugen about it, not pleasant, but convincing to me. And Tirgee, well, our minds are one when we work together and the girl is crazy in love with him. I think it's sweet."

Kati sighed. "Then I suppose it will be. That, and everything else going on."

"You have control over those things, Mother," said Yesui.

"I will be seen as a dictator."

"Only by Jensi City. The rest of Shanji is completely behind you, and you know it. Jensi is a rogue. It must be controlled by any means necessary. I've never seen such a mess of corruption. If it were up to me I'd send the Moshuguang in to take control, close down Fangzi-yin and arrest all the corruptors right now before things get hotter."

"And what if Jensi's police resisted you?" asked Kati.

"Shoot them down, use the purple light, whatever. The police are also criminals. I think you're acting with considerable restraint, and nobody appreciates that."

Kati looked solemnly at her daughter. "You've talked to Yesugen about this. You sound like her again."

"Yesugen has kept order on Meng-shi-jie for a long time, Mother, and they still have a democracy there, but nobody doubts her authority or power as Empress. Jensi doubts you, Mother. You're not real to them, and so they feel free to go their own way. They don't know what you're capable of *doing* to them!"

"Ah, yes, the light of creation. I could come in the night and turn Jensi City into a piller of fire," said Kati, her sarcasm dripping.

"Well — that's extreme, but you *could* do it. You know what I mean," said Yesui in defense.

Kati's eyes glowed emerald green, and Yesui raised an eyebrow. "What?" she asked.

"You've never taken a human life, Yesui."

Yesui squirmed a bit in her chair. "Well — maybe. Some ships were reported missing after I destroyed one of the rings around Lan-Sui, but if I killed someone it was by accident."

"You've never brought forth the light to fight an enemy bringing his rifle to bear on you, or seen his face at the instant his body becomes ions. You've never heard the screams of men — of horses, caught in that terrible light."

Yesui lowered her eyes again. "No — I haven't," she murmured.

"My prayer to First Mother is that you will never have to see it," said Kati, "and if you do, it will not be done by me."

"Yesui nodded. "I understand your feelings, Mother. It's just that —"

"I'm doing all I can do. The Moshuguang garrison is in place and ready for action if the need arises. Quantou has personally heard my displeasure over his inflamatory remarks at the Jensi rally and knows I will not meet with him until there is a public apology."

"If it comes, will you *believe* it?" asked Yesui. "He called for your *removal*! And while you wait, the arrests, beatings, corruption, all of it will continue. They grow bolder each day. Why can't you see —"

There was a soft knocking at the door, startling both of them.

"Come!" called Kati.

The door opened, and Mengjai was standing there in his military blues.

"I think I'm interrupting another argument," he said, and smiled.

"Darling!" cried Kati, and quickly rushed to crush him in an embrace.

"Oof," grunted Mengjai, and laughed. "You haven't lost any strength, I see. Where is Tanchun?"

"She hasn't felt well for several days, and I had to insist she get some rest in her room," said Kati.

Yesui joined them and gave her brother a more subdued hug.

"Your timing is flawless," she said.

"Glad to see you, too, sister. How are the twins?"

"Busy creating a new universe," said Yesui, and was gratified by his look of surprise. "I'll tell you about it later, if you can stay long enough."

"I'll be here a week, and then I have to get back home," he said.

Yesui rolled her eyes at him when she saw the stricken look on her mother's face.

"Home? I thought your home was here, Mengjai," said Kati.

Mengjai put an arm warmly around his mother's shoulders. "Let's sit down. I have something for you."

Kati sat in her place. Mengjai pulled up another chair to the desk, sat down and pulled something from his vest pocket. It was a photograph, encased in clear polymer, and showed two people standing by a stone bench fronting a stand of young *Tysk*. One of the people was Mengjai. The other was a woman nearly as tall as he. Her long face was finely chiseled, lips full, nose prominent and arched. Her hair was long and pulled forward to drape down her right chest, a cascade in black. The eyes were deep-set and black as night, giving her an intense imperial look, but her generous mouth was opened in a lovely smile showing short blunt tusks.

Both of them were smiling, holding hands, and they were dressed in black Moshuguang robes.

"That is Tirgee," said Mengjai.

"Oh, Mengjai, she's beautiful," said Kati softly, and studied the photograph a long time before handing it to Yesui.

Yesui looked at it, handed it back to Mengjai. "She doesn't look so young. Somehow, I thought she was smaller than that."

Mengjai again handed the photograph to his mother. "It's for you," he said softly.

Kati grasped the photograph hard, and looked sadly at her son. "A keepsake," she said, then, "I think you have something to tell me, Mengjai."

"Yes," said Mengjai, smiling, then looked at his sister.

"Do you want me to leave?" asked Yesui.

"No, no. I want to tell both of you," he said, then paused.

"Well?" asked Yesui, grinning.

"Tirgee and I are going to be married. It will be a civil ceremony, right after I return to Meng-shi-jie."

There was a long silence. Kati struggled within herself, and fought back tears, while Yesui only grinned and looked at both of them.

"Well, that wasn't so hard, was it?" said Yesui. "It's not a surprise, Mengjai."

"It *isn't*?" he said.

"There's been talk about you two in and out of the gong-shi-jie for years," said Yesui, but Mengjai's eyes were now fixed on his mother.

Kati mustered a resolve of acceptance, stepped around the desk and hugged Mengjai's head to her breast.

"I'm happy for you, dear. She's a lovely woman, and you have my blessings for a long and happy life together."

And then she began to cry. "You'll be living on Meng-shi-jie, of course."

"Yes, but we'll come back for visits; you can be sure of that. Tirgee wants to meet you, and also see Yesui in person."

"She'll think I'm a runt," said Yesui.

Kati sniffled, and sat down again. "So far away," she said. "Was there nothing left here for you, dear? Did you have to go so far to find a life for yourself?"

"Ah," said Mengjai, "so *that's* it. Well yes, I did, but it's not your fault or anyone else's. I've spent half a lifetime here. Working with Yesui on Lan-Sui was an adventure, and then the space program and flying with Father, but it's all finished. There's nothing more for me here, Mother, but I'm not unhappy about the past."

"Things are changing for all of us, Mother," said Yesui.

"They certainly are," said Kati, and then lost control for one instant. "My Empire is in upheaval, and now my only son is leaving!"

Tears gushed, and Kati covered her face with her hands.

"Oh, Mengjai, I didn't mean to say that!"

Mengjai and Yesui came around the desk to hug and comfort her. Mengjai looked at his sister.

"Is it really so bad? I've heard rumors of trouble, enough that Yesugen is concerned."

It's Jensi City," said Yesui. "They're trying to form their own state and we'll probably have to take military action to stop it."

Kati cried harder, her shoulders shuddering, but after a minute or so she suddenly straightened up and was calm again.

She wiped her eyes dry. "Well — that's better. I think I've been needing that. Now sit down again, dear, and tell me all about what you've been doing on Meng-shi-jie."

They talked for nearly an hour, then arranged for supper together when a servant brought them tea and honeycakes.

"Have you seen Tanchun today?" Kati asked the servant.

"No, Madam," said the servant, a chubby woman of middle age. "She has kept to her room."

"I will see her after we're finished here," said Kati to her children. "She has become frail, poor dear, but refuses retirement. I do worry about her; when I was a little girl, a captive, her face was the first friendly one I saw in the palace."

When they were finished talking, Kati set a time for their meal. "Your father and Gong-gong will be *so* surprised by your news," she said.

"Father already knows," said Mengjai. "I saw him in his mountain lab before I came here."

"Oh," said Kati.

"Now it's time for *our* talk," said Yesui, taking her brother by the arm, "and I won't let you eat until you've visited with Bao and Shaan. They've become young ladies, you know, and you can save your talk with Nokai until suppertime."

Yesui escorted her brother out of the room, and the door closed.

Kati was alone again at her desk, the photograph perched in front of her. She picked it up and studied Tirgee's image again.

Such a strong face, she thought. The face of both a Tumatsin and Moshuguang ancestor. The bloodlines will now mix in a new way. Our worlds will now be together in a new way. It is like Yesui and Nokai, such an unlikely match in the beginning, but the two of them overwhelmed by their love for each other. And now the twins, so far beyond me and even Yesui in what they can do. Oh, First Mother, I see your influence in these things. If you have a plan I will not question it. I only ask that my children live happy and fulfilling lives.

Kati placed the photograph on a stand at her bedside, then worked for another three hours at her desk. She returned four land grant applications to their senders, without approval, and signed an order from the Economic Ministry to freeze all assets of The House of Fangzi-yin pending further investigations.

There was another call from Rani-tan. A rally was scheduled in Jensi-City to petition for all ties to Mengnu City to be broken unless the Empress agreed to attend negotiations. And Rani's bills regarding currency and local police were being well received in the Peoples' Congress. The Jensi delegation had walked out during the morning's debate.

Kati bit her lip in resolve, and called Congress City to put the Moshuguang garrison there on full alert. At the end of it she felt dispirited, and exhausted. There could be no true negotiations with separatists, but perhaps the average citizen could be swayed by her appearance in Jensi. Still, she could not allow them to think she'd been forced into it.

Kati was still thinking about this when she left her desk at last. She walked the long corridor to the elevator taking her down one floor to where Tanchun and the other servants kept their rooms.

The odors of food cooking were strong there, for the kitchen was only meters away behind metal doors at the end of the hallway. Tiled floors, white walls and numbered doors. She went to number two, near the elevator, and knocked softly on it.

"Tanchun? It's Mengnu, dear. Are you feeling better? May I come in?"

There was no answer from inside. Kati pressed her ear to the door, and knocked again.

"Tanchun? Can I bring you something?"

Kati pressed the door latch, and the door opened.

The room was small, and windowless. There was a chair by a lamp, a small table and a bed. Tanchun was lying there on her back, dressed in a yellow robe. The only light in the room came from two large candles on metal stands on both sides of the bed. Smoke from smouldering sweetgrass trailed slowly from a green bowl on a small stone altar in one corner of the room.

The walls were unadorned except for photographs pinned there, photographs of the people in Tanchun's life: Weimeng, with Kati as a little girl, then Kati with an infant Yesui, with Mengjai, then a plethora of imperial portraits.

Kati walked to the bed, but Tanchun did not move. "You must eat something, dear. It will give you strength."

Tanchun's eyes were closed, and there was a peaceful serene smile on her face. A greenstone pendent was centered at her throat. Her arms lay relaxed at her sides. One hand was open, and a smooth green stone had fallen out of it onto the bed.

"Wake up, dear," said Kati, and touched Tanchun's cheek.

The skin there was icy cold.

"Oh — Tanchun," sobbed Kati.

The screaming went on for minutes, and Quantou could only sit staring.

"I did what you asked me to do and now you've changed your mind. You're not being fair with me, Sheng-chih," he finally said.

"You egocentric fool!" screamed Sheng-chih, and leaned so close he was spitting on him. His hands opened and closed in spasms and at the moment it would have given him great pleasure to strangle the plump little man where he sat.

"I asked for a rally of support for economic independence, but you couldn't be satisfied with that. You had to be a great revolutionary leader and demand her removal if she refused to negotiate! You have put her in an inferior position, you idiot, and it is you who will correct the error!"

"I am in charge of Jensi City, Sheng-chih, not you," said Quantou.

"I put you in your office and funded your military. Without me, you'd still be selling clothes to rich ladies, but now your stupid tongue has put both of us in jeopardy and invited military action by Mengnu!

Why couldn't you *wait* for negotiations before calling for her abdication? I gave you a complete *plan!*"

"She will not negotiate, Sheng-chih. You know it, and so do I. You've not rallied the peoples' support. I have, and they applauded my call for Mengnu's abdication. We are together. We are a revolutionary state fighting for independence from a distant tyrant. Why hide it any longer? Mengnu moves against us. The freezing of your assets is just another act of war against a sovereign city, and next will come military occupation if we don't fight. There is more than economics at stake here. It is our freedom we fight for!"

Quantou's face flushed red as he said it. His chest puffed up in pride and his eyes blazed with fury.

Sheng-chih looked down at him incredulously. "You are a zealot, a — a revolutionary," he said.

"From the beginning," said Quantou. "Our reasons for independence are not the same, Sheng-chih, but we share the goal. And I am *not* involved with the fiscal irregularities within the House of Fangziyin. I only want our freedom from an absentee ruler."

Sheng-chih was suddenly calm. "And how will you achieve that when Jensi is occupied and you are in prison?"

"Then all the people of Shanji will know Mengnu as the despot she is. Others will rally behind us when they see what can happen to them. It is the beginning of the end for a royal family on this planet," said Quantou.

"In the meantime my troops are deployed, as of early this morning. I have no allusions about overcoming the Moshuguang force she'll send against us, but when it's over people will know we were willing to shed blood for our freedom."

Sheng-chih's lips curled into a smirk. "How noble," he said, and picked up his telephone. "Tell Mao and Zang-li to get in here."

The office door opened instantly, and two men stepped inside. Both were dressed in black tailored business suits, one man tall and gaunt, the other much shorter, but muscular.

"We have a problem here," said Sheng-chih, and gestured at Quantou. "Our Mayor does not wish to follow my instructions."

Quantou laughed. "Save your threats for the shopkeepers, Sheng-chih. If you harm me, you'll disappear forever."

"Really? Oh, I forgot the loyalty of your police force, but it's to me, not you. The honors ceremonies, the bonuses for good service, and so many other things, all paid for by Fangzi-yin. My name is in their hearts, Quantou. And how will they know I've harmed you? No, it will be yet another unspeakable act by Empress Mengnu, a small force of Moshuguang elite, perhaps, infiltrating Jensi to kill the mayor and his family and demoralize our defenses. I think it's an excellent way to rouse the ire of our people, and you have suggested it by your insolence."

"I think Mengnu will know otherwise, and have you executed," said Quantou.

"I'll take my chances with that," said Sheng-chih, "and alas, you will be dead, and your family with you, your lovely wife, the little girl. Do they share your cause? Will you allow them to die horribly for it?"

Real threat, or a bluff? Quantou could not decide, but the presence of Sheng-chih's two hoodlums on either side of him was real enough. They stood there silent and rigid, like two pets awaiting instructions from the master. Even so, Quantou managed to keep his composure. He looked up calmly at Sheng-chih, and smiled.

"What would I have to do to prevent such an atrocity?" he asked.

Sheng-chih smiled back. "Ah — better," he said. "It's simple, in fact, and does not detract from your goal of independence. Your pride will be wounded, but it will heal."

Sheng-chih sat down on the edge of his desk and looked over Quantou's heard as if speaking to himself.

"It is absolutely necessary that Mengnu come here for negotiations before she has an excuse to order a military occupation and have Jensi filled with her troops. Now she has been wounded by your careless remarks and will not come. That must be corrected. The rally you've planned will collect signatures asking for her removal. You will change that to a petition pleading for her presence here to settle our differences. In your speech you will support this by making a public apology to her for the hastiness of your words. You urgently desire negotiations. You do not want the blood of your people to be spilled needlessly in a confrontation. You only want freedom for them. Words of a truly noble man, I think."

Quantou agreed, but was bothered by something Sheng-chih had said.

"So she comes to Jensi for negotiations which I feel will be fruitless. Then what?"

Sheng-chih's eyes narrowed. "If she survives long enough to negotiate, you will do your best to persuade her. Your police will be kept in defensive positions around the city. Mengnu will provide her escort, and be responsible for her own safety. Our police will not be involved if the people show her their displeasure. There will only be a token force for crowd control."

"A riot, perhaps?" said Quantou.

Sheng-chih pursed his lips. "It's possible, but I'm sure her escort will be well-armed."

"There is her daughter, who calls herself Mei-lai-gong," said Quantou.

"Oh, she must also be invited. She is next in line for the throne. We wouldn't want to exclude her."

The picture in his mind was now clear, and frightening. "Your plan is even more reckless than mine," said Quantou.

"But more conclusive," said Sheng-chih, "and of course both of us will be innocents in any case. Well — what do you say?"

"I will do it," said Quantou. "I will do it for our freedom."

"And that is a good thing, my friend," said Sheng-chih.

He escorted Quantou to the door, and closed it before turning to the two men who remained standing by the now vacant chair. Their eyes shifted nervously when he stepped in front of them.

"So, you see what is to be done?" he asked.

"Yes, sir," said Mao.

"I will need six of your best men, but nobody we've previously used for enforcement. They must be unknowns to all businesses, including the casino. Bring them here in two days, at this time, and I will tell them what to do."

"Yes, sir," said Mao. The shorter man, Zang-li, had no grasp on what had been said and just stared ahead, saying nothing.

Sheng-chih waved a hand. "You may go," he said.

The two men left the office and closed the door behind them.

Sheng-chih sat down at his desk, took out pen and paper, and began scribbling on a plan for his escape from Jensi City and The House of Fangzi-yin.

Nineteen

Preparations

Those who remained faithful numbered well over two thousand.

They had gone underground since the first arrests and the burning of their church. Their little red books had been put away in secret places and were brought out only for cell meetings held in individual homes or back rooms of small shops. Cells of a dozen members each were scattered all over the city, and only one man knew all of them.

His name was Wan-gu.

Wan-gu had been one of several Elders under Lui-sun. He was a quiet man with a strong faith in First Mother, a man who practiced the teachings of Mengnu in his everyday life. Physically he was small, with greying hair and thick eyeglasses. He lived alone, a middle-aged man who had never married. Theologically he was a moderate, a man who refused to stand in judgement of those who did not accept his religious views. To Wan-gu all people were children of First Mother and shared equally in Her Love, even when they strayed from Her.

Wan-gu owned a small but exclusive antiquities shop near the Peoples' Park. Since the burning of Mother's Church he had kept all religious artifacts from display, for his customers included city officials, nobles, and people highly placed in The House of Fangzi-yin. He was regarded as a quiet scholar of antiquities and a man of exquisite tastes; he was a chameleon who blended in well with the New Order of Jensi City.

Still, he was a chameleon who had become the high priest of Mother's Church, and he led a cell meeting in the back room of his shop once each week, long after dark. Tonight's meeting was different, and even more risky than usual. The usual parishioners would not be there, replaced for this one night by selected cell leaders from all over the city.

Wan-gu had not gotten along well with the more conservative Lui-sun. He'd nearly left the church over their squabbles. Others *had* left, but were now returning in increasing numbers as moderates regained control over the congregation. They were without a church, but still had an Empress who remained their intermediary to First Mother. They had called upon Wan-gu to be their high priest. He'd accepted the call with great humility, but warned them that even a moderate might ask for the shedding of their blood in defense of Mother's Church.

And the time for that seemed to be approaching soon.

It was midnight when they arrived, thirty six of them, men and women from all walks of life. They entered by a service entrance at the rear of the shop and crammed themselves together in a windowless storage room lit by a single oil lamp over a thousand years old. They sat silently on boxes and a wooden floor until Wan-gu entered the room and sat down on the floor next to the oil lamp.

"The blessings of First Mother are upon us," he said.

"And on Her Church," the others murmured in unison.

Wan-gu looked around at the faces in the room, then said, "The time has come, my friends. We stand or perish together. Are there any of you who wish to be excluded?"

No hand was raised; not a single voice was heard.

Wan-gu nodded in satisfaction. "Our timing will be critical. We must move in at the exact moment of her arrival, all banners folded in our clothing. She should see them before reaching City Hall, but close enough that Her Moshuguang might offer us protection. Cell Three, what have you learned?"

A man spoke from the gloom. "She is expected at ten, and with a substantial escort. The military police will be in defensive positions around the city in a show of defense, and only a handful will be in the streets. Quantou has hired agitators to stir up the crowd. There could be violence before we even show ourselves."

"The casino is giving out chits for people attending the rally, and the crowd will be packed tight. We should arrive early and mix in with them. Otherwise, we'll not be heard," said a woman.

"My people will be armed," said another man. "We should all be armed, even if it's only sticks and stones. Let Her see we're willing to defend ourselves and not to be herded away like sheep."

The cross-talk and arguments went on for an hour, and Wan-gu listened patiently to all of them. And when it was over he presented a plan slightly modified by their discussions, a plan requiring minimal compromise. In another hour the plan was approved, a time-table set and cell assignments made, many by proxy.

They stood, Wan-gu standing with them, and each held hands with his or her neighbors, heads bowed.

"First Mother, we are not soldiers," said Wan-gu, "but we go forth to defend Your Name and She who speaks for us. Give us the strength and courage we must have, and take those of us who must die into Your Loving Arms forever."

He raised his arms in benediction. "Go, now, and keep Her in your hearts. Her blessings are upon you."

"And on all Her children," they said together.

They left one by one, a single sentry keeping watch on the street. When they were gone, Wan-gu locked the door and went upstairs to his rooms above the shop, rooms packed with selected antiquities from two thousand years of Shanji history. He poured a cup of tea and sipped it while preparing for bed and a short night's sleep ending with first light coming in through his windows facing east.

He slipped into bed, lay on his back and covered his face with his hands.

If I do wrong, then take me in my sleep. If I do right, then hold me, for I am afraid, he prayed.

He fell quickly asleep, and in his dreams that night there was a calming vision of swirling colorful clouds and a single point of golden light, like a star, twinkling down on him.

Two nights before the visitation Quantou was working late in his office when the final call came from Mengmoshu, Chancellor of the Moshuguang, to verify their arrangements.

"Nothing has changed here," he said. "Security will be in your hands. I'll not have my police accused of provocation while Mengnu is here. Just remember an escort is not an army. The bulk of your troops must remain at the flyer field as before."

"The buildings around City Hall must be secured," growled Mengmoshu, "or there will be no meeting. A few police officers will not be enough."

"You are changing your requirements at a late date, sir. What do you propose?" asked Quantou.

"Just before dawn, a detachment of twenty Moshuguang will arrive to take up positions overlooking the street. There will be controlled entrance and exit to all buildings adjacent to City Hall from one hour before Mengnu's arrival until after she has left the building. Their presence will only be visible during that time, and I'm assuming that City Hall itself is well covered by your people."

Quantou thought quickly. What Mengmoshu proposed would make no difference in the outcome, not with the huge milling crowd expected. And a show of his complete cooperation was equal in importance.

"I see no problem with this as long as your people are unobtrusive, sir, and I can assure you absolute security will be in place for my building on all floors," he said.

Mengmoshu seemed satisfied; they set an arrival time for his advanced security guard, and the conversation was ended.

Quantou sat for a moment, thinking about whether or not he should tell Sheng-chih about the new arrangement, but then the memory of the man's threats while two thugs stood there prepared to enforce them came back to him.

You think you are my master, but you are not, he thought.

So it was that Quantou did not tell Sheng-chih about the call from Mengmoshu, and thus brought about the man's destruction.

Bei-Tong had died at the age of nine and was reborn as a forty-two-year-old man.

He was a distant cousin of Shiang liaw; his birth certificate and other papers had been found by Sheng-chih while preparing the Shiang estate for auction. If nothing else, Sheng-chih was a visionary. He planned in the long-term, and imagined possibilities. One of these possibilities was that he might someday want to disappear. Armed with his newfound documents, he'd obtained travel papers and identity cards in the name of Bei-Tong and opened bank accounts in both Wanchou and Dahe with large deposits to which he added substantial sums regularly, all from transfer accounts.

Bei-Tong, a wealthy recluse, owned two walled estates, one at the eastern edge of Wanchou and another just north of the newly incorporated Dahe Zone. Each was maintained by twenty servants who lived well and waited on the occasional presence of their master, usually only days at a time, in summer.

Sheng-chih had chosen the estate near Dahe for his permanent home, because of its isolation. His current home, furnishings, collections, would be his sacrifice, left behind to satisfy, in part, the people he had stolen from.

He had no illusions about the outcome of tomorrow's visitation. Even if the attack on Mengnu was unsuccessful, the city would be fully occupied within hours. He had approximately an hour by limousine to reach the mag-rail station and be on his way.

Now he worked by lamplight to clean up the remaining pieces of evidence. He opened his briefcase, then dialed the combination of his safe. The copy of Tuen's transfer files was garbage, the information already in Mengnu's hands, he was certain, but he tossed it in the briefcase, then added a considerable sum of legal Yuan notes stored in the safe.

The red accounting book containing his own transfer files in fluorescent ink was stacked with others. He slid it out and hastily tossed it into his briefcase without opening the book to check its contents.

The collection of artifacts in his office had given him quiet pleasure in ownership over the years, but these too were a part of his sacrifice. He selected two things: a small *Shizi* in pure gold, and a golden figurine that had come from the Shiang estate. The picture of his father was left where it was. He wrapped the artifacts in paper and shoved them deep into the briefcase, closed it, and turned off the lamp.

The limousine was waiting, as it would be in the morning. He would make an appearance in his office and then be gone, without looking back. By this time tomorrow he would be Bei-Tong, a quiet patron of the arts, living out his days in peace and privacy in a place far from the chaos taking place in Jensi City.

That was his plan.

Kati had never before flown at night, and was both thrilled and frightened by it.

The canopy was closed, but cool air swirled around her. Only her face seemed cold; Huomeng and Yesui were pressed warmly against her and a woolen blanket covered their legs. Mengmoshu sat in front with the pilot and occasionally grumbled commands into his throat mike as they headed east.

They had lifted off from the flyer field alone, the escort too large for it and assembled on the butte at the west end of the valley overlooked by Mengnu City. Ten minutes out from the city's bubble the escort had joined them, a vast matrix of flashing lights until they came close in the darkness. There were seventy flyers loaded with Moshuguang Elite troops and twenty of the much larger vee-winged craft loaded with personnel carriers. A large force, as seen from the ground, but certainly not large enough for an occupation of Jensi City, and that had been Mengmoshu's promise to Quantou.

What Jensi's mayor did *not* know was that the Moshuguang garrison at Congress Center had been ordered into the air and over five hundred troop-laden flyers would be hovering just beyond radar range during the entire time of Empress Mengnu's visitation.

The escort pulled in closer, flying above and below them. Kati looked out at the flashing lights and said, "This should be intimidating enough."

"On the ground is where it counts, and I see us surrounded by thousands of screaming people," said Yesui. "We should have occupied the city first, and then held negotiations."

"Yes, dear, but it was my decision to make and I made it," said Kati firmly. "The people have to see I'm not their enemy. I won't have it any other way."

Yesui only sighed loudly to show her frustration, and said no more.

Huomeng squeezed her arm. "Use your aural protection. It will be safer."

"In the car? It would fry the canopy and anyone sitting next to me. No."

"Out of the car, then."

"I couldn't even shake hands with people. No, Huomeng. No!"

Now it was her husband who sighed.

Mengmoshu looked back over his shoulder. "Stop it," he growled. "You'll be surrounded by troops on foot, and the cars closely-spaced. The response to any physical attack will be automatic and instantaneous. You agreed to it, Kati."

"Yes I did, Father," Kati said sadly, "but only because I have faith in it not being necessary."

Mengmoshu nodded curtly at her, and turned around again.

Faith, grumbled Yesui. Right now I have faith in laser cannon and the purple light of the gong-shi-jie.

You would do better to put your faith in the goodness of people's hearts, returned Kati, and Huomeng again squeezed her arm gently.

The eastern sky glowed orange, but the disk of Tengri-Khan had not yet broken the horizon as they descended towards the flyer field from the south.

They had flown over the city before making their turn south and then north to the glide path. The streets below seemed empty, but on the perimeter of the city they spotted several clusters of vehicles and men blocking major thoroughfares.

Obvious and pathetic, said Mengmoshu. *So where have you put the rest of them, Quantou?* He mumbled his observations into the throat mike, and they were received by the vast formation of flyers now only an hour out from their holding point at the limit of Jensi radar.

His question was answered minutes later as they made their final descent, an echelon of twenty flyers going in ahead of them.

The flyer field at Jensi City was now an armed camp.

On the tarmac side of the sprawling terminal complex, walls of stone fronted with sandbags had been erected in a great semicircular arc, and the area behind the walls was filled with vehicles and men. There was one break in the walls, a single checkpoint allowing access to the tarmac.

Mengmoshu mumbled again into his throat mike, and the message was received.

Twenty Moshuguang flyers, with laser cannon, went in first and hovered far out on the tarmac, ready to respond to the first flash of light from the barricaded 'defenders' of Jensi. The transports went in next, slipping beneath the hovering battle craft and settling to the ground. The rest came in together, a diamond-shaped wedge with the royal flyer in its center, and they touched down closer to the terminal. Kati covered her ears to dull the scream of the turbines.

Moshuguang Elite piled out of their flyers and formed ranks. Ramps came out of the maws of the transports like great tongues, and vehicles rolled down them to the tarmac: bubble-topped cars, open trucks with benches for seating, and two armored personnel carriers with twin laser cannon. The troops of the Moshuguang mounted up, while their Empress sat patiently in her flyer and felt the first heat from the disk of Tengri-Khan.

The process took over an hour, and all the while twenty flyers still hovered several meters above the tarmac, their laser cannon pointing at the barricades of stone and sand.

Finally, two bubble-topped cars pulled up beside Kati's flyer. The bubbles were black and totally opaque from outside, reflective interference films giving partial protection from laser blasts, super-carbon reinforced polymer offering even greater protection from projectile weapons.

Kati and Yesui got into one car, Huomeng and Mengmoshu into the car behind them. There was another half-hour of waiting while the caravan was formed: four cars ahead of the royal vehicle, seven behind it, followed by troop-filled trucks and the personnel carriers.

They moved out slowly. Heads appeared above the barricades to catch a quick look. When they reached the checkpoint a heavy wire gate on wheels was rolled aside and they were waved through by two guards with helmets, flash visors and chest armor, both of them with laser rifles slung and looking grim.

Yesui sighed. "Well, at least they let us out of the flyer field," she said.

While Kati remained calm, Yesui seemed ready to jump out of her skin. Her head swiveled constantly on the alert for potential assailants, her protective aura barely contained and threatening to explode in the small cabin of the car. Kati could feel its near presence by the bristling of fine hairs on her forearms.

"Control yourself," she said sternly, but Yesui only glared at her.

They drove out of the parking area and sped past mansions towards city center. But when they reached Church of The Mother they stopped again, and it was another wait while Moshuguang troops piled out of the trucks and came to form ranks two-abreast on both sides of the royal vehicles.

Kati looked sadly at the church, with its boarded-up entrance and walls blackened with soot. She remembered the cheering crowd, amulets waving, and the love in their hearts. Where were these people now? What had happened to change them so much they would ask for the abdication of their Empress? This was even more distressing to her than the corruption in Jensi. Somehow she had lost the hearts of the people who mattered the most, those who remembered First Mother and believed in Her.

They moved slowly now, the troops marching in cadence beside them and holding their rifles across their chests. They marched for blocks along a side street, the buildings single-storied, then two, then ten stories high. Except for the caravan, the street was empty, the side-walks clear, and there was only an occasional face peering out at them through a shop window.

Kati looked straight ahead. A single police officer with helmet and armored vest stood in the middle of an intersection, gesturing for them to make a right turn. As they made it, the hairs on Kati's arms bristled again and there was a crackling sound. Yesui was leaning for-ward, her face a grim mask, and the air right next to her body had begun to glow faintly blue.

Ahead, a long section of the main street, four cars wide, had been cordoned off with thick rope stretched between heavy posts of steel along both sidewalks. A huge crowd strained at the ropes, people leaning forward and craning their necks to see the oncoming caravan.

Several policemen rushed to remove wooden barricades blocking the street at the edge of the crowd. The first thing Kati noticed was that none of them were armed, except for long black sticks dangling from their belts.

They passed the place where the barricades had been, and the crowd pressed towards them on both sides. A voice blared, and she saw a man with a megaphone, shouting to the crowd. Another loud voice came from further down the street.

Banners were raised.

GO HOME!

NO MORE ROYALTY!

FREEDOM FOR JENSI!

The collective mind of the crowd struck her like a hammer, and she gasped, putting a hand to her mouth. The air in the car crackled fierce-ly, and seemed to glow blue.

The venom of distrust, anger, even hatred assaulted her, and there were lies, lies, lies —

And Kati heard the first vengeful cries of her people.

Twenty

Revolution

Sheng-chih arrived by private limousine at seven o'clock. The briefcase in his hand was now lighter than the night before. The transfer records had been burned and the ashes well stirred in his fireplace at home.

He checked in with the guard near the entrance to The House of Fangzi-yin and took the elevator up to his office. Traffic was normal in the foyer of the building, faces familiar, nothing indicating anything special about the day.

Jie-mei had tea waiting for him in the office; she smiled and bowed as he entered.

"An important day, Jie-mei," he said.

She beamed. "Oh yes. I've prepared a small greeting if I may use your office window when she arrives, sir."

Jie-mei showed him a box filled with colored paper shredded into long strips which she intended to dump out of his window when the Empress was passing below. She'd been raised in Wanchou and still held Mengnu with affection, saying the difficulties were not her doing, but those around her.

"Of course," said Sheng-chih. "I'll be in a meeting, and the office will be free."

Indeed there was an eighth floor meeting on his calendar for the time at which Mengnu would arrive. Only later would people realize no such meeting had taken place.

Sheng-chih sat down at his desk, sipped tea, and placed the briefcase at his feet. He booted up his machine and randomly selected a file. More files were on his desk, and he riffled through pages without seeing them. Jie-mei came and went with things for him to sign.

Her excitement was growing by the minute as she anticipated Mengnu's arrival.

In a way he felt sorry for her. She had been a loyal and efficient manager of his office for ten years. She was now happy and excited, but only hours away from terrible shock and then grief if things went as he'd planned.

Sheng-chih appeared busy at his desk until shortly before nine, left his machine on and picked up his briefcase. Jie-mei didn't even look up when he passed her on his way out; she knew his full schedule for the day.

He took the elevator down to ground floor, turned to see if the guard at the reception desk had seen him, and stopped with a shock.

Two Moshuguang troopers with full battle armor and slung rifles were standing by the front entrance. As he watched in horror they turned away two people who were trying to enter the building.

Security for the Empress, of course, but he was surprised. The rear entrance was where the limousine waited anyway, was away from the parade route and should be open. He walked briskly down a corridor to the small foyer by the rear entrance to the building and its revolving doors.

Two Moshuguang troopers were also standing there, and stepped in front of the doors as he approached.

"Sorry, sir. There is no exit or entrance at this building for the next two to four hours," said one trooper politely.

Outside, the limousine was there, the driver leaning over to peer out the passenger window as a trooper walked towards him.

"But I have a meeting in Wanchou, and a train to catch. Nobody told me about this!" said Sheng-chih. "My limousine is waiting for me!"

"You'll have to catch a later train, sir. There is no exit from this building," said the trooper, and fingered the shoulder strap of his rifle. "The mayor was informed about our security requirements," he added.

The trooper outside was motioning to the driver to move his vehicle away, but the driver saw Sheng-chih and waved.

Sheng-chih suppressed an urge to press further, to identify himself as CEO of Fangzi-yin and insist on leaving. Instead he waved back to the driver and then jabbed two fingers downwards, hoping the man would understand.

"The mayor will personally hear about this from me!" he said, and turned away.

He went back to the elevator, took it down to the basement. There was only one other exit by the loading dock; the door there was usually locked, but he had the master key to the building.

The bare concrete hallway was empty, the loading area quiet. The sliding metal door was rolled down shut. He went to the door next to it, looked outside. His heart jumped when he saw the limousine coming down a steep driveway towards the loading dock. He fumbled the keys from his pocket and inserted a key in the door's lock.

His heart nearly stopped when a broad armored back suddenly blocked his view through the polymer window of the door. Another trooper, waving his arms. There were four of them on the loading dock, two with unslung rifles and brandishing them at the approaching vehicle.

The limousine didn't even slow, and sped away.

Sheng-chih jerked back from the door without being seen, went back to the elevator, mind racing. It was nearing nine-thirty. Thirty minutes, perhaps more to hide himself in the building before the chaos. Perhaps they'd think he'd managed to get away in time. Where to hide? Play out the ruse, he thought, go one minute at a time. The penthouse was obvious, but there many places. They could tear the building apart and not find him for days. Think!

He took the elevator to floor eight and went to an empty meeting room, laid out papers and scribes at several places for people who would not be arriving, then sat down at the end of the table to think quietly. The building was like a familiar glove, much of it his own design, and he'd spent hundreds of hours with the architects. In his mind he began going down the building, floor by floor, beginning at penthouse level.

A clattering in the hallway, hard soles striking marble.

The door flew open, and Jie-mei was standing there puffing hard, her face flushed.

"Oh, sir, you *are* here! You must hide, sir! They say they've come to arrest you!"

"What?"

"The Moshuguang, sir. Six of them. They barely missed you and I said I didn't know where you were but you were expected soon.

219

They're going through your safe and confiscating *everything*! I hid your appointments calendar, but they'll —"

"You opened my safe for them?" growled Sheng-chih.

Tears gushed, and she was wringing her hands together. "I *had* to, sir. They said they'd arrest me if I didn't do it."

She pulled at his arm. "We have to get you hidden. It's your enemies in the Ministry. They do this while Mengnu is distracted. *Please*, sir!"

He stood up and grabbed his briefcase while she tugged at him, babbling.

"Not the penthouse; they'll know about that. The lower floors are filled with Moshuguang and they're waiting for me. I said I'd look for you. There's the private lounge, your master key, one floor below the penthouse. You'll be safe there for a while and I can get you when they're gone. Hurry! In a few minutes they'll begin searching for *me*!"

Jie-mei dragged him to the elevator and they went up, getting off on a floor used primarily by cleaning staff, with plain white walls and an uncarpeted floor of concrete. All doors were closed and locked, most of them storage closets. A generator for energency lighting whirred behind one of them, another radiating warmth from the heating tower rising above them.

Jie-mei went to a door and unlocked it with her own key. "I'll bring food and tea when I can, sir. I'm so sorry about this. I was so happy to see Mengnu coming, but now I'm not so sure she doesn't have something to do with this."

She was angry, and practically pushed him inside. Closed the door, and he heard the lock click, then the sound of her hard-soled shoes as she ran back to the elevator.

The room was small, windowless and warm. There was a cot, a chair, a light panel in the ceiling and a sink with a counter on which lay a tray with a few aging honeycakes and a half-filled pot of cold tea. Sheng-chih had used the room on many occasions to escape the chaos of his day and take a welcome nap. He was here to escape again, but for a far more serious reason.

He sat down on the cot and began to think about his next move, or moves, depending on the possibilities. The briefcase full of cash and golden artifacts say by his feet.

Sometime later, even through walls of concrete and stone, he heard a series of whumping sounds telling him the chaos in the streets of Jensi City had begun.

And he waited.

Outside the car, people shook fists and waved banners. Kati looked left and right, hugging herself as the wave of her people's anger assaulted her. She pressed her back against the cushioned seat and let out a soft moan as the sounds of their shouting penetrated the car. The troopers on foot moved closer to the car until their shoulders were nearly touching the windows. The car jerked forward, speeding up to a fast walk, the crowd now surging against the rope barriers and leaning over it to shake closed fists. Kati felt the first fear for her safety. She leaned away from Yesui, whose aura was now purple and barely restrained, and there was a sharp odor in the cab of the car.

There was a mix in feelings coming from the crowd, but the angry ones were the majority. There was also fear and anxiety and some whispered prayers for her safety. Megaphones blared from men obviously planted to stir up the people and they were doing it well, drowning out any welcome that might have been there for her.

Something thudded against the car. A trooper turned to level his rifle.

"Now they're throwing things," growled Yesui, and her aura flashed.

Ahead of them, missiles were coming out of the crowd from both sides of the street, striking troopers and bouncing off the lead cars of the caravan. Troopers pressed up against the cars and swung their rifles back and forth, the crowd recoiling from the muzzles but then surging forward again. City Hall was only a block ahead, on the right, and the mass of people there seemed even more dense. A few people had gotten through the barricades and were running back and forth across the street.

The car sped up again to close a widening gap in the caravan, and the troopers were now trotting.

Yesui turned to snarl at Kati. Her eyes glowed so brightly the pupils could not be seen. "There will be a payment for this insult," she hissed.

Kati leaned further away from her to escape the crackling aura. "Only from those responsible for it," she said firmly, "and if Quantou thinks we can talk seriously after this, he is badly mistaken."

Something hard hit the car, making them jump, and then a softer thing that splattered against the canopy next to Yesui and oozed a brownish goo. City Hall was now tens of meters away and the street beyond it was suddenly blocked by people walking towards them in a mass, their arms locked together.

Kati saw them, and then heard their battle cry.

We shed our blood for First Mother! We shed our blood for Her Church! We fight for the cause of Empress Mengnu, and offer our lives in her name!

"Get out of the street!" growled the driver. "We're supposed to have a clear exit!"

A few policemen ran towards the new crowd, brandishing long sticks, the first sign Kati had seen of any local effort to control the demonstrators. Instead of shrinking back, the new crowd filling the street charged them, the front line swinging sticks and throwing rocks. In the back ranks, cloth banners went up, stretched between hands.

'dOWN WITH QUANTOU!'

'CHURCH BURNERS BE GONE!'

'MENGNU SAVE US!'

The police went down as if sucked under a huge wave and now there was fighting within the crowds on the sidewalks beyond City Hall, people slashing at each other with sticks and rocks and tumbling into the street. The car jerked forward in spasms, passing The House of Fangzi-yin and jockying for a position in front of City Hall. Troops from the lead cars of the caravan jumped out to form a line across the street in front of the rioters and were pelted by rocks and garbage from both sides. They ducked, but held their fire.

Missiles still struck Kati's car as they slowed before City Hall, but the attention of the crowd seemed drawn towards the fighting further down the street, and much of the angry screaming had subsided.

Their car stopped. Troopers had reached the doors of City Hall and were forming a rank leading to the car when things happened with such suddeness they could not even be followed by the mind of a Chuang-shi.

There was movement from Kati's left. Something sailed out of the crowd in a high arc and landed with a splat on the short sloping hood of the car. A satchel, like a purse, smoking and hissing. It started to slide off.

And exploded.

There was a burst of fire in the cab of the car. The driver screamed and began beating at his legs with his hands.

Behind them there was a terrible explosion that echoed from the tall buildings.

Kati's protective aura came to her without thought and sizzled against her daughter's as they huddled in the back seat of the car. The front door flew open and a trooper was pulling the driver from the car, flames leaping towards the man's face. The rear door was jerked open, and a trooper was thrown back screaming when he tried to grasp Yesui's arm.

Yesui jumped out, and Kati right behind her. The troopers moved in as close as they could without being seared black by the auras; they gestured for her to move quickly towards the doors.

Kati took a step, looked to her right — and saw the horrible thing that had happened behind her.

The car carrying Huomeng and Mengmoshu was on its side and burning fiercely. Two faces smashed against the cannopy were dark splotches in the flames.

Kati screamed.

Nobody dared touch her. She whirled and rushed towards the burning car. Brave troopers crawled over it in the flames, had a door open, were pulling at something. As she neared the car, something green flashed at the periphery of her vision and her aura brightened with new energy. Another flash, from a third story window in a building across the street, a laser pulse coming straight at her face and absorbed in aural purple. The window exploded in laser fire instantly directed at it from troopers in the street.

The crowd was in panic, their screaming changed, fear and outrage not directed at their Empress, but at what was happening. A man was on the ground being stomped and kicked as two troopers tried to reach him. People had fallen to their knees, wailing. Others were running away and two of them, men dressed in black suits, went down scorched in laser fire that had deliberately sought them out.

A Moshuguang officer was shouting orders into a radio as Kati reached the car, and he held up a hand.

"Please, Madam, the car might explode!"

He jumped back as she passed him, her eyes fixed on a horror inside the car.

Two faces were smashed against the canopy, their flesh blackening in the flames. One was the driver, a Moshuguang trooper.

The other was Mengmoshu, eyes closed, his neck twisted at an impossible angle.

Kati screamed. Yesui screamed behind her, for she had followed her mother.

More screaming — from the car. The troopers standing on it by the open door grunted and pulled hard. Two feet, then legs appeared, then a burning robe. Huomeng was a burning match, his clothing and hair in flames. His screams were awful. Without time for gentleness, the troopers pulled him out roughly as he shrieked in pain. The car was hissing with fire. A jet of new flame issued from the rear and troopers on the street jerked backwards.

"It's going!" shouted one of them.

The troopers handling Huomeng ignored the warning, took him beneath his arms and lowered him towards the street. Blood oozed from his blackened face, but his eyes were open and he saw Kati. His mouth moved, but no words were there to be heard.

Kati's aura snapped off. She leaped forward to help just as one trooper jumped down to the street.

"Mother, DON'T!" screamed Yesui.

She got an arm around her husband. He smelled like cooked meat. A trooper took him from the other side and then they dragged him one step, two. The boots of the other trooper struck the street behind them.

There was a loud hiss, and then a terrible explosion.

Kati was sent sprawling to the ground on top of Huomeng. There was a flash of terrible heat on her legs and back, and the sudden acrid stench of hair burning.

Before unconsciousness she was only aware of a terrified, enraged shrieking, both in her ears and in her mind.

It was Yesui.

Captain Zao watched the grounded flyers carefully, for he had orders to open fire immediately if they attempted to advance on the terminal. His men remained tense behind the barricades and he walked back and forth to calm them with his presence and remind them to fire only at his command.

The Moshuguang had formed ranks around their flyers and had been standing at a brace for over an hour, their armor gleaming in the morning light. Elite troops, all of them, but only their officers had seen combat in the great war of decades past. It was still more than for Zao and his young contingent. Most of his men were barely old enough to show fuzz on their cheeks. And the laser cannon on those flyers would tear apart the barricades in less than a minute.

Zao did not say these things to his troops. They were frightened enough as it was.

And quite suddenly, the Moshuguang force far out on the tarmac began to move.

Troopers broke ranks and piled into their flyers as the scream of turbines filled the air. Ramps were pulled up into the transport ships, and loading doors closed. Two flyers lifted off to hover meters above the ground, their weapons directed at the barricade.

Men were sighting their rifles over the stone walls. Others looked at Zao with wide eyes as he hurried past, repeating, "Hold, hold. Only at my command."

Behind the hovering craft, two other flyers lifted off, then one of the transport ships. They turned and headed east, only meters from the ground, and passed out of sight beyond a small forested hill near the city. The hovering craft remained where they were, but the shrill whine of turbines grew louder as the engines of the grounded flyers came to life.

Watching the hovering ships, Zao caught sight of something else. Out near the southern horizon, a dark cloud was moving in fast.

He watched in horror as the cloud came close enough to be resolved into black specks — flying in formation.

An orange ball of fire engulfed her mother and father, and Yesui screamed.

One trooper staggered away, a torch on legs, and was tackled by two others who covered him with their bodies to smother the flames. The explosion sent fire across the street and the crowd was stampeding in two directions, people trampled flat, others on their knees and screeching. There was only a single blast, leaving the car a burning ruin with the shadows of two bodies left inside.

Mother and Father were flat on their faces, the arm of a trooper draped over them, and all three were on fire. Troopers beat at the flames and quickly put them out, but not before scorched flesh showed where there had once been robes.

Yesui screamed in shock, then rage, her aura extending a full meter from her body, and her eyes were like hot blue stars. She came back to her senses when a Moshuguang officer began shouting commands.

"Off the street! Get them inside and off the street, and shoot *anyone* who gets in the way!"

Armored men lifted the charred bodies of the trooper and Yesui's parents. Her father cried out, but Mother was silent. The sight of them brought new rage to Yesui, and she was losing control. Meters above her head the air crackled, glowed. A light purplish mist fell and fused spots of pavement to glass all around her. The crowd saw it and went into total panic. Even the troopers shrank away from her.

Her parents were being carried into City Hall past a phalanx of troopers blocking the still rioting crowd farther down the street. She must first see to her parents, and not the evil around them. Yesui let out a loud sigh, regaining some control, and she followed the Moshuguang officer who had dared to get close to her.

Beyond the line of troopers people were still beating at each other with sticks and rocks, and there was the occasional flash of a blade. Strangely, one portion of the crowd seemed organized, massed in front of the troopers and actually aiding them.

"Quickly!" said the officer, and Yesui went inside the building, her aura searing the doorway black as she passed through it. People inside quickly jumped aside to make a large empty space around her.

Mother and Father had been laid out on a cold marble floor. What little remained of their robes still smouldered. Their hair had been burned off to the scalp and great blisters were forming on their faces. A small portion of Father's chest was crisp and black. His mouth was opened wide, sucking air, and then he coughed weakly. Mother did not move, or make a sound.

"Mother!" called Yesui. *Mother!*

No answer or other response came.

There was new pandemonium in the street outside.

The people who had been helping the Moshuguang were trying to come in the building, but the doors were locked shut. They pressed their faces against the windows and screamed to be let in. The street behind them lit up in green bursts, laser beams scorching in a rushing swath down its center, a flyer coming by so fast it was only a blur. Another followed seconds later, sweeping the street clean in bursts of green fire while the people pounded on the windows, begging for entrance.

"Let them in!" cried the Moshuguang officer. "Whoever they are, they were trying to help us!" He looked at Yesui as he said it, and she nodded, for the mental cries of these people had washed over her, and she realized who they were.

The door was opened; men and women pushed through inside. Two of them dragged a beaten and bloody man between them and threw him roughly to the floor at Yesui's feet. "That is one of the assassins," said a man, pointing. "Another one is dead, and we left him outside, but there were others."

The new people fell to their knees in a circle around the bodies of their Empress and her husband. They put their foreheads to the floor and began wailing prayers to First Mother just as a flyer rushed past to sweep the street again with laser fire.

The man at Yesui's feet moaned, and turned over on his back. He was dressed in black. His lip was split open, one eye a purplish mess and swollen shut. His good eye opened, looked up at her. He shuddered, and his fingernails raked at the marble floor. Yesui leaned over to look closely at him, and his face was brightly lit by the glow of her eyes.

"This is the one who threw the bomb at your car," said someone. "The man who bombed the car behind you is the dead one."

There was a loud whine from outside. Yesui looked up, saw a huge flyer landing in the street, men leaping from a partially deployed ramp before it even touched down.

"Make way for the medicals!" shouted the Moshuguang officer. "Clear the area around the patients!"

Yesui forgot the man lying at her feet, but only for a moment. She watched helplessly as the medical team arrived with stretchers and cases with polymer tubes and bags of liquids, dropping to their knees to work frantically on her parents. The looks on their faces, the haste in their movements, all of it told her it was bad, very bad.

Mother, Father, your help is here. Can you hear me?
Nothing.

It seemed tubes were inserted all over their bodies, and they were wrapped in gauze soaked in a foul-smelling chemical before being placed on the stretchers. The church people were still on their knees, wailing prayers. Something about that was making Yesui angry. These were the people who had filled the street ahead of them, slowing their progress and making them an easier target, and now they were praying over the results of their interference.

A Moshuguang officer came inside, an older man with grey hair, and a scar across his chin. All troopers, including the other officer, snapped to attention as he stepped up to Yesui and bowed.

"Madam. I am Major Duan. The flyers from Congress Center have arrived and we are prepared to occupy the city at your command."

Yesui realized with a start that she was now Empress of Shanji.

"Then do it," she growled, "and kill anyone who opposes us. I want Jensi under our complete control by dusk."

Without answering her, Duan took out a hand-held radio and relayed her command into it. Yesui thought of something else.

"Quantou has not appeared here, but was supposed to be waiting for us in his office. I want him brought to me — right here."

Duan barked an order, and two troopers raced up stairs to fetch the mayor of Jensi.

Duan tried to reassure her. "The transport ship has good facilities for emergency treatment, Madam, and your parents are in good hands. In two hours they'll be in Mengnu City; the hospital has been alerted. Do you wish to go with them?"

"No. I'm staying here until I find out who's responsible for this. Secure this building for a command post. And there is a man named Sheng-chih. He was supposed to be arrested this morning in the building right next to us. I want him brought to me for questioning."

"Yes, Madam," said Duan.

The stretchers bearing her parents were being carried outside to the waiting transport flyer. Yesui went to the window to watch the loading, her aura fainter now, but still there. To her right, dozens of bodies were blackened in the street. To her left an overturned car flamed weakly, with the charred remains of her beloved Gong-gong still inside. Tears came to her eyes and her aura flared again. The wailings of the church people continued, and suddenly made her furious. She whirled on them, most of them still on their knees.

For some reason she chose a frail looking older man with thick eyeglasses, and vented her rage directly at him. Her aura raised the hair on his bowed head as she stepped up to him.

"In your words to First Mother you'll do well to include a prayer for your own lives," she growled. "There are no innocents here, and if my mother dies I will return as Mei-lai-gong to reduce this city and every living thing in it to a cinder."

The kneeling people only wailed louder, prostrating themselves, and even Duan looked at her fearfully.

Yesui pointed at the beaten assassin who still lay where she'd left him.

"I will begin with this one," she said.

Captain Zao gaped in shock and disbelief at the cloud of flyers approaching from the south. There had been no warning of any kind, yet there they were, in close formation, so close to each other they were nearly touching, and the sound of their engines had not yet reached him.

When his men saw the flyers they did not aim their weapons or show any other sign of bravado. They hunkered down behind the barricades and looked at him fearfully, a silent plea showing in their eyes.

Zao stood tall and defiant, but only for a moment. The flyers reached the southern edge of the landing field and the sound of their turbines reversing for braking was an explosion in his ears. They were only tens of meters above ground level, spreading out into a vast arc before him, and it seemed there were thousands of them. The two flyers over the tarmac had maintained their hovering position close in, waiting for motion or a flash of fire from the barricades.

Zao could visualize what two laser cannon could do to the barricades and the men behind it, but what a thousand could do was beyond his imagination.

He was a career military man, and intelligent enough to have obtained a high rank at a young age. But his loyalty was first to the men who served under him, and not to his masters. He was also a man blessed with considerable common sense.

Captain Zao ordered his men to lay down their weapons, and he led them out onto the tarmac with their hands on top of their heads.

Twenty-One

Consequences

Yesui's aura flared again as she approached the man lying on the floor. Her rage was now cold and contained. Behind her, turbines shrieked as the transport flyer lifted off to carry her mutilated parents away to hospital. They were alive, but barely. Neither had answered her mental call, and her Gong-gong was turning to ashes in a burning car.

One man responsible for it was dead, but another was here, lying again at her feet. The prayers of the church people had ceased with her outburst, but they were still whimpering. Otherwise there was silence, people just standing as far away as they could from her and waiting to see what she was going to do.

Yesui leaned over the man, and his face was illuminated blue by the glow of her eyes.

"You are a hired assassin," she growled, and entered him.

The man's one good eye opened wide. His mouth moved, but no sound came from it.

Yesui crawled into his mind like a parasite, sucking. "You and others were hired to kill us. Tell me who hired you, and I'll spare you the pain you deserve."

The man moaned, and kicked out at her with his legs, then screamed when his feet touched her aura.

Yesui smiled nastily, and clamped down on him with all the power of an old Searcher.

His body went rigid, and shuddered. His good eye rolled up towards the eyelid. In seconds his back was arched and his feet were drumming the floor, his entire body writhing in spasms. A trickle of blood oozed from both nostrils.

Behind her, people began sobbing, and Major Duan dared to come close, saying, "Madam — please. We need his testimony."

Yesui only clamped down harder, and scoured the man dry. Blood came in a gush from his nostrils and ears. He cried out once, then suddenly relaxed and was still.

Yesui stood up straight and turned away from the man as Major Duan leaned over to examine him.

Duan looked up at all of them. "He's dead," he said.

It seemed to them all that Yesui hadn't heard him. She was looking up the stairs where two troopers were descending on either side of the mayor of Jensi City.

"There is a man named Mao. The name isn't familiar to me, but perhaps our good mayor can tell us who he is and where he can be found."

She stepped around the body on the floor, and smiled at the sight of an approaching mayor shrugging off troopers' grasps on his arms. A shrill whine behind her and she glanced over her shoulder, saw another flyer descending to the street outside. Several troopers were entering the building, and they carried more bodies with them, three of the corpses blackened by laser fire. The laid them on the floor where her parents had been only moments before.

Yesui turned to face Quantou, and streamers of blue reached out towards him from her aura without conscious control. He fell backwards against the troopers and clenched his hands together over his chest, his eyes filled with tears.

"Madam — oh, Madam," he sobbed. "I could not imagine such an atrocity, yet I saw it with my own eyes. After — after the explosions — I saw it from my window, and — and when I looked, a laser pulse nearly hit me! It blackened the wall in my office. You can see for —"

"YOU!" screamed Yesui, and clenched her hands into fists at her sides. For one instant her aura seemed to fill the entire room, crackling dangerously and raising everyone's hair.

Quantou sprawled forward on his face as if hit from behind with great force. He cried out and struggled to his knees, a cut on his forehead oozing first blood.

"STAND UP!" ordered Yesui, and he stood, shaking. Yesui pointed to the body of the man she had just executed.

"Do you know that person?"

Quantou looked, really looked, and gasped, "No, Madam. I've never seen him before."

It was the truth, for already she was Searching him.

"Then perhaps you know the person who hired this assassin — a man named Mao," she said, and probed hard, without subtlety.

His eyes widened as he sensed what she was doing.

"Mao — yes — I think so. I saw him once in the office of Sheng-chih, the chief executive of The House of Fangzi-yin. He works for that man."

Also true. Quantou's mind was amazingly open to her, but only out of fear for his life. Feelings, scenarios, snatches of memory whirled in his mind and were difficult to sort. One memory was recent, and perhaps explained his openess to her. There really *had* been a laser blast directed at him in his office, and he remained terrified by the experience. He'd hidden beneath his desk until the Moshuguang troopers had come for him.

Yesui pressed in harder, and Quantou gasped again.

"So Sheng-chih is responsible for attempting to murder Shanji's royal family, and you know nothing about his plotting."

Ah, getting clearer, things sorting out in the terrified man's mind.

"There was one time — a meeting — he said something that made me suspicious — but I couldn't imagine he would really — oh!"

Quantou cried out in sudden pain, and grabbed at his head.

"You could imagine it if it served your purpose as well as his. Well, I've seen enough."

She released him. Quantou fell to his knees and held his head with his hands, moaning.

Yesui turned to Major Duan, who was receiving still another message on his radio.

"Arrest this man," she said. "The charge is treason against the Empire. I want him flown to Mengnu City and imprisoned in the Hall of Ministries for further questioning."

"Yes, Madam," said Duan. He gestured, and two troopers grabbed Quantou beneath his arms, hauled him to his feet and began dragging him away.

"Sheng-chih will not be so fortunate," snarled Yesui. "Bring him to me."

Duan looked distressed. "I'm sorry to say he hasn't been found, Madam. He wasn't in his office when our people arrived. An informant took us to his hiding place, but he wasn't there either. We're searching the entire building, Madam. The guards remained at their stations at all times; I see no way he could have escaped to the street."

Yesui stamped a foot in frustration. "I cannot wait here *forever*! I must see to my *parents*! When you find him, take him to the Hall of Ministries and make sure he's put in an isolated cell. Is occupation underway?"

"It is. There was no resistence at the flyer field. The first columns should be here within the hour. There's still a small crowd rioting a few blocks east of us, but a flyer is hovering near them and they're slowly dispersing to their homes. I see no problem in achieving total occupation by nightfall."

Yesui pointed to the corpses lying side-by-side on the floor. All were dressed identically in black body suits. "Why are these bodies here?" she asked.

"Assassins, Madam. Two had sachel charges with them when they were shot down. The other was killed while firing from a window across the street. We've searched the bodies, but there's nothing to identify them," said Duan.

"Five men," said Yesui, "working as a team."

"Maybe more," said Duan, then, "It's best if you leave, Madam. A flyer is ready for you in the street and I'm sure you want to be with your parents. You'll have our first report soon after you touch down."

Duan walked her to the doors, past church people who flinched back from her aura, but then a woman cried out, "Forgive us, Lady. We only meant to support our Empress. We didn't know this would happen."

Yesui ignored her, kept walking, and they were outside. The fire in the overturned car had been put out, and troopers were lifting the charred remains of the driver and her grandfather from the ruins. Tears again came to her eyes when she saw it, and her rage simmered at the sight.

"There is one more thing," she said as they stepped into the street. Duan looked at her expectantly.

"When the city is fully occupied I want an evacuation to begin. I want the hotels, casino, all businesses closed in the downtown area. All buildings are to be emptied, people sent to their homes or the hills. I don't care which, but I want this city empty within a day, and that includes your troopers."

"That is difficult, Madam. So many people, and —"

"The downtown area only. That is perhaps thirty six square blocks, centered on City Hall. Few people actually live there. Be as thorough as you can, but have your people out by midnight tomorrow night."

Duan shook his head. "I don't understand your purpose."

"It is simple, Major," hissed Yesui, and her aura brightened. "This atrocity has been committed by a city, not just one man. My parents might well be dead before reaching hospital. At best they will be scarred for life. I will be returning to Jensi City. I will not come as I appear to you, but as Mei-lai-gong. I will come to cleanse the cancer this city has become. Two midnights from now, Major. If people resist your evacuation efforts, tell them two midnights from now the Mei-lai-gong comes to bring the purple light of the gong-shi-jie down on Jensi City to destroy it."

Duan looked at her incredulously, then smiled uneasily. "I see," he said. "It is a threat."

The sudden glow from Yesui's eyes wiped the smile from his face. "It is a promise," she said.

Duan was stunned, but bowed stiffly. "We'll do our best, Madam," he said, but in his mind he found her harshness most extreme and he was thinking mostly about the monumental cost of rebuilding an entire city.

A small part of Yesui's mind took note of his concern.

She stepped into the flyer. The pilot leaned forward to escape her aura and looked afraid. Yesui breathed deeply several times, and the aura shrank closer to her body, brightening as it did so.

Duan took a step back and saluted smartly. "My best wishes for your parents' recovery, Madam, and my condolances for the loss of Chancellor Mengmoshu. All Moshuguang feel his loss sadly."

Turbines whined and the flyer jerked upwards. Yesui gave Duan a nod as she was lifted off. The flyer went straight up above the tallest buildings, hovered, then turned west and suddenly accelerated, pressing her back into her seat for a long moment.

Breathing was difficult until they came up to speed. She had never flown so fast, and suddenly other flyers appeared beside and above her craft. She counted twenty and knew there would be others below her. They were moving in tight formation at attack speed, trails of vapor streaming from the leading edge of each flyer and forming a hollow cone behind them.

Reality struck her again. Yesui was gone, for a while, perhaps forever. For the moment it was Wang Yesui Shan-shi-jie who struggled for breath in her flyer and fought back the tears of worry. Her parents were now nearing Mengnu City. In an hour, perhaps more, Yesui would be with them. She wondered if she would find them alive, or dead. Rage, and a terrible sadness fought for control within her. Her aura disappeared as she began to cry.

She cried all the way to Mengnu City, but dried her eyes quickly as they came down through the open panel in the city's protective bubble.

A contingent of twelve heavily armed troopers was there to meet her at the flyer field.

And they took her directly to the hospital within her golden-domed palace.

He remained in the closed and locked room for only a few minutes, and not because of a lack of proper food or drink. It was the idea that *someone* knew where he was, even if she was loyal, for loyalty is a fleeting thing. The Moshuguang could threaten, or search her mind, and he would be trapped in this room with only one exit.

After he heard the muffled explosions outside the building, Sheng-chih allowed himself minutes to think about where he might go, for he had the master key to every room in the building. To change floors would be folly. He could be trapped in a stairwell or elevator. The rooms on this floor were mostly storage. Access to air conduits was by ceiling panels in the hallway, and he had no ladder.

There was only one place.

He put an ear to the door and listened. It was silent in the hallway. He unlocked the door and opened it slightly, his briefcase in one hand. The hallway was empty in both directions and the lights above the elevator were unlit. Sheng-chih stepped outside, closed and locked the door behind him.

One light above the elevator suddenly glowed red, and Sheng-chih's heart thudded hard. He hurried down the hallway to the one terrible place they might not bother to search, a place where he should also have access to the roof of the building. He reached it, put a hand on the door. It was warm.

When he opened the door, a blast of heat seared his face. He gulped air and stepped inside, clinging to his briefcase, closing and locking the door behind him. He pulled a handkerchief from his pocket, covered his nose and mouth and breathed shallowly. In seconds it seemed all moisture had been sucked from his eyes.

The space was lit by a single red bulb above the door. He was on a catwalk with a railing waist high. Below him the main ventillation shaft fell out of sight; above him was a twisted matrix of copper slabs attached below the radiator on the roof of the building. The constant stream of air coming from below was a dull roar in his ears and carried his sweat away before he could feel it.

There were two catwalks above him, connected by steep metal stairs. The top level was just below the roof of the building, with hatch access to it for work on the radiator. He climbed one flight of stairs, shoulder sliding along a hot wall for balence. The heat was now worse, the next set of stairs even steeper. He held his breath, took the handkerchief from his mouth, but still scalded his hand on the railing as he climbed. At the top he collapsed against a wall, hand over his face, and gasped for air.

Suddenly the blast of heat from below stopped with a thud vibrating the wall at his back. The system was cycling. It would only be a minute or so before the heat came again. He gulped welcome breaths of still air, saw a vertical ladder leading three meters up to a hatch nearly above his head. He put down his briefcase, climbed one rung, then two — and froze.

There was a rattle from the door meters below him. The catwalk clanged softly as his feet hit it, and he pressed back against a wall out of sight from the door.

The door opened and there were voices. Two men, and a woman.

The woman was Jie-mei.

Boots scuffed the catwalk below him.

"Hot in here, and it's a long way down. Can we get to the roof up there?"

"I think so," said Jie-mei, and her voice quavered.

"The roof is covered. If he went out this way we'd have him by now."

"But he was in that *room*! I swear by First Mother he was *there*!"

Jie-mei was now sobbing, frightened, and under their control.

"So you said, and also believe, but it's no longer true. Where else could he be?"

The man's voice was low, and ominously threatening.

"His suite the next floor up, but he wouldn't go there. Everyone knows about it," sobbed Jie-mei.

"Then take us there, and be *quiet* about it!" ordered another man.

Just as he said it a loud thunk announced a new rush of air coming up through the shaft. Sheng-chih covered his face as it struck him.

"Woof!" said the trooper below him.

The door slammed shut.

Sheng-chih remained huddled on the catwalk for what seemed an eternity, counting ten cycles of rushing then swirling hot air before he dared to move. The roof was guarded. He could only go back the way he'd come, and play a cat-and-mouse game to avoid capture. He hoped they'd eventually think he'd escaped the building. Until then he could only proceed minute by minute.

He climbed down the ladder when the air was still, and tried the door. It was locked. He opened it slowly, peered out into an empty, silent hallway. Went to the lounge he'd occupied, and opened it. The scraps of food, the cold tea were still there. A tempting bait, but he dared not take a single bite or sip to satisfy his grumbling stomach.

He locked himself inside a cleaning closet, sitting on the floor in darkness amidst wet mops and smelly chemicals until his mouth was like paper and pain gnawed at his stomach. He turned the light on three times to check his watch, then turned it off quickly again.

It was three in the morning when he left the closet and took the stairs up to the next floor, pausing at each step to listen for a voice, a boot scuffing concrete, anything.

The hallway was bare, the suite unguarded. He went to it, put his ear to the door and listened for a long time before opening it. Inside it was dark. There was a grumble of heavy machinery from outside. He threaded his way to the window and looked out. All buildings were dark, not a single light in a window at a time when cleaning staff should be busy. Below him, heavy personnel carriers roamed the street, and there were many troopers on foot.

Jensi was occupied. Was Mengnu dead, or alive? At the moment it made no difference. He could not leave the building.

He went to a sink and gulped water directly from the faucet, but there was nothing for him to eat.

When it was required, Sheng-chih was a patient man. He filled his stomach with water to dull the pains of hunger, paced the room and checked the view outside often to keep himself awake.

He kept his mind occupied with new plans for his escape, and was confident in the possibilities remaining for it if he could rely on his noble friends for help.

The troopers were still with her when she reached the floor where her parents had been taken. They followed her wherever she went. A crowd was there: Ministers, high ranking Moshuguang officers, her family. Bao and Shiann were crying hysterically, and brought terrible fear to Yesui. Nokai came forward arms outstretched, and crushed her in his embrace.

"Are they dead?" asked Yesui.

"Not when they were brought in. They're both in surgery now. The entire hospital staff has come in, Yesui. Everything possible is being done."

Bao and Shiann came to them and they embraced together while the people around them bowed their heads and looked sadly at each other. "Why? Why?" the girls kept asking, but Yesui could not answer them.

Nokai whispered into her ear. "I'm so sorry about Mengmoshu, but I think he would rather have died this way then by languishing in bed. He was a true soldier, and many here are grieving for him."

Yesui's eyes filled with tears, and she hugged her family to her.

Two men elbowed their way through the circle of troops around Yesui. One was Minister Shui, whom she knew. The other was a Moshuguang officer, a Colonel, dressed in formal leathers. He was middle-aged, his hair still black, eyes deep set below the prominent veined bulge of his forehead, and he had a broad square jaw. He bowed stiffly as Shui introduced him to Yesui.

"This is Colonel Damoshu, Madam. Mengmoshu named him his successor as Chancellor some years ago, and it's supported by a vote of the Moshuguang Council. The appointment, of course, will require your approval," said Shui.

"Colonel," she said softly, and studied him, probing.

"My sincere regrets about your grandfather, Madam. He was a fine man and will be missed by all of us," said Damoshu, then smiled when Yesui raised an eyebrow at him.

"The fact that our Empress Mengnu is his daughter was common knowledge among us, even though he made every effort to hide it. Our prayers are also for your parents, and we stand ready at your service."

"Thank you, Colonel," said Yesui graciously. In two heartbeats she'd searched this man so consciously open to her, and she liked what she saw there. "You have my oral appointment as Chancellor of the Moshuguang according to the judgement of my grandfather, but we must meet and talk more before I put it in written form. I hope you understand."

She had felt his probing of her, and been open to it.

"Of course, Madam. We must understand each other's views," said Damoshu, "and now is not the proper time. Major Duan has contacted me only minutes ago. Jensi is fully occupied, and the evacuation has begun as you ordered. We'll begin pulling our troops out of the downtown area by noon tomorrow and set up a perimeter around the city. Most people have fled to their homes outside Jensi, or to the surrounding hills. There's one group congregated in Peoples' Park, religious people, and they refuse to leave. They say they await their deaths at the hands of The Mei-lai-gong."

"Leave them where they are," said Yesui quickly.

"Yes, Madam," said Damoshu, but in his mind Yesui again felt a great concern, even opposition to what she might do to the city.

"I will do what must be done, Colonel," she said.

He bowed formally. "I await your pleasure, Madam," he said, and took a step back. Minister Shui moved in front of him, held out a hand to her and she took it. She thought him a kind man, loyal and honest in her dealings with him.

"My prayers go out to First Mother for your parents. And if I might distract you from your worries for just a moment, I have some interesting news about Sheng-chih."

"Have they found him?" asked Yesui, squeezing his hand.

"I'm sorry. No. But I received something in the mail this morning. It came by mag-rail and was addressed to me, a red accounting book with a note saying everything we needed regarding Sheng-chih could be found on apparently blank pages if we tested for fluorescent ink. We did it. All his transfer accounts are there. We have everything we need to prosecute him when he's found."

Prosecution won't be necessary. There will be no trial, thought Yesui.

"Who sent the note?" she asked.

"It was signed 'A Friend of Mother's Church'," said Shui.

The metal doors at the end of a long hallway opened, and two doctors in surgical gowns walked towards them. Yesui excused herself, locked one arm with Nokai's, draped the other around the twins' shoulders and met the doctors halfway along the hall, four troopers only a step behind her.

The doctors looked grim, and bowed to her.

"Are they still alive?" she asked anxiously.

"Yes, Madam," said one doctor, "but their condition is unstable, and you cannot see them now. Both are badly burned. We're putting your mother in a saline wrap, and she's unconscious. I would call it a coma, but the brain activity is not right for that. She has gone far into herself."

"And my father?"

"Much more serious, I'm afraid. He's still in surgery, Madam. We're removing his spleen, and there are other internal bleeding points we're trying to reach. There's hope, Madam, but his condition is critical. He could last a day or recover completely. We simply can't tell at this time."

The girls began sobbing again, and Nokai squeezed Yesui's arm against him.

"I'm sure you're doing your best," Nokai said softly. "Please notify us of new developments, and let us see your patients as soon as possible. Are you a believer, sir?"

"In First Mother? I am. All of us who heal are Her followers."

"Then may She guide your hands," said Nokai.

Yesui felt an ache in her throat. People were crowding in around her again. "I want to go back to our rooms," she said to Nokai. "I can't think with all these people here, and I have decisions to make."

Nokai frowned at her, for he knew the dark struggle going on in her mind.

"We must talk about it," he whispered, then turned and spoke to the people gathered behind them.

"We're retiring now, but we'll be here again in the morning. Thank you for being here with us. Your support, and prayers are most appreciated."

They threaded their way through the small crowd, and four troopers followed behind them along a hall, down an elevator, another long hall to the palace wing that was private quarters for the royal family. The troopers set up station at the entrance to the wing.

Once in their quarters the twins refused to be left alone in their room and joined their parents in their sitting room. Their sobbing was terrible. Nokai held Bao to comfort her. Shiann sobbed on her mother's shoulder while Yesui stroked her hair.

Not a word was said, but Yesui's eyes were suddenly locked on her husband's without consciously doing it.

Do you hear me, husband? she thought.

Always, my love. There is a struggle within you that frightens me. There are dark thoughts that surprise me. I did not think you a vengeful person, and First Mother would not have you be one.

The girls' sobbing ceased. They opened tear-filled eyes and looked back and forth at their parents' faces.

"We'll discuss it later," said Yesui. "It's late. You girls should be in bed. We'll be getting up early in the morning."

"Please, Mother, not in our room," said Bao. "We don't want to be alone."

"Not tonight," said Shiann.

Nokai kissed the top of Bao's head, looked at Yesui for any sign of disagreement. "There's room in our bed for four, but you must go to sleep right away. Your mother and I will come to bed later."

"Get your sleeping robes," said Yesui, and the girls rushed from the room. They were back in a minute, dressed for bed, kissed their parents good night and went to the bedroom, whispering to each other.

Nokai came over to cuddle Yesui on the plush reclining lounge where she'd been sitting. She put her face against his shoulder and sighed. They remained that way for a long moment, and then —

"I keep forgetting you see my every thought. You are always in me, Nokai, but you say so little about it," she murmured.

"I try to be unobtrusive, dear, but now is not the time for it. I think what you're considering for Jensi City is wrong. You're not just the Mei-lai-gong. You're Empress now, at least for a while. An Empress who cares for her people does not destroy a city for what a few have done."

"It's more than a few," said Yesui.

"A few hundred, then, even thousands. The city is under military control. What more is needed? It's vengeance you're thinking about, not order. You heard the Colonel. There are people who await death by your hand. And they are believers."

"But not innocent," said Yesui. "Their church was part of the problem that brought Quantou to power, and their demonstration blocked a possible escape route for us. I hold them accountable for that."

"Oh Yesui," said Nokai.

They argued for nearly an hour, hearing and considering each other's words, but it ended when Yesui suddenly masked herself so strongly even Nokai could not see what was there. His eyes widened when she looked up at him, and then she kissed his cheek.

"I hear your words, darling, but at midnight tomorrow the people will know an atrocity has been committed not just against an Empress, but against the Chuang-shi. They will see the true power behind the throne of Shanji, a power they've forgotten or no longer think is true."

Nokai looked at her sadly. "Your power is First Mother's, and She is merciful. I pray She will come to you tonight in your sleep," he murmured, and kissed her lips softly.

When the parents went to bed, the girls were pretending to sleep but were wide awake. They lay in the middle of the bed, hands clasped. Yesui and Nokai slipped in on either side of them and nestled in under the coverlet.

Nokai fell asleep quickly and the twins began drifting towards sleep once their parents were there beside them. Yesui remained awake, awaiting the matrix of purple stars, a golden cluster, any sign of the First One of the Chuang-shi coming to advise her.

She dozed.

And the Chuang-shi were there, in one being.

Yesui. Oh, Yesui, I'm so sorry for you.

Yesui stirred, on the edge of sleep.

'Mind'! I thought you were gone forever.

Not yet, but soon. I was sent to tell you your mother is with us.

Oh, NO! She's —

Not dead, Yesui. Her body lives, but the part of her that is Chuang-shi is now under our care. It is all we can do. The rest is up to her physicians.

But if she dies, I will —

If she dies you will know she is with us forever, but there will be no time for goodbyes to be said. Your mother has not come to us by her own will. First Mother has brought her here. If her body begins to heal, she will be returned and be whole again.

Yesui was nearly awake. *Oh 'Mind', tell me what I should do! I have a terrible decision to make.*

You have already made it, said 'Mind'. *It is harsh, but must be done. Now sleep, and know First Mother is with you, and all the Chuang-shi.*

'Mind's' presence was gone before Yesui could even respond. The sudden absence brought her awake. She turned her head to see if Nokai had awakened.

Nokai was sound asleep, but not her daughters.

Bao and Shiann were looking at her with huge eyes.

"You heard," whispered Yesui.

The twins nodded together, then looked at each other in a most curious way as if each expected the other to say something.

Yesui relaxed her head against the pillow, and closed her eyes again.

"Then you know grandmother is in their care," she murmured, and fell quickly asleep.

She dreamed of blue fire, consuming a city.

In the morning she rushed to hospital, and found her parents were still alive.

Twenty-Two

Coma

Heat, a bright flash of orange light and then terrible pain. Yesui screaming.

Oblivion.

Kati's mind stirred, as if wakening. The sight of her father burning, Huomeng's screaming as he was pulled from the flames, all of it was happening again. She wanted to scream, but had no voice. All physical feeling was gone from her. She was floating in a black void, disembodied, without form or function.

All she had done, the war saving Shanji from bondage to Tengri-Nayon, her reforms, new democracy, fair treatment of the poor, all of it had ended in the hatred of her people. A part of her tried to rationalize it by saying the hatred came only from a few, but it seemed she had simply failed as an Empress. The people didn't want her anymore. She had also failed First Mother and Abagai, for the people of Shanji were no longer united in harmony.

Kati recognized her musings for what they were, an exercize in self-pity and grief over something that had gone terribly wrong. But there were truths she now faced for the first time, truths about the errors she'd made, and going back to the beginning. Her strong compassion for people had swayed her judgement, for it had extended to those who did not deserve it. Her desire for democracy had been an excuse for not exercising her power over people who sought to destroy the Empire. Her ego had allowed Jensi to be elite from the beginning so that she might have that one bright jewel in the monument of her reign. She had trusted the nobles, even pampered them, and they had only conspired for personal gain with a new noble class arising to flaw that jewel.

All the arguments with her daughter over these things, yet Yesui had been correct in many of her judgements. The thought brought Kati a sudden new fear. Yesui's screams had been as much in her mind as in her ears. There had been surprise, shock — and a terrible rage. Wherever Kati was, it was certainly not Shanji. Was she dead, or in transit to transfiguration in the gong-shi-jie? Wherever she was, Shanji was not part of it. Yesui was now Empress, and on her own.

And Yesui was not like her mother in most ways.

Kati felt a terrible fear of what the Mei-lai-gong might do.

She floated in the black void, helpless, saddened and without hope for what seemed like a very long time.

Until the Chuang-shi came for her.

Kati. We are here. You're torturing yourself needlessly with regrets, for you have done everything First Mother has asked of you.

In the blackness, three wisps of color flickered into view, then grew in brightness and form until they were wavering columns of red, green and blue.

Have I died? asked Kati. Is this to be my transfiguration — alone?

She remembered Abagai's transfiguration, when all the important people in the woman's life had been present to say goodbye.

No, Kati, that time comes when you will it. Do you want to die? The red manifestation flared bright with the question.

Kati thought carefully, was surprised and disturbed by the seriousness of her consideration, for it was a question she would have rejected as rediculous — before now.

I don't think so. No. I haven't given up on my life, but it's suddenly going quite badly for me. I'm afraid for my husband. I'm afraid of what my daughter might do. And I don't know what has happened to me. Where am I?

Now the blue manifestation flared.

You are within yourself, but in a state beyond sleep. This is why we have come to call you. The matrix of lights you're used to seeing will not be here for your focus, so we will guide you to the place of creation.

For what reason? asked Kati, still anxious.

The green manifestation brightened as the third member of the Chuang-shi answered her.

Your body has already begun to heal, but your mind must remain in a dormant state for a time. While it is there we have an opportunity to show you

245

new things and increase your perspective. Your physical being is but a tiny part of your life, Kati. In this universe, the rest of life will be in a different form, with us.

But I've already seen the gong-shi-jie and worked within it, said Kati.

Others have not, said Green, other Chuang-shi who've not yet been called. They are the first in their line; there is no member of their species to bring them to our dimensionality and show them the way back. Not all of us have been as fortunate as you, Kati. You were first called by a being like yourself.

Abagai, said Kati.

A name said with much affection, said Red, flaring. Emotion is so strong in your species. It is — pleasant.

We are all different, Kati, said Blue. In all of this universe there is only one species like yours. It is time for you to see others unlike you, but beings who are still Chuang-shi. Are you ready?

Yes, said Kati. All worry, self-pity and doubts were suddenly gone, the flashing of the three manifestations somehow mesmerizing in her dark place.

Follow us, they said together, and she was drawn to them, coming together with them in a whirl of colors, and then there was a flash of green, and —

The swirling mists of the light of creation surrounded her.

It was her usual place of entrance, the vortices of Tengri-Khan and Nayon quite near, but there was no purple vortex showing the way back to herself.

We'll guide your way back, Kati, said Blue. Now come. There is a creature in your own galaxy you must see.

They moved towards the galactic core along a route Kati had not traveled before. The vortices of stars were dense, then sparse, then dense again as they left one spiral arm and entered another. Many of the vortices were large in this zone, and a deeper red, a gravitational signature of hot, blue stars.

She is a water creature who lives deep in a gaseous world with a hot star that will not last long, said Red. Her people have evolved quickly to their present form, but now grow and reproduce slowly. It will only be a few generations before their star explodes and destroys them all.

She is different from her people, Kati, said Green sadly, a spontaneous mutation that usually begins a new line of Chuang-shi.

She senses our presence, but is detached from her own kind. She is lonely.

Her people think she is strange, said Blue. They are quite social, and travel together in schools.

She must breed to continue the line, said Red.

Kati sensed some urgency in what they were doing, and at that instant first noticed she was traveling without manifestation of any kind. The Chuang-shi saw her concern in a blink.

In the current state of your physical being there will be no manifestation, Kati, said Blue. You are totally detached from your body, but you can make a simple form from the light of creation if you imagine it. A sphere, a fan, any simple shape will do.

A deep, deep red, said Red. This creature senses only sound and heat. It is only through heat that she can see us.

Try it, Kati, said Blue.

It had been years since Kati had moved the energies of creation, but she remembered that in doing it she must relax and only imagine what she wanted and it would be so. She remembered the simple fan of green that Yesui used, imagined it in red, called forth that light from the clouds around her and it was there.

Too hot, said Green. It will frighten or repel her. It must be a deep, deep red, like this.

The great column of green in front of Kati turned red, then brown, then black against the background of vortices and swirling mists of creative light.

Kati thought of the deepest red she'd ever seen, the first dim glow of a piece of steel being forged into the blade of a sword.

Better, said Green, but still quite warm. It will have to do. Your physical senses do not allow your imagination to go deeper in redness. So hold what you have.

They were approaching a huge vortex, deep red, and something stirred in Kati, a feeling, an ache that was disturbing.

We are here, said Blue, and her manifestation turned instantly black. Red followed her example, *Do you feel her?*

I feel something, said Kati. It is — sad.

She tries to call us back. We were here just before we came for you, said one of the Chuang-shi.

Feelings exploded in Kati, a terrible anguish turning to euphoria in an instant. *Oh*, she said.

She knows we're here, said a Chuang-shi, and now you must call her to us, Kati. We feel your empathy as she does. It is your empathy and not so much your signature that will bring her to us. But you must show her the way.

For Kati, first contact had been an image of Abagai's emerald green eyes, and then the matrix of purple stars, one flickering to give her a point of entrance to the gong-shi-jie. But none of this would work with a creature who could only sense heat.

Keep it up. She feels you. Imagine an oblong glowing cloud, first in brown, then turning to black, over and over again. It might simulate the heat signature of her kind.

Kati imagined it. Feelings overwhelmed her, a terrible mix of happiness and sorrow, fear and excitement. She tried remembering what it had been like when Abagai had come, when little Kati had seen her mother dead and was in the arms of her Moshuguang captor, ready to give up her own life in sorrow and loss. The emerald eyes had been there, then —

Know that I am with you, for there is something I would have you do for me when you're a woman.

One life had ended, another begun, a new life beyond her imagination.

We are here. You are not alone, and there is so much for you to see and do. Come to us and we will guide you. We will be your friends. We will —

She was babbling, thoughts expressed in a way only her own species could understand, and suddenly she felt foolish.

But something was happening.

At the edge of the vortex of a hot blue star a spot of purple appeared, grew into an oblong shape and began to spin.

Move back, said a Chuang-shi. You are much, much warmer than the rest of us.

Kati moved back as the spinning oblong spread out to form a small purple vortex, dimming until barely visable, a thing she'd seen so many times but had never watched during its formative phase.

And something black oozed out of the vortex.

A single tendril of something coal black issued forth from the center of the vortex and split into two parts, like a forked tongue. It wavered there for a long moment, still attached to the vortex. Kati drew back while the other Chuang-shi came in closer, their vertical black manifestations flattening into oblongs and wavering in synch with the movements of the new visitor.

Kati followed their example, her fan reshaping itself as she thought it. *Welcome to this place*, she thought, and again felt foolish. She also felt the quiet fear and awe emanating from the newcomer.

The forked tongue in black seemed to flow, coalescing into an oblong and then detaching from the vortex. It floated there a moment, then flattened out like a membrane stretched between the corners of a rectangular frame.

Kati imitated the shape, and the other Chuang-shi followed her. She was working by instinct, trying to retain friendly feelings and an empathy for the sorrow she had felt, but thoughts of her husband, daughter, her own injured body were threatening to intrude again. She tried to suppress them. The three other Chuang-shi came over to stand beside her.

You are the brightest, the hottest. She sees you as the leader here, said one of them.

The creature's manifestation suddenly sagged, the upper corners of it drooping, folding into flaps, then straightening up again.

Kati could only imitate the gesture, and wondered what it meant. As she did it, another gesture came to her mind, but one requiring cool light. She thought red, deep red, deeper until nearly black, a tendril of light snaking from her manifestation and encircling her companions.

We are Chuang-shi, she thought. We are one.

She sent out a black tendril towards the creature, who shrank backwards and again touched the vortex from which she'd come. Kati advanced the tendril slowly, not touching but encircling her with it until they were all connected within a single black thread.

We are all one, thought Kati.

And she ached with sudden joy.

She understands, said a Chuang-shi.

She's very quick, said another, and excited. But something's disturbing her. She's going to leave!

Instinct, again. Kati thought an oblong, brown to black, then brown again, the first sign she'd shown the creature. Our call, she thought. We'll come again. She still felt joy, but also anxiety. It suddenly occured to her that something had disturbed the creature in real space and time, and she was returning to a waking state.

There was barely time to repeat the calling signature before the creature's manifestation had sunk into the vortex, and was gone.

One of the Chuang-shi went after her, dropping into the vortex before it was gone and reappearing at a nearby point an instant later with the full color of her manifestation.

It was Blue.

She is safe. There is a crystalline shell of frozen water and gases around the ocean she swims in, and she was pressed up against it. A few of her people had come up close to see what was wrong with her, and she sensed them. She is swimming again.

I want to see! said Kati.

You cannot make the transition in your present state, said Blue. I'm sorry.

But what does she look like?

The Chuang-shi thought together for a moment. As they did it, both Green and Red regained the colors of their manifestations.

On your world, Green finally said, there is a large fish in your sea. It is flat and uses part of its body like wings to propel itself. She is something like that, but has many heat-seeking organs, like whiskers, that give her depth perception in all directions. You must heal yourself, Kati, and come back to see her again. We want to leave her in your care.

There are others, said Blue. Three others in your own galaxy.

It is something a First Order like yourself can do, added Red, and it's important. There are many ways to serve First Mother, Kati.

Kati's interpretation made her suddenly sad again. *Have I failed Her so miserably as Empress of Shanji?* she asked.

You haven't failed, Kati, but perhaps your work on Shanji has run its course, said Blue. There is more to this universe of ours than a single planet, and both you and Yesui have been most distracted lately by your political squabbles. As a Chuang-shi the universe is your home and Shanji is a speck of dust in it. It is only a single speck out of billions where life exists. We must nurture this life and seek out all Chuang-shi evolving from it. Our numbers decrease with each new universe.

I have nurtured life on Shanji, and my daughter is a Chuang-shi, Kati said defensively.

You've done well. I'm only saying there are other things for you to do. Yesui is prepared to be Empress; let her do it so you can pursue some of this work in the gong-shi-jie. There are other things Yesui should be doing as well, and she will soon hear about that from one of us, said Blue.

The Chuang-shi began moving, and Kati followed.

Memorize some markers, Kati, said Green. We won't be with you the next time you come here, and she will be expecting you again soon.

If you will care for her, said Blue, a bit nastily, Kati thought.

The creature's star was in a cluster of six at the edge of the galactic arm and only a few markers for direction were necessary, most of which she'd already noted in coming from her own system.

I'll do it, but I don't think it's going to be a simple task. Now where are we going? How long am I going to be here? I'm worried about my husband!

Beings with high metabolic rates are always in such a hurry, said Red, and two of the three Chuang-shi seemed amused.

Kati was not, and neither was Blue.

Worry is useless. Leave that to your physicians. We cannot help your husband, Kati. We were sent here for you, to give you new purpose in your life. Now please let us do that!

Blue was clearly miffed, and in charge. She sped ahead, and the rest of them hurried to follow her. But Kati herself was angered by Blue's outburst. She felt it selfish, and uncaring. Huomeng was in my life before I ever saw the gong-shi-jie, and now I'm the only one here who cares about him, she thought.

Kati! called Blue, and Kati hurried faster.

And they took her to another place to introduce her to a creature far more bizarre than the one she'd just met.

Twenty-Three

Mei-Lai-Gong

When evening had come and it was dark, the city was empty. The buildings stood tall, without a single window lit, looking like tombstones in a vast cemetery.

People had fled to their homes in the outskirts of the city, beyond the checkpoints and patrolled perimeter where the Moshuguang invaders walked their posts. They locked themselves in. Those who did not believe ate their meals and were in bed as midnight approached. Those who believed remained awake to say their prayers by candlelight in the hope they would be spared.

The Mei-lai-gong would come at midnight, and with her the vengeance of First Mother for the crime committed against Her emissary the previous day.

The few people who had homes inside the guarded perimeter had been taken in by friends. Even fewer watched from verandas overlooking the city as midnight approached, verandas of great homes in marble and quartzite high up in the surrounding hills. Within these homes an atmosphere of cautious gaiety prevailed. There was good food and drink. Wagers were placed on the Mei-lai-gong's coming or not, and the exact time of her coming if the myth were true.

These people were also unbelievers.

Down in the city, near its center, to the east, there was only one place showing signs of human activity and that was in Peoples' Park where the religious zealots of Jensi had fled to chant their prayers. From the hills they could not be heard. There was only a long snaking line of dull points of light from lit lanterns in procession throughout the park to show their presence.

As midnight approached the procession changed, moving out of the park and along streets south and west of it, well within the guarded perimeter of the city.

The prayers of their atonement were finished, and the time for their judgement was at hand.

Wan-gu led the faithful from the park and they followed him like lambs, singing. He prayed he was not leading them to slaughter.

He had looked into the glowing eyes of Mei-lai-gong, had both heard and felt her rath. He believed her powers to be even more terrible than those of Mengnu. There had been no compassion in her when she'd spoken to him, but the scorched bodies of her parents had been in her view, and her dead companions burning in a car. She was human, and what human could show compassion at such a time? He could think of only one.

Mengnu.

He'd heard no reports to tell him whether the emissary to First Mother was alive or dead, or if her husband had survived. The Moshuguang troopers told him nothing when he asked, and the fact they'd allowed Wan-gu and his people to remain inside the guarded perimeter could be interpreted to two ways. Either their lives were to be spared, or they were to be destroyed with the city. Where they were would not matter.

If death was at hand, the judgement of First Mother against them, there was only one place appropriate for them to be received into Her arms for eternity. Wan-gu was taking them there.

He was taking them to the ruins of their church.

The faithful were strung out in a long line behind him. Most were adults, men and women, but there were also many children, even babes-in-arms. The adults were aware of their possible fate, and had the courage of their faith. The older children were confused, the babies unaware of anything except the singing and the cool night breeze. They marched behind him down a street heading south, then turned at a Moshuguang checkpoint and went west, the eyes of glum, armored troopers following them.

They think we march to our deaths, singing, thought Wan-gu, as his people again burst into song.

It was only a few city blocks to the church, and they arrived several minutes before midnight. The parking area and courtyard in front of the church would be sufficient to hold all of them. They could not enter their burned and gutted sanctuary, and would accept judgement on their knees, beneath the stars.

Wan-gu halted at the edge of the parking area a hundred meters from the church, and remained there until his congregation had crowded in behind him. When all were there he lifted his lantern over his head to gesture them forward.

As he did it his skin suddenly tingled, as if cold. The hair on his head seemed to be stirred by a breeze, and his mind blanked. His muscles suddenly refused to move.

The hallucination appeared only meters in front of him, two huge eyes opening up and glowing brightly in metallic blue.

People gasped, and someone screamed behind him.

The commanding voice in his head blew all other thought from his mind, and made his knees sag.

STAND WHERE YOU ARE!

And the people of First Mother's Church dropped to their knees in unison, lanterns clattering beside them.

All day he'd kept himself awake by frequent peerings out the window to check the street below. Gradually, fewer vehicles were there, and fewer troopers on the sidewalks. As street noise diminished it was harder to stay awake. He paced the suite and drank from the faucet until he was bloated, but still it felt as if his stomach were eating itself from inside. Sometime in late afternoon he sat down on the edge of the bed to rest his aching legs.

And awoke in darkness.

Sheng-chih was awake abruptly, lying on his back, his feet on the floor. He sat upright, heart pounding, listening for any sound in the room. There was nothing but his own ragged breathing. He went to the window and looked out. Darkened buildings, the street empty, not a single vehicle or person on foot there. He refused to believe it and watched for several minutes, but nothing moved in the street below him. It was not what he'd expected. In an occupation there would be patrols, a curfew of some kind. But the city seemed empty, the silence absolute. Internment? Could a city of over a hundred thousand souls be emptied in a single day? And then what?

There was a terrible foreboding within him, urging him to flee when he saw the empty street. Would there be a better time than now?

The absence of patrols was surely transient, and he did not have far to go, a block west, then several blocks south to the walls of the Zhentou estate. The man owed him, would surely hide him for at least a little while. After that — well — a step at a time. He could have been visiting from Dahe. He wished to return home, this noble recluse, and had all necessary documents to prove his identity once things were settled a bit and travel restrictions lifted.

It was a risk, but one he had to take. By morning the streets could be filled with troopers again.

Sheng-chih took his briefcase and left the suite. The hallway was gloomy, only two battery-operated emergency lights glowing there. It was cold, and the elevator lights were also off. It seemed the entire building was without power.

He took the stairs down, pausing often to listen, the stairwell lit in dull red. When he reached ground level he opened the door slightly to peek out. More energency lights, and the lobby was empty, the guard's station deserted and dark.

Sheng-chih could not dare to leave by the front entrance. He went to the back of the building, watched from the shadows. Nothing moved outside. He let himself out, locked the door behind him and walked west. Even the street lights were out; he did not go into the street, but stayed close to the buildings as he moved.

One block, then a left turn and he had to cross the street. He darted across it and that one sprint left him breathless with effort and fear. He looked back once. Up in the hills were the lights of homes there, so it seemed power had been shut down only in the downtown area. For what purpose? Again foreboding, and he hurried along, his left shoulder brushing shop windows.

At an alley his heart nearly stopped. There was a clang to his left, and a man staggered towards him, mumbling. Sheng-chih sprinted again and hid in a doorway as the man stumbled out into the street and moved north.

He reached the Y where a street ran east by the church and its gardens, the main street heading south to the flyer field past the walled mansion of Zhentou. Another five blocks and he would be there. Without hesitation he stepped into the intersection and began crossing it.

He was in the middle of the street when two bright lights suddenly came on from a block ahead of him, and froze him in his tracks.

He heard a distant shout, and the grumble of an engine.

And Sheng-chih sprinted for his life.

He sprinted left down the center of the sidestreet, then right to finnish crossing it. There were only a few trees in the church gardens, scattered among carpets of flowers separated by low hedges in a labyrinth pattern of stone walkways. The Moshuguang truck was nearing the intersection he'd fled from when Sheng-chih reached the first hedges. A searchlight on the truck was already turned on and sweeping the street in search of him.

He crashed through two hedges and threw his entire body into a third, crushing it. Sharp stems and tiny hard leaves stung his face and poked into his nostrils as he lay perfectly still in the folliage.

The truck rumbled by in the street. The searchlight beam swept by his place, and the truck kept going. Sheng-chih rolled out of the hedge and peered over another. The truck was sitting at an intersection east of him, playing its light back and forth across the street and buildings. It backed up, turned south and sped ahead. Sheng-chih ducked as the beam again swept the gardens of the church, slowly, more deliberately this time. *They've seen nothing, but know I must be here*, he thought. *They'll be back again. I can't stay here.*

And before the truck was completely out of sight, Sheng-chih grasped his briefcase tightly and sprinted towards the ruins of the church.

He pressed his back against cold stone and smelled charred wood. The back entrance was boarded up with a single sheet of wood and only a few nails. There was a screech as he pulled it loose at one side. A light swept the street to his right. The truck had quickly circled the church, and was coming back again.

The sheet came loose. Behind it, the door had been burned away. Sheng-chih slipped past the loosened barrier and felt a nail tear at his clothing. Another jabbed his hand as he pulled the sheet back into position. He heard distant voices, and a light swept past the boarded entrance. The truck rumbled by, again heading east.

The interior of the church was darker than night and smelled like charcoal. The floor was a crazy tumble of charred wood and debris. There was a faint flickering glow coming from cracks in the boards over the front entrance, and now the sound of singing voices in the distance. Sheng-chih stumbled his way to the center of the church. A downdraft of cold air made him look up and he saw stars beyond the huge hole that had been burned through the roof.

He could not hear the truck, now, only the singing. Suddenly it stopped. The only sound was his raspy breathing. People were outside, perhaps near, and he dared not move for fear of banging into something and making a sound.

Safety was only blocks away. He would wait here until first light. The Moshuguang checkpoint was at a street intersection, and now he knew where it was. At first light he could slip past it and sprint the rest of the way to safety if there were no other patrols in the area.

That was his plan.

Sheng-chih sat down on the floor amidst the charred remains of the church, looked up at the stars overhead, and waited for morning to come.

The wait was not as long as he expected. A few minutes later, morning came suddenly, and its color was purple, a brilliant sun descending upon him through the opening in the roof.

In the last nanosecond of his life, Sheng-chih felt warmth.

I HAVE NO DESIRE TO TAKE YOUR LIVES. TURN YOURSELVES TO THE SOUTH. WHAT I DO HERE IS NOT FOR YOUR EYES TO SEE.

Wan-gu shuddered, and bent over to place his forehead on the ground. It seemed all the hair on his body was standing straight up. The chill of the air was gone, and he felt bathed by warmth from above him. He looked up towards the stars. At first it seemed a cloud was there, but it was something else, a shimmering mist colored richly in purple and then there were flickering streamers in red and green. The mists began rotating far above his head and there was a brightening in their center, purple, then blue and the people around him began crying out in fear. The center of the swirling vortex flared to a blinding brightness and was suddenly descending on him. Wan-gu closed his eyes and turned away from the church as Mei-lai-gong's command came again.

TURN AROUND! AND PROSTRATE YOURSELVES IN THE PRESENCE OF FIRST MOTHER'S POWER!

People cried out. Wan-gu turned south and prostrated himself on concrete suddenly warm to the touch. There was heat on his back, not burning, but hot. The hair on his head was struggling hard to pull away from his scalp and now there was sound, a terrible sound like rushing water, a cascade coming down to crush him. He squeezed his eyes tightly shut, but it was if they were open and staring at a purple sun. The heavens rumbled, growled, then shrieked and he was deafened by it. Hard pellets, like hail, struck his back and face. One got in his mouth; it was searing hot and burned his tongue before he could spit it out. He pressed his mouth against concrete and gasped for breath as the world around him shrieked and howled for an eternity that was only seconds.

The sound went away as quickly as it had come, and with it the stinging pellets and the heat on his back. The purple light showing through his eyelids was still there, but dimming. Wan-gu dared to open his eyes, and rolled over on his back. The bright vortex above him was fading fast, replaced by a roiling mass of air glowing green, then dull red, then becoming a moist cloud misting lightly on his face.

YOU WILL BUILD AGAIN, said Mei-lai-gong.

Wan-gu sat up while the others dared to open their eyes, and he looked at the place where the ruins of his church had been.

Glowing bright orange, there was a great mound of something transparent, but with faint shadows inside it. It was like a huge dollop of glass just taken from a furnace, a dollop four meters high and a base nearly covering the space where the church had been. Wan-gu's face felt hot from its radiation, even with falling mist to cool him.

THE NEW CHURCH WILL NOT BE A PLACE OF WORSHIP, BUT A SIMPLE STRUCTURE FOR MEDITATION AND STUDY. FIRST MOTHER IS NOT A GOD. SHE NEITHER REQUIRES YOUR WORSHIP OR DESIRES IT, spoke the supernatural presence of The Mei-lai-gong.

The sight of the glowing crystal was awesome and terrifying to him. *We hear your words, and will obey them*, thought Wan-gu. The crystal was now cherry red in color. There was another glow further away, a red glow reflected from buildings ordinarily not visible from this location. And then it struck him.

The great structure of The House of Fangzi-yin, tallest in the city, was no longer there.

I LEAVE THIS MONUMENT TO YOUR PAST ERRORS. YOU WILL LOVE AND RESPECT ALL PEOPLE, AND LIVE IN HARMONY WITH THEM FROM THIS DAY FORTH. THIS IS THE WILL OF FIRST MOTHER.

It will be done, thought Wan-gu, then said it out loud, and there was a chorus of voices behind him.

And Mei-lai-gong was gone.

The people arose hesitantly, and stood silently to watch the crystal cool until it was nearly dawn. A few picked up the pellets that had fallen from the sky. Most were black, like highly compressed charcoal. Others were clear and very hard, tiny pieces of a dead star brought to them from far away by First Mother's right hand.

If they could have probed the diamond hard surface of the monument Mei-lai-gong had left them they would have found inclusions of blackened wood from their church.

They would also have found a few pieces of carbonized human bone.

Far up in the hills, people remained in shock on the verandas of fine homes. They stood in silence, wagers forgotten, their vision still blurred from the sight of two bright vortices that had formed over the city exactly at midnight to belch forth columns of gas and hot dust in an explosion of sound.

In the distance there was a glowing ember to show where the ruined church had been. Closer, two glowing mounds of slag, in many colors, were all that remained of City Hall and The House of Fangzi-yin.

The people watched the mounds of slag cooling.

And they believed.

Twenty-Four

Awakening

The news of what had happened in Jensi City was known planet-wide by noon the following day. But outside of Jensi, Nokai was the first to know it.

Shortly after midnight Yesui returned to herself from the gong-shi-jie to find Nokai wide awake and nestled against her on their bed.

"It is done," she whispered, and then showed him what it was.

Nokai caressed her bare shoulder, and smiled. "It is imaginative," he said. "I think First Mother will be pleased."

"It was probably Her idea," said Yesui, and kissed him.

They fell asleep immediately in each others' arms, and awoke at first light.

Mother! called Yesui, but there was no answer.

They dressed quickly and went straight to the hospital, leaving the twins asleep. A Moshuguang surgeon met them, his eyes puffy from lack of sleep. He'd been in surgery all night, fighting for Huomeng's life.

"The spleen is out, and we've stopped the internal bleeding," he said. "His blood pressure is rising, and that's a good sign. But the hot gases your father breathed in have badly damaged one lung, and we might have to remove it. He's a strong man, Madam. The trauma to his body would have already killed most men his age."

"My Mother?" asked Yesui.

"The same. Comatose, but her vital signs are good. The burns are second and third degree, especially on her back. We already have skin and nerve mats in solution for her. I'm more concerned about her coma. The brain signals are most abnormal."

Yesui put a hand on the man's shoulder. "I will explain it to you when you've had some rest. And I'm very grateful for what you've already done."

"It has been my privilege, Madam," said the surgeon, and they left him to his search for an empty bed or a gurney on which he could take a well-earned nap before resuming his duties.

Nokai returned to their quarters to get the girls up and ready for their tutoring, and then a day of his analysis with Sheng-chih's red accounting book.

Yesui went straight to her mother's quarters to begin her second full day as interim Empress of Shanji and spent most of it with telephoned reports coming in.

Rani-tan was first to report. By unanimous vote Jensi City had been expelled from The Peoples' Congress in special session the previous evening, and Yesui had been acknowledged as Empress. There were already anxious murmurings among representatives regarding her dramatic show of power in the rogue city.

Jensi was fully occupied and closed. Troops had begun patroling the downtown area at dawn. And Sheng-chih had not yet been found.

Yesui could only hope he'd been hiding within The House of Fangzi-yin the previous midnight.

There was a report of a slave labor camp operating in the forests north of Jensi; she authorized the dispatch of twenty flyers and a transport ship to investigate it.

Quantou had been brought to Mengnu City and locked in a cell in the basement of the Hall of Ministries. He was refusing to eat, and babbling incoherently to the guards, who thought him mentally ill.

Perhaps I pressed him too hard in my questioning, thought Yesui, but for the moment she didn't care. She would let him sit there for months before granting him a first hearing. Or wait until Mother was well enough to do it.

She buried herself in paperwork and exchanged data with Nokai by computer the rest of the day, building their cases against noble families and The House of Fangzi-yin. She went with Nokai and the twins to hospital that evening, but nothing had changed and the physicians would still not allow her to see her parents. Both were unconscious, they argued, and the sight of them would cause needless trauma to their family. Yesui accepted this on behalf of Bao and Shiann, for she knew even if the girls were kept from seeing the injuries, and Yesui saw the horror, they would also see it through their mother's mind.

The days turned into a week, then two. Father's vital signs stabilized, and there was hope, but it was now likely he would lose a lung. The tissue and nerve mats for Mother were growing well, but she was still gone to wherever the Chuang-shi had taken her.

After the fourth day the doctors allowed visitors for the patients, but excluded Bao and Shiann because of their age. The visits were short, the patients unconscious and unresponsive.

Huomeng looked like a cybernaut with tubes sprouting from his chest and every orifice. Occasionally he would roll his head, eyelids flickering, and moan. Mother lay still, like a statue of stone, the left side of her face swathed in moist gauze. She lay on her stomach, her back covered with a soft polymer bristling with tubes carrying liquids and gases to her injured tissue.

The visits were unpleasant. Yesui could sit there only a few minutes, touching a hand, a face, saying some words of comfort she knew were not heard.

In the second week, Tirgee called with Mengjai from the gong-shi-jie and Yesui went there to jump the newlyweds' ship. Teacher showed student a new goal when she brought them out only a hundred thousand kilometers above the surface of Shanji, and they had to nearly empty their fuel tanks in a long burn to slow down.

Mengjai was critical again. More than a tad close, sister, and a two gee deceleration for forty minutes is not a pleasant way to spend a honeymoon, he grumbled.

A shuttle brought them in from orbit, and Yesui met Tirgee face-to-face for the first time in a shuttledock lounge deep in the mountain. She thought the way Tirgee clung to Mengjai's arm was sweet, and their emotions with each other were wonderful and soothing to her troubled mind. Tirgee was even more beautiful than her image in the photograph on mother's night table, and she towered over Yesui by twenty centimeters. She seemed shy at first, bowed politely, then blushed fiercely when Yesui hugged her. It would take her a while to get used to the spontaneous show of affection between Mengjai's family members.

Yesui put them up in quarters near her own. They had a meal together, with Nokai and the girls. Bao and Shiann were quiet, and a bit sleepy. They'd just returned to themselves from a long session with the Chuang-shi they called 'Lady', and were still thinking about it. They were also thinking about losing their teacher when she was First Mother of a new universe, and wondering about who would come after her to show them even more in the place of creation.

That evening they all went to the hospital to stand beside the beds. Tirgee was not shaken by it, but tears came to Mengjai's eyes when he touched his father's face, and he had to leave the room. Outside, the twins consoled him, and he hugged them hard.

Tirgee gave Yesui a questioning look. "Mengjai cries as if he's mourning them, but they're alive and have the finest care. I don't understand," she said.

"He cries for their suffering," said Yesui.

"Ah," said Tirgee, and she learned something new about her husband.

They returned to their quarters and talked until late. Bao and Shiann listened quietly for a while, then excused themselves and went to bed. Nokai retired soon after, leaving Yesui, Mengjai and Tirgee to talk at length about the events in Jensi. Tirgee strongly supported the Mei-lai-gong's show of power there, and was likely repeating the words of her own mother. Mengjai felt it harsh, yet restrained, and wondered if Jensi would again be a problem in the future.

Tirgee led Mengjai off to bed, her head against his shoulder. Their masks were useless against Yesui's probing, and she was inspired by their intentions. Nokai was sleeping lightly when she joined him, and in seconds he was wide awake.

They made love for nearly an hour, and fell into dreamless sleep.

In the morning they went to the hospital again.

Yesui and Mengjai were standing at their mother's bedside when she suddenly awoke.

We have no more time, said Blue. You're fading on us.

What? said Kati.

Your manifestation is fading. You're being called back, and we cannot work against it. We'll have to come to you another time.

Blue sounded impatient, and annoyed.

That's good, isn't it? I was only able to make one contact. The other creatures wouldn't even come to me, said Kati.

In Kati's state of mind, one contact is astonishing, said Green. When she's healed she can penetrate real space to see them physically and formulate an attractive calling sign by observing their behavior. Why are we in such a hurry?

This is the work of first or second level Chuang-shi. Our time is better spent on other tasks, said Blue.

Now, now, said Red. It's not so long since all of us were second level, and this is the task First Mother has given us.

Impatience is a human trait, said Green.

I beg your pardon? said Blue, then, Very well, one more time. After that, Kati, you're on your own. But will you commit to it? Otherwise, we're wasting our efforts.

Kati thought slowly, her mind blurred as if being drawn to a new reality beyond the place of creation. The sign was familiar; something was drawing her back to herself in the four dimensions of real space.

Yes, I'll work with the Chuang-shi I've felt here, but only those beings. I'll be fortunate to do what you want with even one of them.

In your physical lifetime, you mean, said Blue, but that is only the beginning for you. Very well, it's a start.

They were far from the vortex of Tengri-Khan and Kati's instinct was to reach it before returning to herself, yet the Chuang-shi seemed in no hurry.

There is no purple vortex awaiting you, said Blue. We will return you from here, and call you again when you're healed. Remember your promise to us, Kati. It is also your promise to First Mother.

I'll remember, said Kati, suddenly detached, and the colorful manifestations of the Chuang-shi were fading fast, along with the vortices of stars and the clouds of creative light around her.

Light swept by her as if she were falling, and then blackness and a voice crying out.

Kati! Kati, my darling, where are you? Where am I? I can't see, but I feel you near me. Kati!

She was lying on her stomach, her head turned to one side. She felt the pricks of a thousand needles on her back, and something moist there. There was a loud beeping sound right next to her, and motion within her blurred vision, the sound of footsteps.

"Mother!"

Huomeng! You're alive!

Oh, I feel awful!

A high-pitched ringing sound struck Kati's ears, and she blinked hard to clear her vision. Footsteps were all around her.

"What is it? Nokai, see what's going on!"

"Mother, are you awake? Say something!"

It took her mind forever to identify the voices.

"Well — I'm still alive," she mumbled, then twisted her neck to look up as her vision finally cleared.

Yesui and Mengjai were standing there shoulder to shoulder, grinning down at her, their eyes filled with tears.

"Mengjai", she whispered, surprised. "I thought you were getting married."

Mengjai laughed, and touched her face. "I was. I am. Tirgee is here with me.

What's going on? I hear voices. I can't seem to open my eyes or move my arms! I hurt everywhere, Kati.

The children are here. We're in hospital, dear. Oh, Huomeng, I thought I'd lost you!

Nokai was back. "The alarm was from your father's vital signs. He's waking up!"

Kati heard her husband groan from close by, but she couldn't turn her head to see where he was. "Huomeng!" she called weakly.

I hear you. Something is covering my face, and my eyes are stuck shut. Ouch!

"The doctors are with him, Mother," said Yesui, and streaks of tears stained her face. "You've both been badly hurt, so don't try to move. I have to see Father."

Yesui moved away. Mengjai took her place, and next to him was a beautiful young woman with a long face and coal black eyes.

"Tirgee," said Kati, and tried to move her hand, but the woman grasped it with her own.

"We are relieved, Madam, and I bring you warmest regards from my mother," said Tirgee quite formally.

Kati squeezed her hand.

Oh, Father, we were so worried!

Touch me, Yesui. Let me know I'm really alive!

You are, you are. Mengjai!

Now Mengjai left to join his sister.

"When I look at you I see a young Yesugen," said Kati, "but your eyes are much darker than hers. You're a beautiful girl, Tirgee."

Tirgee blushed.

Father, lie still. They're trying to clean out your eyes so you can see, and you're a very sick man. Can you feel my hand on yours?

Yes. At least I still have feeling. Where's your mother?

Two meters away. You're in the same room, but her injuries are far less than yours. You're the difficult patient here.

Listen to your son, dear, said Kati.

"Both of you are fortunate to be alive," said Tirgee. "The attack on you was well planned and coordinated."

Mengmoshu! said Huomeng. He was in —

He's gone, Father, said Yesui. Nothing could be done.

"Father," whispered Kati, and her eyes suddenly burned.

"Yesui has restored order in Jensi City, Madam," said Tirgee quickly. "The people behind the assassination attempt have been killed or arrested, and Yesui has —"

Tirgee, not NOW! said Yesui, and Tirgee's mouth snapped shut. I'll tell you later, Mother. You just need to rest and heal, both of you. There's nothing for you to worry about.

Tirgee looked hurt, and Kati squeezed her hand again. "Please call me Kati, dear," she said. "I'm so happy to see you here."

Yesui was back, and put a hand gently on Tirgee's shoulder. "The doctors aren't pleased with all the visitors, Mother. If we don't leave, you won't rest. We'll be back again this evening."

Yesui was euphoric with relief. "I understand, dear," said Kati, "but we'll be expecting to see all of you this evening."

If you can stand it, said Huomeng. We must look awful right now.

Gauze head to toe, Father, said Mengjai, and yes, you look terrible. But we'll keep on coming back until you're on your feet. Now squeeze my hand. Ah — that's good.

The Moshuguang physicians had heard everything. "That's enough for now. Out, out — everyone," said one of them.

Even Yesui obeyed. There was a shuffling of feet, a door closing, and it was quiet again. A doctor with graying hair leaned over to look at Kati.

"Peace at last. Welcome back, Madam," he said smiling, and patted her hand.

"How is my husband?" she asked sleepily.

"Serious, but no longer critical. He gave our surgeons quite a race there for a while. Now relax. No thinking about work, and let us pamper you as much as we please. Now that you're awake we'll have you both in suspension harnesses by tomorrow, and you can see each other, I promise. Just think of this as a long vacation."

"How long?" asked Kati.

"At least several weeks," said the doctor, "but we'll have both of you on your feet long before then. Burn tissue is slow to replace, even with our present synthesis systems. We don't want to leave you with scars."

No scars, he says, and I feel like I've been pulverized, said Huomeng.

"You *have!*" said the doctor quite loudly. "Now get some sleep!"

He left them, and closed the door. There was only the click and hum of equipment monitoring their bodies.

He's pleased, said Huomeng. I'll take that as a good sign, but I think I've aged fifty years.

When I'm up and around, I'll use my hands on you, dear, said Kati.

Mmmm, those warm, healing hands. Kati, can you let go?

What?

Can you let go of your rule, and let Yesui do it for a while?

Yes, dear. I'm worried though.

I know, said Huomeng.

Tirgee started to tell me something, and Yesui cut her off.

If it has to do with Jensi City, I don't care, said Huomeng. Let the place rot in isolation until we're well again.

Yes, dear.

There was a pause, and Kati felt herself slipping away, then,

Kati?

Yes?

I love you, darling.

I love you too, Huomeng. You are my life, said Kati.

Both of them fell quickly asleep.

Yesui worked quickly and efficiently at her mother's desk. Her attitude was not what it had been before Mother's awakening. There had been that awful two weeks when Yesui had thought she might be Empress of Shanji for the rest of her life, and she'd made many decisions on her own, including the flaming of Jensi. But now, with

Mother healing, she saw her duties as temporary, good training for the position she would assume permanently, but later in life.

She organized her work into three major files: immediate decisions, decisions after consultation with Mother, and issues delayed until Mother was returned to her duties.

Mother was not particularly cooperative, and Yesui interpreted this as an effort to increase her self-confidence by forcing her to make decisions on her own. If Mother disagreed with Yesui's views she did not say so, but she had cried when Yesui told her about the retribution brought to Jensi City by the Mei-lai-gong.

They met regularly, but it seemed at times that Mother didn't care about the affairs of Shanji. She would listen, sitting at Father's bedside with her hands moving over his gauze-wrapped body so lovingly to bring healing energy to him while Yesui babbled about affairs of state. Occasionally she'd offer a suggestion: consultation with a Minister, or Rani-Tan, a vote of the Moshuguang Council in naming a military governor of Jensi. But all final decisions were left to Yesui, and Mother voiced no opinions of them, even when they were sought.

The decisions were many. A Moshuguang Colonel, Piendimoshu, was recommended by the Moshuguang Council as Military Governor of Jensi City and Yesui made the two-year appointment. She formally affirmed Colonel Damoshu as Moshuguang Chancellor after several long meetings with him. The evidence of corruption within The House of Fangzi-yin was now overwhelming, thanks to Nokai's careful analysis. The company was closed, its funds returned to many investors and confiscated for others. She had the heads of four noble families arrested for fraud against the Empire, and jailed them with Quantou in the Hall of Ministries. One of them had been responsible for the slave labor camp north of Jensi; the half-starved political and religious prisoners there had been returned with much public ceremony to their families.

All of this Yesui did in only weeks, but there were other things she thought necessary, things that Mother stubbornly refused to advise her about as if she didn't care. There were appropriations to make for two new buildings and a church in Jensi City. Yesui wanted the land grant system for investment by the nobles to either be ended or extended to all people on Shanji. She wanted to federalize the banks, not through takeover but by insuring deposits, which would require an annual audit of all accounts.

Mother would help her with none of these things. "The advice of your Ministers is better than mine. Listen to them," is all she would say.

Such changes in policy were major, and permanent, the decisions inappropriate for an interimEmpress. Yesui put these issues aside. She intended to lobby hard for her views on them when Mother was well again.

And Mother was healing quickly.

Father was slower in recovery. He was on his feet in six weeks after an operation to remove a portion of one lung. Each evening Mother walked him up and down a hallway and then used her hands on him while Yesui visited with them. Their faces were bright red with fresh new skin.

Other family members visited during the day, but Mengjai and Tirgee were gone again. They had left for Meng-shi-jie after staying long enough to see Father on his feet, and then Yesugen had called Mother from the gong-shi-jie to say she'd visit them soon.

After another visit with her parents, it was again late when Yesui returned to her quarters. Nokai had waited for her, but the twins had eaten and were in their room. A servant brought strips of lamb over rice, and a hot barley soup. They ate in silence until Nokai finally spoke.

"The girls missed you again. They've been depressed the last two days," he said.

"About what?" asked Yesui. "Mother and Father are healing nicely."

"It's not that. It's the Chuang-shi who teaches them. She's leaving."

"We've been expecting that for a long time," said Yesui.

"It's tonight," said Nokai. "The girls are with her now. They've been gone for nearly two hours, Yesui, and I'm concerned. They're never gone for more than a few minutes. Anyway, Bao and Shaan were both crying about losing her, and hardly ate a thing."

"Two hours is unusual, but not long," said Yesui. "I was out of my body nearly a day when I moved Lan-Sui City and then had to search everywhere to find it. I'll check on them, dear."

She finished her meal and went alone to the girls' room, opened the door slowly and peeked inside. The only light there came from a computer screen. Bao and Shaan were on their bed in the usual position, hands clasped together. Yesui sat down on the edge of the bed, watched the slow rise and fall of her daughters' chests, both of them breathing only a few times each minute.

So far away. I wish I could be with you, she thought sadly. I wish I could do what your Lady does for you.

She reached out her hand to touch Bao's cheek, then pushed an errant lock of hair up from Shaan's forehead. The girls lay deathly still; there was not even the flutter of an eyelid. The only sound was a high-pitched buzz from the computer.

Yesui.

The call itself was faint, but the presence was strong and familiar. When she felt it, Yesui's heart jumped. It was not the usual joy she felt with the call, but anxiety that seemed to come from a secret place inside her, a place beyond conscious thought.

Yesui, I have come to say goodbye. My time has come.

I'm with my daughters, 'Mind', said Yesui. I'm waiting for you to give them back to me.

Ah, said 'Mind', you've made a good guess.

It's more than that. The affection they have for their Lady is the same as mine for you, and now we're all losing you.

Our memories of each other are forever, Yesui. Now come to me in the gong-shi-jie. There is one last matter for us to attend to. But remain physically with your daughters. That is important.

Yesui lay down next to Bao and closed her eyes. The matrix of purple stars was instantly there and rushing towards her. She focused randomly on a single point, then the flash of green as she dashed through the interface and the swirling clouds of creative light, the vortices of stars all around her.

I am here, said Yesui. 'Mind' had never shown her a manifestation, and so Yesui did not look for one, only waited for the Chuang-shi's presence.

It was there. The last time for us, Yesui. My universe is ready to be born, and your daughters have helped while I taught them. They still don't accept the fact I must go alone. They do not understand the void between universes.

I will try to explain it to them, said Yesui, but I have my own questions, 'Mind'.

Yesui hesitated to ask the question, for she feared the answer she might receive.

What is it? asked 'Mind'.

If — if my daughters have helped you prepare the birth of a new universe then they know how it is done. Does this mean they will be first mothers during their lifetime with me?

This has been your fear since I began working with them, said 'Mind'.
Yes, very much so.

But unnecessary, said 'Mind'. No, Yesui. They, you, your mother, all Chuang-shi must first live out their full lives and be transfigured before the final step in First Motherhood can be made. I cannot explain it fully, for it's beyond your physical senses or imagination, but in transfiguration one becomes a kind of pure energy in a higher dimensionality than yours. A new universe and First Mother are one entity at their birth. Your daughters have the abilities, but not the proper form. But until then, there are other things they can do, and that is one reason we're meeting here — all of us.

All of us? Yesui was confused, thinking all the Chuang-shi might be coming to her.

The four of us, Yesui: you and I — and your daughters. They have seen the smallest there is to see in the gong-shi-jie, but have not seen the whole of it. I promised them a lady would come to show them the whole when I was gone.

They told me that, said Yesui, and an old dream swelled within her, filling her with anticipation and an aching joy.

Yes, Yesui, that lady is you. It has always been you. First Mother would have it no other way.

Oh, 'Mind', said Yesui, this has been the strongest dream of my life!

She was filled with such joy that her concentration wavered, and the green fan of her manifestation flickered wildly.

I will bring them here, for they are far away, but you must call them, Yesui. You must be the first to bring them forth in the whole of the gong-shi-jie. Your presence will be enough if you call them. Are you ready?

Yes, oh YES!, said Yesui, and focused hard to calm her unruly manifestation.

It will be a moment, said 'Mind'. Her presence faded, but was not gone while Yesui regained control over her excitement.

In front of her a golden mist appeared as if condensed out of the clouds of creative light. It swirled, then condensed further into bright points like a cluster of stars.

Call them, said 'Mind'. They are here.

Bao and Shaan, said Yesui, it's Mother. Do you hear me?

Mother? Two presences in one, and strong. Are we waking up? Lady is with us, and she's leaving!

I am also with you, but in a place you haven't seen. Think of the green fan of my manifestation in this place, and come to me.

You're in the gong-shi-jie! said the girls together.

Come, now, and show yourselves; give me a manifestation so I can know where you are.

The girls seemed hesitant and confused, and then 'Mind' spoke.

Hurry, girls. This is the lady I promised you, the one who will teach you further when I'm gone.

It's MOTHER! they cried out, and between Yesui and the swirling cluster of golden stars a new manifestation burst forth, two columns in red and blue intertwined like a double helix.

Ohhh, said the twins.

And we are finally together in the gong-shi-jie, said Yesui, fighting back emotions. It has been my dream since you were little girls.

It's so beautiful, said Bao, and the red column of the double helix flickered.

And your green fan is just like we imagined it, said Shaan, flickering blue.

But where is Lady? they asked together.

I am here, said 'Mind'.

We can't see you.

It has been my choice to travel without manifestation here, but now is the time to show you something. It will also answer a question your mother once asked me a long time ago.

Your Lady is the Chuang-shi I've always called 'Mind' because I thought she was a part of me when we first met, said Yesui quickly. She has also been your mother's teacher for many years.

To her left, a roiling, red mist appeared with writhing streamers in green. The streamers moved chaotically at first, then slowed, branched, organizing themselves into a pattern. The memory of myself is so old, Yesui. I can only approximate my image when I was an organic creature, but it will be close to what I was.

The image of something vaguely insectile formed within the roiling red mist. There was a large head, with four antennae and no visable mouth, two arms ending in clusters of four small pincers. The body was upright and in one narrow piece like a snake's; it balanced on a long smooth tail, and had two legs ending in claws.

Both Yesui and the twins were shocked at the sight, and drew back in surprise.

We were small, my people and I, said 'Mind' wistfully. Our bodily secreations were mixed with sand to build our little cities, and we lived happily there without higher technology. We did not travel in space, Yesui. Our senses could not even detect the stars in our sky. Our universe was much simpler than yours, yet two of us were called as Chuang-shi. We lived and were transfigured. Only the two of us are left. My species ended with the explosion of our sun before your people had reached the age of simple toolmaking. The Chuang-shi are spread over many species, Yesui. First Mother does not favor one over the other.

The image flickered, faded, was gone, leaving only roiling, red mist.

I could not hold it longer. It is — painful, said 'Mind'. Now I go to nurture a universe of my own, and all the wonderfully new creatures that will evolve with it. Do not feel sorry for me, any of you. I will not be alone for long.

But we will miss you, said Yesui. The twins seemed unable to speak, and their manifestation flickered dimly as she spoke.

Come, now. I will take you to a place where you may see the signature of my new existence, said 'Mind'.

The swirling cloud of golden stars led them straight up and out of the galactic plane, and the twins had their first glimpse of the great wheel of vortices and violet light as a whole entity. Far out was the dim glow of another wheel that was Abagai's galaxy, their nearest neighbor.

Look in the general direction of that galaxy you've visited, Yesui, and you'll see the event of my passage, said 'Mind', then quickly, I will miss you, too. Think of me.

The cloud of golden stars whirled in a blur, shrank to a single point, flashed once, and was gone.

Beyond Abagai's galaxy it was as if the universe exploded at that instant, a flare in purple so bright it seemed to fill the void there. It was transient, dimming rapidly until appearing as a single star with color changing from blue to orange and then deep red before fading to nothingness.

It would be months before Shaan would bring her mother a report of something the astronomers had seen, the apparent explosion of an elliptical galactic core several billion light years from Shanji.

And Yesui would be reminded there is no time in the gong-shi-jie.

They watched the star fade to blackness, and felt the absence of the Chuang-shi who had taught them. Then Yesui led them back to the purple vortex leading to herself and coaxed them into it with her.

They awoke together, and found Nokai sitting on the edge of the bed, waiting for their return.

Bao and Shaan rolled into Yesui's arms, squealing with joy and crying at the same time. Nokai looked astonished, but smiled at them.

"What's *this* all about?" he asked.

And so they told him.

The girls were too excited to sleep, but Yesui was tired. She took Nokai's hand, and they left the twins to chatter the night away, going to their own room. When they were in bed, Yesui sighed and snuggled up against him as his hand found her breast.

"Your heart is pounding," he murmured.

"It's a dream come true, Nokai. I've waited years for this day," she said.

"I know."

"I can hardly wait to tell Mother," she said.

"In the morning, dear," said Nokai.

But when morning came, the conversation with Mother was not what Yesui had expected it to be.

The bandages were gone. Father was sitting up in bed and Mother was going over his chest with her healing hands, a thing she'd first practiced in Wanchou before being Empress of Shanji. Father was obviously enjoying it, but Yesui could not contain herself. She burst into their room and excitedly told them what had happened in the gong-shi-jie the previous night.

Father smiled. Mother took Yesui's hand warmly in hers, and squeezed it. "I know how much you've wanted this, dear, and I understand why. When I was a young Empress my happiest times were those spent with you and Abagai in the gong-shi-jie. They were often a welcome relief from the affairs of state."

"The girls are so far beyond me in ability. It will take me a lifetime to show them everything and explore what they can do there," said Yesui.

"You will make the time for it as I did, dear," said Mother calmly, and went back to work on her husband's chest.

"Oh," said Father. "You keep that up, and I'm your slave," he groaned.

Mother smiled. "All mine," she said tenderly.

Yesui sat down on the edge of the bed, feeling suddenly uneasy. "What do you mean 'make the time'? I'll have plenty of time. In a few weeks, at most, you'll be well enough to resume your duties and I have everything ready for you, all the issues and policies that require your attention up to now. There are certain things — "

Father's laugh interrupted her. "Kati, your Tumatsin propensity for understatement doesn't work with Yesui, and never has. You must be direct with her."

Mother blew out a deep breath slowly. "It seems so," she said, then turned to Yesui and held out her hands. Yesui took them in her own and felt the lingering heat there. Her mother's eyes turned emerald green in an instant. A sign of love. A sign of war. Yesui gulped nervously.

"Yesui, the news about you and the twins is wonderful, but I have some news of my own. You surely know by now that when I was first brought to hospital a part of me was somewhere else."

"Yes," said Yesui. "I recognized the signs. I had to explain it to the doctors."

"I was taken to the gong-shi-jie, Yesui. There were two Chuang-shi present to meet me, and at first I thought I was there to be transfigured. They even asked me if I wanted to die. Sad and depressed as I was I said no, Yesui. I hadn't given up on life, and when the Chuang-shi saw that, they showed me wonderful things I'd never even imagined. When I tell you this I think you'll understand why my life, and yours, are about to change again."

Mother held Yesui's hands tightly for the next few minutes while she told everything that had happened during her comatose state. Her mask was down, and Yesui began seeing things coming before they were said.

"They said you'd also hear about a new task from First Mother, and now you've heard it, Yesui. We both have new things to do."

"Mother, you've never quit anything in your *life*!" said Yesui in desperation. "Jensi is under control now, and the rest of Shanji is totally loyal to you. It's Mengnu the people love and revere. How can you — "

"I'm not quiting anything, Yesui. I've done what I can, and I'm moving on to new things in the years your father and I have left together. I'm retiring as Empress, not quiting. It's time for new ideas, new policies to come from the throne. I've worked years to prepare you, Yesui. You know what you want to do, and now you should do it. It's no longer necessary for me to agree with you."

"Oh, Mother," said Yesui. "I didn't want this to happen so soon."

"You are Empress of Shanji," said Mother. "I'll announce it as soon as they let us out of this hospital."

"Well, that was direct enough," said Father.

"You *agree* with her?" asked Yesui.

"Absolutely," said Father, "but she neglected to say we have complete faith in your ability to rule, as long as you can keep that temper of yours in check. Love rules better than fear, Yesui. What you did to Jensi City was pretty dramatic."

"Now, dear," said Mother, then squeezed Yesui's hands and released them.

Father grinned. "Well? Are you resigned to your fate?"

"Yes, Father. As usual I'm not being given a choice, but I knew I'd have to do this someday. I'm a bit frightened by it coming so soon."

Mother suddenly looked sad, and there were tears in her eyes.

"I've given my last order as Empress, dear, but I would like to ask a favor from you. It's about my father," she said.

"His ashes were interred in the Moshuguang Vault of Honor, Mother. I was there to represent us," said Yesui. Already she knew her mother's request.

"I would like his remains to be placed in the Imperial Crypt, dear, and to have him acknowledged as my father," said Mother, and a single tear ran down her cheek.

"It will be done," said Yesui, and smiled. "It will be no surprise to the Moshuguang, Mother. Your little secret was not well kept over the years."

Mother smiled faintly. In a flash her mind had played back a lifetime with Mengmoshu as first captor, then teacher, then that night in a Tumatsin village when she'd first learned he was her true father.

The visions made Yesui's heart ache. She leaned over, put an arm around Mother's shoulders, and said, "I miss him, too. He was my Gong-gong."

They enjoyed a few relieving sobs together, and Father reached out his hands to touch both of them in a soothing way, but it was over quickly.

Yesui sat up straight and wiped her eyes dry with a hand. "Well, I'd better leave you two alone for a while. It seems I have much more work to do than I thought."

Mother continued sobbing softly; Father held her tightly against him and smiled. "Love — not fear," he said.

Yesui smiled back at him. "Yes, Father. I heard you."

She left them there cuddled together on the hospital bed, and felt the wonderful love they had between them. She thought of her own love for Nokai and the twins.

Yesui returned to the royal suite.

But it was Wang Yesui Shan-shi-jie who sat down at the desk to deal with the files which had awaited her mother's attention.

Twenty-Five

Transfiguration

There was one more decade remaining for them to be together as a whole family.

Wang Yesui Shan-shi-jie was crowned Empress in a simple ceremony held in a throne room unused since Mengnu had come to power. The event was televised for the public, attended by Ministers, representatives of The Peoples' Congress and the highest ranking officers of the Moshuguang. The royal family was present, Nokai in his white robe of the Lan-Sui priesthood, the rest in Moshuguang black. And it was Mengnu herself who placed the tall crown of gold filigree on the head of the Mei-lai-gong.

All over Shanji people sat close to their television sets, crying over Mengnu's words of farewell, nodding thankfully at Yesui's promise to retain her mother's traditions and values, then straining for a close look at the pair of lovely and identical young girls rumored to have powers even exceeding those of the Mei-lai-gong. But when the ceremony was over, the people went back to their everyday lives and waited to see what their new Empress would do.

Yesui did not disappoint them in what she did, but her relationship with the people would never be what they had enjoyed under Mengnu: the gentle countenance, the touching, the loving voice in their minds when they were near her.

Yesui was never seen to smile in public. Everywhere she went she was surrounded by a protective aura in purple that crackled dangerously if one approached her too closely. That and the blue glow of her eyes was a constant reminder of the terrible cosmic power on the throne of Shanji, and her presence was soon familiar to all the people.

Unlike Mengnu, Wang Yesui traveled extensively, visiting all major cities and select villages in the rural provinces at least twice each year. She traveled to Congress Center where she presented her views in person at the opening and closing days of each annual session of Congress. The general public heard her arguments for or against issues on monthly television programs broadcast from the throne room, her aura there not real but a digital effect to avoid signal interference in transmission. She openly lobbied for support of her views, and the people responded. In all the years of her reign she would never be forced to veto a single bill passed by Peoples' Congress.

Jensi was rebuilt under a military governorship that lasted two years. A mayor and city council were then elected under Yesui's close scrutiny, and representatives were welcomed back into The Peoples' Congress. But the city would never again be the financial jewel of the Empire. It returned to its beginnings as a city of science and technology, and opened its gates to all citizens of Shanji.

Outside of Jensi, life continued unchanged under the second Empress of the Chuang-shi dynasty on Shanji. The people would enjoy nearly three generations of peace and prosperity under her reign. They did not love or revere her, for she would not allow it, but they respected her judgements and held her in private awe for as long as she was with them. For Yesui was not the last of the Chuang-shi dynasty; when she was crowned, her successor had not yet been born.

The twins, Bao and Shaan, grew to become lovely young women who attracted many suitors from the Moshuguang. None were satisfactory to them, and Yesui began wondering if she would ever have grandchildren. She organized parties, receptions, and events attracting the artistic elite of Shanji, but nothing seemed to work. The twins charmed everyone, but showed no interest in a relationship leading to marriage. Their days were spent with other artists frequenting Stork Tower, their evenings with Mother in the gong-shi-jie or at their computer, and they were content with it. They learned the whole of the place of creation, watched Tirgee jump the great freighters to and from Meng-shi-jie, and went with their grandmother to observe her work with newly called Chuang-shi. They began a project of their own to produce a new planet beyond the gaseous giants by condensing the icy debris there onto a massive singularity brought by them from a tiny place beyond Mother's perception in the gong-shi-jie.

There was no time for love.

After Yesui's coronation Nokai resigned his post as Lan-Sui ambassador and became a citizen of Shanji. His work on the Jensi problem had been highly regarded by the Economic Ministry; he was offered an accounting position there and accepted it. Within a decade he was named Associate Minister on the basis of his work, and there were no outcries of nepotism to be heard.

The case against Sheng-chih remained open during all the years of Yesui's reign.

He was never found.

Mengjai and Tirgee built their home on Meng-shi-jie, a sprawling ranch outside the capital city. Dispite Tirgee's royal status, they lived as middle class citizens. They kept horses, and rode often to inspect the greening of the planet as more and more aquifers were tapped for use. Both had civil positions in the Environmental Ministry, Mengjai as engineer, Tirgee as analyst. The fact that Tirgee was second in line for the throne and could move great ships in spacetime was never brought up by the people they worked with. They enjoyed a peaceful, private life together, much of it outdoors, and it was five years before Tirgee gave birth to their first child. They named him Sacha, and he was born Moshuguang. And it was another five years before Tirgee was pregnant again.

For Kati, most of the decade passed peacefully in quiet retirement. Her body was totally healed within a year, but the trauma had aged her and her hair was now white as snow. The same thing had happened to Huomeng, and now there could be no doubt they were grandparents.

It was soon apparent that Huomeng's injuries had taken a terrible toll on his body. Kati's warm ministries had sped his recovery only to a point of functionality, but there was nothing she could do for his damaged lungs. One partial lung was badly scarred and next to useless, and the whole one had lost much of its elasticity. Breathing was a conscious effort for Huomeng, even when he was sitting down.

But Kati would not allow him to sit for long. Their last decade together would be lived to the fullest.

For over a year their only activity was walking up and down the winding paths on the steep hillside below the palace to spend quiet times talking or reading in the hanging gardens there. Huomeng hobbled along bravely without complaint, but often became congested from the effort and Kati would draw the energy of Tengri-Khan through her hands to soothe him.

When Huomeng was stronger they began to travel, but always by flyer or freighter. They spent four summers in the Dorvodt ordu on the northern shore of the great lake in a ger near the grave of Kati's mother and foster father.

Goldani had passed on, and after two terms in Peoples' Congress, Rani-Tan now led all the ordus.

They ate meals with the elders and told stories to the children, and went out to sea twice on Baber's boat to watch the activities of a fisherman's life. Both times Huomeng became so congested from the cold sea air that Kati momentarily feared for his life, and the heat from her hands brought up great gobs of bloody mucous from his injured lungs.

But Huomeng did not complain. Each day with Kati was a blessing to him. He would not leave her side, or disappoint her.

They visited Meng-shi-jie twice, and Tirgee jumped their ship in both directions with breathtaking precision. Yesugen and Kabul hosted them the first time, and took them by flyer to see the results of Mengjai's work, the surface of Meng-shi-jie now dotted with farms and mature forests of *Tysk* as far as the eye could see. The second time they stayed with Mengjai and Tirgee, and bounced baby Sacha on their knees. Tirgee coaxed Kati onto a horse, but the ride was short. The strength was gone from her legs, and her knees ached after only a short trot on the animal.

They visited Wanchou and Dahe City several times, but never returned to Jensi. The memories of that place remained bitter to Kati until the end of her physical life. But the people in Wanchou and Dahe both remembered and revered her wherever she was seen. They brought forth babies and young children to be touched by her, and asked for her intercession with First Mother. In return, she gave them the feelings of great love and affection they remembered from years past.

The trips were exhausting for Huomeng, since there were many short walks in the cities, and even Kati's legs ached for days after they returned home. But the last trip to Wanchou was the worst; they'd attended the opening of the new cultural park there and walked kilometers to see everything. When they returned to the palace Huomeng was coughing hard, every breath a wheeze. He went straight to bed without eating anything. Kati ate a light meal before joining him.

Huomeng was lying on his back. Kati stradled him and brought the healing warmth through her hands, rubbing his chest, shoulders and neck. As she did it he ran his hands lightly up and down her forearms and looked up at her with half closed eyes.

"It seems we've been together forever," he said suddenly.

"It's over half a century, dear," she murmured.

Huomeng closed his eyes, and his voice was a wheeze. "It's not long enough," he said.

In his mind he was playing back their entire life together, all the way to when she was a little girl who thought of him as an arrogant Moshuguang tutor. Kati followed his thoughts, and smiled.

"We were a bit livelier in those days," she said.

Huomeng opened his eyes, and grasped her hands gently. "You once asked me about when it was I knew I loved you. I think I know, now. It was in your room, that time when you first saw yourself as a changeling."

"I was hysterical, and you held me," Kati said softly.

"You leaned back against me, and I looked at your face in the mirror, and — and I knew," whispered Huomeng.

Kati took a deep breath and sighed to ease the constriction in her chest. "I knew it, too, Huomeng. That same moment. Are you feeling better now? Can you sleep?"

"Not alone," he said, and squeezed her hands.

Kati slipped into bed beside him and turned off the nightstand light. They cuddled together in darkness, and she could hear his raspy breathing at her shoulder. His arm slid over her stomach; he grasped her waist to pull her tightly against him, and kissed her ear.

"I'll love you forever, Kati," he murmured.

Kati turned her head and kissed him softly on the mouth. "Me, too," she said.

They fell asleep pressed tightly together.

In her dreams that night Huomeng called out to her from a place so brightly lit she could only see his silouette, and he told her again that he loved her.

But when she awoke in the morning, Huomeng did not move. His arm was draped across her chest, and the flesh was cold. His presence was gone from her mind. And a part of her had gone with it.

She cuddled him until a servant came with their breakfast and rushed away to notify the physicians. And only when Huomeng's cold body was taken away did she allow herself to cry.

Something went out of her that morning, as if a piece of her soul had stolen away during the night. She was numb during the funeral and interment, but feeling returned when she was alone in her suite and facing an empty bed she had shared with a man for over fifty years.

The walls closed in on her. She spent days walking the terraces below the palace and sitting by the garden pools, but even there the memories of family exercises and quiet conversations with Huomeng and Mengmoshu came back to haunt her. She felt herself withdrawing from everything around her. Yesui sensed it, was constantly inviting her for meals with Nokai and the twins.

Hearing the twins chatter excitedly about their plans in the gong-shi-jie was a turning point for Kati. With Huomeng to care for, her flights to the gong-shi-jie had been infrequent. In ten years she'd only been there a few times with Yesui and the girls, and had made little progress with the fledgling Chuang-shi First Mother had called her to work with.

Kati withdrew from the world of Shanji, and returned to the place of creation, the place that had been the center of her life when Abagai was alive. She retired to her room, lay down on her bed to close her eyes and the matrix of purple stars was there for her day or night. She began working regularly with Bao and Shaan, even when Yesui wasn't there. She took the three of them to Abagai's galaxy and Yesui told the story of their encounter with the Chuang-shi in the nursery for new stars, all of which were now fully born and glowing brightly.

The twins watched her work with the sea creature she had named Flicker because of the way she communicated through pulsations of her manifestation. Kati took Flicker as far as Tengri-Khan and showed her Shanji from real space. But Flicker could only see or imagine in the far infra-red region of the spectrum, and Kati could not imagine what Shanji looked like to her. It was the feelings of mutual awe, adventure and joy that bound them together, and parting was always difficult.

She called two other Chuang-shi: a bird-like creature with diaphanous wings the size of sails, and eye-stalks with hair-like rods that sensed infra-red, then a deep sea animal that was many creatures with a group mind, looking like a spine covered rock anchored to the sea floor and sensing local changes in electric fields which Kati accomplished with her aura.

Communication was difficult at best, and mostly impossible. Kati was too limited by her physical form; she was a being capable of sensing only a tiny part of the electromagnetic spectrum, while the transfigured Chuang-shi had no such problem. She couldn't even go with Yesui to see the green threads of space-time, or with the twins into the tiniest places where new universes were born. When Bao and Shiann showed her where they'd placed a tiny but massive object in the gong-shi-jie she could not see it. But when they jumped to real space she could see the cloud of icy debris whirling as it condensed around a singular point by mutual attraction.

Kati suddenly yearned for transfiguration.

She was neglecting her body, spending long hours of real time in the gong-shi-jie. She did not exercise, and began missing meals. She was rarely seen outside her rooms. Yesui became concerned, and began nagging her about it.

"I'm doing First Mother's work, dear," she said, "and I'm preparing for the rest of my existence. This old body is no longer relevant."

Yesui sent two nurses to watch her around the clock. They fed her, and she ate to keep them happy, but they could not prevent her flight to the gong-shi-jie.

Kati prayed to First Mother for transfiguration.

And First Mother came to her.

It was night, and she'd just dreamed of Huomeng again, feeling his hands on her from a time long ago in a ger by the sea. She awoke, and cried out, *Oh, First Mother, please take me. There's nothing left for me to do here, and I'm useless in my present form. There's so much more I want to do for you.*

In the darkness, a whirling cluster of golden stars appeared as if projected on the ceiling above her bed, for her eyes were open.

Kati, oh Kati, your sorrow is so deep. If your wish is truely for transfiguration, then it will be so. When you are ready, I will be there to guide you.

The golden stars flickered once and were gone. Kati shivered, suddenly cold, but felt as if a great weight had just been lifted from her.

She couldn't sleep the rest of the night. Early in the morning she went to Yesui, told her what had happened, and the decision she'd made.

Yesui argued, cried, became hysterical. "I'll never see you again!" she cried. "You have years left if you just take care of yourself."

"We are Chuang-shi, dear. We'll be together again, but in a different form," said Kati, holding her daughter like a little child.

"There's no guarantee of that," cried Yesui. "We might not even recognize each other!"

Kati kissed Yesui's forehead. "But I think we will, dear, and my decision has been made."

So when the arguing and the crying was over, Kati went to the gong-shi-jie, called all of her family and Yesugen from there to give them the time of her transfiguration, and asked for their presence at the event. There was more arguing and crying from as far away as Meng-shi-jie, but it did not come from Yesugen, who understood Kati's decision and was considering the same thing for herself. It was Tirgee who cried, and then explained she was pregnant again.

The time she chose was at dawn on Shanji. Kati slept well and awoke at first light, her usual time to begin a new day. She hobbled to the wide doors of her room and went out onto the balcony to watch the orange disk of Tengri-Khan come up over the horizon. She watched the coming and passing of the red glow on Three Peaks, the Mei-lai-gong's shrine there, and then she went back to bed to lie down on her back and fold her hands over her chest. She closed her eyes, took a deep breath, and sighed.

They were waiting for her.

Yesui's fan of green flickered wildly. Nokai was with her, for she had called him. The double helix of Bao and Shaan also flickered, but it seemed they were not so upset as their mother. Yesugen showed her usual manifestation of the warrior she'd once been. Kati herself had never changed her image in the gong-shi-jie, and was still Mengnu at age twenty.

It was Tirgee she noticed first, a simple green fan with Mengjai also present as a mental apparition the way he'd done with his sister. It was not the fan she noticed, but the tiny blue flame wavering next to it.

We have a visitor, said Kati.

Her name will be Naya, said Tirgee.

A new generation of her line. Kati was pleased.

Kati led them away from the vortex of Tengri-Khan. I have chosen a place Yesugen and Yesui will remember. It's not far, she said.

Where Abagai was taken? asked Yesui.

Yes.

Yesugen traveled beside her. The years have passed so quickly. I will follow you soon, Kati, she said.

First enemies, then friends, and now here we are, said Kati, and I don't even know where I'm going.

You were always somewhat rash, said Yesugen, and smiled.

Kati led them to the edge of the galaxy where star vortices disappeared and there was only the hazy violet manifestation of matter unseen there.

Kati turned around to face all of them. There could be no greater blessing for me than having you all here. I will miss you, all of you, but I have faith we will all be together again. I hope you understand why I must go now. I've always required meaning in my life, and this is the way for me to have it.

Oh, said Yesui, and Yesugen scowled, for both had been present at Abagai's transfiguration and knew the signs.

Kati looked behind her, saw a swirling, green cloud condensing into an enormous vortex shaped like a funnel. She was being drawn towards it, her own manifestation fading and being replaced by a metalic blue glow.

Mother! cried Yesui and Mengjai together. *We love you!*

Goodbye. Goodbye my darlings. I love all of you.

Green light rushed past her, the manifestations of her family, a friend, the galaxy of her world, all she'd ever known receding in the distance, then gone, and she was falling, falling, falling ...

Yesui cried out as her mother was sucked into the green vortex and disappeared. The vortex remained for only an instant before becoming a swirling cloud again, then a green mist, then gone and there was only the violet haze beyond the rim of the galaxy and, far out, another dim wheel of stars.

They remained there a while, but not a single word was said. Yesui led them back to Tengri-Nayon and Khan, and one by one they returned to themselves. Yesui awoke beside Nokai on their bed, and the first thing she heard was the twins crying in their room.

She cuddled with Nokai a few minutes, then went down the hall to her mother's suite. The balcony doors were open, the room bright in morning light. Mother lay on the bed, veined hands folded on her chest. All breath was gone from her. In profile, with the full lips and finely arched nose, she was still the youthful Mengnu.

Yesui sent out word that Mengnu had passed into the loving embrace of First Mother. The people mourned her, and erected new monuments to her name in every city on Shanji.

Wang Yesui Shan-shi-jie moved forward with her physical life. Her reign was long and firm, but fair. Shanji prospered greatly under her leadership.

Among most of the people, she was still called Mei-lai-gong, the Empress of Light.

But to the people of Jensi City she would forever be known by a different name.

They called her Huo Di Wang.

Empress of Fire.

Epilog

She remembered riding Sushua at full gallop across the high plateau, the wind whiping at her face and hair.

Now it wasn't wind rushing past her, but light, first green, then blue turning to purple. Ahead of her, a golden orb like a tight-packed cluster of stars was leading the way, twisting, turning to follow a glowing tube with no end. Kati followed, drawn on by the orb, her own manifestation now a bright sphere in metalic blue, her consciousness intact, memories still there but pushed away by the thrill of the moment. Enthralled by the view, she did not feel The Change, though her new manifestation was the first signature of it.

Kati did not sense the occurance of her transfiguration. She only saw the results of it.

There was a bright green glow ahead, rushing towards her, and suddenly the great tube of light was gone. The golden orb was still ahead, drawing her on. The space was not constrained, stretched far in every direction and was anything but empty. Three realities flickered back and forth, producing a single scene in her view. The orb plunged straight ahead, but off to Kati's right was a vast wheel of stars, an immense spiral galaxy surrounded by a halo of star clusters, all of it flickering between images of vortices and swirling mists as seen in the gong-shi-jie, and a lace of fine green threads woven in a tapestry with bumps and depressions. Three images flickering to form one, and in the center of the galaxy where the star vortices became red beyond red the fine, green threads pinched in to form a singularity.

All of this with only a glance, for the galaxy moved past her quickly, and ahead another green vortex opened up to swallow her. Another tube of light, twisting and turning, narrow then broad then narrow again. The golden orb was still there, but now the lights within it were flickering and Kati suddenly felt a powerful presence that seemed to come from all around her.

We're nearly there, Kati, and you're not alone. This is only a new beginning for you, and I'm most pleased by what you've done for me.

Kati was stunned, and could not answer at first, then thought, *I follow First Mother wherever she takes me.*

They came out of the tube in a field of stars, most of them small and red and scattered throughout clouds of dust and gas. Far ahead, the green threads came together in a deep depression in the tapestry of lace and there was a huge vortex in deep red. Again only time for a glimpse as another green vortex opened up, and she fell into it. Light streaked by her, but immediately there was a bright green glow ahead. The lights within the golden orb guiding her now flickered wildly, becoming a blur, then expanding to a spherical manifestation in gold as they came out of the tube.

It was as if she had returned to Abagai's galaxy, for around her was a nursery for new stars: billowing clouds of dust and gas with scattered dark globules and pillars topped with faint glows from stars about to be born. The pattern of green threads was a myriad of bumps and depressions. Clouds of violet light swirled and moved in small fragments throughout the region, each fragment accompanied by what seemed to be a metalic blue star.

The great golden manifestation drifted ahead of her, slowed and came to a halt.

Welcome, Kati. You will begin here, and there are many Chuang-shi willing to help you learn our ways.

And Kati was suddenly aware of a thousand new presences in her consciousness.

It's Kati!

Kati is here!

Ah, the human has arrived.

Kati, oh Kati!

Something stirred within her, a memory, a feeling, a connection to someone dear in her life. Metalic blue stars rushed towards her from every direction; as they came close, she could see they were not stars, but manifestations like her own — the manifestations of Chuang-shi.

All of them stopped at a distance from Kati, but one rushed on, heading straight towards her.

Kati, my darling, you've come at last, and I have missed you so!

The presence was so familiar, so dear. Abagai! cried Kati. Oh, Abagai, it's really you! It has been such a long time for me!

Two spherical manifestations in metalic blue came together and whirled with cosmic joy. Around them, at a point some ten billion light years from a place called Shanji, the cores of two galaxies came together, sending out pressure waves giving birth to new stars. Distorted clouds of dust and gas condensed into dense globules, warming, heating, giving off first light and streamers of hot gas before bursting forth in full glory.

Around them, the Chuang-shi all rejoiced as Kati and Abagai came together again.

Biography

James C. Glass

James C. Glass read and wrote science fiction as a kid and published a fanzine while in high school, but then came college, a degree in physics and starting a family while working on ion and arc-jet engines at Rocketdyne.

Graduate school followed, and a thirty-five-year career as a professor of physics, department head and dean at North Dakota State University and Eastern Washington University. The writing during this time was seventy-five technical papers on his research in molecular biophysics and superconductivity. But the fiction writing bug bit hard again when Jim was well into his forties. His first published story was in Aboriginal S.F. and soon after he won the 1990 grand prize in the Writers of the Future Contest. He retired from his academic job in 1999 and now writes full time.

Printed in the United States
938100001B